The familiar voice didn't startle Mairie, for she was
expecting him. "Jack

He held his finger u
in her ear, the sound
shivers up her arms.
I said when I found yo

Dear Reader,

I truly never expected to make a career out of writing, especially about the magical possibilities of time. Yet, I have always been fascinated by the connection between past, present, and future, and I can vividly recall the words with which my father inspired me. "Connie," he said, "don't ever be afraid of dying. It's only falling asleep in one world and waking up in the next." Twenty years later, that wisdom became the basis for my first time travel romance.

After writing ten books, I decided to take a break, to step aside and write contemporary fiction, but time continued to haunt me. . . . Then one extraordinary day when my daughter challenged me to skydive with her, it slammed into my consciousness with such a force that I knew I'd return to my first love. Time Travel. That experience of skydiving begins this book and has led me on an incredible adventure . . . to discover that time is an illusion we are only just beginning to glimpse.

I've often been asked to define time travel fiction. To me, it enables one to experience the past or the future without sacrificing the present. It is unpredictable, mysterious, adventurous, hopeful—just like love, its natural complement.

I hope you enjoy this new journey where anything is possible. It could happen . . . *Anywhere You Are.*

Kindest regards,

Constance O'Day-Flannery

Constance O'Day-Flannery

ANYWHERE YOU ARE

AVON BOOKS  NEW YORK

AVON BOOKS, INC.
1350 Avenue of the Americas
New York, New York 10019

To Christine Laidlaw, Ann O'Day, Patricia Woollett, Colleen Bosler, Patricia Trowbridge, Helen Breitwieser . . . for their friendship, support and their loyalty to purpose. I will treasure each one, each memory, each unique view that broadened my own. All are "memory makers," gifted women, and I am honored to call each of them friend. Thank you, ladies.

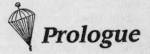 *Prologue*

She was doing it for love . . . and sometimes love got you into trouble. Deep trouble. What else could explain her being suited up like a spaceman and seated on this narrow bench, ready to hurl herself from a perfectly good plane out into the universe? It simply had to be love. Or . . . she was crazy.

Mairie Callahan preferred to think it was love, for she had fought for her sanity in the last few years since her divorce. She was sticking to her story. Love . . . that was it. Only this time it wasn't for a man who promised to honor and cherish her in sickness and in health, and then turn around six years later and find a younger version to replace her. She was through with unfulfilled bogus dreams. This time it was for a deeper love, a love that reso-nated within her DNA.

Breathing hard in a futile attempt to release anx-iety, Mairie glanced at her brother, who was grin-ning like a fool as he looked out the small window down to the earth. Despite the mounting fear that seemed to crawl over her body like a monstrous snake and squeeze her breath, she knew she would do anything for him. Anything. Whatever he wanted, she was a willing participant. Every day, every experience, was now a miracle and she was going to file each one away in her heart.

1

Bryan looked away from the window and laughed. "We're really gonna do this, kiddo! Thanks . . ."

She tried forcing her lips into a smile, yet her stomach was screaming out to her that she was the fool. What kind of people did this? Skydiving was no sport. It was for those who needed a thrill beyond what life offered. Maybe that's why Bryan wanted to do it so much. He was determined to experience everything he ever wanted in whatever time was left to him.

He brought his arm around her shoulders and hugged her. "C'mon, you're going to be fine. I'll go first and you follow me," he yelled, over the roar of the engine.

She merely nodded. Right . . . just as she had followed him to Peru to climb Machu Picchu. To Australia, to scuba dive at the Great Barrier Reef. To Alaska, to kayak with the whales. She would follow him anywhere. Do anything he wanted. As long as he drew breath, she would be there cheering for him. As much as she tried to repress the memory, in a matter of moments her mind ran through scenarios of Bryan telling her that he was terminal. Her shock, anger, grief. She saw herself quitting her job, withdrawing all her money, and taking off with her older brother like two middle-aged hippies determined to find the meaning of life and experience it. With both their parents killed in a fire when she and Bryan were in college, he was her only family now, and she loved him unconditionally.

Glancing at him as he checked his harness, Mairie again wondered how someone so handsome, so loving, so vital could be dying. It didn't make sense. And it was so unfair. That was it. It was the unfairness of it all that ate away at her gut. She felt helpless to stop this unseen, silent invader, but as long as there was life she would stick by Bryan's side and tell it to screw off. Together, they would live to see another day.

When the instructor slid open the door and yelled at them to get ready, all Mairie's bravado against death seemed to disappear as her own loomed as a distinct possibility. What if the chute didn't open? No matter that she had packed and repacked the damn thing fifteen times. What if something happened? She could have a heart attack or a stroke. It wasn't unheard of at thirty-seven. It could happen . . . she could really die doing this! She almost lost her nerve as the small cabin filled with a tremendous force of wind and her body felt paralyzed with fear. Love, or craziness? Both, she finally decided.

"You can do it, Mar," Bryan yelled at her.

He could always read her, she thought, hearing him call her by her nickname. It was just like when he was teaching her to ride a two-wheeler. Holding the back of the seat to help her maintain balance, he had kept pace with her all around the block. *You can do it, Mar,* he had shouted, when he'd let go and she had been on her own, fighting gravity. And he'd been right. She had done it.

How she loved him. He was intelligent, kind, funny, compassionate—a human being of worth. And he was dying.

"Look out the door and see your marker," the instructor yelled.

Mairie tried to rise, yet all the gear she was wearing made it feel as if she'd gained thirty pounds. Bryan helped her and she grabbed hold of the door handle to stand upright.

Her brain seemed like a crashed hard drive, spinning crazily, as she looked down to the earth so very far away. A mountain range, partially obscured by haze. A desert spread out below her. The gaudy glitter of Las Vegas a mere outline of buildings in the far distance. It was surreal. Thirteen thousand feet

. . . how the hell was she supposed to do this? As the wind robbed her of breath, every instinct was urging her to sit back down, to call this off, for somehow she knew that if she went through that door her life was going to be altered. It was like a primal warning.

"I love you, kiddo."

While the instructor checked their gear, Bryan pulled back the Plexiglas shield of his helmet and smiled at her with such joy that Mairie's heart constricted. She pulled back her own so he could see her eyes and together they gazed at each other for a timeless moment. It had to be true that the eyes were the windows of the soul, for what she was feeling went beyond earthly love. They were family, but it was even more profound than sharing genes. It was a knowing. They were eternally connected.

"We're both crazy, you realize that," she yelled back.

Laughing, Bryan nodded. "Yup . . . crazy. But we're *alive*, right? We've left the rest of the tribe to their own devices and struck out on our own adventure. This is it, kid. Right here, right now. Nothing matters but this moment. Remember it. You're about to experience terminal velocity firsthand." Still grinning like a ten-year-old on Christmas morning, he closed his shield and said, "I love it! I love you. And, Mar—you can do this."

No one, nothing, could have prepared her for it. It didn't matter how many hours of ground instruction she had endured. Her brain refused to function as she heard the instructor yell at Bryan to go, and watched her brother disappear into thin air. *She hadn't even told him she loved him.*

The man motioned for Mairie to come closer to the door, yet her feet refused to move. No matter how hard she tried to command them, they seemed rooted to the floor. She saw his hand reach out for her and he pulled her to the open door at the same time he slammed the Plexiglas shield over her eyes. Standing at the doorway into the unknown, she swore she knew what death was like. Never in her life had she experienced such fear. She couldn't do this! She couldn't!

Then, from someplace inside her mind that was struggling to break through, she thought of her brother out there in space and knew it was love that would make her leave this plane. If she faced death, she would do it for him. And in that moment, in a startling flash of clarity, she knew that the love in her heart was far stronger than the fear.

"Go!"

The slap on her back was more than a little push. It was like a Mack truck had slammed her from behind. Unprepared, she was shot out into space, vulnerable, terrorized, and her body instinctively curled into a fetal position.

And then it happened . . . she had a brain freeze, a moment out of time where one knows one has left everything considered normal and entered another sphere of existence.

Earth. Sky. Earth. Sky.

On and on it went as she tumbled and became more disoriented. She closed her eyes against the dizzying sight as the wind stripped her of breath, and then something even stranger happened, something she had never experienced. A bright light flashed behind her closed lids and she thought for a moment that she truly had died, for she felt a frisson of heat saturate every cell of her body and infuse it with an odd energy. Then she seemed to enter a most peaceful state, a place where she heard herself saying to arch her back.

Immediately, she straightened out and opened her eyes. Spread-eagled and falling at two hundred miles an hour through space, Mairie Callahan knew what it was like to be *alive*. Every sense was acutely activated. Every nerve ending was picking up vibrations and sending them back to her brain. Her jumpsuit was flapping furiously against her body as the law of gravity reminded her of its power, and the earth lay spread out below her like a crazy quilt.

She looked at the altimeter on her wrist and saw that she had still two thousand feet to travel before she pulled the chord. Her instructions came back to her. From that place of peace she gathered her courage and lowered her right arm. Immediately she turned right and soared in that direction like an eagle. It worked! She pulled down her left arm, and suddenly she was a human bullet shooting out into space. Incredible . . . hormones raced through her body and she wanted to giggle at a sensation that boarded on sexual. Fighting the force of the wind, she managed to raise her arms back into the spread-eagled position and check her altimeter. Six thousand feet.

It was time.

Her fingers clutched the handle at her chest and her heart constricted in a flutter of fear for just a moment . . . right before she pulled it out.

It was like she was shot out of a cannon, straight up. A human rocket. Again her brain seemed to freeze and she was held in a place without time or space, a place she couldn't comprehend. Just as suddenly as it happened, she was dropped like a two-ton anvil. The heavy straps around her upper thighs and under her arms dug into her muscles. Every organ in her body felt as though it had been rearranged. Realizing she wasn't breathing, Mairie grabbed hold of the straps in front of her, took a deep breath, and looked up to the canopy of green and white above her.

It was magical.

The silence that followed was so breathtakingly

beautiful that Mairie was stunned. Never had she experienced such perfection. Her breath left her body in deep appreciation and she grabbed hold of the two handles dangling before her eyes. Pulling the left one, she was turned toward the distant mountain range. Cool, she thought, loving every second of this and knowing it was worth it. She should have just jumped and immediately pulled the chord and forgot about the terminal velocity insanity. The panorama of nature was spectacular. She experienced a moment of true perspective, of realizing how tiny and insignificant she really was compared to Mother Nature, that she was merely a visitor here in this time and place.

Bryan . . . she wanted to connect with her brother and searched the sky for his parachute. She looked below her, yet he wasn't in sight. Unable to see over her shoulder, Mairie pulled on the left strap, her only guidance system, and found that it took all her strength to turn the chute.

Nothing.

Where was he? And where the hell was the marker, that huge white cross in the desert? Frantically she tried to find it. It had disappeared, or she had wandered far off course. She fought the panic, the bile rising in her throat, and looked out to find the outline of the city.

It was gone. All of it . . . *gone.*

Nothing looked the same. *Nothing.* Not even the landscape.

Over and over, around and around, she kept twirling, desperate to find something familiar. Anything! There was nothing except the desert floor rushing up to meet her. Dear God, what had happened? Where was Bryan? The city. *Anything.*

She had known it from the moment she'd agreed to this adventure, and here she was . . . in trouble, deep, deep trouble.

* * *

A man sat cross-legged on the narrow precipice that reached out over the desert. He was still, silent, barely breathing, alone unto himself . . . at the pinnacle of his world. He had been sent on this vision quest by his adopted brothers three days before. Hunger had left him more finely tuned to the movements of the earth. Thirst had forced him to go inward and battle his mind for control. Finally, after days of purification, he had stopped at the sacred rock and lightly touched the strange images etched into the red stone by the ancients . . . leaving some message not revealed to him. Yet his brothers knew.

There he had surrendered. Finally, irretrievably surrendered. Only then did he place the ritual peyote button on his tongue and chew. He'd felt at one with nature, ready to receive her wisdom, and had proceeded to this narrow ledge. He had come to this place, climbing without stopping to reach the highest ground, and had dared to look out over the valley so far below. Here he would wait for his answer. Here he would get his sign. He came without fear, without shame. Stripped of all human desires except one. He wanted hope.

As yet . . . there was nothing.

He refused to give up. He had come back to the place of his youth to seek refuge with the Indians who had taken him into their hearts when he was an abandoned twelve-year-old. He felt abandoned again, this time by his soul.

They called it the War Between the States . . . brother fighting brother. He had been wooed by the call to honor, filled with bravado, and joined the North to protect the Union. Three years later he knew he had lost a far more personal battle, for the carnage he had witnessed screamed at him that there was no honor in death. It was insanity, and he had been a willing participant. He'd returned hollow, a mere shell that functioned. Life no longer held interest. And so he had made his way back to this desert, to the only people he could think of who still knew of balance, who were sane.

Now he sat . . . waiting.

Casting out the memories and centering himself within the elements of the earth, Jack Delaney called out to the Great Spirit not to desert him, but to reveal his vision. For he had no intention of leaving this mountain without completing his quest. He was prepared to meet his death rather than fail. There was no meaning to it all any longer, and he had lost his fear long ago on a forgotten battlefield. His brothers, the Paiutes, had recognized the sickness within his soul and had instructed him in the cure. The balm, they had assured him, was within himself.

Opening his eyes, he blinked in disbelief. His heart began racing and he held his breath in awe as he gazed over the valley spread before him.

What was that, falling out of the sky?

He brought up his hand to shelter his eyes and squinted as the thing twirled and slowly, gracefully, fell toward earth. Something powerful took hold of his body, infusing it with a tingling force that demanded his full attention. Whatever effects the peyote had were long since worn off. The small button from the mescal cactus had produced some colorful dreams, but this . . . this was no dream.

This was his answer. His vision!

It had come out of heaven.

Standing up, he brushed the dust from the seat of his pants and started the long descent to meet his future. He had called out for help and been given an answer. Gratitude and hope, strange emotions thought to have been lost, entered his heart as he realized all he had to do was find his gift and he would somehow again be whole. A vitality he couldn't remember ever having filled his lungs and raced through his aching muscles, as he seemed to leap down the rocky mountain surface. His body lengthened and expanded, reaching toward the desert floor like a thoroughbred stretching toward the finish line. His quest was almost complete.

Find the gift, his mind kept repeating.

He knew once he did, life as he had known it would never be the same again.

Now . . . what the hell *was* that?

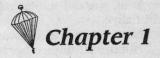

Chapter 1

It was like a bad dream, the kind where you don't wake up before hitting the ground.

Her body was curled into a jumping posture, and the muscles in her legs were screaming from holding the position as the desert seemed to rush toward her. Her arms were strained, pulling both handles together until they were between her thighs. She could feel the muscles in her arms trembling from the force she was applying, yet she knew her life depended on her slowing down the descent. She was getting too close to the mountain, and she didn't dare look up to the parachute to make sure it was working and the material was narrowing. She thought she was slowing down, but her gaze was riveted to the desert floor dotted with sagebrush. Wherever she was . . . she was about to land. And by damn, she was going to make it alive!

When it happened, when her feet slammed against the hard surface, she stood for a moment out of time staring at her Nikes, sure that her ankles were broken. And then she was suddenly pulled backward and landed on her backside, as the wind dragged the chute and her along with it across the dry, scrubby ground. It must have been instinct that caused her to roll over and start gathering up the lines to stop the momentum. When she had the material around

11

her like a huge silky blanket, she stopped and regained her breath.

Well, she did it. She was alive. Bruised. Rattled. But alive.

Now, where the hell was she?

Hot dry air burned her lungs. An ominous silence surrounded her. What had happened, she wondered, as she stared out to the mountain range before her. When she was playing up there and soaring like a missile through space, did she wander *that* far off course? She had expected to land at the big white cross, or close to it, attended by the people from the skydiving school, with a four-by-four waiting to take her back to civilization. And champagne, chilled champagne, was part of the deal. She'd settle for good ole H_2O now. And the sight of another human being would be nice. Real nice . . .

What was she supposed to do? Obviously someone had to have been tracking her. They would know she was off course, right? She should stay here until they found her; no sense in trying to find them. She didn't have a clue. Suddenly she thought of Bryan and how worried he would be and tried mentally to call out to him that she was all right. At least she was in one piece, a little bruised but still alive. Attempting to stand, she yelped as her right ankle gave out and she fell back down. Damn, she must have injured it when she landed. Just what she needed now, a swollen ankle. Knowing she should keep her shoe on, she fought back the tears and wondered again why the hell she had ever left her normal, predictable life back east. She'd had a cute little apartment on the Delaware River, a decent job as a computer sales rep, even if it meant dealing with anal retentives all day. Still, it paid well, sometimes real well. She had friends who would never think of skydiving . . . normal people, who went to the theater and to Starbucks and perhaps took to rollerblading for adventure. Immediately she thought of Bryan and sighed, knowing everything she had left behind was meaningless compared to her brother. Okay, her motivation was definitely love *and* craziness. But this . . .

This was scary.

She had no idea how long she remained hidden from the blaring sun beneath the makeshift canopy, because time held no meaning for her. Her watch was left behind in a locker, along with her purse, the car keys to the rental—everything. She kept the jumpsuit on to protect her skin from frying. Once she had tried taking off her helmet, but found that the shield cut down the intense glare of the sun and had put it back on. Where were they? Where was the group from the school? Bryan? She couldn't just stay out here all day. She needed water. She wanted to strip off the stifling jumpsuit and imagined jumping naked into the hotel swimming pool. Closing her eyes, she tried to concentrate on the delicious image—plunging into cool water, having it surround her and lower her body temperature in seconds, feeling it wash over her face, through her hair . . .

"You came."

Hearing the words, Mairie stopped breathing and lifted the edge of the canopy away from her head. She had imagined that, right? Maybe she was starting to hallucinate from the heat and lack of water. Dehydration could do that . . .

"I knew you would. Thank you."

This was too real. She pulled the canopy completely away and looked behind her, just to make sure she wasn't delusional. What she saw didn't help confirm her state of mind.

A man, some kind of man, was staring at her. All he was wearing were dirty heavy pants and boots. He was naked from the waist up. His chest and face were painted in some sort of Indian zigzag sign that was smeared, and his hair hung below his shoulders in a matted mess. He looked . . . wild. Crazy. And he was staring at her as if he'd seen a ghost.

Fear entered and made the adrenaline start pumping fast. She had to stay calm. This guy was definitely not from the skydiving school. He didn't look like he had attended any school, ever. He looked . . . *feral.*

"Hi." She tried smiling. "Thank God you found me. I've, ah, sorta wandered off course, and I need to get back to civilization. Can you tell me where I am?"

"What are you?" The man's voice was low, as though he might be frightened of her, yet he walked around her to stand in front. He squatted down and stared at her as if she were an exhibit in the zoo.

How do you answer that question? she wondered. He must be a hermit, or something. He wasn't an Indian, not with brown hair, sun-streaked, and blue eyes. Maybe he was crazy. Really crazy. Damn . . . what kind of luck was this?

Stay calm, she told herself. The best way to deal with crazy people was to stay calm. She had no idea where she'd heard that, but it seemed like good advice, considering the person before her. "You see, I was skydiving, and like I said, I must have gotten off course, so if you could just point me in the right direction, I can—"

"You dived from the sky?" His tone was filled with disbelief.

"Well, yes. Actually, I jumped from a plane and *then* dived, but that doesn't matter . . . I just need some help here, and then I can—"

"What is a plane?" he interrupted again, tilting his head and staring at her with the intensity of someone examining a bug under a microscope.

She stared back at him, wondering if he was messing with her mind. How could he not know what a plane was? *"You know . . . an airplane."* She pointed to the sky and made hand gestures.

"What *are* you?"

Suddenly she remembered that she was still wearing the helmet and pulled it off. Of course, he hadn't been able to see her face; that was it. Maybe he'd been alone out here for so long that he'd forgotten modern things. Dropping the helmet to the ground, she pulled her long hair out from between the collar of her jumpsuit and twisted it on top of her head. Holding it up, she tried smiling.

"I'm a woman. See?"

He fell back onto the ground in awe.

She couldn't help it. She laughed. Seeing his startled expression, Mairie attempted to get serious, but found that his reaction to her still made her giggle. How long *had* this guy been out here, if the sight of a woman had that effect on him?

"Are you God, the Great Spirit?" The words were barely audible.

She heard them and looked around her to see if something else was causing him to ask these questions. Surely it couldn't be her! Turning back, she decided to keep it light. No sense in trying to reason with a person who had obviously been in the sun too long. "I'm not God," she said with a grin, "though I do like the fact that you would consider God might be female. Pretty enlightened." Compliments wouldn't hurt. "However, I'm just a woman who's lost and looking to get back to civilization. So if you could just point me in the right direction, I'll leave you and—"

"You're my gift. I saw you fall from heaven."

Mairie started unhooking her harness and gathering the parachute to stuff into the sack. Maybe he was one of those mountain people who had lost all touch with reality, those weird men who haven't seen a woman in years, and kidnaps them. Whatever he was . . . she was getting as far away from him as possible. "Look, mister . . . I'm not your gift, okay? I'm lost. My brother is waiting for me, and I've got to find him. If you can't help me, fine . . . but I need to get back now."

Immediately he got up and started to help her gather the material of her chute. "What is this?" he asked, running the silky fabric through his fingers.

Yanking on the strings, she pulled it out of his hands. "It's a parachute," she answered, realizing she must be addressing a mentally challenged adult.

"Is this how you came from heaven?"

"I didn't come from heaven. I came from a *plane*." She tried curbing the exasperation in her voice, yet knew she'd been unsuccessful. This was *way* too weird. When she found Bryan, she was going to tell him it was time for a hiatus from this adventure business. She needed a break. Maybe they could go to Hawaii and be beach bums for a while, commune with nature, watch sunsets . . .

"What's your name? Do you have one?"

Annoyed that he had interrupted her fantasy, she looked up at him and snapped, "Of course I have a name. *What do you think I am?*"

He slowly stood up to his full height, over six feet, and stared down at her. "You may be a woman, but you're not of this world. I saw you coming from heaven. You tell me what *you* are and *who* you are." The awe had left his voice and expression. Now he sounded annoyed.

She figured she might as well pacify him. What else could she do? There wasn't another human being in sight, and besides, she had snapped at him. "Look, mister . . . my name is Mairie Callahan. M-a-i-r-i-e." She spelled it for him, hoping to break through to reality. "I'm a woman, just like any other, and I came from Pennsylvania to Nevada with my brother on . . . on a sort of holiday, I suppose you might call it. I was skydiving and I guess when I was experiencing terminal velocity I . . . well, kind of experimented, and got off course and landed here. That's it. The whole story. There's supposed to be a truck to take me back and even champagne to celebrate my first jump. So you can imagine how disappointed I am to find myself stranded in the desert."

He was just staring at her.

"What's wrong?" she asked, concerned by his expression. She was trying to get him to understand her predicament, yet he was looking at her as if *she* were the one warped by the sun.

"What the hell are you talking about? Terminal . . . what? A truck?" He shook his head in disbelief and put his hands on his hips as he looked out to the desert. "What kind of answer is this? None of it makes sense. You were to be the answer to my vision quest. You are supposed to be my gift. But what are you?"

"Okaaay . . ." Mairie drew out the word as she continued to stuff the material into the sack. Obviously there was no reasoning with this man. She would simply get up and walk away from this madness. There had to be a road somewhere. She would rather sit by the side of it than continue this useless discussion with a crazed hermit.

Once she had managed to stuff enough of the parachute into the bag, she stood up and tried putting her weight onto her right foot. Pain tore through her, willing her to sit back down, yet she ignored it. Fear of the man overrode even that. *His gift.* Right! This guy had no idea who he was dealing with. A divorced woman with an attitude was not about to become any man's gift! Ever again!

"What are you doing?" he demanded, watching her pick up her gear.

She hoisted the satchel over her shoulder and

looked at him. "I'm leaving. I am not your gift. I am not your vision. You can stay out here and play Geronimo, if that's what gets your rocks off, but I'm not about to enter into your game. I'm going back to civilization, and when I find my brother, I'm gonna punch the shit out of him for getting me into this. So . . ." She raised her right hand and held up two fingers. "Peace, and may the force be with ya, 'cause I'm outta here."

She turned and started walking, limping, away from him. She kept her gaze on the horizon, praying that she was heading in the right direction. If she kept her focus, concentrated on it, she might be able to obliterate the agonizing pain in her ankle. Suddenly she heard the sound of his footsteps behind her and held her breath as she waited for him to make a move.

"Geronimo is an Apache. I've been adopted into the Paiutes. There is nothing but desert before you for twenty miles. You should come with me into the mountains. I need water, and you will soon. I can't leave you here to die."

She stopped and turned around. He was looking at her with resentment, as if she'd taken away his birthday present. Maybe he was luring her into a kidnaping. She'd heard stories . . . gazing out to the glare of the desert before her, Mairie fought the burning at her eyes that signaled the onset of tears. This could not be happening. What were her choices? To walk into the unknown, perhaps to her death, or to follow him into the mountains and risk whatever that held? Before her was the desert, cruel and unyielding. Images of herself crawling in dehydration across its floor made her shudder in horror. "There's water in the mountains?" Already her tongue felt too big for her mouth.

He nodded. "Several streams. There is even one close by, but too dirty to drink because it's the runoff from the mountain pools above. I have fasted for three days and I must get to one of those pools soon. I cannot stay here with you much longer."

Beyond the smeared yellow and red paint, she could see the strain in his face, a deep sadness in his eyes, and knew he was telling the truth. This man needed water more than she did. He didn't have the strength right now to kill her or kidnap her. A spark of compassion entered her heart. So he was a little crazy. He had come to her and offered help. Sighing, she again looked around her.

The man? Or the desert?

"There's a small waterfall less than forty minutes from here. But we must climb. Are you able?"

That did it. A waterfall.

She was so thirsty and hot she would climb over cut glass to reach it. "Okay, I'll do it," she said finally, and exhaled deeply, having made a decision. She could only pray it was the right one. "But I'm just going to refresh myself and then I have to find my brother. I don't want any funny business. Understand?"

He smiled slightly for the first time, and she caught a glimpse of white teeth behind his parched lips. "Mairie Callahan, the only funny business here is *you*. But standing on the slope of this mountain, under this sun, is not the place to figure you out. Follow me." He turned and started walking in the direction of the red rock outcroppings that led to the pass now in view above the mountain range.

Adjusting the sack over her shoulder, she looked once more toward the horizon and took another shuddering deep breath . . . then turned and limped after him.

They had gone no more than twenty yards when he stopped and waited for her to catch up. Pointing to the parachute, he said, "You are in no condition to carry that bag. Leave it. Your foot is hurt and the weight of that thing is adding to it."

"I can't leave it," she answered, dropping it to the ground for a respite as she caught her breath. "I signed papers and I'm responsible for this equipment. It'll cost me two thousand dollars if I don't return with it. They have my VISA number."

He squinted. "What are you talking about? What is a veeza number? Is that Spanish? You are a strange woman." He said the last word as if he still wasn't sure that she was human.

Her lower jaw hung open in disbelief. "VISA! Credit cards! Eighteen percent of legalized robbery! How long have you been out here?"

"Six days. What difference would that make?"

"Oh, you've been gone longer than six days, my friend. You've been gone a *long* time if you've never heard of credit cards." She pushed her hair back off her forehead and picked up the sack. "Never mind. Forget I mentioned it. Let's get to the water."

When they finally came to the base of the mountain, Mairie had almost bitten through her bottom lip to stop the tears. Pain shot up her right leg until it went numb, and that scared her more. The crazy man hadn't spoke to her, except to grunt and take the parachute and fling it over his shoulder. And the closer she got to him . . . well, clearly the man hadn't bathed in some time. In truth, he reeked. She told herself that she'd crossed some invisible line in reality. Skydiving, that was bad enough, but this— trekking up this desert mountain slope, with some deranged feral being who thought he was an Indian on a vision quest and had absolutely no knowledge of modern life, was beyond belief. Wait till she got back and told Bryan. She knew they'd laugh over it eventually, but right now the nightmare continued.

"How much farther?" she asked, knowing she sounded like a kid on a car trip.

"Less than a mile," he answered, holding out his hand to pull her up the incline.

"A *mile!*" Dear God . . . she just wanted to cry out and surrender. Her body felt like a bruised rag doll. How was she supposed to endure this for another mile? She placed her hand in his and felt the strength in his darkly tanned fingers. Maybe he did have enough of it left to harm her. Pushing the frightening thought out of her mind, she concentrated on the climb and hoped she wasn't doing permanent damage to her ankle. How could she have let Bryan talk her into this? She swallowed the painful lump in her throat. He would find her soon; she had to believe that. She refused to accept that her last picture of her brother would be of him jumping from the plane and disappearing. They would be reunited; she knew it. She would never rest until it happened. In the end it was love that gave her the strength and resolve to keep going.

And a waterfall. She figured she might as well at least admit the truth to herself.

He was certainly a man of few words, Mairie thought, as she broke yet another nail and cursed under her breath. He hadn't spoken since they'd left the foothills an hour ago, but he did go to the trouble to find a gnarly branch and break it in two places to make a primitive cane for her. Another grunt was his only communication when he'd shoved it in her direction. She tried to figure out why he was so angry at her and thought perhaps it was because she had laughed at him. Male ego . . . she could never figure that one out with the men in her past life, so attempting to analyze this one was far beyond her comprehension. What did it matter, anyway? In a few hours she would find civilization, phone her brother, and that would be it. Maybe she should report him to some social agency . . . maybe they could help him adjust to modern society. She wanted to repay him—that is, if they actually ever got to this water. He could be leading her on some wild-goose chase, confusing her so she couldn't find her way back. He said she was supposed to be his gift... whatever the hell *that* meant. Anything could happen.

Was she becoming paranoid as a result of dehydration? Well, any normal person would agree that she had reason. Her guide on this impossible trek was...was weird. Really, really weird. Suddenly, just as she thought she would collapse from heat, thirst, and exhaustion, she heard it. To her, at that moment, it was the most beautiful sound in the world.

Water. Running water...

Smiling, she looked up to say something but saw that her quasi–Indian hermit had disappeared. For a split second she thought he had deserted her, but she realized, as she clawed at the striated red stone before her, he had just gone on ahead. When she came over the top of the boulder, she saw him running toward the stream. He stood for only a few seconds before falling backward into it.

That was all she needed. Hobbling the remaining distance, she dropped her cane and knelt before the clear mountain stream in deep homage. It was the most wonderful sight she had ever beheld. Water. Beautiful, life-saving water.

Her hands were shaking as she reached down to scoop it to her mouth. She didn't think about bacteria, diseases, or the man downstream. She felt almost crazed by the desire to taste water and, frustrated by her flimsy efforts, she stretched out until she was lying on the ground and her head was inches above it. She kept splashing her face and gulping in the delicious, precious liquid, feeling she would never be sated. From the corner of her eye, she saw that the man rose from the water and was walking upstream. He didn't say a word as he passed her, and Mairie stopped drinking as a strange thought entered her mind. Here she had called him feral, and she was doing a pretty good imitation of an animal herself. Funny how when technology disappeared, instincts kicked in. She continued to watch him through the long, damp strands of her hair. He moved toward the small waterfall and began unbuttoning his pants.

Oh, shit! Now he's going to make a move, she thought, as terror raced once more through her system. She should have known she couldn't trust him! Her fear kept her paralyzed at the bank of the stream as she watched him. He stepped out of the water and pulled off his boots, then, with his back to her, he removed his trousers. Her breath seemed caught in her throat, as though if she didn't breathe he would forget she was there and leave her alone. Fighting panic, she continued to watch him as he reentered the water and began unbuttoning those longjohns. She felt frozen in fear. A part of her brain was saying that she should get up, find a weapon, do *something* . . . yet he walked away from her toward the outjutting of rocks, and even though her rational mind was telling her that this could not be happening . . . it seemed within moments she was watching a nude man bathing under a waterfall. He used the silt from the bottom of the stream to wash off the paint. His back was turned toward her, so she couldn't actually see him wash off the paint, but she remembered what it had looked like on his chest. Come to think of it, his chest had looked rather strong . . . like living out here had given him a definition that most men would spend a fortune in a gym to achieve. *Don't think of it*, she told herself, and raised her head from the water. Better to sit up and turn her back on the embarrassing scene.

Mairie found that she was breathing heavily and

made herself concentrate on her predicament. Now
that she was here and they could rest for a while in
shade, she decided it was safe to remove her jumpsuit. Besides, she needed to soak her ankle in the
cool water. She unzipped the sleeves and pant legs
and pulled her arms out of it, wincing at her sore
muscles. Throwing it to the side, she couldn't help
but again glance in the direction of the waterfall. It
wasn't like she really wanted to, really—it was just
that her gaze seemed to wander there of its own
accord. Dear God . . .

His hair was hanging straight past his shoulders.
The muscles in the back of his body were clearly
defined. He wasn't really big, not like those men
with no necks. He was built like a runner . . . lean,
with every muscle chiseled in marbled movement as
he continued to wash himself as though it were the
most natural thing in the world to stand out in nature and bathe. He really was feral, like some wild
creature. Ashamed at spying on him, Mairie concentrated on removing her Nikes. Really . . . she'd been
on the brink of responding to him like some sex-
starved woman beholding a buff male body. She
wasn't starved, at least, not for sex . . . and especially
not for some weird mountain man who painted himself up like an Indian. She had some standards.
Traveling with her older brother for seven months
hadn't exactly provided her with opportunities, and
she'd found that in those months of celibacy she'd
lost all desire. It was like any other appetite. It could
be controlled. It could . . . yet as she struggled with
removing her sneaker, she was keenly aware of the
man behind her. He'd better not even think of trying
anything. Eight years ago she'd taken a self defense
class, so he wasn't dealing with some helpless female here.

She sucked in her breath through clenched teeth
as she finally got the Nike off and the pain seemed

to expand, along with the size of her ankle. She carefully removed her sock and pulled up the hem of her Spandex legging before plunging her foot into the stream. She couldn't help crying out as the cold water enveloped the bruise and pain shot up her leg. How was she supposed to walk away from this mountain if one leg was out of commission? Maybe it wasn't sprained. Maybe it was only badly bruised. It still hurt like hell. She thought of the naked man behind her and then her self defense class. Since kicking was the main defensive action, with only one working leg, she was at a distinct disadvantage. Damn . . . what was that old cliché? If it weren't for bad luck, she wouldn't have any luck at all?

Well, it didn't matter how clearly defined his pecs were, he was still unstable and she didn't trust him for an instant. She would be polite, distantly polite, and figure some way out of this mess. Closing her eyes, Mairie focused her mind on more practical matters. She was going to find her brother and normalcy. It was her only plan.

"How's the foot?"

Startled at the sound of his voice, she opened her eyes and looked up through the dappled sunlight to the man standing at her side. He had put those longjohns back on and rested his hands on his hips. She squinted, held her palm up to shelter her vision, and when her pupils dilated sufficiently to allow the light in, Mairie Callahan found that for the first time in her thirty-seven years of being on this planet . . . her voice had deserted her.

His dark, wet hair was slicked back off his face and hanging behind his shoulders. Contrasting against a deep tan, his blue eyes looked wide and . . . and almost normal without paint surrounding them, as if the water had infused them with intelligence. His lashes were damp and spiked, defining the clarity of deep blue irises. And his mouth held a knowing hint of amusement, as if he knew that she had been spying on him. But what robbed her of the ability to speak was a simple plain fact that she couldn't ignore.

He cleaned up well, real well.

In fact, the man was *gorgeous*, like some rugged hero out of a romance novel.

Yup . . . she was in trouble, she thought, hating the fact that her gaze was drawn to a jagged scar on his chest beneath the dark hair that seemed to form a vee and disappear below the two open buttons of his underwear. She smelled it. Felt it. Even tasted it at the back of her tongue.

Trouble. Only this time she didn't know from which one of them it was coming . . .

Jack Delaney continued to stare at the odd woman who sat, in her underwear, speechless before him. He had never seen anything quite like it before. Tight black material clung to her legs and a white cropped sleeveless vest of the same fabric covered her breasts, yet revealed her stomach. She seemed to have no shame in displaying herself, so he couldn't figure out her condition.

"Your foot," he repeated. "How is it?"

She seemed to swallow and search for her voice. "It's killing me. And it's my ankle, actually," she added and looked to it, dangling in the stream. "I think it's sprained, or severely bruised."

She lifted her leg slightly and he saw she had painted her toenails red. He had never seen such a thing. Looking at her swollen ankle and the deep purple color of the skin surrounding it, he sighed. How was she supposed to walk to the encampment? If he did not return at first light, his brothers would begin searching for him. He had no idea how he was going to explain *her* to the Paiutes. He himself was desperate to find any reasonable explanation for her.

If he'd not seen with his own eyes that she'd fallen from the sky, he would think she had wandered off some wagon train and was afflicted with prairie fever. But he could find no explanation for her strange equipment and there was no denying that she was different from any other woman he had known, or even read about. She was . . . otherworldly, eerie, and he couldn't shake the uncanny feeling that somehow, in some preposterous way, she really was his gift. Though how such a perverse creature could be called a gift was beyond his comprehension. One thing Jack had learned in his adopted family was the unwise path of taking everything at face value, that Spirit might use anything to get his attention. At the exact moment of calling out to the Great Spirit in total faith, he had opened his eyes and beheld a sight that robbed him of breath and set his heart racing . . . this incredibly rude and confused being slowly falling from heaven. As much as he wanted to leave behind what felt like a major problem and get back to the camp, how could he desert her?

"What are you staring at?" she demanded, grabbing the strange suit she had discarded and holding it in front of her chest, as though for protection.

He immediately picked up what her actions were implying, and his back stiffened. "I don't know yet what I'm looking at. What kind of woman are you? Where are you from? How did you fall with that material out of the sky? Why were you dressed in men's clothes? What is that hard hat you were wearing when I found you?" He took a deep breath and exhaled his exasperation. *"Who the hell are you?"*

She pushed the long black hair off her face and he could tell she was angry as a deep flush of resentment spread beneath the light dusting of freckles on her cheeks. Her chin tilted, as if she were descended from a royal lineage and merely suffering his presence. And her eyes, those remarkably light eyes, seemed to ignite the blue into a darker shade of outrage. She was near bristling with indignation, and even though she was far from young, she looked like a warrior maiden. In fact, under any other circumstances, he would have found himself mighty attracted to her. But until he got some answers, he didn't even want to remain in the same stream. Not for the first time since he'd encountered her on the desert mountain slope, near the sacred gathering place of red rocks, Jack wondered if the woman were insane. It was for that reason that he wanted to put as much distance between them as possible. He'd seen men lose their minds in the war. He'd come close himself. A woman, especially this impossible woman, made him want to run.

Yet he stood his ground.

"Well? I believe I deserve some answers now. You cannot complain of heat or lack of water, and your foot is receiving the only treatment available. I have done as much as I can, and for this, all I ask is clarification. Who are you? *What* are you?"

She glared up at him, her eyes blazing for battle. Yes . . . definitely a warrior, perhaps not a maiden after all.

"I've already told you my name, and where I'm from. Now, let's turn the tables, shall we? Hmm . . . obviously, once you took your little shower, you ended your Indian game, and now you're supposed to be the big bad cowboy? C'mon, how many more roles do you have to play before we can find the real you? Oh, and speaking of the real thing, try really, *really* hard and see if you can answer my questions for a change. Who the hell are *you*, and what the hell is *your* name?"

His hands dropped to his sides as he stared and fought the urge to dump the rest of her into the water. "My name, madam, is John Fitzhugh Delaney. If you wish, you may address me as Jack."

She seemed triumphant to have gotten that out of him and he didn't know why her reaction annoyed him so much. But it did. Highly.

"Well, how do you do, Mr. Delaney," she said, in a proper voice that barely hid her annoyance. "I appreciate your assisting me and leading me to water, but now I've had enough and I need to get back to civilization. If you'd just point me in the direction where I can find a phone or a fax, I'd be grateful. I need to contact my hotel in Las Vegas. I'm sure I've been reported missing, and pretty soon there will be helicopters out searching for me. I'm actually surprised I haven't seen any yet."

She was looking up to the sky, as if believing something was going to magically come out of it and rescue her from the mountain. She *was* crazy.

A *phone*? A . . . a *fax*? *Heli* . . . something? Surely now there could be no doubt about it. He was obviously stranded on a mountain with someone who belonged in an asylum.

He wondered how to return this gift, and imagined the Great Spirit of his brothers laughing. This god was a Trickster. A Coyote.

And in that moment, staring into the angry eyes of the woman, Jack Delaney realized his quest must be complete.

He got his answer. He was cursed.

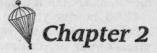

Chapter 2

"Well . . . ? Cat got your tongue, Delaney? Where's the nearest phone?"

He was just staring at her, as though she were a Martian, and Mairie felt whatever shreds of patience she had left dissolving. "C'mon . . . no more games, okay? I have to find my brother."

"And where is this brother of yours?"

Thankful that he was at least speaking again, she answered, "Probably still at the landing zone, or back at the school, or maybe he's even gone into Las Vegas and is talking to the police. I know he won't rest until he finds me." There. That should put some fear into him if he still entertained any ideas about kidnaping her. Although from the look in his eyes, he didn't seem to want to be anywhere near her. Really . . . what had she done, except try to reason with him? It wasn't her fault that he seemed to be living in the past.

"Are you speaking of the Las Vegas ranch?"

"The ranch? You mean that . . . that whorehouse?" Mairie threw back her head and laughed. "I doubt my brother would find anything of interest there. I'm talking about the city—you know, hotels, gambling, shows. I'm staying at the Luxor. I'm sure you've seen the light coming out of the top of the pyramid, even out here. What . . . ? Why are you staring at me like that?''

''You are claiming that you saw a pyramid out here?''

She tried not to giggle. ''A pyramid . . . yes. Haven't you ever gone into Vegas and seen it? It's a hotel. A fabulous hotel.''

''Out here?'' he asked again, as if trying to make sure he'd heard right.

''Well, not here in the mountains, but out there in the valley. A huge pyramid, with the face of a painted pharaoh before it. Come on . . . you have to have seen it, or heard about it.''

''I have heard that Napoleon discovered pyramids in Egypt. When I was back east I even saw drawings of them.''

She look at him, realized that he was serious, and warning bells went off inside her head. ''Delaney . . . how long have you been out here?''

''I told you. Six days. I was on a vision quest.''

''Were you on drugs, or something?''

''Drugs? What are drugs?''

She lifted her numbed foot from the water and wished he really had something on him. Morphine would do for this kind of pain, she thought, as she placed her heel gingerly on the ground. ''Did you smoke anything? Eat anything to make you . . . well, forget things?''

''I followed the ritual and chewed the sacred button, that is all. And that wore off yesterday. Exactly what are you attempting to say?''

''*Peyote?*'' She tried to hide her shock. ''Well, that explains it. You're still hallucinating, Delaney. You've forgotten everything modern and think you're living in the past.'' Somehow the explanation made her feel much better. So he experimented with drugs on his vision quest. Who was she to judge? She didn't understand anything about Indian ritual, but she had read enough about peyote to know that it was a hallucinogen. All she had to do was be patient and see if she could reason with him until the effects wore off.

"I know exactly where I am living, madam. Do not use that excuse to explain your appearance. I know what I saw, and you have carried the evidence of it up this mountain because of a veesa number. You are the one who is speaking in riddles."

She looked out to the water and sighed. "Okay. Then tell me what year it is." She held her breath, waiting . . . when he spoke, his words had a chilling effect.

"It's 1877. You don't know that? What year do *you* think it is?"

Her empty stomach clenched in fear and a frightening heat spread over her chest. This guy was really out of it. How was she supposed to reason with him? Stay calm, the voice inside of her advised. Don't excite him. Just answer truthfully and maybe it will connect with reality for him. "Mr. Delaney . . . please believe me . . . it's 1999. You're a hundred and twenty-two years behind in your mind."

He merely stared at her for a few moments before cursing under his breath and abruptly walking away toward his boots.

"What?" she demanded. "I'm telling you the truth. You can't keep going around believing you're living in the past. If you've been out here for six days, then surely you've seen planes at night coming in and going out of McCarran Airport. You have to be able to see the lights from Las Vegas from this high up in the mountains. How can you deny all that?"

He picked up his boots and emptied the water from them, ignoring her question.

Mairie figured she might as well try again to break through. If she didn't, she'd be out here all night

waiting for him to come down off his trip . . . and
she needed direction to the nearest town. A real
town that existed now, not buried in the past of the
Old West and this man's confused mind. "Can you
just try and think of a town with a phone? That's
really all I need."

He spun around so quickly that his damp hair
whipped around his face. "Woman, what the hell is
a *phone?*"

The last word was shouted so loud that Mairie
swore it reverberated against the nearby boulders
and slammed into her solar plexus. Stay calm, she
told herself. He's . . . tripping, or something. "A telephone. You know . . ." She held up her hand in a
poor imitation of holding a receiver to her ear. "You
speak into it and someone answers. Your voice is
carried over wires, or sometimes shot up to a satel-
lite in the sky. I know you must have used one. Try
to remember."

"Shot up to the sky? Your *voice* is shot up to the
sky?"

"Yes. I mean, I don't know exactly how it works.
I just know it works. Like television." When he again
spoke, his voice was so low and so serious that despite the heat of the day . . . Mairie shivered.

"I don't want you to talk anymore, do you understand? Can you possibly understand me through
all your incoherent rambling? Be quiet. *Quiet!*" He
sat at the water's edge, about ten feet away from her,
and stared into the stream. "I need to think."

"Yes," she whispered. "You do that. You think."

"Quiet!"

She clamped her lips closed and pushed the hair
back off her face. She would keep quiet, watch him,
and pray that he *could* think . . . rationally. What
dumb luck that her only hope of surviving this ordeal was a druggie hermit who thought he was living a hundred and twenty-two years ago. Nobody

was going to believe this. Nobody. She found it hard
to believe herself. In the silence that followed, Mairie
went over everything that had happened since she
left that airplane. Where *was* the city? Why hadn't
she seen Bryan's chute when hers opened? Why had
everything normal seemed to have disappeared?
Down deep, in a place that she knew she was denying, she was terrified that her brother might not
find her, that she might never look into his eyes
again.

She had no idea how long she remained battling
the frightening thoughts. Time as she had known it
seemed to have disappeared. Alone with this man,
up here on this mountain, with nothing but nature
as a reference, time held no meaning. Maybe that's
why Delaney had mentally slipped back into a time
that had seemed to him more simple. He sounded
educated, if a little proper in his speech. He could
be a disillusioned corporate executive who had finally burned out. Just her luck, to have stumbled
upon his private nervous breakdown.

"Can you walk?"

Turning her head, she saw him dressed and staring at her. "I think so," she said, and began putting
on her sock. "God, it hurts," she mumbled, as she
attempted to slide the heavy white cotton over her
swollen foot. When she tried putting her Nike back
on, she almost yelped in pain and frustration. She
couldn't get it on.

Tears she'd been holding back since the airplane
came forth and burst from her eyes. It was impossible to stop them, nor did she even try. She merely
sat with her shoe in her hands and allowed the tears
to come. What was she going to do now? How was
she ever going to get out of this mess? And why . . .
why was all this happening to *her?*

"You can't walk, can you?" His words were more
of a statement than a question.

She shook her head and swiped at her nose with the back of her hand. "I don't know. I . . . I can't get my Nike back on."

"Your shoe?"

She merely nodded, no sense in trying to explain brand names now. "Maybe I can walk with only my sock."

"Not in these hills. Your foot would be further injured by the sharp rocks." He stood up and walked toward her. Picking up the parachute, he said in a resigned voice, "We'll have to spend the night. There's a cave not far from here."

"A *cave?* I can't! I have to get back to the city. My brother . . ." Her mind refused even to contemplate what he was suggesting.

Dropping the bag, he raised his hands to the sky and started waving them. "There is nothing . . . do you understand. . . . nothing in the valley that can be called a city! There is only the old Mormon fort in the middle of it that O.D. Gass took over and renamed Las Vegas Ranch. He has about four hundred head of cattle and trades supplies with travelers, but there's no city, woman. Try and get that through your head. You are not living in the future. . . . in . . . in 1999! There is no device that will shoot your voice up into the sky so you can call out and find your brother. Look around you. You are here, on a mountain, in the middle of a desert, with a useless foot. What would you have me do, carry you down? It would take days."

She couldn't stop the tears from falling. Either he was totally crazy, or she was. There had to be an answer. There had to be a way back to sanity. It would obviously be up to her to find it. "Are you saying that this . . . this Gass person doesn't have a telephone on his ranch?" she asked, sniffling like a wounded child. She didn't care how she appeared anymore. This was serious now.

He was staring at her as if he wanted to make her disappear. "I can't believe you asked that," he muttered, sitting down and shoving his foot into a boot. "Look, I'm going to check out the cave and see what I can find to eat. You stay put. Don't even move, because I swear to you, if you're not here when I get back, I'm leaving. I should be halfway to the Paiute camp by now, instead of stuck with some crazy woman who thinks she's living in 1999!" He jammed his other foot into the remaining boot and muttered, "Some gift!"

"I'm not crazy!" she nearly shouted at him. "And I'm not your *gift*. So you can just put that one out of your mind. And if you think I'm thrilled to be spending the night in a bloody cave with some lunatic on peyote, think again!"

He looked like he wanted to strangle her so she wasn't all that surprised that he didn't answer. He just got up and left.

She sat by the water and cried. Cried for her brother. Cried for her ankle. Cried for the hotel room with a Jacuzzi that was waiting for her . . . somewhere. It seemed like the perfect time to indulge in self-pity. She'd put up a brave front long enough. The crazy man was gone, and . . . and what did it matter any longer? She'd known in the airplane. She'd known when her brain had frozen up on her, after she'd jumped. She'd known when she'd landed. And she'd have to be as nuts as Delaney not to know it now. She simply had to acknowledge the gravity of her situation.

She was in danger.

There was no one to turn to. She was on her own and would have to use her wits to get herself out of this mess. Trouble was . . . she was in a battle of wits with a lunatic.

She needed a plan. That was it. It had worked for her in the past. When she'd thought she'd lose her mind at the breakup of her marriage, she'd formulated a survival plan and had focused on it. That's what she needed now . . . a survival plan back to sanity.

He returned to the stream a half hour later, telling her that the cave was prepared, and she silently accepted his help in hobbling to it. That was her plan: silence. She figured she would not let him goad her into another argument. She would silently spend the night, endure whatever awaited her, and in the morning she was getting off this mountain if she had to roll off it. Resting her foot all night made sense, considering her predicament, and she was sure that a search plane would be out before dark. If she didn't see one before nightfall, then it would come tomorrow. Thinking of Bryan and the anguish he must be enduring, she mentally called upon the strength of her brother to help her accept whatever happened. Bryan was the bravest person she knew, and his love would see her through this. It simply had to—it was all she had left.

Love. Right then it seemed the most powerful force in the universe.

Delaney told her they were following dung trails left by burros and mountain sheep which led to a unique outcropping of massive red sandstone boulders above. There they would find the cave. She suffered her pain in silence as she slowly made her way over sand, silt, and gravel. The ground was dry, harsh, and baked in earthen tones of umber. Sagebrush, small succulents, aloe, weeds, oleander, and Joshua trees dotted the trail. She couldn't think, wouldn't think, what she was hiking into. She kept her gaze in front of her, not daring to look at the edge of the boulders that dropped off to the valley far below. Not yet . . . when they reached the cave, she would have the advantage of being so far above the valley that she would be able to see the city and know what direction to follow. But until then she would keep quiet, endure the pain each time her heel touched the ground, lean on her makeshift cane, and accept the help of Delaney while privately formulating her plan of escape.

They rounded the side of the boulder and Mairie was breathing heavily as they stopped in front of strange figures etched into the red stone.

"The ancients," Delaney answered her unspoken question. "They carved these out before recorded history. This is a sacred place."

"Petroglyphs," she whispered in awe, forgetting her vow of silence. She could feel the almost mystical energy surrounding her as her finger reached out and lightly touched a stick figure drawing of a man with a halo above his head. "These have been here for thousands of years . . ."

"Probably." Delaney breathed deeply as he stared at the etchings. "The ancestors of the Paiutes. There's a story here, though it hasn't been revealed to me. What is that name you called them?"

"Petroglyphs," she repeated, studying the other drawings of more strange figures with more halos and fallen animals with Spirits rising from them. There were cryptic images she couldn't decipher. One almost looked like a figure with a parachute. Another appeared to be pointing to a craft of some kind. She wondered who had left them. What story had they been trying to leave behind? What were they saying to their children, great grandchildren, their lineage, and to us? "They're beautiful. So primitive, yet still powerful."

He nodded. "I left my things here when I performed the ritual. They're in the cave. Come . . . it's not far now."

She started to follow him and then stopped. Suddenly she knew that if she turned around from this vantage point she would be able to see for miles in all directions. It was her moment of truth. Now, she would know . . .

Lifting her head, she took a deep breath and gazed out over the valley spread below like an unfurled earthen blanket.

Nothing.

It was as if she were on top of the earth and able to see forever. She turned east, north, south, and finally lifted her face to the setting sun and felt her legs shaking, her heart racing, her head throbbing as the truth slammed into her brain. Try as hard as she might, she couldn't deny it.

"Where did it all go?" she whispered.

"What?"

"The city. What happened to it?" She stared into his eyes and tried to keep her voice from trembling. "What happened to *me?*"

He looked uncomfortable at her reactions and her words. "Come, let's go to the cave now. You need to get off that foot."

"Yes." She wouldn't think about it now. She couldn't think about it. Reason, sanity, had deserted her. Cities didn't just disappear. She didn't free fall that long. She couldn't have been that far off course. The city should be there. There was no logic to this. Where was everything? Maybe it was the energy of this place. She needed to get away and think clearly. "Let's go to this cave." Her voice held the distinct tone of fear. She heard it. She knew Delaney felt it. And now . . . it no longer mattered.

She felt like she was still free falling. This time into madness.

He led her away from the boulder and she concentrated on every step. If she focused on her movements, she wouldn't have to think of what she'd just seen. Or, what she hadn't seen . . . a city, a way out, a reinstatement of normalcy.

"This is it?" she asked, seeing the opening in the red sandstone.

"Yes, it isn't big, but we'll be sheltered from the elements and I can build a fire out here to cook."

"Cook, what?" she asked, remembering she hadn't eaten since last night. She'd been afraid to have breakfast before skydiving. She was hungry. Really hungry. She peeked into the cave, saw a cloth bag in the corner and something else, something furry. She shrieked in fright before backing out. "There's a . . . an animal in there!"

Delaney stuck his head inside for a brief moment and then turned to her. "It's supper."

"You mean . . . ?"

He merely nodded and she hesitantly looked back into the cave. Mairie recoiled in horror when she realized what he meant. "What is it?" she asked, already feeling sorry for the poor thing that looked like its neck had been broken.

"Prairie dog."

She turned and stared at Delaney. "You killed it?"

He stared back at her. "Unless you know of another method of eating . . . yes, I killed it."

She couldn't keep the shudder from running through her body. She had a hotel room somewhere, with a telephone that she could use to order room service, and here she was, about to spend the night in a cave with a crazy man and eat a dog. How much more bizarre could this become?

In the back of her mind came a tiny voice whispering that she would soon find out.

An hour later she gave up trying to figure out the unusual turns in her life. She had just returned from hobbling around the boulder to relieve herself and was seated on a flat rock overlooking the valley. Delaney squatted in front of the fire, slowly turning the poor skinned little prairie dog over a makeshift spit. The sun had set and darkness was quickly descending, turning the sky from orange to pink to violet purple. At any other time she would have appreciated the show of nature.

"Here," Delaney said, and held out a plant that looked like strange white string beans, about five inches long, bunched into clusters.

"What are they?"

"Mesquite beans. You grind them."

"You want me to grind these?" She almost laughed. "Sure. Show me a Cuisinart and I'll be happy to." She held the hard beans in her hand and wondered what on earth he thought she could do with them.

Bending down, Delaney picked up two rocks and started to show her how to crush the beans. After he had one ground down to meal, he picked out the white shell fragments and handed the rocks to her. "Now *you* do it. Make sure you get all the shells out, or you might lose a tooth."

She stared at the rocks, at him, back to the ground bean, then back again at him. "You're kidding, right?"

"No, madam, I am not. Since you're sitting here, you can grind the beans while I gather more wood for the fire. It can get cold up here at night."

"Delaney, what in the world are you going to make with these?"

He looked at her as if she were brain dead. "Cakes."

"We're having cake?" Prairie dog and cake . . . what a meal.

He merely shook his head, as if deciding her question wasn't worthy of a reply and got up. "Just grind them," he muttered before walking away.

Not caring for the man's condescending attitude, Mairie's pride rose once more to the surface and she figured she'd show him. So what if he was good looking? He was still nuts. He actually was treating her as if *she* were the one who was delusional. She broke three more nails, scraped two fingers, cut her thumb when picking out the razor-sharp shells, and increased her vocabulary by making up words that a sailor would have trouble figuring out. Yet when Delaney had returned, she had a small pile of ground meal on one side of the flat rock and the shells on the other. And she had to admit that she was proud of her accomplishment. Plus . . . it made her feel better to contribute something to this high desert dinner al fresco.

He merely grunted and scooped up the meal into his hand. Not even a thank-you or an acknowledgment that there wasn't a single speck of shell to be found. Well, obviously, when someone was teaching him proper speech, they forgot to instruct him in manners. What did it matter? After tomorrow, when the plane spotted her and a rescue team got to her, she'd never have to see him again. She'd make sure that she and Bryan did something nice for him, maybe give him a reward for helping her . . . but after that, it was *adios, amigo*. One night. That's all she had to get through. Just one night. Alone with a good-looking crazy man. In a cave. In the middle of nowhere.

She knew she would laugh about this one day.

All thoughts of laughter vanished as she watched him add water from a canteen to the meal and form flat cakes in his hands. He placed them on the hot rocks of the fire, wiped his hands on his thighs, and picked up his knife.

She knew he must have used one to skin the prairie dog, but he'd done it while she was behind the boulder. This was the first time she'd seen it, and it looked frightening. It was long and gleamed dangerously in the firelight as he held it before him and examined the blade.

Okay . . . she had to get through just one night in

a cave with a good-looking crazy man *who had a knife*. As fear once more entered her system, Mairie knew she would never find anything humorous in this situation. This had the potential to be terrifying, and as tired as she was, she knew she wasn't going to sleep.

It was going to be one long night.

He glanced at her across the fire and seemed to read her mind. Beneath that rough cotton shirt was a scar on his chest. She vividly remembered it and wondered if he'd received it in a knife fight. Darkness had now closed in around them and she was glad that she'd put on her jumpsuit, for the temperature had dropped. Still, she knew it was not the cool air that caused her to shiver. There was a look in his eyes, as if he were peering into her soul, and she felt relieved to break eye contact. "How much longer?" she asked, to make conversation. To heck with her plan of silence.

"The cakes will be done soon. Then we can eat." He was still staring at her, holding the knife out to the fire.

"Ah . . . how did you learn to do all this?" She desperately wanted to get him talking, to stop studying her. To put down the knife. "Do you camp a lot?"

His eyes narrowed, as if not understanding her question. "I told you. I was adopted into the Paiutes when I was young. This is . . ." he looked to the fire, ". . . basic survival out here."

"Really? You were adopted when you were young? By Indians? I thought you meant that it was simply some kind of honorary thing. But you were really adopted into an Indian tribe?"

"Yes."

"Wow. I'm impressed." And she was, if he was telling the truth. "How old were you?"

"Twelve."

He certainly wasn't offering anything personal. It was like root canal, digging for information from him. "That is young. You . . . you lived with them?" It didn't makes sense to her. A white child, almost a teenager, adopted by Indians. She wondered what social agency had placed him in such an unusual setting.

"Yes. I lived with them."

"Are you part Indian? Is one of your parents Indian?" It was the only thing she could think of to explain the situation.

He shook his head. "My parents were white."

"White. Hmm . . . they died? I'm sorry, that's too personal." Conversation was one thing, but she could see that he was getting uncomfortable with her questions.

"They were killed while we were traveling to California."

Her heart lost some of its fear and opened slightly to him. "I'm so sorry. Car accident?"

"What?"

"Car accident." It seemed a reasonable assumption.

"We were traveling on a wagon train. A war party of Mojave Indians from southern Arizona attacked us. My mother hid me inside a water barrel that fell over during the assault. It must have been two days before the Paiutes came and took me back to their camp."

Mairie simply stared at him. She wasn't going to touch that one. Okay . . . let him continue to fantasize if he wanted. While he held that knife, she was not about to contradict him. Obviously, the residue of peyote was still affecting him. Maybe it was like LSD with flashbacks. Granted, she was from the East and not familiar with western tradition, but she was pretty damn sure wagon trains had not been a common form of transportation for quite some time.

"How 'bout that dinner?" she asked, forcing her lips into a big grin. "I am truly starved."

He stuck his knife under one of the cakes and lifted it to a rock outside the fire bed. He then cut into the meat and pulled it from the carcass, licking his fingers when he'd dropped it onto the same rock. She realized it was her dinner plate when he stood up and offered it to her.

"Thank you," she said, and inhaled the gamy aroma. It didn't matter what it tasted like. She had to eat to keep up her strength for whatever awaited her through the night. And there was no way she was going to insult him now. Not when she was spending the next ten hours in the dark with him and his knife—a man who continued to stick to his story of living in the past.

She ate in silence, forcing herself to chew the stringy meat and dry tasteless bean cake. Both were protein, and even though her stomach rebelled, Mairie was determined to keep each bite down. She took deep breaths and finished every single crumb.

As if reading her mind, he handed her the canteen. It was old, dented, and the leather strap was soft and worn. Unplugging the top, she brought it to her mouth. The water was warm and tasted of metal, yet she took several gulps and handed it back. Delaney drank from it and placed it on the ground next to him. He tore the carcass apart and handed her a leg. Looking at the tiny limb, Mairie shook her head.

Delaney shrugged and bit into it. She watched as he cleaned the bone and sucked on it as if to extract every bit of nourishment. He made a good Indian, she thought. He didn't waste a thing. Finally, when he sat back against a boulder and sighed, she knew he was satisfied. Well, she thought . . . it appeared that dinner was over. *Now* what?

Intense darkness surrounded them. There were no lights in the distance. No city. No planes . . . only the most spectacular display of stars that she'd ever seen. She'd been watching him so closely for the last hour that she had almost missed it. Lifting her chin, she stared in awe at the sky above her. Thousands of stars formed a canopy of brilliant beauty.

"God . . . it's beautiful," she whispered.

"Yes."

She heard his voice, yet kept her gaze on the stars. She had never seen anything like it in her life. Without the reflection of city lights, the stars seemed to come out and display all their magnificent glory. "Doesn't it seem surreal?" she murmured. "What we're actually seeing is the past."

"The past?"

She nodded as she continued to take in the glittering show of bright jewels against the night sky. "I read somewhere that there are more than two hundred billion stars. Imagine that. And they are discovering more every year. This book said it took years for the light from the stars to travel to our atmosphere. Light years, millions and millions of miles. So what we're looking at is not that star as it appears right now in this moment, wherever it is in the universe, but as it appeared years ago, millions of millions of miles ago. Amazing, huh?"

"Where did you learn this?"

She blinked and looked at him. He was staring at her with an odd expression.

"I told you. I read it. In a book. You know . . . a book? Maybe when I was in college."

He seemed surprised. "You attended college?"

Her spine stiffened. "Yes. Is that so surprising? Don't tell me you're a male chauvinist, too."

"A what?"

"Male chauvinist. A man who doesn't believe that women should have the same equal rights as a man. You know . . . equal pay for equal work. The right to hold office. No discrimination because of sex. All the rights granted under the law to males. Of course, I've always thought that women who seek to be equal to men . . . lack ambition." She tried not to laugh.

"And how can a woman hold office, if she can't vote?" He seemed pleased, as if he had punched holes into her argument.

Obviously, he didn't get her joke. "Hey . . . ever hear of the Nineteenth Amendment?"

"No."

It was one word, one simple word, and yet it had a startling effect on her. For she knew he was telling the truth. He had no idea what she was talking about. What had happened to him? How had he lost all memory of history?

"May I ask you a question?"

He nodded.

"How did you get that scar on your chest?" She wanted to know. She needed to know.

He simply stared at her for a few moments, as if deciding whether or not to tell her. Finally, he sighed deeply and said, "In the war."

"The war? Vietnam?"

"What?"

"The war in Vietnam." He seemed a little young for Vietnam. "Or the Gulf war?"

He was looking at her as if she were speaking a foreign language. "Gettysburg. The war between the North and the South? Where have *you* been for the last ten years?"

She tore her gaze away from him and looked back to the stars. It was getting cold, yet she couldn't attribute the chill in her body to the night temperature. He had to be crazy. He *had to be!* For if he wasn't, she was. What was happening here? If she listened to him for one moment, if she believed his words for one instant, then she was the one out of time. She was the one traveling into the past. Like the light from the stars . . .

She shook herself from the irrational thoughts. This simply couldn't be. In the morning she would laugh at herself for even considering such a concept.

"I'm going to sleep," she announced, and stood up. Every muscle in her body rebelled at the movement, yet she ignored the pain as she limped toward the small cave. "Good night, Delaney. Thank you for the meal."

Once inside she arranged herself, using the parachute as a ground cover and blanket. It wasn't much, but she left a goodly portion of it to her side, in case Delaney wanted to cover himself. She would not wait for him to join her. Secretly she hoped he sat in front of the fire all night. She knew she wasn't going to sleep.

Gettysburg! None of it made sense. And she was too tired to figure any of it out now. Tomorrow . . . tomorrow everything would be put in its right order. She would be rescued. Look into her brother's eyes. Get a real bath, real food. She was even going to get a facial and have her nails done, at least what remained of her nails. That was it: she would find a spa and spend the day being pampered. She certainly deserved it. Studying Delaney's profile as he sat before the fire, Mairie fought the dread his words had brought. Something . . . something really strange had happened. Either to him, or to her. Right now, at this moment, in a cave on a mountain in the high desert with a man before her who lived in his head, it was too scary to let it all play out in her own mind.

Life as she had known it seemed to have disappeared.

It was that sense that creeps up on you in sleep, a warning that someone is watching you. She felt it yet was too tired to open her eyes. It persisted and she tried pushing it away, but her instincts were beginning to activate and she felt herself surrendering. As much as she didn't want to lose the warm comfort in front of her, the dream of sleeping next to a handsome cowboy with long brown hair and laughing blue eyes who pulled her against his chest for warmth, something was nudging her to wake up. She felt safe. Protected. Wanted. It was too good to last and Mairie reluctantly opened her eyes. She was immediately confused. Why was she snuggled up against Bryan? Was it still a dream?

Oh . . . my . . . God!

Mairie froze for just a moment before lifting her arm off a man's chest, a man who definitely was not her brother. The heat of humiliation rushed through her body and she blinked a few times, attempting to make some sort of sense out of her surroundings when she again felt that creepy sensation. Lifting herself up on her elbows, she turned her head toward the daylight and stared for a few seconds at the strange figures crouching in front of her at the entrance to the cave.

And then she screamed at the top of her lungs.

Terror slammed her against the back wall as she tried to pull away from them yet she only managed to entangle her feet in the silky parachute as she yanked it up to her chest.

"*What?* What the hell is going on?" Delaney shot upright into a sitting position next to her and pulled the material away from his face. He looked sleepy, irritated, confused.

She stuck out her arm and pointed a shaky finger toward the men.

Delaney turned his head and she couldn't believe how his expression changed. It softened immediately as he called out to them in a guttural language. The men nodded and laughed and moved away from the cave opening.

"They are my brothers," he said. "They came looking for me when I didn't return yesterday." He shoved the material away from him and added, "Get ready. We're about to break camp."

"Who . . . who are they?" Mairie demanded, trying to make her heart stop slamming against her rib cage.

"I told you. My brothers. The Paiutes. We're going to their camp."

He slid out of the cave as nonchalantly as if he'd just delivered the morning mail. She could only clasp the silky chute to her chest and fight back the tears as the truth entered her brain and refused to be denied.

The nightmare was about to continue.

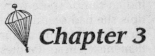 **Chapter 3**

It was bizarre. Truly bizarre. And Mairie wondered how she would ever relate this to Bryan when they were together again. How could she explain being hoisted like a sack of potatoes by three men and taken down the mountain? The grunts and laughter. The look of awe in the eyes of the Indian men when Delaney explained how he had found her. It didn't matter that she didn't understand the language, or that she protested and tried to interject reason. She could see in their expressions that they too believed that she came from ... from heaven ... like some angel, or something. Even Delaney must be questioning it, or why would he have sarcastically muttered that she certainly was heavy for an angel, even one with a bruised wing?

He introduced the two young men as his brothers and gave them names she knew she wouldn't remember, like *Waits for the Sun*, or something. They were shorter than Delaney and stocky, looking more like Mexicans than like the Plains Indians she had read about in her youth. Their hair was long and matted. Their clothing, shifts and pants, really, was made of crude fiber. They seemed very poor, and Mairie decided to be as polite as possible, until they reached this encampment and she could figure out her next course of action. Somehow, she *must* reach her brother and get out of this madness.

All plans seemed to evaporate when she saw the Indian camp. These were not the colorful and exotic tipis she had seen in pictures and movies. This was far different from the romanticized Plains Indian settlements. These Paiutes lived in brush shelters, lodges made from the earth, situated near a creek. Fires were already smoking with some morning meal. Men, women, and children were moving about, all dressed in the same poor clothing. It was quite depressing, and Mairie knew she would not find anything modern to communicate her distress to the outside world. She saw a horse attached to a line that ran from two mesquite trees and wondered if Delaney would take her to civilization with it. At least it was a mode of transportation, although provincial. She would ask later, but not now, not when people were noticing the returning men and beginning to walk toward them. Her body stiffened with apprehension as the tribe crowded around them.

She was lowered to the ground with surprising gentleness and everyone began talking at once in a strange language that Mairie thought was more like sounds than words. What did she know? She was at the mercy of a deranged mountain man and a tribe of Indians that appeared to have turned their backs on any modernization. It was as if she had stepped back in time.

No, she wouldn't think of that. She refused to consider that possibility, for then she truly would be mad and Delaney would be right about her. Instead, she tried smiling at the children who were staring at her with a look of wonderment. What were these men saying to their tribe?

She turned to Delaney and saw he wasn't pleased. "What is being said about me?" she asked, wondering if he would tell her the truth.

He shrugged, pushing the hair back off his forehead as if he were highly annoyed by her question. "My brothers are saying that you came from heaven as my gift. That the gods have smiled on us, and Wolf has outsmarted his brother Coyote in bringing a messenger of hope."

"Me?" She looked at the faces of the Indians and couldn't find it in her heart to contradict their words. If ever a people needed hope, these did.

Delaney spoke the dialect rapidly and she could see that the Indians were not pleased with his words. He turned to her and translated. "I told them that you insist you are not my gift and that you didn't come from heaven. I have said that you are . . . well, the best way to translate is . . . you are confused in your head."

She glared at him. "You told them I was crazy, didn't you? How could you?"

Again, he shrugged, and Mairie wanted to punch his shoulder. "I am *not* crazy, Delaney. I know where I come from. I just don't know how to get back . . . yet. You tell them that. Go ahead, *tell them.*"

Delaney wasn't even listening to her as he spoke with an old man. A small child, a little girl dressed in a rough shift, bravely reached out and touched Mairie's leg and then retreated with a giggle. Looking down to the child, Mairie smiled, and when her gaze connected to the innocence of the girl, Mairie experienced an intense wave of compassion. What kind of life awaited this beautiful child? Her depression set in deeper and she stood quietly until Delaney turned to her.

"You are to go into the elder's lodge. There you will be given food and afterward he wishes to speak with you. He knows little English, so I'll translate."

Her back stiffened. "Delaney, I need to get off this mountain."

His eyes narrowed, as if he were speaking to a disrespectful child. "Look, this is an honor. You can't refuse his hospitality. It would disgrace him."

She gazed to the older man at Delaney's side and saw in his eyes an ageless wisdom. Perhaps this man could help her if Delaney continued to prove difficult. Besides, she wasn't about to stand here in front of all these people and argue with a delusional man who took drugs and thought he was an Indian and then a cowboy and is back being an Indian. Really . . . she had some sense of reality, even if he had lost all concept of the word. Nodding, Mairie reluctantly used her makeshift crutch and allowed herself to be led away.

Entering the largest dirt lodge, she was struck by a wave of pity while looking around the dark, humble shelter. A woman smiled at her and indicated she was to sit on a rug made of rabbit fur. It was soft and worn in places and Mairie gratefully sat down by the dirt wall, keeping her parachute by her. She looked around at the crude structure. Weapons or hunting tools were placed in leather. Baskets were filled and covered by the same rough material that was used for clothing. Looking up, she saw a small smoke hole in the top and was grateful a fire hadn't been lit. The last thing she needed was to be smoked out. Herbs hung from the wall, drying, and she smelled something pungent and slightly citrusy.

Soon she was joined by other women. Some carried in water and bowls of food. Mairie was stunned to realize that the baskets had been woven so tightly that they could contain water without leaking. She smiled her thanks to each woman and they squatted down on the opposite side to stare at her.

It took her only a few seconds to figure out that they were like women anywhere, at any time. They wanted her to taste their food and were waiting for her reaction. She picked up the bowl and looked at the mashed stuff. It didn't look appetizing. She again smiled as she brought it to her nose and inhaled. The women seemed pleased, and Mairie had to use every ounce of willpower not to show how distasteful the aroma was to her. How in the world was she supposed to eat this? Her stomach began rebelling even before she tasted it. For a moment she thought of the Luxor Hotel in Vegas, of the luxury and the delicious food, and felt guilty. She couldn't hurt the feelings of these women. Somehow she would do this.

Mairie scooped out some of the paste and stuck it into her mouth just as the women shouted and began covering their mouths to stop peals of giggles.

Mairie stared at them and almost choked as she held the lump of foul mass on her tongue. Gagging was a distinct possibility.

One of the women came forward and shook her head. She pantomimed spitting. Mairie didn't need further instructions. She spit out the paste and wiped her mouth and tongue with the back of her hand. Another woman came closer and covered the mess with dirt. Then the woman touched her own ankle and pointed to Mairie's.

It took only a few seconds for Mairie to get it. The paste was for her ankle. She giggled at her ignorance and smiled into the faces before her. Such a simple act of human kindness and frailty. Already she felt herself opening to these women.

Hey, maybe they could help her if a friendship could be nurtured . . .

She untied her Nike and gingerly slipped her foot out of the shoe. Inhaling sharply at the pain, Mairie placed the sneaker beside her and removed her sock. The women were murmuring at her actions, and now some gasped at the purple and green bruise that marked her ankle. Or maybe it was her nail polish. They were staring at her toes as if they'd never before seen painted nails.

The woman closest to her held out her hand, as if to show that nothing was inside of it, then slowly she sat in front of Mairie and picked up her heel. This stout woman placed Mairie's foot into the warm water and bathed it. The woman's focus was entirely on Mairie's ankle, as she created tiny waves in the water to run over the bruised part while whispering words Mairie couldn't understand even if she heard them. It was almost as if she were performing some sort of ritual. After a few minutes, the woman used her shift to dry Mairie's foot, then placed it in her lap and began scooping up the paste, lathering it on so gently that Mairie felt soothed by the delicate action.

Never before could Mairie remember someone being so selfless, so sincere in wanting to be of service.

"Thank you," she murmured, and the woman smiled compassionately.

Suddenly an anger rose up inside of her when she thought of all the history books she had read, all the movies she had seen while growing up, depicting all Indians as barbaric and uncaring. She had been in their camp less than a half hour and already they had shown her more empathy than if she had hobbled into a modern convenience store. She realized that for all society's so-called advances, this simple grace of personal charity had been lost. She wondered if we're so afraid of encroaching on another's space, of maybe being sued, perhaps we're afraid to reach out to another in need, to actually touch them? She had little time to ponder these thoughts as two more women joined them. One carried more water and another placed a basket by her side. This one definitely contained food. She recognized those cakes made from mesquite beans.

Her ankle was wrapped tightly in a long strip of the crude material that seemed to be woven from some kind of plant. She gratefully ate the meal cake, the crushed pine nuts, a few berries she couldn't name and drank the cool water. One of the younger women touched her Nike as if it were a curious thing, until an older woman chastised the younger and made a motion that all should leave. Mairie was given a primitive comb and left alone in the dirt shelter.

Sighing, she leaned back against the wall and figured it might be okay to stay for an hour or two and show her gratitude. She would talk to this elder, this chief, and maybe they could make some sense out of everything. Surely he would know about Las Vegas, about how she could get back to her own people. She ran the wide toothed pick through her tangled hair and waited. Soon . . . soon she would have her answers.

Less than fifteen minutes later, the elder entered the lodge, along with two other men and Delaney. They sat before her in a half circle and stared. Mairie stiffened her shoulders and stared back, waiting for someone to speak. Two middle-aged men sat on either side of the elder, whose face was wrinkled and leathered from the sun, like a shelled walnut. Yet his eyes were warm, friendly, hopeful. Delaney sat by the entrance, with the sunlight behind him. Finally, the leader sort of grunted and said something directly to her. She couldn't understand the language and looked to Delaney to translate.

"He said, 'Welcome to my humble home. We are honored that you would make your appearance to us.' "

She bit the inside of her lip, while her brain seemed to run wild in attempting to make sense of the words. "What does he mean, make my appearance?"

Delaney sighed, as if he were again losing patience with her. "It would be proper if you thanked him for his hospitality before you begin ranting."

She glared back at the man. It didn't matter that the sun was creating almost a halo around him, that he was so good-looking he could have been a western model. It didn't matter that at any other time she would have been struck by that haunted look in his eyes . . . none of it mattered in that moment. What did matter was that he was right. She should have thanked the man first and it galled her that Delaney's manners were better than hers.

"Yes," she murmured. "Please thank him for his hospitality. And tell him I am honored that his people would show such tender care to a stranger."

She watched as Delaney translated and saw the pleasure in the older man's expression. She had said the right thing. The man spoke and she could see Delaney didn't want to tell her the answer. "What did he say?" she asked, before Delaney could add his own words.

"He said, 'You are not a stranger. You have been expected. Generations have spoken of you appearing, coming from the sky. A messenger for the people.' "

She was stunned. This must be corrected before it got out of hand. "Tell him for me I am no messenger, that I am lost. That I need assistance in getting back to my brother, my people, and can he tell me how to do that? Does he know where there is a phone, or even a road I can use?"

"I am not asking him that." Delaney looked at her as if she were an escapee from an institution.

Mairie's back straightened with indignation. "Hey . . . you're just the translator here. You tell him what I said."

Their eyes locked in battle as he muttered words she couldn't understand. The elder seemed confused and then very pleased. He said something in an excited voice.

"You didn't tell him!" Mairie accused, frustrated by her inability to communicate herself. How maddening, to depend on a druggie hermit who seemed to be in his own delusional *Dances with Wolves* scenario.

"I told him you can only stay until you are healed and that you bring great blessings to his people. He is planning a celebration tonight for you, to honor your arrival." The last words were said with such distaste that Mairie felt as if he had mentally assaulted her.

"I can't stay the night," she whispered. "I must leave." Holding her hand to her heart, she looked at the old man. "Listen to me, please ... I need to get back to my own people. Can you help me? Please, I need help."

All three men seemed confused by her words and looked to Delaney for translation. She didn't want to do it, yet she couldn't help following the old man's line of vision. What she saw wasn't reassuring. Delaney looked furious.

"You will stay and be honored. I will not disgrace my brothers by telling them that you are a madwoman, seeking to throw her voice out to the sky and expecting her brother to hear her."

"I am not mad," she said through clenched teeth. "You tell him that. I am not mad."

Delaney said something and all of the men laughed. They rose to their feet and abruptly left. It was obvious the meeting was over.

"What did you say to him?" Mairie demanded, feeling a rush of anger creeping up her throat to settle on her cheeks.

Delaney leaned back against the dirt wall of the lodge and sighed. "I told him that you are like a wounded bird, yet you will dance with joy tonight for falling into the nest of such a great wise man ... that your steps may be awkward since, by your costume, you haven't yet decided if you are a warrior or a maiden."

She could only stare at him as she attempted to

repress the urge to crawl over and slap that satisfied smirk off his face. "Get out," she barely managed to mutter.

He raised an eyebrow in question, while lowering his head to stare at her. "I beg your pardon, madam? Since I have no lodge of my own, when I visit my brothers I remain with one of them. Until you leave, this is my lodge. We are both honored to share it this night and any refusal of such a gift will be seen as an insult. You're stuck with me, as I am with you, until this celebration is over."

She was stunned. "Wait, wait . . . you're telling me that you and I have to remain together—*here*?"

He looked like he wanted to laugh at her predicament. "Until the women come to prepare you."

"Prepare me? For what?" She didn't like the sound of this at all.

"You cannot participate dressed like that. You are a woman and tonight you will look like one. Everyone wears their best when they speak with the gods. To do less is to dishonor life."

"I want out of here." Her words were said with as much force as she could muster. Right, like she would be dressing up in some Indian costume to please him!

"And, quite honestly, madam, I want *you* out of here. Had you not injured your ankle, you would be on your way. But since you are unable to manage travel today, I was forced to bring you to this camp. If you think I am pleased by this turn of events, you are mistaken, madam. I cannot help that my vision of you falling from the sky signals to my brothers that you are a messenger for them. But, you will go along with it, and you will give these people a message of hope."

She looked around her and nearly shrieked. "Hope! These people don't need hope. They need a miracle. Look at them, look at their poverty. This

way of life is disgraceful ... it's below poverty
level.''

He sat up straight and glared at her. "What do
you know of these people? What they have gone
through? You are blinded by European standards
and you cannot see beneath the surface of your vision. What you see as acrid, barren and inhospitable,
the Paiutes see as a land of great variety ... if you
have eyes to see and ears to hear the earth. They
gather pine nuts, mesquite, screw beans, Indian
spinach, agave. They plant corn and squash. They
hunt rabbits, desert tortoises, bighorn sheep, deer,
quail. They weave baskets from the grasses by the
creeks. They make jewelry. They're farmers, husbands, wives ... families. They're peaceful, wanting
only to live and feed their children, even though the
white man has come in and driven them from their
traditional grounds. You see them as a poor and
simple culture. I see them as the most resourceful
people on earth. And the most balanced. They see
the earth as our mother, providing us with food, the
air we breathe, clothing—even this lodging." He
touched the dirt wall with reverence. "And now
traders come, miners, and wagon trains heading for
California. They run their herds over the land and
damage the delicate plant life. They camp at the Paiute home sites near the springs and streams and
shoot at the Indians to keep them away. They kill
the game and deplete the supply. They even kidnap
Paiute children and women and sell them as slaves
in New Mexico and California. And yet the hearts
of these people remain pure."

He looked at her and slowly shook his head. "Disgraceful, you say? No, Mairie Callahan. The Paiutes
are full of grace ... if you are willing to open your
eyes and really see them. How they live is heroic."

She felt like a properly chastised child and lowered her eyes to the dirt ground as she felt him stand and move to the opening.

"You will find a way," he said, in a low, controlled voice. "You are their messenger. And tonight you will give them hope." He left without another word.

As she sat in the dirt lodge, her depression slowly became anger. Nothing was turning out as she had thought. She was too isolated. Maybe Delaney really *had* kidnaped her, and she was just now realizing it. This entire thing was ludicrous. Why were there no airplanes or helicopters looking for her? She knew Bryan must have notified everyone possible. Her brother would not abandon the search for her. He wouldn't. Something was very wrong, and at that moment Mairie was too angry to analyze it further. Now she was pissed. She needed to become proactive. Instead of sitting around waiting for women to come prepare her for some Indian dress-up dance or for Delaney to come back and insult her, she should just get up and walk over to that horse outside and ride the hell out of here.

The more she thought of it, the better it sounded.

All she had to do was get up and sneak out of this lodge. If she kept to the woods, she could circle the camp to where the horse was tied and take it. She would only be borrowing it. It wasn't really stealing. Okay, so she hadn't ridden a horse since she was thirteen years old at summer camp, but she knew she could do it. She had to, for she couldn't see any other means of escape from this madness. Better to take a horse, get back to civilization, and make a donation to these people than lie to them about a hopeful future.

A small part of her brain told her that she sure knew how to rationalize her way out of a tough situation. She stood at the entrance of the lodge with her bag in hand. She'd have to leave the helmet, since Delaney had been carrying it and she didn't know where it was. Big deal. She'd either get it back later or pay for it. The only thing that mattered now was making her escape.

It was like she was in some freaky cartoon, for as she stood watching the Indians who were preoccupied with preparations for the celebration, Mairie felt like she had two angels on her shoulders. One dark. One light. One whispering to take the horse and ride as fast as possible, and the other telling her to stay and honor her hosts.

Go or stay?

Steal or honor?

Dark or light?

"Madness or sanity?" she whispered, hating the fact that her conscience was pushing toward one end of the polarity. When she saw all the tribe running toward a hunter who had entered the camp with a small lifeless deer across his shoulders, she muttered a profanity and slipped out of the lodge.

It must be the right decision, she thought, as she quickly hobbled her way through the mesquite trees to the horses. No one had seen her. She scratched her thigh against a thorn and her legging snagged, but she couldn't take the time to indulge in pain. She had to untie the horse, who was shying away from her approach.

It was a lot bigger than she remembered from her teenage years at camp. Big and powerful. How was she supposed to ride the thing without a saddle? She hadn't thought of that.

"C'mere, horsie," she whispered, reaching out her hand. The brown-and-white-spotted animal snorted heavily and backed away from her. "It's okay," she continued in a soft voice, taking baby steps closer. "I'm not going to hurt you. I just want to ride you for a while. You can take me away from this craziness and then I will return you. I promise."

Was she certifiable, or what, talking to a horse like that? She couldn't think about it now. Later, when she was soaking in a warm Jacuzzi, she could decipher her precarious state of mind.

She teetered closer to the horse and managed to grab hold of its rope bridle. "Come on, big boy, you and I are going to take a little ride." She untied the rope from the line and started to walk it toward a fallen tree. Now, if she could just climb up on the thing and pull herself onto the horse's back.

Trying to mount the horse, while it jerked back and forth and she hopped on her good foot with an unwieldy parachute sack slung over her shoulder, was nearly impossible. She'd have to leave the sack, she thought regrettably. It was either ditch it, or never mount up. Besides, the skydiving school was responsible for her mishap. Something weird had happened and it wasn't her fault. She would contest the charges if they attempted to bill her for the equipment. Throwing the bag behind a clump of brush, she took a deep breath and turned back to the nervous horse. "Okay, buddy . . . you and I are going to do this. We're going to be pals . . . *amigos*, and whatever the Indian word is for we're stuck and in this together."

Using the horse's back for balance, she steadied herself on the large log, walked up the incline to a higher level, and grabbed hold on the horse's thick, coarse mane. She raised her leg and had to bite her bottom lip to stop a yelp of pain as her ankle throbbed in protest. She couldn't do it. She was too short for her leg to reach.

Damn, her mind screamed in frustration. There was no other choice. She have to throw herself onto its back and then straighten out. She told herself that she could do it. On the count of three, she would hurl herself up onto the horse and hold on for dear life until she could turn her body and swing her leg into place.

"One . . ." *If she could jump out of a plane at thirteen thousand feet, she could make it onto a horse's back.*

"Two . . ." *But* look *what had happened when she jumped!*

"Three . . ." *Do it! Just do it!*

She stood there breathing like a defeated hurdler, wanting to slap herself for her lack of courage. She could do this. She *had* to! It was fear, that's all. Was her fear of falling worse than her fear of being caught? Determined, she squared her shoulders and counted again.

"Three!"

Using her good leg, she pushed off the log and flung herself at the horse's back like a crazed trapeze artist. She landed with a thump and the horse started prancing in protest. Mairie hung on, grabbing its mane, and struggled to bring her injured foot over its rump. They went around and around in a circle, and even in her panicked state, she knew she must look like a fool.

It took every ounce of strength to right herself and when she finally managed, she collapsed against the horse's neck in relief. "Oh, thank you," she gasped, trying not to cry. "We did it. We did it . . ."

From somewhere over her left shoulder she heard that dark angel whispering to stop feeling sorry for herself and get moving. Gathering what little composure remained, she reached down for the loose rope and sat up. "Okay, horse . . . let's go."

Nothing.

She tried moving her behind up and down in a riding stance. "Giddiup, come on."

The horse refused to move.

Damn . . . what if this was one of those horses that refused to obey commands if they didn't come from the owner? What kind of luck was this? It was too incredible to believe that she had gone through all this for nothing!

All thoughts of bonding with the animal vanished. Desperate, she kicked her heels into its belly with more force than she'd intended and was startled when it jumped and broke into a frantic run. Gasping for breath, Mairie felt her entire body become rigid with the whiplash jolt. She held on for dear life as branches lashed her face and shoulders, as if punishing her for her actions. It was almost as disorienting as when she was pushed out of the plane. She couldn't think of anything, except not being thrown to the earth, as the horse ran wild . . . straight for the creek.

From somewhere behind her, she heard yelling, and then a shrill whistle pierced her ears as she desperately tried to hold her balance.

Suddenly the horse stopped abruptly, as if a switch had been turned off and all motion ceased. Like a rag doll, Mairie found herself flailing though the air, in an eerie silence of terror. Her only thought was *oh, shit* . . . before landing with a huge splash into the stream.

It was deep enough to break her fall, and she gasped at the shock of cold water that filled her nostrils, making her brainstem feel as though it were burning, the back of her throat on fire. She felt herself floundering like a trapped fish, as she attempted to stand up upright and lost her footing. Down again she went, fighting the water and her own inability to remain above it.

It felt as if the strong, secure hand of God had reached down and grabbed hold of her upper arm, pulling her to the surface and life-giving air. She sputtered and pushed her hair out of her eyes only to see Delaney standing right next to her. Coughing, she tried to pull her arm out of his grasp, yet was unsuccessful as his iron clasp tightened. The animal was standing right next to her, as peaceful as if that had been its intention all along, to wander into the creek for a drink.

"What did you think you were doing, stealing my horse?" he demanded, as if she were a juvenile delinquent.

"I . . . I didn't know it was . . . yours," she gasped at her captor. Trying to regain some measure of composure, she tried to still her pounding heart. "I have to get away, Delaney. I have to find my brother." She wiped at her nose with the back of her hand. "You can't understand. Whatever this is you're living in, isn't my place and time. I have to get back to my own time. My own people. My own version of . . . of reality." The tears were burning her eyes and she felt helpless to fight them and him together.

His blue eyes darkened with more annoyance, if that was possible. "Time? What madness are you talking about? There is no time but right now."

Pushing her hair back again, she sniffled while noticing that most of the tribe was gathering at the shoreline and watching. She knew she was making a spectacle of herself, yet it didn't matter. "Something's happened. I don't know what. Either you're mad or I am, and I have to get out of here and away from you to prove it isn't me!"

He stared at her as if she were speaking a foreign language. His gaze traveled down her body, and suddenly, Mairie was acutely aware of the thin wet Spandex outlining every detail of her breasts. Every detail, and she cursed her body's reaction to the cold water.

Delaney's eyes darkened with something more than anger and she managed to pull her arm free, crossing both arms over her chest for protection.

"It's high time you bathed," he muttered in a thick voice. "You saved the women from doing it. Now, get back to the lodge. I will think about taking you tomorrow to the Las Vegas ranch, but tonight you

are the honored guest of these people and you will
not insult their hospitality."

Knowing she was defeated, Mairie tried walking,
but stumbled, and Delaney reached out to help her.
She shrugged off his hand and hobbled a few steps
through the water when the horse, as if startled by
her action, moved its rump into her shoulder and
down again she went under the surface. Within seconds she was lifted not only out of the water but up
into the air and flung like a sack over Delaney's
shoulder as he walked out of the creek.

"Put me down!" she demanded, with a punch to
his back. Outraged by his macho behavior, Mairie
tried kicking him with her good foot. "How dare
you? How *dare* you treat me like this?"

She felt a muffled grunt from her assault and then
her legs were captured in a tight hold as Delaney
walked out of the creek and back toward the camp.
His shoulder cut into her solar plexus with each step
and Mairie whimpered her useless protest. She tried
pushing her hair away from her face, yet since her
face was upside down, it too appeared useless, and
besides, it helped to hide her shame, for she could
hear murmurings and even a few chuckles from the
spectators.

She would get Delaney for this. She vowed that
somehow she would get even.

He dumped her in front of the lodge, allowing her
to slide down the front of his body, and held onto
her waist for just a moment too long. Mairie felt his
strength, his power, rushing from his large hands
and racing through her body.

"You will go inside and wait for the women," he
said with a deep breath which hinted to more than
exertion. "I'm posting a guard here, so don't even
think of making another attempt." His eyes scanned
her face, as though searching for sanity.

Mairie felt his gaze move over her and suddenly

she knew exactly how to get even. Her lips moved into a smile of shy surrender and she whispered, "I'll behave, Delaney. But you'll take me to the ranch tomorrow? You promise?"

He seemed startled and suspicious by her sudden change of mood. "I said I would think about it. I will come when the women are finished preparing you. Do not disgrace yourself or me, madam. Or that promise to think about it is null and void."

"You needn't threaten me," she whispered. "I'll be good."

"Hmm . . . well, that would be a welcome change, now, wouldn't it?"

She could tell he didn't believe she was capable of such behavior, so she merely smiled again, trying to hide the rush of pleasure that ran through her when she saw Delaney's reaction. Now why didn't she think of this before? Feminine wiles . . .

Turning without another word, she entered the lodge and sat down to formulate her plan.

A throughly modern woman, she felt it went against her principles to resort to hormonal subterfuge. She knew all about the communication war between men and women, about sexual harassment and intimidation, and all that was fine and good when one was in a sane, or near sane, environment. This was neither. This was not a place of equality. Here a man had power over her, not power she had given, power assumed. This must be how women had felt before laws had tried to protect them against such abuse of power. So since the scales were unequal, and so out of balance, she would simply use what women had used for thousands of years . . . her innate feminine power.

Now, how was she going to do that, since Delaney was convinced that she was a crazy woman? She thought for a few moments and then smiled as she flipped her wet hair off her face. Hah . . . as hard as he'd tried to hide it, she had seen that look of male interest first at the creek with the wet top and then just now before he left. He might think she was crazy, but it was obvious he was not above being attracted to a crazy female. It was kind of flattering, since it had been so long since she'd even entertained the thought of male interest, and she had to be honest . . . he was gorgeous, but he was also nuts, so she'd have to proceed cautiously.

First things first, she thought, as she looked around for the primitive comb. Spying it on the rabbit skin rug, she reached down and started dragging it through her damp hair. Well, soon the women would come and she'd figure out what else she might use to transform herself into an Indian maiden. She already had the black hair. All she needed was a little help, and . . .

Her thoughts stopped and her hand froze midway through her hair.

A part of her didn't like the plan. It was deceptive, and she knew enough about cause and effect to know that whatever she gave out could have a boomerang effect and come around to slam her in the back of the head. But what were her options? She simply had to get him to promise to take her to that ranch tomorrow. She had to find civilization again. A phone. A car. A *modern person!* Enough was enough, and she'd played by his rules way too long.

Now it was time to even out the playing field.

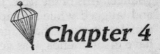 *Chapter 4*

His breath caught at the back of his throat as the women left the lodge with big smiles of accomplishment. Fires burned brightly, illuminating the circle of stones in the middle, and Jack found himself still not breathing as *she* finally made her appearance. It wasn't possible . . . It wasn't! Mairie Callahan, incredible wild gift from the heavens, was magically transformed into a . . . beautiful Indian maiden. No other description suited her. She wore a light shift to her ankles that was gathered at the waist with a wide beaded sash. A choker of brightly colored beads surrounded her neck, with matching beads braided into the tips of her dark hair. The shy smile on her face seemed to soften her features until he was hard pressed to remember the angry woman he had dropped at the lodge earlier.

Finally releasing his breath, Jack couldn't pull his gaze away from her. The women motioned for her to move closer to the fire, and once seated, she slowly lifted her face and stared across the flames at him. Her eyes seem to sparkle in the firelight and he swore an unseen force entered his chest, infusing him with a tingling heat.

Dear God . . . she is exquisite.

The steady beating of a drum signaled the beginning of the ceremonial meal. The women sat on one side of the fire, the men on the other. Mairie was surrounded by those who had prepared her and the younger girls of the tribe. Jack watched as she smiled and laughed while attempting to converse with the females through hand gestures. She appeared to have made friends, was very polite, was even enjoying herself. While the food was passed around, he continued to watch her from under the cover of his lashes. As hard as he tried, he simply couldn't seem to tear his gaze away.

A part of him realized he was making a fool of himself, that all those surrounding him must surely think he was besotted with the woman. He told himself to pay attention to the talk of the men . . . the recounting of the successful hunt, the coming celebration, anything to distract him from the woman who also was sneaking glances in his direction. What was happening? He didn't want to think that she could actually be his gift. He reminded himself of her perverse nature, of her stubborn insistence that it was over a hundred years into the future and she was capable of miraculous things such as flying and speaking over great distances.

Perhaps she was a witch.

That thought hadn't occurred to him before, and suddenly it made a bizarre kind of sense. He had never believed in such superstitions. Witches were fanciful characters used to frighten children into behaving. They were not beautiful women falling from the sky. But it was a thought . . .

Tonight the Indian shaman would travel into the other world and speak with the Great Spirit of the Wolf, and express his gratitude for the appearance of Mairie Callahan. If a shaman could enter another world, why couldn't a witch enter this one?

Damn, he could use a long drink of whiskey. Of course, from the way his mind was wandering with such fantastic thoughts, he could already be drunk

... drunk with the vision of a beautiful, beguiling witch who was ... yes, who was now glancing at him, with a definitely seductive smile playing across her lips. She was teasing with her eyes, toying with her smile. He'd had enough women and enough experience to recognize a blatant flirtation.

He took a deep steadying breath and concentrated on his brother's tale of expert tracking. Male companionship was safe. Hunting made sense. He had enough worries as it was ... he would not be bewitched, too.

Yet as he selected his portion of roasted deer meat, he suddenly felt like the one being hunted. It was not a comforting premonition.

Mairie had almost forgotten what it felt like to flirt with a man, to focus all her energy inward and capture the essence of seduction and then to project it outside herself. Somehow, over the last several months, she'd lost sight of the rush of pleasure to be derived when a direct hit was scored. And in the last fifteen minutes, she'd had several direct hits. The flirtation had not yet been returned, but that didn't bother her in the least. Delaney's reaction was satisfaction enough ... for now.

The poor man's expression changed from stunned appreciation at her appearance to confusion and just now settled into a strained discomfort. The time spent on her costume had been worth it, and to be honest, she actually enjoyed the company of the females. It was soothing to allow them to attend her. She had always been so self-reliant, so independent, and these simple, giving people were teaching her to receive without guilt. Amazing.

It was then she stared into the fire, wondering what in the world she could say to them to encourage them, when she knew that the modern world held little for the Indian. She thought about the history books she had read in school and again felt a stirring of anger. America . . . land of the free and home of the brave. Dear God, Americans had stolen a continent and nearly annihilated an entire race of people and felt justified. And how much better was she? She enjoyed those freedoms, those luxuries . . . but at the expense of the rightful owners? She had never really thought about the plight of the Indian. Maybe she hadn't wanted to, maybe she was the ignorant one, uneducated in truth. But what could she say?

Certainly, not the truth.

She thought back to when the younger women knelt around her and wove the tiny beads into the ends of her hair, when she had experienced a feminine bonding that went beyond the color of skin or culture. There wasn't a separation of *them and me*, of being different, and when she'd seen her reflection in a small silver bowl, she'd felt like a pampered Indian princess. How natural the transformation. She knew it was a silly thought—ridiculous, really— yet she kept that image when she left the lodge, wanting Delaney to see her as one.

If she was supposed to be this visitor from the heavens, a messenger from above, then she was going to play the part with gusto.

She would mesmerize him tonight and extract his promise to take her to the ranch in the morning. She felt like Helen of Troy, Cleopatra, and Anne Boleyn all rolled into one. Of course, one committed suicide, one lost her head, and another was portrayed as a deceitful woman driven by passion or an innocent victim of her own beauty, depending on the male or female version. Not exactly promising endings to extraordinary lives, yet they had *lived*, not settling for a passive, servile existence, submissive to men. They knew about feminine power.

Shyly glancing at Delaney, she lifted the corners of her mouth in a flirtatious smile and almost giggled at his startled reaction. As he was about to bite into a piece of meat, his hand froze in mid-air.

This was definitely going to be fun.

She thought about all her struggles with him since he had appeared in the desert, her anger and frustration. Scenarios ran through her mind. She envisioned him bathing in that waterfall and then smirking at her confusion. She almost heard his laughter once again when he explained her to his Indian brothers and said she didn't know if she was a warrior or a maiden. Well, tonight she was both. Her stomach muscles could almost feel his shoulder digging into her as he humiliated her at the creek earlier. How could she have forgotten that old adage?

Don't get mad, get even.

Yeah . . . tonight she would have some fun and accomplish her goal without his even knowing what happened. Where reason failed to penetrate, femininity would prevail. Her smile was filled with impending victory. Soon. Soon, she would prove to him she was right, and a reunion with her brother would take place.

She just loved being a woman.

Once the meal was over, the dancing began. To Mairie, it seemed disorganized at first, as though everyone was doing his own thing, but she soon realized that the Indians were slowly forming a circle. She was asked to join and reluctantly stood. Looking across the fire, she saw that Delaney was already beginning to stamp his feet lightly in time to the drums. She noticed that he was graceful for a man and tried to make her movements match his. Soon everyone was joining hands and moving very slowly to the left. The dancers moved in a circle, with clasped hands and, dragging their steps, singing with a rhythmic swing the songs of the dance, over and over in a dizzying trancelike movement.

Mairie was always a decent dancer and, even now as she dragged her bruised foot, she picked up the rhythm quickly. She found the beating of the drums soothing—hypnotic, even—as her ears and mind were filled with a song that she couldn't understand, yet expanded her heart. Something special was taking place; she could feel it in the energy surrounding her. She looked across the fire and found Delaney staring at her as he moved in the dance, and she automatically smiled softly at him. From somewhere in the recesses of her brain came the realization that her smile wasn't planned or forced. In that instant she had actually felt affection for him, maybe even a thread of gratitude for this incredible experience with the Indians. It was as if she were now falling under a spell . . .

Round and round went the circle, slowly, entrancing her even more. It was tranquilizing. Suddenly a young man staggered from the ring and swooning, fell to the ground. Mairie was immediately concerned, yet the woman holding her hand on the left smiled and nodded, as if saying it was all right, that it was to be expected. The dance continued, the singing was uninterrupted, and Mairie searched out Delaney. He was looking at her.

Their gaze connected with such intensity that Mairie was stunned. Across the fire, Delaney seemed to be speaking, communicating with her. It wasn't words. More like concepts that filled her mind. It was as if he were saying, *Don't be afraid.* She watched as he withdrew from the circle, making sure those on either side of him clasped hands to keep the circle intact. He slowly walked around the others until he came to her. The women on either side of her joined hands, leaving her outside the circle, next to Delaney.

"Come," he whispered. "Let's sit down and I'll explain what's happening."

She followed him back to her place behind the dancers. She felt a strange kind of energy running through her body, as if she were in a church, or a sacred place of worship.

He sat next to her, clad in his jeans and a vest made of deerskin and rabbit fur. His long dark hair was swept away from his face and fell behind his shoulders. His eyes were intense in the firelight, yet Mairie found it hard to concentrate on anything but his mouth as he began to speak.

"This is the Spirit Dance," he said in a low voice. "It's an invitation to the Great Spirit to communicate, and it opens a window for that exchange. The young man who fell into a trance is now taking a journey into that world of Spirit and will come back with a message. The dancing and singing continues until he awakens and describes his vision of the spirit-world."

She simply nodded, as if it made all the sense in the world. A part of her, that irascible dark angel, seemed to whisper in her ear that she was being naive, actually falling for a primitive hypnotic suggestion . . . that she should laugh it off and merely observe it all as if she were watching a documentary. She mentally shrugged her shoulder and shut up the annoying voice of fear. Something was happening here, something inside of her, some part that was telling her to pay attention, to learn, to grow, not to judge what she didn't yet understand.

"See through the dancers . . . see him begin to awaken." Delaney pointed to the man who had collapsed. "His name is Wovoka. His father was a disciple of Wodziwob, who began his own form of the Ghost Dance, sometimes called the Dream Dance. But first, from what I've learned, there was Smohalla, from the northwest. Smohalla was a . . . a mystic. He was kin to the Nez Perce and Yakima. After taking part in the Yakima wars, he believed that he had died and been resurrected by the Great Spirit. His followers gave him the name of *the Dreamer*."

Delaney paused for a moment, as if recalling what he had been taught by these people. "His message was peaceful, and it spread to all the tribes. Then there came one from the Paviotso Indians in western Nevada, a prophet, Wodziwob, a man I'm told of commanding character and stature. His message too from the dream state was one of peace. He had many disciples, and Wovoka's father was one of them. It is only natural that Wovoka be the one to journey this night."

Delaney took a deep breath after his long explanation and turned his head to look at her. "This is not naive spirituality. This is older than all the churches and temples, all the religions from across either ocean, and in my time with these people I have come to respect it as the only source of balance that I know of. I have learned to listen." And then he smiled.

For the first time he smiled, really smiled . . . and Mairie felt something pop inside her heart, infusing her body with warmth. She tried to remember her plan of getting even, to recapture that feeling, yet all she could think of was how magical this night seemed. Dressed in an Indian costume, seated next to this man of mystery, she wondered exactly what was reality and illusion.

It truly felt as if she had traveled back in time.

"What are the words they are singing?" she whispered, watching the dancers slow even more and their voices lower until she had to strain to hear them.

Delaney waited until the repeated verse began again to translate.

> *Mother, oh come back*
> *Mother, oh come back*

> *Little brother calls, as he seeks thee*
> *Weeping*
> *Little brother calls, as he seeks thee*
> *Weeping*
> *Mother, oh come back*
> *Saith the Father . . .*

"What does it mean?" she asked, suddenly feeling sad.

Delaney smiled. "I suppose it depends on who is singing. It could be used to reconnect with those who have passed on to the spirit world before us, or it could mean, as I take it, that the Indian knows the earth is his mother and is calling out to Her to come back in peace, to restore abundance to the people as before the white man came."

Mairie saw that Wovoka was rousing, beginning to sit up. The others began to take their places, as when they had been eating. It was obvious that this young man had something of great importance to impart to his people, and she found herself as eager to hear him as his brothers and sisters. "You'll translate for me, won't you, Jack? I want to hear this."

He didn't answer and she turned her head slightly to look at him.

"That is the first time you have used my name," he said, gazing at her mouth, her cheeks, her eyes. "Yes, Mairie . . . I will translate."

It felt like a caress, as if he had actually touched her, and she sighed as they both turned their attention to the young man in the center of the tribe.

"He's saying . . . *'I journeyed to the land beyond where the sun sets and then I went to the spirit-land, where I saw the spirit encampment. I drew near and stood outside a spirit lodge. A spirit man came out, one of the rabbit robes, of us Paiutes, and he stood beside me. He spoke to me and said: "Behold, I give you something holy." Then he said, "Whence come you?" And I told him of us, of the Paiute in the land of the setting sun.' "*

A murmur of approval spread through those seated in the wide circle, and Mairie felt herself being drawn into this story. She couldn't wait to hear what came next.

Delaney listened and repeated, " *'Then said the spirit man, "Go we together in a cloud, upward, to the Father." So we rose in a cloud to where there was another camp and a man and a woman, a husband and a wife, married in thoughts, body, and spirit, came forward. "I will speak with you now. Behold, I will tell you something for you to tell to all the people. Give this dance to all the different tribes of Indians. White people and Indians shall all dance together. But first they shall sing. There shall be no more fighting. No man shall kill another. If any man should be killed, it would be a grievous thing. No man shall lie. Love one another. Help one another. Hear me, for I will give you water to drink. Thus I tell you, this is why I have called you. My meaning, have you understood it?" ' "*

There was a pause.

" *'And I did. I understood.' "*

Mairie let out her breath and was filled with awe. Wovoka was like Moses, coming down off the mount with instructions to live in peace. The man started speaking again and she turned to Delaney for the translation.

" *'In the spirit camp I have seen those who had died, and when I came homeward there came with me two spirit companions. These journeyed with me and will stay with me evermore. I hear their counsel, even now.' "*

"Wow." The word escaped Mairie's lips as she looked at the remarkable man. He seemed so composed, so peaceful . . . as if he were in this world, yet not of it.

Everyone started talking at once and Mairie turned to Delaney. She was so excited she grabbed his arm.

"Questions are being asked," he said, looking down to her hand on his arm and smiled. "Wait, one is asking how they can be brothers to the white man, who won't listen to Spirit, who carries guns and destroys Mother Earth."

She watched as Wovoka seemed to go inward and listen. Finally he began his answer.

" 'It is true all men should love one another. It is true all men should live as brothers. Is it not we who do not thus? What others demand of us, should they not themselves give? Is it just to expect one friend to give all the friendship? We are glad to live with white men as brothers, but we ask that they expect not the brotherhood and the love to come from the Indian alone. The red man alone cannot continue into infinity to hold the source to Mother Earth. A prophecy handed down from tribe to tribe, from family to family, need not be fulfilled if the white man would open his heart. The white man has come to our land raping and plundering our Mother, and we try to defend her, yet the red man is outnumbered by this aggressive human. I have seen how this will continue like a plague upon the earth for generations upon generations until a deadly enemy overtakes them . . . a deadly enemy that they can not see, nor fight. As the white man continues to be a plague upon the land, so shall a plague remove him from it. White and red must be in balance, or a disease, an affliction, will teach respect for our Mother Earth. There is hope, for we have our white brother with us and he has brought us a messenger from the heavens who has come from the land of our tomorrows.' "

Mairie was reeling. She was aware of the attention of the tribe, yet her mind was almost shouting at her to pay attention. She grabbed Delaney's arm again and muttered, "I have to speak to him. Ask if I may speak."

"What will you say? You have such a message?"

"I have questions . . . I think I know what he is

talking about." She felt her heart slamming into her rib cage, her pulse in her fingertips. "Listen, there is a plague in the land of your tomorrows, but it doesn't affect only the white man. It's called cancer. My brother has it, and he is dying. What Wovoka said about the white man and the red man can also be applied to this plague, the form of it my brother has. Leukemia."

He was shaking his head as if she were speaking in riddles.

"Okay, look . . . when my brother got sick, I researched this disease thoroughly, not wanting to accept the negative prognosis, so I know what I'm talking about here. We have white and red blood cells. Even if you don't understand, take my word for this. Red blood cells carry oxygen. The white blood cells are the defenders of the body against infection, but if the body starts producing too many white blood cells and they become aggressive, they destroy the red, and when there are not enough red blood cells to carry the oxygen that feeds the body, that keeps us alive, the person dies. The white has overdefended and killed off the red. Completely out of balance."

She was breathing heavily as she stared at him, desperately seeking to see understanding in his eyes.

"This is confusing. Are you talking about blood, or about the white man and the Indian? I don't think I understand."

"Both!" She was excited that he was at least thinking about it. "When Wovoka started talking about the aggressive white man and the red man holding the source to Mother Earth . . . it made such sense to me. This disease, this plague, could it be a symbol of when we become aggressive, when we overdefend and kill off the red man and lose their teachings? I listened and heard teachings tonight that could challenge established religions in its simple truth. Dance. Sing. No more fighting. No more wars. No more killing. No more lies. Help one another. Peace. What will happen when the Indian teachings are gone? Will we die because we won't have the food of life . . . the connection? It seems to me that the red man is holding our connection to *the* source. Mother Earth, a living organism."

"Mairie . . ." He almost breathed her name, as he continued to stare into her eyes. "What you say feels like truth, yet I am confused about the blood. What are these . . . these cells you speak of?"

She sighed and closed her eyes for a moment. "I can't explain science, especially biology, but take my word that your blood, my blood, everyone's blood contains them and they are so tiny they cannot be seen with the naked eye."

"They are spirit based? From the invisible world?"

She opened her eyes and held his intense gaze. "You know something . . . without a piece of powerful machinery, a microscope, you would have to say they are from an invisible world. When they're out of balance they create illness, and when the aggressiveness of the white against the red is way out of balance, in many cases . . . death. This is a plague, a real plague that has killed millions, and it's so small no one can see it with the eye, or successfully find the way to stop it. Just like in the Indian's prophecy." Their gaze intensified with a deep connection. "And my brother is dying, Jack, from this plague. I need to speak with Wovoka and ask if there is anything that can be done, if there is a cure. It's my brother, Jack. My brother . . ."

And then suddenly Mairie stopped speaking as the realization slammed into her that she was talking to him as if she believed he really was living in the past and that she came from the future. Where were the planes? Where was the city? The lights? Anything modern . . . ?

Jack began speaking to Wovoka and Mairie had no more time to ponder this incredible situation as the two men conversed. She could see that Jack was having trouble explaining what she had told him, yet Wovoka kept nodding as though it made sense to him.

Turning to her, Jack said, "He asks what is your question."

She took a deep breath. "Ask him if he knows of a cure. Tell him I have come from the land of his tomorrows to seek his wisdom."

Wovoka listened to Jack and then seemed to meditate. After a few moments, he opened his eyes and looked directly at Mairie as he began speaking . . .

" *'I have seen the land of tomorrow and it is troubling. The Indian disappears until only a few are singing songs of the Father Sun and Sky and dancing to the rhythms of Mother Earth. Mother seems sick, ill-used, violated, forgotten . . . it pains my heart to envision our Mother raped, yet she is all wise and will find her own remedy, for she contains the cure. You ask about your brother and I tell you that Mother has the answer. It is here, growing from her womb, for would she not care for her children, even if they no longer recognize Her? Does the love of any mother cease? Her love is endless. There is a plant, an herb, growing at the sacred stones that would provide understanding of our Mother's concern and love. From this plant would come answers. However, my sister, I must also reveal that as this plague descends, I have seen that by man's greed and disrespect for his Mother he will have destroyed his own cure. For in your land of tomorrow it no longer could obtain the air and life from Father and Mother and has died away.'* "

Mairie sat listening to every single word that Jack translated, taking each sound and meaning into her heart for another deeper translation. "So you are saying there is no cure? That because we've been so greedy, so forgetful of the earth, we've destroyed what we now need to stay alive?"

Wovoka smiled at her. Even though he appeared younger than her, he seemed like an older brother, one who was patient and loving. She thought of Bryan, and immediately her heart opened to this Indian. She trusted him.

" *'I am saying that in the land of tomorrow there is always hope. Our white brother knows this, yet is now fearful of even himself for in his heart of hearts he knows he must change. He has forgotten the many times he has walked this land and that he will walk it again and again, reaping what he has sown. He is his grandchildren's grandchildren, living his own errors of judgment. His heart must change. And only he can do that. Remember, you are not walking the land of tomorrow, my sister. You are walking this moment. And in this moment, there still grows the herb of understanding. It is there by the sacred stones of the ancients, for this moment is the conception of your tomorrow. In this now, the numbers of the white man are not enough to destroy this connection to the source. It is here now, not in your land of tomorrow.'* "

Mairie's mind was spinning. It was as if he were speaking to her on a level that was familiar, trusting. It felt so right, everything he said. Part of her wanted to call it madness and another part calmly whispered that it was truth. Simple truth. Man had destroyed his connection to the earth. She wasn't an environmentalist, had even been a bit suspicious of their zealotry until she read that the seeds from a pine tree in the Pacific Northwest were being used to fight breast cancer. Did the earth contain the cure? Was Wovoka right? Was there a plant growing now by the petroglyphs that could provide some understanding into this plague? Was there hope for Bryan?

Her heart sang *Yes!*

She didn't care that it seemed naive to believe an

Indian who appeared to be living in the past. Something, some inner guidance, told her to find that herb and bring it to her brother. Maybe this was why she had landed off course. Why she met Jack Delaney. Why he brought her here to this camp. Maybe she was meant to hear this tonight. It wasn't just desperation.

It was hope.

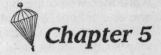

Chapter 5

How her heart changed so quickly. It amazed her.

She had started the evening wanting to get even, to make Jack pay for infuriating her and wound up being grateful for the opportunity to learn about a simple people who seemed to have a profound message. She felt shy, embarrassed by her arrogance, and thought she was the naive one among so many of wisdom. The Paiutes impressed her with their clear common sense and she felt privileged to have witnessed this evening. She knew, deep within, that had she not wandered off course, none of this would have happened. She was so excited to find Bryan and tell him this information. Soon she would see her brother . . . she simply had to believe that.

When Jack turned and asked her if she had any words of hope, any message for the people, Mairie took a deep breath as she saw his look of encouragement. It was almost as if they were no longer at odds with each other . . . more like a team now. United in hope.

She had already thought of the only truth she could impart to these people, who appeared to be caught in the past.

"Many generations of the Indian will suffer, yet in the land of tomorrow the Indian begins to receive the respect he should have always had. One day many tribes will own casinos, gaming establishments, and they will become rich, richer than the white men who come to play." She said her message was one of hope, and that it was very important the Indians continue to teach their children the balanced way so that in the land of their tomorrows, their children's great-grandchildren would be able to teach the white man. For many whites are finally open to hearing truth.

Even though she had spoken about suffering, everyone had seemed pleased with her words of eventual respect, even Jack. Wovoka claimed she was an honored traveler from another world and that the people were honored in return that she'd chosen them to hear her message. She didn't have the heart to contradict him, or take away the hope of these people.

Arrangements were made to gather the herb in the morning, and then she sat listening to the Indian songs of celebration. As the stars appeared to dance above her head, she realized that she was the one moving. She was traveling on this beautiful life-giving planet at astonishing speed through the universe. Why had she never thought of this before? So many new thoughts were running through her mind. Not the least was seeing the earth as our ultimate Mother. That was a new concept for her. Once she had mourned the concreting of the world as just the loss of beauty and nature. Now she saw it as threatening our very lives. Most synthetic drugs were based on nature. Like aspirin from a willow tree. Could it be that in trying to dominate the earth, we're actually creating an artificial means of destroying ourselves?

Where were these thoughts coming from?

Geez . . . she felt like a recruit for Greenpeace, or something.

Shaking her head, Mairie looked across the fire to

Jack and saw that he was in animated conversation with the elders of the tribe. He had left her after the plans were made for a party to travel to the petroglyphs and bring back the plant. She'd stayed with the women and had listened to the singing—smiling, wondering, marveling ... and thinking some pretty revolutionary thoughts. Soon her eyes became sleepy and the woman at her side motioned toward the lodges. Mairie smiled her thanks and withdrew from the circle.

Inside the lodge, she saw that a small fire had been lit. She looked up to the smoke hole and sighed. What an evening, and she still hadn't obtained Jack's promise to take her to the ranch after she received the herb. Somehow, she knew he would. She sat for what seemed like a half hour, thinking back on what had just happened. It was so powerful, yet so simple. Sing. Dance. Peace with the earth, and each other. Why was this so scary to the white man? Why had they tried to wipe out the Indian teachings? Knowing she was pondering questions far greater than her mind was ready to handle at the moment, Mairie reluctantly stood up to get undressed. It was then she realized her ankle felt so much better. She wondered what the Paiute woman had administered.

Untying the beaded sash, she laid it in a basket with loving care. Removing the necklace, she held it in her hands and admired the intricate work. How many hours had someone persevered to create such beauty? Placing it on top of the sash, Mairie smiled at herself while remembering how she grew up with the notion that "store-bought" was somehow better than handmade. How curious to now appreciate the art and mastery of the individual craftsman. So many things, so many lessons, she was learning. Even though she missed her brother terribly, even though she knew he was worried about her, perhaps this incredible detour was actually serving her?

She didn't feel like the same woman who had been pushed out of that plane.

"I'm sorry. I thought you would be sleeping."

Startled, Mairie jumped at the sound of his voice. He stood at the entrance to the lodge with a questioning look on his face. A sigh almost escaped her lips when she thought about the sleeping arrangements, for Jack Delaney was just too handsome to be spending the night with her *again*. Especially this night . . . this night when she felt so open to the unexpected.

"I was . . . thinking," she muttered, as she turned around and sat down on the rug of rabbit fur. Better not to stare at his deep blue eyes, or the way his trousers fit snug over his hips . . . or the fact that he wore only a vest and his tanned muscled arms were gleaming in the firelight. Suddenly, her plan seemed to backfire on her.

Yup . . . this was going to be another long night.

"And what were you thinking?" he asked, coming into the lodge and sitting down on the rug opposite her.

Startled by his nonchalant actions, Mairie cleared her throat. "I was wondering . . . well, if both of us are sleeping here, where is the elder going to sleep? This is his lodge, after all."

Jack grinned, as if he knew what was racing through her mind. "He is spending the night with his brother and his family. It's an honor to give over his lodging to a visitor from the heavens."

She shook her head. "That really is ridiculous. You know that. I am not from heaven. I'm from Pennsylvania. I just didn't have the heart to disappoint everyone tonight. They seemed . . . no, they deserved some message of hope, at least for future generations."

He smiled. A real smile again, and Mairie felt like

warm honey was running through the inside of her chest and down her body.

"Thank you for that. It was a good message. But you forget, Mairie Callahan, I saw you fall from heaven, so I know that much of it is true. I can't decide who or what you are after tonight." His smile was gentle and seductive.

Staring at his lips, Mairie attempted to bring herself back to the discussion. "It's simple, Jack. I'm a woman who is lost, and I'm seeking to get back to my own people . . . even my own time it appears." There. That sounded relatively intelligent, which surprised her, considering she was still wondering what his lips would taste like.

"Where in Pennsylvania do you live?"

She was slightly surprised that he switched the conversation and really had to focus. "Yardley. Not far from Philadelphia. It's a small town and I can commute easily by train into the city for work."

"You work?"

He seemed amazed, and Mairie couldn't stop a tiny giggle from escaping. "Of course I work, or at least, I used to before my brother became sick. I'm a computer sales rep. I don't suppose you know what computers are . . ."

He merely stared at her, and she found that she didn't have the energy to explain, nor to argue. "Forget it. It was just a way to make a living and keep the lights on."

"Keep the lights on? You mean, to buy provisions? Candles and such?"

Oh, brother . . . they were back to this again. "Jack, will you take me to the ranch tomorrow after I receive that plant from the petroglyphs?"

There. She finally asked the question.

Jack stared into her eyes and tried to fight the growing attraction. "Yes, Mairie. I will take you," he answered. "I was hoping that you would want to spend another day with the Paiutes. They would be honored." He wondered if he were really asking for his brothers, or for himself.

She shook her head and looked determined. "I must reach my brother. Especially after hearing what I did tonight. I'm on . . . I guess a mission. A mission of love. You see, I quit my job right after finding out that my brother had this disease. We had . . . adventures, Bryan and me, traveling to different countries . . . swimming with sharks in Australia, kayaking alongside whales in Alaska, climbing mountains in Peru. I never really wanted to do any of these things, but Bryan did . . . so I went with him. He's all I have left. He's my only family. I'm sorry, Jack, I have to leave and reunite with him."

He nodded, feeling the love she had within her for her brother. "I understand. Tomorrow I will take you to O. D. Gass's place and you can wait there for transportation west. It shouldn't be more than a week or two."

Her jaw dropped. "A *week* or two? You can't be serious. What kind of transportation are you talking about?"

Why was she so surprised? "Wagon trains going west on the Los Angeles–Salt Lake Emigrant Trail. It's right in front of Gass's ranch, and everyone stops there coming out of the desert whether they're going east or west. I just assumed you'd be going west. You aren't thinking about going back to Pennsylvania, are you?"

"I can't go back without my brother. I have to find him." She ran her fingers over her forehead and sighed deeply. "God, I hope the same thing didn't happen to him." Her eyes suddenly appeared frightened. "What if he's lost, too? What if he's wandering around in the desert? Why didn't I think of this before? That would explain why no one is looking for me."

He wanted to reach across the small space and touch her, calm her, yet he kept his distance out of respect. Plus, he remembered her temper and didn't want to see it flare up again. Still, the urge was nearly irresistible. "Mairie . . . didn't you say you were supposed to be met by someone when you landed?"

She stared at him for a few seconds and relief flooded over her features. "Of course, you're right. Someone from the diving school. Yes . . . even if we're both lost, someone would have notified the authorities. But why hasn't there been anyone looking for me? It doesn't make sense."

He didn't want to tell her that nothing she was saying made sense. A diving school? What authorities? There was nothing out here except O.D. Gass's limited power as justice of the peace. "You'll find your answers tomorrow when you get to the ranch," he said with encouragement, though he had no idea what answers she would actually find.

She appeared thoughtful, as if wondering the same thing. How could she deny what she'd witnessed tonight? How could she still think she was a hundred and twenty-two years into the future? Surely by now she must realize that no one from the sky was going to come looking for her? He knew he should be thankful that by this time tomorrow she would be in the hands of Gass and his wife and be their problem, yet something, some tiny nagging instinct, was telling him it wouldn't be that simple. Besides, after tonight, after watching her, listening to her, he didn't exactly want to walk away.

It was that last thought that shook him the most.

Mairie Callahan, woman of mystery, was capturing his mind.

"I'll leave for a few minutes and you can change,"

he offered, wanting to create some space between them. Suddenly, the lodge seemed far too small for them both. She moved, as though to make room for him to rise, and they brushed each others' arms in the process. Jack froze, feeling the silkiness of her skin, and stifled a groan.

She looked up at him and whispered, "I think I'm supposed to sleep in this shift." She touched the thin material and grinned. "The women were so nice to me. I'm ... well, I guess this might come as a surprise, but I'm actually grateful to you for bringing me here. It was quite an experience tonight, Jack. Thank you."

The last words were said so softly he had to strain to hear them. Her expression was sincere, her smile was almost shy. Was she doing it again? Was she initiating a flirtation?

All he had to do was move a few inches to kiss her, to capture her mouth and taste what he had been desiring all day and night. Damn ... he must have been too long away from white women to recognize the coy, subtle moves in the mating dance. Or he could be delusional himself. Considering their interactions, the latter was most likely.

"So, tell me of your life, Mairie Callahan," he said, in an attempt at composure. "You have worked and secured your own income. What else? You have never married? No children? No family, other than your brother?"

"Who said I was never married?"

Surprised, Jack shrugged. "I assumed you made your home with your brother."

She toyed with one of the beads in her hair. "My brother and I didn't live together. I was only traveling with him since he was diagnosed as terminal. Right now he's in remission, but the outlook isn't hopeful."

"What is remission? I don't understand."

"Remission..." She crossed her legs before her and sighed. "Seems like false hope where my brother is concerned. It's when the white cell count lowers. He was feeling so much better, he decided to do all the things he's always wanted to do... while he still had time. I was just his sidekick. I didn't want him to do them alone."

"He is fortunate to have you for his sister," he said. "You do love him."

"Yes..." she murmured, while looking into the dying flames. "I do love him."

She seemed so sad suddenly that he again wanted to reach across and touch her, to let her know that he understood loss. "What was it like to see whales?" he asked, trying to change the subject and take away her pain.

Immediately, she smiled. "Oh, Jack... it was spectacular. Imagine, being in such a small boat and this... this magnificent creature is swimming less than thirty feet away. I mean, I was terrified at first, sure we were going to capsize. And then there was this... peace. I guess that's the best way to describe it. A noble peace. Far better than swimming with sharks."

She giggled, a wonderful childlike giggle, and Jack felt any resistance melting with it. For just a moment, she seemed so natural, so real. There wasn't any defensiveness about her. She wasn't striving to make a point or understand his. She was... earthy and genuine. And he found himself on dangerous ground. He didn't need this, this feeling of connectedness, not now and not with her. How laughable, that he had gone on his vision quest to find hope and he'd found Mairie Callahan, a mysterious and quite possibly mad woman.

The gods must love laughter.

"Tell me of your husband. Is he not concerned that you have been gone with your brother?" He asked the question to stop the strange feelings from growing within him. Better that he should remember this woman was not his hope. She belonged to another.

She shoulders stiffened and her chin lifted. He recognized that expression coming over her face and took a deep breath to brace himself for her answer.

"My husband," she began, emphasizing the last word, "is no longer my concern. We are not married any longer."

"I'm sorry." He said the words, yet something inside him was oddly relieved by her answer. Why should he even care?

"I'm not." Shrugging, she added, "I respect the institution of marriage. I'm just extremely grateful to be out of an institution."

"You were in an institution?" He had been afraid of that.

Her jaw dropped. "I'm talking about the institution of marriage. Marriage . . . that most respected state of matrimony where almost no one is happy. What did you think I meant? You still think I'm crazy?"

"No." Even though he said it, he really wasn't sure of her sanity, or his own at this point.

"Let me tell you something. Being married to that man could have made me crazy. Men! You all think alike."

She said the word *men* as if it were a curse.

"I'm sorry if I offended you. I was confused. You said you were married." He knew he was stepping on thin ice and tried to be careful.

"What is it with you guys? This is exactly what I'm talking about. I said, 'Who said I was never married?'"

He could only stare at her, wondering if she was slipping into incoherence again. Was she married or not? How could a simple question have turned into this debate?

"Look, I'm almost to the point of believing that men and women will never communicate successfully. I've read all the books. I know that men are from Mars. It would just be nice to meet up with an earthling for a change."

He merely stared at her. One moment she seemed quite sane, and in the next she began speaking in riddles. "Mairie, perhaps you should rest now. The evening appears to have wearied you."

Her eyes narrowed dangerously and he realized that somehow, no matter how carefully chosen, his words were about to set her off again.

"That's right, I am tired. Tired of trying to justify to you who I am and where I come from and that I am not crazy, and tomorrow when we get to that ranch, I will prove it. There must be a road that leads to modern civilization. I'll hitchhike if I have to, but I am getting out of this and finding my brother. I appreciate all you have done and everything, but enough is enough." She slid down onto the rug and turned her back to him. "Goodnight."

He continued to stare at her and felt certain that tomorrow she would be even more troubled by what she found. Jack wanted to stroke her hair, to soothe her, yet he knew he couldn't help her anymore. He could only lead her where she wanted to go and bid her good-bye. Better to put her out of his mind than allow her to seize possession of it.

Maybe she really was a witch after all.

An earthling? Now, what the hell did she mean by that?

They came off the mountain slowly. Mairie rode the horse and Jack led by foot. She felt guilty, seeing that it was Jack's horse but he insisted that the horse would need its strength to get through the desert.

The plant was wrapped in a damp cloth and in a saddlebag on the side of the horse, along with Jack's filled canteen and another container of water that Mairie swore was the bladder from some animal. Little did she realize that before the morning was over, she would be grateful to drink from it.

When they finally left the mountain, Mairie stared out before her. There was a long green patch in the middle of the valley, yet it seemed so very far away. How would they ever make it there? To reach it, they followed a crooked trail that wound through dry washes. Her throat burned from the dry heat. Her face stung from the blazing sun. Her spirits plummeted from the lack of anything modern in sight. This was not the country she had left two days ago.

She and Jack didn't speak, for it seemed a mutual agreement to save their energy for movement. He rode behind her when they left the mountain for a short period in order to cover more ground, and then dismounted to give the horse a break. Her guilt deepened every time he took off his hat and wiped his forehead on his sleeve, yet he refused to tax his horse with two riders for any long period. Realizing the water was for the horse, Mairie stopped herself from asking for more. Jack insisted she ride for her injured foot. Still, it bothered her that he would push himself so hard under the desert sun.

"You need to rest," she called out. "Let's stop and take a break."

He shook his head. "Soon. There's a spring at the west end of the trail. We'll stop there."

They must have traveled over twenty miles; at least, it felt like that to her. The desert seemed to go on forever, while the green oasis tantalized her like a mirage that always appeared further away. Her mind felt like it had closed down. Even thinking took too much energy. Her gratitude toward the

man before her increased when she realized that
without him finding her, without his assistance, she
might have died a horrible death in the desert. For
no one ... *no one* had come looking for her. Her
mind couldn't put any of it together any longer. She
closed her eyes to the glare of the sun and envisioned this spring ... somewhere out there in the
merciless land.

"Mairie ..." The sound of her name was almost
breathless and she seemed to come out of a comatose
state. Her lids opened slowly, as if dreading the assault of blinding light.

What she saw lifted her spirits.

The oasis of green no longer beckoned from an
endless distance. It was before them, within reach.
Shelter, water ... sustenance. Dear God, they had
made it. They would live.

Neither spoke as they closed the remaining short
distance. Even the horse sensed that the torturous
journey was nearing its end and a renewed vitality
entered its step. Mairie sensed it spring into the muscles of the animal, propelling it onward with determination.

They stopped beside a tree-shaded spring and, as
Jack reached up to help Mairie down, their gaze connected for a brief moment. No words were necessary. They each understood the other and Mairie felt
a bonding occur. They had banded together and survived an ordeal.

As he gently placed her on the ground, she looked
into his eyes and whispered, "Thank you."

He appeared exhausted, depleted. His skin
seemed covered with a fine dusting of salt. Her heart
expanded with compassion. He merely smiled and
nodded before leading the horse to the water.

She stood for a moment, watching him, ignoring
her thirst, her desire to throw herself into the creek,
seeing him as the man he was. Why was she think-

ing of him as a knight, chivalrous, brave, honorable,
in service? Surely it was lack of water.

She shook the thought from her mind and hobbled
to the water's edge. Too weary to throw herself into
the small running creek, she removed her jumpsuit
and slowly walked in until the water reached her
thighs. Then, instinctively, she fell to her knees,
gratefully, humbly, in complete surrender to the
power of nature. She felt her body temperature
lower immediately as the water enveloped her in its
coolness, and without thought she lowered her face
and began drinking. How precious this gift. Tears
she had been holding at bay sprang forth. No longer
did she know what was happening to her, why she
was on this incredible detour, and she was beyond
rationalization. She only knew that something
within her was altering, something was happening
. . . some tightness in her that she had been carrying
around like a boulder upon her chest was lifting. She
felt tiny, vulnerable . . . losing her preconceived notions of the way she thought her world worked. This
detour seemed necessary now for some unknown
reason. She had no idea where it was leading her,
what she was going to find . . . yet she knew she was
bound to follow it through. Not for Bryan. Incredibly, not for her brother.

Now it was for herself.

Jack scanned the horizon, considering the short
distance left of the arduous journey. The sun indicated it was early afternoon and he knew they
would be at the ranch in less than an hour. Turning
toward the water, he stood transfixed, forgetting
even his intense thirst. It wasn't so much that he was
accustomed to the desert heat . . . what captivated
him at that moment was a vision in the form of a
goddess, much like those he had seen in history
books back east. He watched her intensely, after she

had stopped drinking . . . her long black hair slicked back, her face turned up to the sky, her arms raised as she ran her fingers from the crown of her head down to the nape of her neck, pressing the moisture from her hair. Water droplets glistened in the sunlight as they ran down her skin, creating an iridescent beauty about her more stunning than when she was dressed last night as an Indian maiden.

His train of thought shook him to the core. He would have to release the notion that she was his gift. She was a lost traveler, and as soon as he deposited her at the ranch, he was out of it. Desert survival-instinct kicked in and he noticed that although her body appeared fair, her face had been burned by the sun. He walked over to a huge aloe plant and broke off a thick tip. Stepping boot deep into the creek, he squatted and took a few handfuls of water for himself, then made his way toward her, his steps absorbed by the sound of the babbling stream.

As he was looking down to her kneeling before him in the water, his breath caught. Her eyes were still closed, as though she were away somewhere in her mind and in that moment he felt privileged to observe her silent beauty.

"Your face has been burned by the sun." Even to his own ears his voice sounded raspy, filled with desire, and he cleared his throat. "I have something here that will ease the pain and refresh your skin." He stood looking down at her and felt the stirring of something that was better forgotten in this situation and with this woman. "It's the meat of an aloe plant."

Her eyes opened, her lovely blue eyes, and she stared up at him. She really was a goddess, a water nymph, something unearthly that was mesmerizing him. Suppressing a groan, he squeezed the succulent juices of the leaf onto the tips of his fingers and slowly lowered himself into the water until they were face to face. She didn't move. She didn't say a word. Her gaze followed him as he knelt before her and reached out his hand to her face. He hesitated for an instant, waiting to see if she would allow him to minister to her.

The tip of his thumb grazed her cheek with the moisture, and she winced in pain. He pulled back and cursed the rough calluses of his own hand against her smooth skin.

"I'm sorry. I . . . I'll be—"

"It's okay," she interrupted, with a voice as soft as a whisper.

Their gazes locked in a moment that felt like an eternity. His fingers didn't move. His caress stopped, as he drew in a breath between his teeth, and when his thumb continued to gently soothe her cheek with the aloe his fingers instinctively cupped the side of her face.

He heard her intake of breath, her allowance. The spitfire was gone. In her place was a soft and gentle woman, who was staring into his eyes with a look of wonderment. Nothing else seemed to exist but the water and her . . . her startling wide eyes, her tender silky skin, her full waiting lips.

An unspoken introduction was made.

His thumb softly caressed the corner of her bottom lip and her face turned ever so slightly into his hand. He stared into her eyes, down to her lips, then back into her eyes . . . waiting for permission. Eye to eye, mouth to mouth, he inhaled her breath . . . wanting to take her inside him, to remember this exquisite moment. He kissed her . . . softly, gently, and watched her lids flutter closed. A rush of desire washed over him and he fought the urge to pull her closer, to deepen the connection, yet it felt so fragile, so precious, that he found his body shaking with the intensity of holding back.

How was he ever going to walk away from this?

* * *

Mairie felt every nerve ending come alive. The skin of her cheek received his touch like a gentle magnet, drawing some kind of electrical energy from his fingers. Her lips tingled, as his barely grazed over hers in an exquisite meeting of skin and texture and sensations. Her mind was reeling from the contact. Her senses were screaming at her to open her lips, to abandon herself to the most exquisite kiss awaiting her surrender.

The horse gave a great snort and Jack suddenly pulled away. Mairie almost lost her balance and had to fight to stay upright.

"Let me check the horse," he whispered while standing and hurrying out of the water.

She found herself breathing heavily, as though she'd just run a marathon. What the hell had just happened? And why had she allowed it? Surely she was weak from the sun and she'd had a momentary lapse into madness. Embarrassed, Mairie splashed her face with cool water and rose from the stream. She walked to the shore and stood in the sun to dry. She would not watch him check the horse and surrounding area, as if protecting her.

Lose the knight image, she told herself. This was some delusional man who preferred the past to the present, not a knight rescuing a lost damsel in distress. She'd obviously read too many books. He seemed satisfied that nothing was wrong and walked back to the stream. He filled the canteen and bladder with water and looked to the sun.

"We must be going. We have less than an hour's travel, and then you can get out of the sun."

That was it? He wasn't going to say anything about what had just happened? Typical male . . . to ignore what he couldn't understand. She mentally reprimanded herself for allowing such behavior. What weakness . . .

Shrugging, Mairie decided to play it off casually. So what if she had responded? She'd never see the man after today. What did it matter what he thought? It was weakness, sunstroke or something.

"Sure." She walked toward the horse and he didn't even look at her as he tied the canteens to the horn and then laced his fingers together to assist her into the saddle. Up she went, easily, and settled once more onto the horse's back. Soon they would reach this ranch and then this amazing detour would be over. What stories she would have to tell Bryan . . .

After another three miles or so they passed the lodges of nearly three hundred Paiutes, some of whom worked at the ranch, Jack said. She felt an excitement building inside her as they rounded a bend.

"How much farther?" she asked, seeing a small adobe house with outbuildings.

Jack stopped walking and turned to her. "This is it."

She merely stared back. "This is *it*?" It couldn't be. She was expecting the Ponderosa, or something. Not this depressing version of the Beverly Hillbillies before they struck oil.

"This is it," he said in a dull voice.

Shit . . .

There were no electrical lines running to the place. Nor phone lines. No cars were visible. Nothing modern in sight. A tall man was standing in the front wearing dark trousers and a white shirt. An equally tall woman opened the door and stood on the porch. She was wearing a long white dress . . . a dress that would have been worn a hundred years ago.

Fear slammed into her brain, sending distress signals to every organ. Something was very wrong . . . no search parties. No planes. It was one thing to think Jack might be living in the past. She could even rationalize the Paiutes in the mountains. But this . . . this could not be denied.

It couldn't be possible. Not in her world. Not in her mind. Not in any reality . . .

This was proof, undeniable proof of what she feared the most, what she had been denying since she had landed two days ago . . . proof that she had somehow time traveled into the past.

She no longer knew where to call out for help to stop this madness. She was alone, a stranger in a very strange land. Her body started trembling in the intense sunlight. Her mind was spinning in overdrive. And then it happened, something so weird that she was mildly surprised as the darkness entered her vision.

Slowly collapsing, she surrendered and welcomed the oblivion.

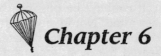 *Chapter 6*

Everything was disorienting.

Her forehead was cold. In what seemed a distance she heard whimpering, the sound of a plaintive cry. Something in her wanted to stop it, to help out, and she struggled from the deepest sleep she could ever remember. Her lids barely opened and she squinted at the sun through a glass that was veined and bubbled with imperfections. A fine dust added to the distortion of the setting sun.

The whimpering began again and she turned her head slightly. A young boy stood at the foot of the bed, his golden hair matching the fur of the small puppy. She saw two warm brown eyes, two big paws, and a fat pink belly dangling underneath the arms of a sweet-faced child.

An innocent voice called out, "Momma . . . she's awake!"

Mairie couldn't figure out where she was, or how she got into this bed. Her head ached, as if a steel band were tightened around it. Raising her fingers to her face, she felt a cold compress had been placed on her forehead.

"Let me help you with that, dear."

A tall woman dressed in a long white dress hurried to her side. A cameo brooch was attached to the high collar. She had dark eyes, dark hair pulled up in a bun, and a kind face.

"Where am I?"

The woman smiled and her slightly worn features appeared almost pretty. "Hush now, my dear, you've had an awful time of it, haven't you? Suffering sunstroke and falling off the horse. Rest now. You aren't the first one the desert has brought to their knees."

"Where am I?" Mairie repeated. Her confusion deepened as the woman removed the cold cloth and dipped it into a basin of water on a nightstand.

"You're at the Las Vegas ranch, dear. Jack Delaney brought you in from the mountains. He said you were lost." She placed the refreshed cloth on Mairie's forehead.

Mairie stared up at her as everything started falling into place. Delaney. The Indian encampment. The pool of water and the kiss. The shock of seeing that where the glittery town of Las Vegas was supposed to stand was merely a rundown farm. She was lost . . . definitely lost . . . in someone else's time.

"Do you have a phone, a telephone?" Mairie whispered.

The woman stared down at her. "I'm sorry . . . you mean a telegraph?" She laughed lightly and shook her head. "No. The nearest one is in Fort Mojave. There will be a wagon train coming in from the fort in a couple of days and you could send your message back with them."

This couldn't be happening. It simply couldn't . . . Jack couldn't have arranged this. He wasn't a delusional executive having a nervous breakdown and living in the past. The Indians weren't isolated in history. She was the one . . . she was out of place, and out of time.

Her time.

"Please," she whispered to the woman. "I am so

lost. I need to get to modern civilization. Can you help me? Do you know what's happened? I don't belong here." She started to rise and the woman appeared worried. "Please . . . help me."

"Now, now . . . lie back down and rest, my dear. I took your clothes, and Lee, my Chinese man, is washing them. Strange clothes for a woman, but I say, never judge another person by appearances. You may use one of my dresses, until you're well enough to travel again." Her smile deepened in friendliness. "I'm Virginia Gass, by the way. And we already know that you're Mairie Callahan from back east. We can talk later and you can fill me in on everything that's news. Besides, you can't go anywhere yet, so you just might as well take advantage of the situation and recuperate while you can. Supper will be ready in about a half hour. Fenton here will keep you company until then. If you feel up to it, you can join us. Or I'll bring a plate in here for you."

The woman patted her son's head and left the room as efficiently as she came into it.

Totally confused, Mairie looked at the child and the puppy.

"What's his name?" she whispered.

The young boy grinned. "I call him Digger, cause he digs in the yard all the time and Momma says if he touches her vegetable plants again, she's gonna plant him pure and proper. But he's a good one. Really . . ."

Mairie tried smiling as the boy came over and let the puppy rest on the edge of the bed. Immediately the dog scampered up to kiss her face and she grabbed his golden fur to stop him. "It hurts too much."

Fenton collared the pup and scolded him. "You had best behave or I'll have to put you out again. Momma says this here's a special visitor and we have to be nice." He looked up to Mairie and grinned. "You want me to show you my kittens, too?"

Children were innocent. Children this age didn't lie. She looked into his big blue eyes and asked, "What year is it? Do you know the year?"

"The year?" Fenton scrunched up his nose and looked at the beamed ceiling. "It's ... uh ... it's ... *Momma, what year is it?*" His voice carried throughout the house.

Virginia stuck her head in the room and scolded her son. "Now, you just leave if you can't speak in a proper tone of voice. We do not yell in the house."

"But what year is it, Momma? The lady wants to know."

Virginia looked from her son to Mairie and smiled in sympathy. "Sunstroke confuses you, doesn't it? Had it myself once, the first year I came here. It's 1877, dear. Now, rest easy, and Fenton, if you can't be pleasant company, then you must leave."

"I'll be good, Momma. I promise."

When they were alone, Mairie simply stared at the rough planked wall. How could this have happened? How could she be in 1877? This ... this was impossible, insane! Yet even as she thought it, everything started to make sense. No wonder no one was looking for her. No one she knew was even born yet! Bryan ... her brother ... dear God, she would never see him again ... what must he be thinking? Did anything of her life in the future exist? She wanted to cry out at the unfairness, to scream at the universe for this trick. Was she insane?

This just didn't happen in her world.

But as she gazed into the true eyes of the child, Mairie realized she wasn't in her world any longer. It wasn't some massive elaborate plot to trick her. Somehow, in some way, she had traveled into another dimension. What was happening in her world, her time? What happened to Bryan, her friends, her life . . . ? Everyone she ever loved, everything that mattered possibly never existed. She was alone. Terribly alone, abandoned into the isolation of the past. Was it her past? Was her life in the future all a dream? It was impossible to consider anymore. It was too overwhelming to comprehend. She stared at the wall, wondering if she could stay in this bed and just die. Nothing seemed to matter.

"I could show you my secret place if you want."

Blinking, Mairie shifted her gaze to the child. She almost forgot he was in the room. "Maybe later, okay?"

He smiled shyly and nodded. "I always go there when I'm sad and it makes me happy again."

She couldn't help it. In spite of all the bizarre circumstances surrounding her, she smiled back. He was so innocent, so sweet . . . how like a child to come to her rescue in this moment. And how like her to respond. If she trusted anyone right now, it might as well be a child. "Later. I would love it if you'd show me your secret place. How long have you lived here, Fenton?"

He shrugged and stuck his finger into his mouth, as if thinking really hard. "I just always been here. Lee tells me of magic places across big oceans, but I ain't never been there. Just here."

"You were born here, then."

"I guess."

Mairie smiled and looked down at the white cotton nightgown she had on. "Is this your mother's?"

"I guess." He shrugged again shyly.

She reached out and touched his freckled cheek. "Tomorrow you can show me your secret place, Fenton. I would like that."

Lifting the patchwork quilt and stiff linen sheet to the side, she eased her legs to the edge of the bed and began slowly to raise herself with her arms. Pain shot through her entire body and into the crown of her head.

Fenton backed away as she grimaced and grabbed her skull.

"Ahh, I've had better hangovers than this."

"Huh? Are you gonna be okay, lady?"

Her eyes still closed, Mairie began to stand. The throbbing in her skull increased as she gained the altitude of her height.

"I'll be fine, just give me a second to get my bearings." She opened her eyes and gave Fenton a forced reassuring smile. Mairie saw there had been a house coat placed on the end of the bed. As every muscle in her body ached, she pulled it over her shoulders.

"Can you show me to the bathroom, Fenton?"

"You wanna take a bath? It's not Saturday. We always take baths on Saturdays."

"I need to use the . . . the bathroom, Fenton. Can you tell me where it is?"

"Oh! If ya gotta go, ya hafta use the pot there, under the bed."

Mairie resigned herself to the situation. She couldn't think about it now. Later . . . much later, she would settle it in her mind, but right now her attention was focused on a priority. "When in Rome, do as the Romans do . . ." she muttered. "Will you excuse me, Fenton?"

"Oh, sure." Fenton grabbed the puppy from the bed, nearly pulling the quilt with it, as Digger had begun to chew on the fabric. Balancing the pup under his arms, he went out the door and before he shut it poked his head back into the room. "You gonna eat dinner with us at the table?" he asked softly.

Mairie turned to the boy and nodded, her face describing the pain that wracked her head and body as she lifted the heavy ceramic pot onto the bed.

Fenton closed the door quietly, then, from beyond,

she heard him shout, "Ma, I don't think that lady's doin' so good. But she says she's gonna eat with us at the table."

Staring at the chamber pot, Mairie let the tears come.

Her body was jolted by the ring of a loud bell. She rose and wiped tears from her tight cheeks. She slipped into the soft white cotton dress with tucked pleats on the bodice and shoulders. It was actually comfortable and the cool fabric felt soothing against her skin. Barefoot, Mairie pulled her hair back with a ribbon she found on the night table and took a deep breath as she saw her reflection in a small discolored mirror. Her face was red and parched from the sun. Sighing, she realized that a day at Elizabeth Arden's was out, so what was left? She'd just have to find more of that aloe and hope she didn't peel. Nothing could be done now about anything. And what did it really matter any longer? She steeled herself to meet her uncertain future in the mysterious past and walked out of the room.

She opened the door to the main house and stared at the table set in the center of the large room. It had to be twenty feet long with seating for sixteen. A Chinese man with a long braid down his back was placing bowls on the table and looked up at her standing in the doorway.

"Come," he motioned, and nodded toward the table. "Come, come . . . you eat, now."

Mairie smiled timidly and slowly walked into the main room. Virginia Gass briskly entered from another doorway, followed by three children. Two girls and Fenton, with Digger still perched over his arms. "So glad you could join us, Mairie. The ranch hands have finished and there haven't been any travelers for a few days, so we're eating early for a change. Please be seated. The men are about to join us. And Fenton, if you don't set that dog out now, you can eat your dinner on the porch with him."

Mairie sat at one side of the table as Fenton immediately scampered to the front door, set the dog outside, then raced back and took the seat next to her. She smiled at the young boy and looked across the wide table to his sisters. Two young girls stared at her with curious eyes until Virginia introduced them. Before Mairie had a chance to say more than hello, the front door opened and a very tall man with a long beard entered. Behind him was Jack . . . washed, his hair combed behind his ears, and dressed in a pressed white shirt. In spite of her situation, she felt an immediate pang of attraction and looked down to her hands in her lap. He looked so . . . civilized.

"Mairie Callahan, may I present my husband, Octavius Decatur Gass."

She smiled up at him as the man held his hand out to take hers. She placed her hand in his and he bent over it in a gentlemanly bow. "A pleasure, Miss Callahan. Everyone calls me O.D. Pleased to see you've recovered."

"Thank you, O.D. I appreciate you and your wife's hospitality. I was . . . desperate, I'm afraid."

"Nonsense. You aren't the first who's come to us in that state, and you won't be the last. Glad we could help out." The man nodded and pulled out his chair at the head of the long table.

"Good evening, Mairie."

Just the sound of his voice sent shivers up her arms. Or could it be the sunburn? It was the sunburn. She was not about to get stupid over a man who had kissed her and then ignored her. However, she was grateful to him for bringing her to this ranch, so she looked up and smiled. "Good evening, Jack. Thank you for all your help."

"Glad to see that you're feeling better."

Why was there this formality now? Was it this

place? These people? She actually felt shy in his presence, and even that annoyed her. Part of her wanted to take him outside and tell him about traveling into the past, and another part knew it would add to his conviction that she was crazy. Who would believe her? And could she blame anyone? These people thought she had sunstroke, but not Jack. Yet he was the only one who might believe her. If she could just prove it. But how could one prove she had time-traveled a hundred and twenty-two years into the past? Even she didn't want to believe it.

Jack was seated next to the girls and he stared across the table at Mairie. She looked very lovely in the white dress and the yellow ribbon holding back her dark hair. At any other time with any other woman he would have pursued the attraction.

But not this woman, and definitely not this time, when he was leaving tomorrow and would never see her again. To do so would only cause further distress.

The dinner conversation centered mostly on the proposed annexation of the ranch by Arizona and how O.D. was fighting it. Jack noticed how Mrs. Gass attempted to draw Mairie out by asking for the latest news from the big cities back east. He could see her uneasiness as she fumbled for answers and volunteered the excuse of sunstroke to save her from further pressure. Yet he could not save her as O.D. asked how she had wound up all alone in the middle of the desert.

He watched as Mairie stared down at her plate before raising her face to stare at him with pleading eyes. A moment passed and she whispered, "I don't know."

Jack was grateful to Mrs. Gass for her sympathetic heart, and for the young boy at Mairie's side, who stared up at her adoringly. Young Fenton, it appeared, had one heck of a crush. He understood the lad.

"O.D., can't you see Miss Callahan has been through so much? Let her rest, now," Virginia chided. "You gentlemen take your cigars to the front porch while we clear the table. Lelah, you and your sister come help me."

He rose from the table and felt slightly worried as he looked at Mairie. He had not seen her feisty spirit in some time. She appeared . . . defeated.

He turned to Mrs. Gass. "Thank you for the most delicious dinner."

Virginia Gass glanced at her husband with one of those looks married people have that speaks in silent communication. She turned her attention back to him and smiled comfortingly.

"Now, Jack Delaney . . . you know that you are always welcome at our table. Have you thought on the job O.D. offered you? We really could use you here at the ranch."

Jack grinned, knowing that the attractive woman from Missouri had left a wealthy family to travel west and discover her own adventure. She was greatly admired by all, even the Paiutes. Virginia Simpson Gass was one tough woman, and one lovely lady . . . who knew how to use her charm when it was needed.

"Mrs. Gass," he said with an appreciative smile. "the offer is tempting, especially since I would be feasting at your table nightly. However, my heart is with my brothers right now. I've been away far too long. I will keep it in mind, though, and thank you for the suggestion."

Virginia laughed. "You are a charmer, Jack. Seems a shame to waste those lovely eastern manners living on those hot and dry mountains."

Jack joined in the laughter. "And I'll return that

back door compliment to you, madam. You are a rose amid this parched desert."

Nodding, Virginia chuckled, then said to her husband, "Now, this is why you must allow us a trip to Missouri. I miss this bantering, O.D. Need to sharpen my social skills . . ." She grinned at Jack. "And my wits."

With a pat on the shoulder, O.D. invited him to the porch. "Well, before you charm my wife, and I suffer a month of Sundays hearing about a proposed trip east, come share a cigar. I'd like to show you my new mowing machine for my alfalfa before you leave tomorrow."

Mairie quickly looked up at him. He walked toward the door eager to share a fine smoke, but couldn't quite shake the expression in Mairie's eyes. He had seen arrogance. Anger. Disbelief. He had even seen laughter.

It was the first time he saw fear.

She felt like a robot, helping Virginia and the girls clear the table. When they went to the kitchen, Lee fussed about taking bowls and shooed them out. Still weak, Mairie was grateful to sit in the parlor and watch Virginia sew a vest. She marveled at this woman, so resourceful in this wilderness. And yet . . . she appeared happy.

Again, Mairie thought of how the crafts of an earlier age were being lost. It was so much easier to run into the mall to buy mass produced goods than take the time to create them. She was as guilty as the next. She remembered her grandmother crocheting pillow covers and baby clothes. The art was lost with her grandmother's passing. Suddenly, Mairie regretted not taking the time to learn. It would have honored her grandmother, and she would have expanded her own abilities. Sighing, she looked at the pleasant family scene. It was something she might never have, and that thought depressed her.

The girls, still shy around her, sat looking at books with pictures while Fenton and Digger played at her side. It was a very domestic scene. There was happiness here, despite the hardships.

It just made Mairie want her own time and place more. Somehow . . . there had to be a way back. If she had traveled into the past, there must be some way to travel into the present, her present. She was merely an observer here. Would Jack understand? He wasn't like ordinary men, especially men in this time. He was looking at a different picture through the eyes of the Indian. He believed in the unexplainable. Surely what had happened to her was unexplainable.

A sharp pain had closed around her heart when she'd heard that he was leaving tomorrow. She shouldn't care. But she did . . . she really did . . . and now she knew she would have to speak with him tonight, tell him the truth, ask his help, his guidance. How ironic that Jack Delaney was the only person she trusted right now. How wrong she had been about him . . . and she wasn't above admitting a mistake.

Like that kiss. She should never have allowed it. Best to put it out of her mind and concentrate on more important matters . . . like finding a way to survive this incredible detour. For that was all she was willing to accept. It was merely a departure from her own world, her own time. She *was* going to find a way back.

Her opportunity arrived when O.D. came inside to spend time with his children. He appeared to be a good father and Mairie excused herself, leaving the family to their routine. She slipped outside and was grateful to see a wide chair. It was made of rough wood, yet the double seat was worn smooth by use.

She sank onto it and sighed as she looked at the night sky, while hearing the faint strains of laughter coming from the cabin of the ranch hands.

Looking up to the huge desert moon, she called out in her mind to him. She must wait for Jack to show up. She knew somehow that he would. In the meantime, she listened to the sounds of the night and tried not to think too far ahead. She could only survive this moment by moment. Anything else would lead to madness.

"How do you feel?"

The familiar voice didn't startle her, for she was expecting him. She blinked a few times, pulling her into the present. "Jack . . . I knew you would come."

He smiled in the moonlight and Mairie felt that tug at her breast.

"That's what I said when I found you."

She thought of his first words. It felt like a lifetime ago. Returning his smile, she said, "You're right. You weren't sure of who or what I was, and I wasn't sure you weren't crazy. You were right, Jack, and I was wrong. I'm sorry. Sorry for thinking you were the one out of place. It was me. It was me all along."

He came onto the porch and leaned against the railing. "What's wrong, Mairie? It's more than the sunstroke. Something's happened."

Looking up at him, she fought the burning in her throat from unshed tears. This conversation must take place and she must have control over her emotions in order to do it. Tears could come later. "Jack, what I'm about to say is going to sound insane to you, but you're the only one I can talk to about it. You're the only one that might possibly understand . . . or even if you couldn't understand, you might believe me."

He sat next to her and leaned his elbows on his knees and rested his chin in his hands. Turning his head, he stared into her eyes. "Mairie, what are you talking about? What is bothering you so?"

"Listen, I'm in the wrong place at the wrong time. You saw me fall from the sky and I tried to explain to you how it happened, but you couldn't understand it. Now I know why. Jack, I really am from the future . . . your future." There. She'd said it.

She waited for a response. When she realized none was forthcoming, she continued.

"I know this is going to sound crazy to you. Now I completely understand your reactions to me and they were justified. How could you possibly understand what an airplane was when you'd never seen one? They haven't been invented yet. But you saw me fall from the sky. You saw it. How could I possibly have gotten there? That far up? Something had to have taken me there to jump in the first place. It was an airplane. A . . . a vehicle of transportation." She struggled to find the right words, just as she knew he was struggling to grasp them.

"What you say is far too incredible to imagine. If this is true, then explain air . . . plane. I ask how such a thing is possible. How does it fly in the sky?"

She was afraid he would ask that. "I wish I knew. Something to do with thrust and air speed, air moving over and under the wings—"

"Wait," he interrupted. "They have wings?"

She wanted to laugh at his expression. "Well, yes. There are wings, but they don't flap because there's an engine. Kind of like the engine that powers a train. That's steam, creating energy to propel something forward. This is the same concept, except instead of coal or wood, there's gasoline, an oil from under the earth."

He was shaking his head, as though he couldn't picture what she was saying. "I don't understand."

"I know," she said in a sympathetic voice. "This isn't an easy concept, and how can I explain it when even I don't understand it? I never realized how much I took for granted until now."

"Hold on . . . you are saying there are trains in the sky?"

She stifled a giggle. "Not trains. Airplanes are single, not linked together. But some are so big that they can hold a hundred or more people at one time. If we were in my time, we could get on a plane in Las Vegas, the Las Vegas that I left in 1999, and fly back east to Philadelphia in five hours."

"Oh, Mairie . . ." Jack's jaw dropped. "This . . . this fantasy is too incredible to believe."

Desperate, she clutched his shirt sleeve. "Jack . . . *you saw me!* How can you deny what you saw? I did fall from an airplane through the sky and something, I don't know what, but something happened to me while I was doing it. And instead of landing where I was supposed to, in *my time*, I landed in yours. In 1877. A hundred and twenty-two years before me."

Jack appeared bewildered, speechless.

"It's true, Jack. I just realized it myself when I saw this ranch. It was one thing to think you were crazy, that the Indians were hiding away from reality in the mountains . . . but this . . . this is too extensive. This really is 1877." She shook her head. "I'm trapped in the past, and I don't know what to do."

She looked at him and pleaded, "What should I do, Jack? You're the only one I can talk to about this because you saw me coming into this place. You are my witness that I'm not crazy. You, Jack Delaney . . . you confirm I am sane."

So why was he staring at her as if that were the last thing he was thinking?

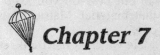 **Chapter 7**

No one so crazy could sound so sane.

Part of him was beginning to actually believe her. He *had* seen her fall from the sky, and his Indian exposure gave him the opportunity to view things from another side, to accept ideas that might not be grasped by so-called educated people. But this... coming from the future? This was asking too much.

Certain things baffled him. The clothes she had been wearing, the equipment she had been using. Even Wovoka had said she was from the land of tomorrows. It was just too incredible... he had been sitting on a mountaintop, waiting to see a sign of hope, and he had got Mairie Callahan... from the future?

"Then tell me this... if you jumped from this airplane, why didn't you plummet to the ground? The material you used was so thin. It couldn't possibly keep you from crashing. Something about this is beyond belief, Mairie. I mean, I know I saw you... but what you're asking me to accept is unreal."

"Well, of course it's unreal to you. It hasn't been invented yet. To me... it's everyday life. People skydive all the time, for fun. It's even a sport, like ... like baseball or horse racing. People compete against each other, though it wouldn't be something

I'd personally choose. I was only doing it to please my brother."

"But how do you keep from being killed? I felt that material, Mairie. It was too thin to save anyone."

He watched her think, staring out to the moon as if it might provide her with the answer.

"Okay . . . have you ever been on a street and seen a lady's parasol get pulled with a gust of wind? It's much like that. I had a huge parasol and could control it with pulleys and handles to narrow it and slow me down."

He tried to picture what she was saying. "So you flew like a bird in the sky and jumped into the air with a parasol for entertainment . . . for sport?"

She shook her head slowly and grinned. "Now I know it sounds crazy, but that's about it."

"I've seen a hell of a lot in my life, Mairie Callahan. I've seen Indian spirits and I've seen men overcome miraculous odds in death-defying situations during the war. All right, I admit there's nothing else I can do but accept what you're saying, because I saw you fall from the sky with my own eyes. I can't deny what I saw. And yes . . . it is crazy."

Her eyes filled with hope. "Then you believe me?"

"I don't know what to believe any longer. Maybe we're both crazy." He turned away and looked at the moon. Why didn't it surprise him that it was full? They were lunatics . . . both of them. Her for thinking she had come from the future, and him for beginning to believe it.

He turned back to her. "If all that you're saying is true, how do you expect to get back? There are no airplanes, or fantastic huge umbrellas here. What are you going to do?"

Why was she looking at him as though he might have an answer? He didn't know what he was going to do tomorrow, let alone how to advise her. He didn't think much about the future. Especially his own. He was just trying to get through today. He was like an empty barrel, drained by the fragility of life, and he hadn't a clue how to refill it. For that, he needed hope.

He had asked the one question that was uppermost in her mind.

Mairie sighed deeply, and stared up at him. "Oh, Jack . . . I don't know how to get back to my own time. I didn't even really believe I was out of it until today when I saw this ranch. If I knew how this happened, I'd have some clue about what took place and I'd try to figure out how to reverse it, or something."

"Have you ever heard of someone else falling into another time?"

Mairie couldn't stop the laughter. "No. This is . . . it's science fiction, or something. I mean, there've been movies about it, books even, but that was fiction. *Not real.* I'm *real*, Jack. This has actually happened to me. And I'll be damned if I ever believed it was possible."

"Well, you're here now. So what do you plan on doing?"

"I don't know." Three words, so simple, yet they had such a profound effect. She got up and started pacing, suddenly annoyed with herself and those three words. She was a self-made woman. She had survived a hell of a lot in her time, and had the guts to leave it all and follow her brother. She was a woman of resource. She hated not knowing how to proceed.

"I need to think about this," she said, still pacing. "Do I go back east? At least I would be on familiar ground. Of course, there's no one I could contact, so I guess it really doesn't matter where I go. I just know I can't stay here in the middle of a desert. I need to find a city, where I can get work. That's it

. . . I should go to LA. Wait a minute, what's Los
Angeles like now? Is it a big city, like back east?"

"No."

"Okay . . . San Francisco, then. I could find work
there, and then—" Her words and thoughts ceased
as a strong wave of dizziness washed over her. Stag-
gering, she grabbed the railing.

"Are you all right?" Jack held her shoulders and
steadied her. "Come, sit back down. You aren't
strong enough to go anywhere yet."

Breathing heavily, she sat in the chair and cursed
under her breath the unfamiliar weakness. Turning
her face up to him, she whispered what frightened
her the most. "Jack, are you leaving tomorrow?"

He stared down at her, and Mairie swore she saw
a momentary look of resignation pass over his features. "I'll stay until you're well enough to travel."

Her breath left her body in a huge sigh of relief.
"Thank you. I know how all this must sound to you.
But you're my link, Jack," she whispered as sincerely
as she was able, her voice trailing off.

He nodded sympathetically and walked toward
the front door. "Mrs. Gass, would you help Miss
Callahan? She's had another dizzy spell."

Virginia Gass rushed onto the front porch.
"You've overdone yourself, dear. The place for you
is bed now and a good night's rest. Jack, help me
get her to the door." Virginia put Mairie's arm
around her shoulder and helped her to stand.

Jack awkwardly grasped Mairie's hand and elbow.

"You're not promenading her around a ballroom,
Jack; put your arm around her waist."

Mairie lifted her right arm around his shoulder
and neck. He held her hand gently and placed his
arm around her waist.

Virginia shouted for her husband. "O.D., we need
your help."

O.D. held the door and Mairie hesitated at the opening, gazing into Jack's eyes. In an instant she realized they were very much alike. Both of them lost, with uncertain futures.

When O.D. assumed Jack's place, she experienced a moment of loss as his embrace left her. In those few seconds she sensed a deep tenderness, strength, and caring from Jack she had not felt before.

"Rest well, Mairie. I'll see you in the morning," he said quietly.

Lying in the dark, her body exhausted, she could not stop her mind from reviewing the entire day's events. Before sleep claimed her, she had come to a conclusion. She had to accept three things . . . that she was unusually weak, that she was living one hundred and twenty-two years in the past, and that she might be falling in love with a disillusioned cowboy.

Talk about dizzy.

Defeated, she surrendered to slumber.

The morning sun made Mairie squint. She was glad Mrs. Gass had given her a large straw hat to wear. "How much farther, Fenton? I may need to rest again."

"It's just over here, Mairie." Fenton pointed toward a flat ridge with mesquite trees.

Mairie looked down at the ever-present Digger, who was now tugging at her long white cotton dress. "You silly puppy . . . let go . . . I've enough trouble keeping myself moving, much less dragging you with me."

"Digs! Come here, boy!" Fenton scrambled up a hill and Digger happily loped behind him.

Another hill . . . just what I need. What am I doing? I should be preparing to leave this godforsaken desert for the nearest big city . . . and I'm off gallivanting about the countryside with a six-year-old boy and his dog, Mairie thought to herself.

Struggling for breath, she rose to the top of the ridge and straightened to ease her back and legs. The view was breathtaking. Early morning sun was painting hues of earthy pastel colors on the distant mountains. "How lovely," she said aloud. She thought about the city lights she had expected the day before. The glitter. The audaciousness of the Las Vegas she knew. This was unspoiled splendor.

"Wait till you see the inside!" Fenton exclaimed with a giggle, interrupting her thoughts.

She looked down at his grinning face from a small opening within thorny branches. "You don't expect me to crawl in *that*, do you, Fenton?"

"Come on, you can do it, Mar."

With a flash, his words struck her like lightning. Bryan had said that just before he'd jumped from the plane. Without hesitation, Mairie found herself hitching up the long skirt of her dress and bending down to crawl through the narrow passageway into the thicket.

Inside, she was able to sit, while the child could stand. Sunlight filtered through the mesquite branches and danced on treasures dangling by strings as she looked up around the ceiling of this hollowed secret place. Fenton began to explain the origin of each article, pieces of colored glass, long feathers, Indian beads, and objects travelers had given him when they'd stopped at the ranch.

She found herself entranced and thought of Bryan.

With detail the child wove tales of all his adventures. How ironic . . . "And a child shall lead them." The quote came to her as she watched Fenton make his way around this magical cavern. How much her brother was like this boy. Embracing all of life's simplicities. Enjoying the experience. Loving his life and everything it offered, no matter how small or grand.

Bryan was as this free-spirited boy . . . fulfilling the instinctual need of all mankind to do more than just survive. To live.

"I have a brother," she whispered, wondering when she'd lost her free spirit. She could remember feeling it as a child, making mud pies, and being fascinated with nature. When had she lost this magic? When had she grown up and thought such things were merely childish? Was this what Bryan was trying to teach her before he dies? To stop being such an adult and remember what it was like to be a child . . . before she had thought in order to get along in the world, she had to accept society's point of view. Childhood was freedom. What had Bryan said that day in the plane? About leaving the tribe behind and experiencing life?

"Are you listening to me, Mar?" Fenton was crouched over her with a puzzled look. "This place is supposed to make you happy, not sad."

She smiled at him and touched his face. "Thank you, Fenton. This is just wonderful. Magical."

Fenton's eyes lit with pleasure. "See? I *told* you."

"Yes . . . yes, you did. I don't feel sad any longer. How could I when I'm here in your secret place. No one knows about this? Not even your sisters?"

He shook his head emphatically. "Nope. Just you now. And Digger, of course."

She looked at the puppy, naturally digging at the base of a tree. "Of course. Digger."

"What's your brother's name? Where is he now? Does he have a boy like me?" He *had* heard her whisper.

Mairie laughed at the series of questions. "His name is Bryan. He's . . . he's . . ." What could she say? "He's waiting for me to return to him, and no . . . he doesn't have any children."

"When will you see him again?"

"I don't know. I'm lost. That's how I came here to your ranch."

"My daddy tells me about the stars. He says if you always follow the North Star, you'll find your way home. The stars will help you, Mairie."

She could feel a lump of emotion gather at the back of her throat and she wanted to hug the child. Mairie knew young Fenton was developing a crush on her and she almost regretted that she would soon leave him.

"C'mere, Fenton," she whispered, as she cupped his chin in her hand and leaned forward. Planting a light kiss on his forehead, she smiled. "You're a good friend. Thank you. I feel much better."

Fenton blushed and shrugged his shoulders. "It *is* magical, Mairie." He swung his arms out and twirled around as he looked up through the trees. "All of it . . ."

Her heart expanded. From the mouths of babes comes truth.

They lazily made their way back to the ranch as the midday sun reminded them it was time for lunch. The busy sounds from the ranch courtyard told them it had not yet been served. Mairie didn't see Jack about. She hadn't seen him since he left breakfast early that morning and they hadn't had the chance to speak again. She wondered if he would be there for lunch. Why was she putting such importance on his appearance? She simply had to fight this attraction and latching onto the man emotionally was not going to help.

Fenton opened the back door to the kitchen and Mairie followed. The aroma of baking biscuits and simmering stew filled the room.

Virginia looked up from the bowl of dough she was kneading and smiled. "How was your morning walk? You must be feeling better."

Mairie grinned down at her friend. "It was magical. My charming escort showed me some remarkable things. Unless you need my help here, I'll freshen up before lunch."

Virginia wiped her hands on the long white apron. "No, Lee can finish the rest. There's something I need to speak with you about in private, Mairie. Let me get you a fresh towel for your washbasin."

Minutes later, standing over the basin, Mairie reveled in the relief of cool water on her face, while wondering what was so private and important. Virginia stood away, looking out the window.

"We had a visitor today," she announced, and turned. "And he was looking for you."

In the midst of patting her face dry, Mairie stopped and stared at the woman. "Me? Are you sure?"

Virginia nodded. "He described you quite accurately and knew you were lost."

Stunned, Mairie whispered, "Did he say his name?"

She shook her head. "No, he wouldn't say, and that's why I became suspicious. I told him to check later today when the wagon train from Fort Mojave comes by. Who could it be, Mairie? Are you married? Have you run away from a husband? Family?"

Mairie felt frozen with confusion, mixed with hope. Someone was looking for her? Could it be Bryan? "No," she insisted. "I haven't run away from anything. I was . . . I am lost. What did he look like, Virginia? Did he have dark hair and blue eyes?"

The woman nodded. "Yes. But there was an unnatural air about him. Very mysterious. He wouldn't give me any more information and . . . I don't know, I felt something was missing in him, in his heart."

It could be Bryan. If he was also lost in the past, he would be hesitant and careful. And scared, just like her. Her heart sang out that it had to be her brother. Who else would even know about her in this time? Only someone else that had experienced the same thing!

"Oh, Virginia . . . where is he? He didn't leave, did he?" She couldn't stop the desperation in her voice. She *must* find him!

Shaking her head, Virginia said, "I don't think he's left the area. He's probably camping by the creek. I didn't invite him into the house, since my instincts were on the alert."

Mairie threw the towel onto the table. "I have to find him. He . . . he may know something about how I can get back home."

Virginia walked up to her and looked into Mairie's eyes. "I have so enjoyed your company, Mairie. I don't get the opportunity to share time with many women. When you leave us, I will miss you . . . but I know you must get home . . . I know how important *home* is. To all of us."

With the woman's emphasis on the word home, Mairie felt the emotion building in her again. If only she could click her heels, like Dorothy, and make it happen. But she wasn't in Oz and there was no wizard to remind her, but she did have a glimmer of hope now. Bryan. He had to be here.

Impulsively, Mairie reached out and hugged Virginia. "Thank you for all your help. You've been so kind to me." Pulling back, she smiled widely. "I've got to find this man . . . please excuse me from lunch. I'll be back soon."

As she left the room, she heard Virginia's parting words, said so softly that it was only down the hallway they registered in Mairie's mind.

"Be careful . . ."

Bryan . . . his name sang out in her mind and heart as she raced from the house and hurried to the creek. He couldn't have left, not yet. Surely he was here. He would have to stay and refresh himself from the desert. All she had to do was find him.

It was easier than she could have hoped. She saw him standing by a grove of cottonwood trees that bordered the creek beyond the house, and she broke into a run. He was doing something with his hands and he seemed to freeze as she called out . . .

"Bryan!"

He slowly turned away from a horse drinking at the creek, and Mairie stopped short.

It wasn't her brother.

They stared at each other for what seemed an eternity, until the man began walking toward her. She could see as he closed the distance between them the resemblance to her brother stopped at height and coloring. He didn't look like Bryan at all. His features were more defined, as if chiseled from granite. He looked . . . dangerous.

His walk was determined as he came closer and Mairie felt the racing of her heart that she knew had nothing to do with her run. Suddenly, she remembered Virginia's last words.

Be careful. . . .

"Mairie Callahan?"

Her brain refused to function properly. How could this stranger know her name?

She merely nodded. "Yes. Who are you?"

He stood in front of her and she leaned on a tree trunk to steady herself. He lifted his hands and continued to roll a cigarette. "I've been looking for you."

"Who are you?" she repeated, watching his tongue moisten the edge of the paper while he pulled something out of his jean's pocket.

He held up a lighter and flipped the top quickly, before holding the flame to his hand-rolled cigarette. "Specialist Fourth Class Robert Lee Harmon," he said, staring into her eyes as if waiting for a reaction.

"Navy Seals." He tossed the lighter to Mairie and her hand automatically caught it.

A part of her marveled at her reflexes, since her brain was desperately trying to put together the man's words with his intentions. This didn't make sense. None of it made sense. Slowly her eyes lowered to the lighter in her hand. It was chrome, with the Naval seal on it, surrounded by words verifying what he'd just said.

"You . . . you're with the Navy Seals?" She knew it sounded stupid, yet her mind was struggling with the fact that there were no Navy Seals in 1877. In fact, she was sure there weren't any lighters invented, either. "How did you get here . . . how did you find me?"

"I was sent in to retrieve you."

"Sent in . . . *retrieve* me? What do you mean?"

He backed against the trunk of the tree and Mairie instinctively moved away from it, wanting some distance between them.

"Look, I know you've been through a tough time. So just listen to me before you ask any more questions. The government sent me to find you and bring you back. You were caught up in an experiment that was being conducted over Area 51. A plane, a test craft, from Edwards Air Force Base was to be involved—"

"Wait," she interrupted, disregarding his directive to listen before asking questions. "You're from the future? From 1999? This . . . this all happened to me because of some experiment *the government* was conducting? The government did this to me? Where's my brother? What happened to him? Does Bryan know about this government experiment?" Anger was replacing fear.

Harmon took a long drag on the cigarette and watched the stream of gray smoke he exhaled. "No, needless to say, this is all highly confidential. Black

Card clearance only, yet there's no way I can get *you* back without explaining it. You'll be debriefed at Edwards when you return. The simplest way to put it is the test craft was flying at 50,000 feet, an area above and west of your skydiving plane at 13,000 feet. Something went wrong, and the testing area was expanded due to a computer error. Your brother notified the police and there were news reports of your mysterious disappearance, so I was chosen to come in and bring you back. Took me some time to find you."

"Back up," she directed, full strength in her voice. "My brother is all right?"

Harmon nodded, while taking another drag. "Your brother was interviewed, along with everyone involved in that dive, by government agents posing as local police. Your brother is alive and in 1999."

Relief swept through her. Thank God this didn't happen to Bryan. "How do I get back?" She asked the question that had haunted her all night.

He flicked his cigarette into the stream, and started walking toward her. Looking her directly in the eyes, he sternly said, "Listen to me carefully."

Grateful there was a way back, Mairie focused on Harmon's words as he told her they must be on the desert floor at a certain time and they must travel all the way back to the base of Mount Charleston, where she had landed. She kept nodding. She would do anything, *anything* to return to her brother. She listened as Harmon told her that they would be leaving in the morning to make the trip back into the desert.

"Now I need to question you," he added. "You must tell me everything that happened since you landed. Everything. I need to make sure you didn't do anything to change the course of history. Nothing, absolutely *nothing*, must be changed."

She sighed and thought back in her head. It

seemed so long ago. "Well, when I landed, I sat in the middle of the desert for what seemed like hours, waiting for someone from the diving school to find me. Then a man came." She thought about Jack and for some reason didn't mention his name. She felt guarded. "He took me to an Indian camp and I stayed there overnight. There was a celebration. I heard something so incredible as I listened to a prophecy. I . . . I have this herb that might help in finding a cure for cancer. The Indians told me about it."

Harmon turned his head sharply and stared at her.

"I know," she stated, already wanting to pacify him. "It sounds crazy, I'll admit, but you'd have to have been there. I have it with me and I can stick it in my jumpsuit when we return. It wouldn't take up much room, and—"

"You can't bring anything with you." His words were hard and final.

"Wait," she said, not about to back down. "You need to listen. My brother is dying from—"

"No, *you* wait," he interrupted. "Where is this man who found you? Did he ask questions about your equipment? What you were wearing? What did you tell him? Did you say you were from 1999?"

Something about his hardened expression made her extremely protective of Jack. If nothing must be changed in history, did that mean even someone knowing about her? Would Harmon eliminate Jack?

"Oh, I don't know where he is now," she said, as nonchalantly as possible, as if none of that mattered. "He thought I was crazy and couldn't wait to drop me off here at the ranch and be done with me. But let me tell you about my brother and what I found. He's dying from leukemia, and these people might have something that could help him. I am bringing it back. I didn't ask to be thrown into the past, but maybe it happened for this reason. I don't care what you say, I'm bringing it. I have to . . . it's my brother's life we're talking about."

She watched as Harmon appeared to metamorphose. He seemed less human and more mechanical as his face set into an even more rigid expression and he turned his head so slowly that she swore it was unnatural. She knew exactly what Virginia's instincts had warned her about. His heart was closed down.

"*You* will listen to *me*," he stated with authority. "I am in charge of this mission, and my orders were to bring you back, dead or alive . . . with nothing in history disturbed." He paused for a moment, a moment of emphasis. "Do you want to return alive?"

"Yes." It was merely a whisper, as fear entered her heart. This man's devotion to duty had robbed him of compassion.

"I'll strip-search you if I have to, to make sure you do not bring anything back with you. Even that dress you are wearing. I was briefed on your clothing when you took that dive, and if you don't have your own things, you'll go back naked. You can't hide anything if you're naked."

She sucked in her breath at the implication. In an instant she knew she would never reason with this man. He was like a government machine, drained of his free will. Somehow, she had to find a way to bring back the herb without him knowing it. But how, if he strip searched her? She couldn't think about it now. Right now she had to make him think that he was in charge of this mission.

Foolish man . . . he thought he had all the facts, everything he needed to be in control. How like a testosterone-based male to discount a woman. She too was on a mission.

A mission of love.

She felt the strength of all females who had re-

fused to be subjugated throughout history . . . even
that word Harmon had said she must not change . . .
history . . . *his* story . . . bothered her. What about *her*
story? What about all those women who risked
everything for love, a love that went beyond what
the poets could possibly define? Where was the story
that told of the role women had played in shaping
the world?

Was it only women who knew that pure love was
the one thing that could never be discounted? In the
end, it always prevailed. Always . . .

"Do you understand me, Miss Callahan?" He
asked the question in a voice that was supposed to
sound official.

Mairie knew what he was doing, and she suddenly realized that she wasn't as scared as she
thought she would be when faced with this fork in
the road. She was talking about life and death here.
She *knew*, every cell in her body knew, if she did not
surrender, this man was not about to let her live.

Virginia Gass had highly developed intuition,
Mairie thought . . . right before looking him in the
eye and saying, "I understand, Mr. Harmon."

He continued to hold her stare and Mairie had to
use all her strength to shield what was running
through her mind. She inhaled through her nose,
held her breath, and slowly let the air pass out
through her nostrils, allowing every ounce of tension
to slip away with it.

"I understand," she repeated.

Harmon tested her for a few seconds longer with
his expression and Mairie mentally sighed in relief
as the man finally said, "Good. Don't make this
hard."

"I only want to get home again."

He nodded. "Then sit on this boulder and I'll tell
you my plan. Tomorrow we have to be two kilometers south of Mount Charleston at thirteen hun-

dred hours, one P.M. There cannot be a second's delay. We'll arrive an hour early to make sure of that. When you rise in the morning at 0500 hours, five A.M., you will meet me out here. I'll spend the night on guard, observing the area. Try not to let anyone see you are leaving. You have the back bedroom, so slip out the window. Do not leave a thing. Sweep the furniture with that dress after you take it off. I'll be on the other side, waiting. I'll take care of anything you might leave on the windowsills. I'll have bought another horse from Gass to use as a pack animal. Won't be the greatest, but it's better than walking. We'll rendezvous at—"

"Wait," Mairie interrupted, much to Harmon's annoyance. "Why do I have to wipe my fingerprints off everything? These people don't know anything about identification through prints. Isn't that a little excessive?"

She knew she had hit a button that he didn't want her to push.

"Just do as you're told. Nothing about this mission is excessive. Everything is precision planned."

"Hmm . . . just as your little experiment was? The one that landed me back here?" She knew she had to challenge him a little, or he would become suspicious of her *surrender.* Pleased to see Harmon's earlier male tactic of disregarding a woman, Mairie tried not to smile.

He raised his chin only slightly in defense, but she caught the minute gesture of uncertainty. "That error was corrected. This mission will be completed successfully."

"Let's hope so," she murmured. "For both our sakes."

"This is *my* mission. I have it under control."

She merely nodded.

"Now, wipe anything you've touched in that room. I'll be waiting at the window and you can hand me your equipment. You do have it, don't you? I didn't find any trace of it."

Again, she simply nodded as she listened to his plans. Thirteen hundred hours. Not one second later. Two kilometers south of Mount Charleston . . . She was focused on his every word, the exhalation of his breath. The entire fiber of her being was alerted that her life depended on it.

She only knew for certain that she had to get to Jack.

Now he was her lifeline.

A half hour later, she returned to the house through the courtyard. She saw the ranch house in the southwest corner, opposite the stalls of horses. On the northeast wall was the Old Mormon Fort that Virginia had told her about at breakfast. How ironic that what had started with missionary zeal would one day be the site of a barn to store beans and raisins and house cows . . . and later to be replaced with bright neon lights and slot machines in post offices and bathrooms. She again focused her attention on the faint plan that was forming in her mind. Harmon couldn't see what took place in the courtyard, since a stone wall surrounded the entire perimeter. The only entrance was the heavy wooden gate. And that she knew was locked at night. She had seen Indian ranch hands do it from the porch last night while waiting for Jack.

Jack . . .

She had to find him.

Turning to the house, she walked a few feet and then, as if she had called him in her mind, he wandered out of the horse stalls leading his animal into the sunlight.

As the light hit his body, he seemed to lift his face to the sun and absorb it. She saw the streaks of blond though his darker brown hair. The way his body moved in a slow, graceful way, as though he were at one with his surroundings. Was it merely the sun that made him appear so . . . so *manly?* Or was it that she knew his heart was pure, that his intentions toward her were honorable? Both, she honestly admitted.

Jack Delaney was quite a man.

Exactly what she needed for this mission of love.

"Jack." She called out his name in a low voice. Knowing he was blinded by the sun, she added, "Over here."

He turned his head at the same time he sheltered his eyes to see better. "Mairie?"

Walking toward him, she smiled. "I must speak with you. It's urgent."

She closed the distance between them until he could see her. She saw him drop his arm and hurry his movements. "What's wrong?"

"Were you going somewhere?" she asked, glancing at his horse.

He shook his head while continuing to stare at her with intent. "Thought I'd take advantage of Gass's blacksmith shop. Now, tell me what's wrong."

"We need to speak privately. May I go along with you?"

He seemed to read her mind as he nodded, while leading the horse across the courtyard. "Are you all right?" he whispered to her as she fell in step beside him.

"Yes. For right now, I am. This is really serious, Jack, or I wouldn't need to have this conversation. Please believe that."

"Come on," he muttered, quickening their stride. "Now *I am* concerned."

"That makes two of us," she said, more to herself than to him.

He led the horse up to the leather line strung before a pit of burning embers. He tied the horse and then reached around to grab several pieces of wood.

Turning to her, he said, "Now, tell me. Everything."

She gulped, trying to bring moisture back into her mouth and began . . .

"Someone's come to take me back, Jack. He's here now."

Jack's body immediately tensed and he faintly noticed that there was disappointment along with concern in his reaction to her words. "Who? Where is he?"

He saw her inhale, as though gathering her strength. "His name is Robert Harmon. Specialist Fourth Class of the Navy Seals. And he's camping at the creek for the night. He expects to take me back to my own time tomorrow. I have all the details."

"Then you're leaving?" Why was he accepting everything she said? What was it about this woman, this incredible woman, that tore down the mortar of his defenses? Everything she had told him sounded crazy. Everything. Yet he had seen with his own eyes that she spoke truth, even if he didn't understand it yet.

"Yes. I must leave. But I want to do it tonight, or in the wee hours of the morning. I can't go with him, Jack. I have something I have to do first. I have to hide the herb the Paiutes gave me, somewhere I know will still exist a hundred and twenty-two years from now. I can't think of anything, except the mountain. I must find a place, a cave, somewhere it can be left until I can retrieve it in my own time."

He tried to follow her thoughts, yet they seemed beyond him. "You will hide it and then find it in 1999? How will it survive all those years?"

Mairie nodded. "I thought about that. I'm going to ask Virginia for one of her earthen jars, one with a stopper. She uses candles. I can seal it with the wax. You would be surprised what modern technology can do with just a speck of—"

"What?" he asked, seeing her expression change, like she was suddenly aware of something more important.

"I know," she breathed. "I mean, I don't know the real reason, but I know part of it, the reason I have to wipe away any trace I may have been here. It's about DNA. Wow . . . this *is* a precise plan."

"DNA?" She was speaking in riddles again. "Mairie, explain."

She shook her head. "I can't. Just something we carry with us. It's like an exact identification of who we are." Staring at her hand, she ran her thumb over her fingers. "It can also be found in the cells of dead skin. The tiniest speck. For some reason I'm supposed to remove as much of my DNA from this time as possible. I'll do it, since this science stuff is beyond me to grasp."

"Mairie, will you please tell me what you're rambling about?"

She looked up at him and her expression became serious again. "I'm sorry, I can't. We don't have time for me to explain, and I probably couldn't get you to understand anyway. Let me cut to the chase here, Jack. This is a matter of life and death. Mine. Possibly yours, and maybe even my brother's. I'm not allowed to bring anything back with me, even the herb. I won't leave it, if it might save my brother's life. I need your help to get to those mountains and then to the desert floor by 1300 hours. One o'clock in the afternoon. That's probably the exact time I jumped. I must be there. I know Harmon will be there for he told me the coordinates are set for two people."

Jack forgot about the fire, about reshoeing his horse. He ran his fingers through his hair and muttered, "For God's sake, Mairie . . . I can take the jar to the cave where we spent the night. You don't have to do this."

She looked at him. "I know you're in my life right

now for a reason. Who better to have at my side in this moment? And I'm learning that living in the moment is the only way I know to get through this. Jack, thank you for offering, but I would have to *know* that jar was placed in that cave. Harmon is going to be watching the ranch tonight. And he wants you, too. He asked me who knew about me. I am so sorry to have endangered your life in this mess. I didn't tell him your name or describe you, but if he finds out that you know about me, about what happened to me, I think he'd kill you without any hesitation. I can't take the chance he would stop you, or possibly kill you. It has nothing to do with you, Jack, or your ability to hide the plant. My decision is made because of him. He's a Navy Seal."

That was it. His patience ran out. "Like that. Explain that. What the hell is a navy seal? This is a human being we are speaking about, isn't it?"

She actually laughed, and he was surprised that she was capable of it at such a time. "Navy Seals are a specialized branch of the military of the future. They are highly trained for survival . . . at any cost. I don't know about all of them, but for some reason the government chose to send a man after me who's almost blind to anything beside his orders." Sighing, she added, "Yes. He looks human, but his heart is closed down, Jack. This isn't an ordinary man. He's . . . very dangerous."

Jack could only stare at her. "You want my help to get to the mountain and hide the plant?"

She returned his steady gaze. Her expression was completely serious. Once more he was reminded of her the night of the celebration. She had the heart of a princess, one whose courage was not questioned.

"Yes. I know it's a lot to ask, but yes, Jack. I want your help. I need you."

Something passed between them. Some unspoken agreement. He had felt it before, years ago . . . right before battle. You always knew the ones you could stand back to back and trust. Imagine . . . to find that in a woman. He was stunned.

"I will help you. But you forget, Mairie Callahan . . . this Navy Seal has yet to meet a man that thinks with the mind and heart of an Indian. Have no doubt about our safe passage. We will not be depending only on human abilities. Mother Earth and Father Sky shall assist us."

He saw her eyes open wide, her expression soften. She was so lovely in her courage. "Now tell me the rest of your plan. Perhaps I could add something to aid us in our journey." Why did he feel like something was rekindled within him? It had started when he saw her falling from the sky, and it had just expanded.

Could this fantastic woman actually be *his* gift?

He felt humbled by the thought. What had he ever done right in his life to deserve knowing her, a traveler from another time . . . from the future?

Suddenly, he felt his life had a purpose.

And in that moment, Mairie knew she wasn't just falling in love with this man.

She was free falling. It was like terminal velocity.

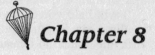

Chapter 8

The gleam in the eyes of Virginia Simpson Gass was unmistakable.

Mairie helped further that sign of acceptance, by adding, "And I know this man would stop at nothing to force me to go with him. He's been ordered to bring me back dead or alive, and I know it might be his act of last resort, but he would even go so far as killing me to fulfill his obligation. It's madness."

Nodding, Virginia rose from the kitchen table and began straightening bowls that were already in alignment on the shelf. "I understand, Mairie. I do. You may not know much about me, but what Jack and I were alluding to in our conversation last night at the table was that I come from another life, too. I didn't always live in the desert. You aren't the only one running from something. Unlike you, I didn't have anyone hired to bring me back to my family. This . . . this hired gun outside won't stop true love."

Virginia turned to Mairie and Jack, then smiled. "I didn't run away with my man. I ran to him. Not knowing he was here. Just had trust."

Mairie had a moment of regret for including Jack in her story about runaway lovers. It was the only thing she could think of that would elicit Virginia's sympathy and convey the urgency.

The woman again straightened the bowls absentmindedly as she said in a thoughtful voice, "Yes . . . I ran to my future. I left behind that unreasonable attitude society insists on placing upon us. Those rules and standards most of us willingly accept . . . as right. My family is wealthy back in Missouri. If I had stayed there, I would have what most of society thinks is a perfect life . . ."

Her words trailed off and she turned around, a slow, thoughtful smile appearing in her expression. "But you know something incredible . . . ? I've never been happier in my life than I am most of the time *right here!* I guess it took me leaving my family, my clan, for me to see I could be happy anywhere. That it was about me, not where I was or how much money or luxuries I had about me." She appeared embarrassed and went back to her seat. "I'm sorry for rambling. Now, how do we create some type of diversion so the two of you can safely leave?"

Mairie heard her words and all she could think about was Bryan. What he had said right before he had jumped from the plane. In a flash that scene played back in her mind . . .

"We're both crazy, you realize that . . ."

Laughing, Bryan nodded. "Yup . . . Crazy. But we're alive, right? We've left the rest of the tribe to their own devices and struck out on our own adventure. This is it, kid. Right here. Right now. Nothing matters but this moment." Still grinning like a ten-year-old kid on Christmas morning, he then closed his shield and said, "I love it! I love you. And, Mar, you can do this."

She remembered staring into his eyes and thinking he was right. They had left what most would consider proper societal behavior. Didn't she even think they were like two middle-aged hippies, leaving everything behind to experience life? Why, she was the exact opposite of Specialist Fourth Class Robert Lee Harmon. She was thinking with *her* mind, not mindlessly following the thoughts of another. She still had free will. And her will was telling her to get the hell out of Dodge as quickly as possible.

Now she knew her opponent.

Harmon was insane. He was unable to create for himself. He must be told what to do; therefore, he had no faith of his own.

He couldn't possibly trust himself.

The thoughts passed through her mind in a few seconds, and she finally let out her breath, as if to absorb this new insight into Harmon's character.

Trust . . .

She had no choice now but to trust herself. And Jack . . . she knew she could trust Jack.

She turned her attention to the man at her side and forced herself to focus on his words and not the almost tangible energy that she felt at the close contact. His thigh was tightly fitted against hers and his arm was around the back of the chair. His fingers lightly brushed the stands of her hair and a shiver ran through her body. Was this merely acting for Virginia's sake? She'd think about it later, not right now when their lives depended on clear thinking.

"I just wish there was a way to get him pissing drunk." He caught himself and added, "Excuse me, but that's the kind of diversion we need with this man, and from what Mairie has told me, he'd never accept alcohol."

"He wouldn't," Mairie whispered.

"Oh, Jack," Virginia said with a grin. "First of all, your language in the presence of ladies has always been appropriate. Right now it's appropriate to find a way to achieve a pissing drunk state."

Her grin widened and Mairie could see the glimmer in Virginia Gass's eyes deepen. "And I have the answer."

Both she and Jack were riveted as the woman explained she would bake a chicken, stuffed with raisins, made from the grapes harvested at the ranch and to make wine. The raisins she would use were soaked from the first extract of alcohol, which made them extremely potent. She couldn't use a large amount without its being detected, but enough to produce a relaxed, sleepy feeling.

They agreed that that would have to suffice and continued to refine their plan. Mairie realized Virginia was actually happy to be of assistance. Somehow, in some way . . . something was looking out for her and placing her in the right place at the right time with the right people. She had no idea what it was and was grateful, actually, that she didn't have time to question it. She'd just have to trust now that it would continue to be there. To guide her home.

Pretty scary, to be flying solo.

And then Mairie looked at Jack's profile and realized she wasn't flying solo . . . she was a copilot. Each respected the other. Trusted the other. No wonder her heart was opening to love again. She had found her equal.

Suddenly she had the irresistible urge to slap herself on the side of the head and laugh.

She resisted it.

But did she have to travel back in time a hundred and twenty-two years into the damn desert to find him? Talk about not controlling love . . . and making things hard.

The rest of the day was spent in preparation. Virginia never even questioned why Mairie wanted an earthen jar with a stopper. Using the candle in her room to thickly seal it, Mairie gave the jar to Jack to put in his saddlebag. Meanwhile, Jack had borrowed a horse from the ranch and was busy organizing his return trek into the desert with supplies.

A little while earlier when O.D. came in to wash for supper, he announced to his wife that the stranger camping out at the creek asked to buy a meal when he found out the ranch was also a way-station for travelers west. Virginia had calmly agreed to take it out, without once giving away that it played perfectly into their plan.

The baked chicken à la Virginia was finished, placed in a basket with fresh biscuits, corn on the cob, and a whole apple pie, with a few more potent raisins baked in for good measure, and a mason jar with homemade lemonade, all covered with a red gingham cloth. Virginia accepted her mission quite seriously, stood straight with both arms under the heavy basket handle, and walked outside to deliver it to Harmon. Virginia Gass was one remarkable woman.

Trying to ignore the debate by Fenton and his sisters over whether Digger should sleep in the house, Mairie paced in the kitchen while fighting the tension creeping into her body. If only Harmon would eat the meal without detecting the alcohol content. She had to trust their plan. It had to work. If only to stop the nagging worry as she waited for Virginia to return, Mairie reminded herself again that everything was falling into place without her frantically directing it.

Moments later, Mairie spun toward the back door and saw the triumphant look on Virginia's face as the woman entered her home.

"Well . . . ?" Mairie couldn't help but ask.

"He tasted it first before he paid me." She winked at Mairie. "Must have liked it. Look what he gave me."

She held out two shiny silver dollars.

Mairie came closer and picked up one. Holding it in the fading light from the kitchen window, she read the date, 1870.

"Can I see?" Fenton asked, pushing back his chair and standing before Mairie.

She handed the coin to the child and watched him examine it.

"I wish I could hang it up," he whispered, and Mairie knew he was visualizing it in his secret place.

"Even though they're seven years old, they look newly minted," Virginia announced, turning the other coin over in her hand.

Mairie mentally agreed it was newly minted. Only not seven years ago. Try over a hundred years into the future. The government would naturally supply him with authentic currency. She remembered seeing a thick leather pouch on the ground where the horse drank from the creek. What else might Harmon have with him?

Mairie looked at Virginia and said, "Now we wait . . . and see."

Virginia nodded with encouragement as Fenton relentlessly begged his mother for the shiny silver dollar. Mairie felt her stomach muscles tighten with tension. She hoped Harmon was starving and ate the entire contents of the basket. Every last morsel.

The family supper proved to be both strained and comical.

Fenton would not let the silver dollar issue rest.

"But Momma, if I do all the chores, even Lelah's . . . ?"

O.D. put his glass of water down sharply. "Fenton Gass, stop pestering your mother. The man gave it to her. She cooked him supper, not you. And she must have cooked him one hell of a supper, too." He looked at his wife like someone had taken away a special gift. "I would have liked chicken myself. Only time we have it is on a holiday. What is the occasion, my dear?"

It was almost funny to see Virginia recover her composure. Mairie watched as the woman appeared startled for just a moment before smiling prettily at her husband. "Oh, O.D., that chicken was so old and tough you would have loosened your teeth. Besides, you raised this beef. Are you saying you don't care for the way I prepared it?''

O.D. immediately shook his head. "It's delicious. Just seemed odd to me, is all."

Virginia continued to gaze at the tall bearded man seated across the long table. Her smile was filled with love. "You've always trusted my reasons, dear. We'll speak again on this subject and you will understand."

Again Mairie observed that silent communication between the husband and wife. Virginia was telling him she would explain everything later and he was content. She wondered if it took years to develop that level of understanding so that one is almost reading the other's mind. Mairie glanced at Jack from underneath her lashes and saw him staring at her. She couldn't stop the blush from creeping up her throat to her cheeks. Hiding the cringe, she could feel heat under her skin spreading like a neon light announcing . . . *I'm falling in love.* It was embarrassing.

Yet in the safety of this family, she allowed herself to indulge in a small fantasy. What would it be like to be loved by a man like Jack Delaney? Hormones she swore had been shut down by months and months of celibacy surged forth into every cell in her body, and she actually felt her legs tingle, her breasts ache, her belly yearn for his touch.

It was hormones. That's all, she told herself. Yet her heart was trying to get her attention. Secretly, in a place she couldn't afford to examine right then, she knew it was more than hormones, and suddenly she felt very sad that she would be leaving him tomorrow afternoon. What irony to find she was capable of love again *now*, here in someone else's lifetime. The wall around her heart, which she had built so well during and after her divorce, was dissolving.

And in that moment, Mairie knew it was going to be hell to walk away from him.

"Tell me again how the Paiutes are doing on Mount Charleston. They're still friendly, correct?" O.D. directed his conversation to Jack. "We've had some difficulty with a few local squaw men. Chief Tecopa tells me they're Mojaves, from Arizona, east of the Colorado River, and make skirmishes into Paiute territory over a longstanding dispute about the wild grapes."

Jack smiled at his host. "My brothers live in peace, Pe-no-kab. As a matter of fact, they are more determined than ever to continue that way of life."

He glanced at Mairie and she somehow knew he was referring to what they both had witnessed the night of the celebration. The message of peace from Wovoka. Was that it? Was this the silent communication she had wondered how long it takes to develop with a man? Wow . . .

Virginia grinned at Mairie. "Pe-no-kab is the name the Indians call O.D. It means 'long back,' given for my husband's broad shoulders."

Nodding, Mairie saw the stature of O.D. Gass and knew it took broad shoulders, and a strong heart, to have survived the tests of the desert. She glanced back at Virginia and returned the smile. O.D. Gass got the balance of heart from his wife.

The moon was still full as its light came through the bedroom window. Mairie used the cotton dress to wipe every piece of furniture in the room. Once more wearing her leggings and cropped top under the jumpsuit, she realized her clothes felt strange and restricting as she methodically accomplished her task. In a little more than twelve hours she would be back in her own time, with her brother. Why wasn't she ecstatic? She should be. It was all she had wanted since she was lost . . . to be able to get home.

Jack. Jack Fitzhue Delaney had changed all that.

How was she ever going to leave him? Never see him again? *Ever* . . .

She couldn't think about it now. Taking one last look around the room, Mairie thought back to her last conversation with Jack and later Virginia. How she would miss them both . . .

She patted the weight in her zippered side pocket. She hadn't expected to ask Jack for another favor, since he had already done so much for her. On top of that, he was risking his life, yet she needed the money. He said he would take care of everything, and he did, she thought, as she blew out the candle on the nightstand.

Earlier, she'd given Jack the rest of her equipment; now all she had to do was meet him.

Slipping out her door, Mairie hesitated only a moment while her eyes adjusted to the dark hallway. She paused at another door and quietly opened it. She could see Fenton asleep in his bed with Digger at his feet.

"Shh . . ." she whispered to the dog who raised his head and started wagging his tail in recognition. "I've got something for our friend here."

Tiptoeing into the room, she unzipped her pocket and took out the shiny silver dollar Jack had bought from Virginia at her request earlier that night. She bent down and stuck it under his pillow, then softly placed a kiss on the boy's temple.

"Good-bye, my friend. When you hang this in your secret place, think of me."

He sighed in his sleep and Mairie smiled as the moonlight showed his peaceful face. So like Bryan. What a lesson this child had taught her.

Life really could be magical again.

Patting Digger's head, she turned to quietly leave the room.

"Mairie . . ."

She jumped at the sound of her name and the candlelight illuminating the hall as she closed Fenton's bedroom door. Virginia stood in another doorway, wearing a nightgown and a crocheted shawl. Her long black hair was braided down her back.

"I know we said good-bye earlier," she whispered, as she closed the door of her bedroom behind her. "I just wanted to wish you good luck again." She placed the candlestick holder on a narrow hall table. "I have to wake O.D. when you two leave, to prepare him for whatever ruckus Harmon might make when he finds you're gone." Virginia looked at Mairie's clothes for the first time and added, "Interesting attire, my dear. From a distance, one would never mistake you for a woman."

Mairie touched the thin ribbon holding her hair in a ponytail. "Thank you for the loan of your dress," she said, handing it back. "I'm sorry it's soiled. I was just going to leave it in the kitchen for Lee to wash. The ribbon will be a keepsake to remember your hospitality by." *Regardless of what Harmon said, a simple ribbon would be harmless to take with me,* she thought.

Virginia held out her hands and accepted the dress. "I'll take care of it. I just want you to know that my prayers will go with you tonight. Though for some reason, my intuition is telling me it will all work out as it should ... whatever that is." She smiled sadly. "I shall miss you and all the excitement you brought into my life. Be happy, Mairie Callahan. That's a choice only you can make."

Mairie thought she might cry, as she hugged the woman tightly. "Thank you so much, Virginia. I don't know what would have happened to me without you. You saved my life."

Virginia returned the embrace for a few moments. Pulling back, she said, "When I got the dinner plate from Harmon earlier, I could see the effect of the wine working. He was fighting to stay alert. He should be asleep by now. Jack's waiting in the court-yard with the horses, right?"

Mairie nodded. "Right. I should leave. I didn't know it would be this hard. All of you have become so important to me."

Virginia chuckled. "Jack gave you the silver dollar and you gave it to Fenton just now, didn't you?"

With a muffled laugh, Mairie again nodded. "He'll know what to do with it."

"Hang it in that thicket of mesquite trees, he will. Sometimes I wonder if that child will ever grow up. He spends so much time in that place."

She looked at Virginia Gass and said sincerely, "Don't let him grow up completely. Fenton knows something many of us have forgotten. Life can still be magical."

"Go create some magic then, Mairie. Go safely into your life."

Mairie squeezed her hand and kissed the woman's cheek then turned to the kitchen door. Beyond it waited Jack . . . and her future, whatever it might contain. All she could do now was trust . . . *in love, and the magic of life.*

Fenton had taught her that.

Jack was waiting for her in the shadows of the stable across the courtyard. Her heart began beating faster as she walked up to him and the horses. Now it began . . . the most difficult part of the plan. Some-how, they must leave the ranch without alerting Harmon.

"Virginia said the wine was taking effect when last she checked. We should be all right," she said, with as much confidence as she could muster.

Jack nodded and handed her the reins to her horse. "We'll walk them for about a hundred yards into the sand. That will muffle the noise of the hooves. Then we'll mount and slowly leave. No point in disturbing the man's sleep, now, is there?"

She looked into his smiling face and returned the sly expression. "No point at all. Listen, before we start, I want to tell you how much I appreciate everything you've done for me and to say again how very sorry I am that your involvement with me has endangered your life. I realize all that you've done to help me since that day when you found me, and—"

He quickly held his finger up to her lips to silence her. "Hush now, Mairie. Everything I did was also for me. You were my gift, remember? I came off that mountain to find you. I brought you to my brother's camp and you returned a gift to them." He looked up to the stars and shrugged. "This . . . this is just a moonlit ride back to where it all began. Stop worrying. Just be quiet now and follow my lead."

"Yes, sir. You're in charge." She gladly assumed the copilot's mental attitude. He was leading this part of the journey. It was his land, his time, and she was the inexperienced one.

"All right, let's go. Slowly . . . remember, until we mount, everything we do must be done slowly and as the coyote stalks his prey. Be alert. Listen. Hear the warm desert breeze moving through the brush and trees. You must be at one with the Mother and Father. You can do it, Mar."

She was stunned when she heard his last words. First Fenton, and now Jack. Both had repeated Bryan's words to her. She didn't need any more proof that she was on the right path.

Now all she had to do was walk it.

Slowly. Very, very slowly.

She could have done without the mention of coyotes, though.

Following him across the courtyard to the huge gate, Mairie realized she was holding her breath and told herself to exhale. Trust. She had to trust that

Virginia's supper had done its job. Seeing that Jack had already removed the heavy wooden crossbar from the gate, she closed her eyes as he reached out and cautiously opened it.

She quickly opened her eyes when her horse jerked to follow the movement of Jack's horse. She moved quietly forward. As she led her horse through the gate, she expected at any moment to hear Harmon's voice, demanding to know what she was doing. Then something inside her instructed she stop thinking of Harmon. Listen to the wind . . . she reminded herself . . . even the coyotes were preferable to that man. Right now she must walk as an Indian, and be attuned to everything.

Jack turned left, away from the camping man, and Mairie deliberately averted her eyes from that direction. She hoped Harmon was deep in dreamland and wouldn't wake until dawn. It would give them the time they needed to get to the cave and back down to the base of the mountain. She didn't want to picture Harmon's furious face at noon when she was waiting for him at the spot where she had landed days ago. Hoping that he would just be relieved to see her, Mairie figured she would deal with it when it happened. Right now she needed to concentrate, to focus, to follow Jack's every movement. To become one.

In silence they led the horses down to the creek and Jack's movement slowed even more. When they passed through the water, Mairie was surprised not to hear any more noise than the soothing rush of the stream itself. The man knew what he was doing, and her respect for him grew.

After they crossed the creek, the night air was cool through her damp jumpsuit. She was glad she had on her Nikes, although she knew the prints would be easy for Harmon to track in the morning light. Hopefully, by that time she would have completed her task and would be coming down off the mountain to meet with him anyway.

Jack pointed southwest of the ranch and Mairie nodded as she caught up to him.

In unison, silently, they continued under the starry night.

Virginia Gass glanced at her sleeping husband as she stood at the window. She knew about love, about what one would do in the name of love . . . what sacrifices one would make to follow its path. But she knew it was worth it. In the end, it was always worth it.

She turned her attention back to the window and saw Mairie and Jack, two lovers, walking under the full yellow moon of the desert. Now there was a perfect match. She grinned, thinking that Mairie Callahan was one blessed woman to have caught the heart of Jack Delaney. She adored O.D. and wouldn't change a thing about him, except for trimming that beard of his a few more inches . . . but she wasn't immune to Jack. What a powerful combination of handsome features, courtly charm, and primal instincts. Living with the Paiutes had added something invaluable to the man's character. It would take quite a woman to be his equal.

Virginia looked at the slim form in the distance and felt Mairie was a good partner for him. She was courageous. Lovely, intelligent, cultured, and her heart was good. And it was plain as day to see that she loved the man. Jack, on the other hand, was more reserved in showing his emotions.

Must be the Indian influence.

Watching the couple until they disappeared from view, she wished them well on their journey to freedom. Freedom . . . she knew about that. It was that which made her leave everything familiar and strike out west all those years ago with her sister and her brother-in-law. Who would have thought it would lead to this ranch in the middle of a desert? Raising children. Teaching Indians to sew. Shooting chicken hawks from her own back door.

Stifling a laugh, Virginia turned from the window and walked to the bed. Affectionately looking down at her husband, she fortified herself for his reaction to her latest adventure. Thank God, he loved her completely.

She hoped he would understand that love cannot be controlled.

It can only be experienced.

"Wake, my love," she whispered, as she caressed the side of his face with the back of her fingers. "I know it's late, but I have a story to tell you . . ."

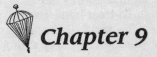

Chapter 9

*Was it because they hadn't really spoken in al-*most an hour and her focus was so intense? The light from the full moon and stars gave the sleeping earth an otherworldly quality. Shadows and light. Dark hidden places and an almost eerie iridescence that seemed to lead their way. Mairie had never felt more alive.

Every sense in her body was attuned to the earth and the current lunar movements. The way the cool desert wind felt on her skin, the sound of the horses' hooves beating and grinding into the granules of dirt, sand, and rocks. Her taste buds were experiencing the distinct flavor of the night that is so different from day. If she stayed in this moment, without thinking of Harmon, or how she was going to find her way back home, if she released her past . . . she was safe. Not just safe . . . she was alive; here was where her life was unfolding.

Mairie figured right then and there it didn't pay to worry about Harmon, or what he might do. How could she predict the actions of someone so insane? Presently, all she could do was stay focused, alert to everything and anything. Part of her realized this was the Indian way, to respect everything . . . the earth, the sky, the animals, the wind. It assisted them in making decisions, choices.

In that graceful moment, Mairie Callahan knew she had taken this incredible journey into the past to find all this out.

To trust herself again.

To know that she was making the best decision she could. To keep riding into the unknown. To have the courage of her convictions. It had to be the right direction for her . . . no matter how it turned out . . . no matter how pissed Harmon might be.

Jack looked at her and smiled his encouragement. They were partners in this now, and she realized she had never felt this before with another. Not even her husband. It was what she had always been striving for, that equal trust. To have found it now, a hundred and twenty-two years into the past, made her want to throw back her head and laugh.

Yet she knew she had to be silent.

Even that was funny to her, that she couldn't laugh . . . when her whole heart wanted to yell out in freedom. On this night of primal awakenings within her body, it was like her mind really *was* letting go of her past. She and her ex-husband were never partners, only working toward that. How could she still be angry at her ex-husband . . . for recognizing it before she did? How funny was that? What an experience to realize that every single relationship she had ever had was preparing her to meet Jack Delaney.

She could only grin back at him with gratitude.

Even if Harmon went berserk on her, she wouldn't have missed this moment, riding in the wind, feeling the earth alive around her and sharing it all with Jack Fitzhue Delaney. No matter what . . .

They continued for another few miles, before Jack pointed to a grove of trees, and in the moonlight Mairie recognized it as the springs where they had stopped on their trek out of the desert. Nodding, she pulled back slightly on the left rein and kept her horse in synch with Jack's. She would have loved to have taken credit for staying in the saddle, but she knew her mount was merely following Jack's.

She *and* her horse obviously knew how to recognize skill.

It wasn't until she slowed down that the memory of what took place here flooded her mind. The kiss. And it wasn't even a real kiss, just a grazing of lips as he held her face, yet it shook the very center of her.

Great, she thought, as she saw Jack pull all the way back on his reins . . . how would an Indian handle this surge of hormones? As incredible and healing as this night seemed, she knew she hadn't learned anything helpful there. On this one she was flying by the seat of her pants.

He dismounted and immediately came to her assistance. Even though her ankle was almost healed now, Mairie knew he would have done it anyway. It was just him. She accepted his help and he caught her waist as she lowered herself to the ground. His touch was very respectful, yet also assuring. Her senses, already energized by the moonlit ride, almost went into overload by his touch.

"Thanks." She gathered all the nonchalance she could and turned around. The muscles in her thighs ached, as though announcing it was some time since they'd had such a workout. Better to concentrate on her aching muscles than on the man.

"I thought we could give the horses a breather and let them drink. They'll need it if we're going to run them hard to the base of the mountain." He was leading his toward the pool of water as he spoke.

"The horses aren't the only ones who need a break." Mairie chuckled, rubbing the back of her thighs.

He glanced at her and smiled. "Are you all right?"

Caressing her horse's nose she admitted sheepishly, "It's just been a while since I rode, Jack. And, quite honestly, I wasn't that good then." Mairie looked directly at him. "I'm sorry if I'm holding you back, but I'm going through with this . . . you're stuck with me."

He dropped the reins as his horse began drinking and stared at her in the moonlight. "Oh, no, Mairie," he said in a thick voice. "I'm not stuck with you. You're my gift, remember?"

Minutes from now she would only recall each of them silently walking toward the other, as if directed by some mutual communication, and falling into each other's arms. This time the kiss was not a mere grazing. This time the meeting of lips was a primitive mating, a graceful dance of movement and emotion. She tasted him, inhaled him, felt him. Hearing his deep moan, she opened her eyes . . . and saw him staring into her own with a look of wonderment.

Time, as she had always known it, ceased to exist as she was held in a state of appreciation she had never before felt. This was love. Dear God . . . this was love. This is what it really feels like, her mind was singing to her. She felt like she had finally come home.

And she must leave this bliss to return to her home in 1999?

How exquisitely ironic.

Don't think, her mind whispered. Don't think of anything but this moment. Bryan's words came back to her. This is it. Right here. Right now. This is being alive. Live it . . .

"Oh, Jack," she breathed, and gave herself fully over to the embrace.

She surrendered.

"Mairie . . ." His hot breath mixed with her name against her neck as he began nibbling. She felt weak, as though floating, and Jack held her tightly against

him "How long I have wanted you," he murmured.
Mairie's heart expanded even more.

She had no idea how long she remained in his
arms, how long she held him to her and looked beyond his shoulder to the moon. She closed her eyes
and was filled with gratitude for this perfect moment. It wasn't until they heard a distant coyote yip
that Jack whispered above her ear.

"We should get moving . . ."

She simply nodded. Words, explanations, weren't
necessary. The feeling of partnership between them
had been strengthened.

Thinking in unison now . . . there would have to
be time later to talk about it.

They could only trust that time would come.

They continued west and Mairie fell into the
rhythmic heaving breath that came through the
horse's nostrils at galloping speed. She moved as
one with the animal, breathing when he did, as
shadows raced past their vision. She spent hours recalling the taste of Jack's lips, the texture of his skin,
the strength of his embrace. It had felt too right to
wonder if it could possibly have been wrong. To
have reacted any other way in that moment
wouldn't have been true. She was leaving this man
today and she wanted to experience as much as he
was willing to share with her. Every minute, every
moment, felt precious.

And she had only a few more hours to treasure as
they rode into the night.

Once they had trekked a bit up the base of the
mountain, Jack directed the horses to a pinyon tree
and they finally dismounted. Taking the reins of
both horses, Jack removed a canteen and handed it
to her. Neither said a word, as he walked the horses
to cool them down.

Mairie drank from the canteen and walked over
to Jack. Extending her arm, she offered the canteen

to him. He brought it to his lips and threw back his head as he gulped the life-saving liquid. Wiping his mouth on the sleeve of his shirt, he muttered, "Thanks. That was a hell of a ride. Well done, Mairie."

Her heart expanded with a sense of accomplishment. She *had* done well. "How are you going to water the horses?" she asked, knowing that their lives depended on these animals.

He grinned and handed back the canteen. Removing his weathered black leather cowboy hat, he held it upside down to her. "Pour."

She did as she was asked and watched as Jack held the hat out to his horse, and then hers. He did it once for each horse, and then tied them to a branch of the pinyon tree. It was the last phase of darkness before dawn began to overtake the night and Mairie suddenly realized she was starving.

She remembered Virginia's delicious biscuits and the sandwiches that had been prepared for this journey. "I'm so hungry I could eat a horse!" She paused, and then joked, "But we need them . . ."

"Sure." He chuckled. "We worked up quite an appetite." He opened one of the leather pockets of his saddlebag and withdrew the food wrapped in a thin cloth. "Here," he offered, handing it to Mairie. "Take it over by that boulder and rest. I'll join you in a moment."

Walking in the direction Jack pointed out, she thought that was the perfect time to hide behind the boulder and relieve herself before they continued. She figured Jack was probably doing the same somewhere. Strangely, since she had accepted this "partnership," she no longer was embarrassed by human needs . . . and the nearest rest stop was one hundred and twenty-two years away. As she returned to the front of the boulder, she saw Jack sitting and opening one of the cloth-covered sandwiches.

Handing it to her, he said, "You're an amazing woman, Mairie Callahan. Yesterday you were barely recovered from sunstroke while nursing a bruised ankle, and here you are today on this adventure. Most women, even men, under these conditions couldn't laugh at themselves, yet you have taken it all in stride. The white man calls that poise. The Indian calls it balance."

"Thank you." She couldn't believe she actually felt shy receiving the compliment.

"Well, it's true," he said, hesitating before taking a bite. "Your dedication is admirable . . . *Woman is stronger by virtue of her feelings than man by virtue of his power . . .*" He paused. "Balzac, Honoré de Balzac." He looked to the east and began his meal.

She bit into her sandwich thoughtfully. *She* had never read Balzac. Thinking back to the bantering between Jack and Virginia at dinner, Mairie marveled that this man who had grown up with Indians could slip into cultured formality with such ease.

"Jack . . . ? May I ask a question?"

"Certainly." He responded without hesitation, taking another bite of his biscuit.

She paused a second to formulate it in her mind so it wouldn't sound intrusive. "You said you were adopted into the Paiutes after your parents died, and I was wondering . . . I mean, I can't help but wonder where you received your education. You continue to amaze me by the way you can transform from the mind set of an Indian, to the rugged cowboy, then to the courtly gentleman. I know you were back east. Did you go to school there?"

He took another bite and looked out to the fading darkness. Swallowing, he said in a somber tone, "It took some time, but eventually I adjusted to Indian life. I became so happy with the Paiutes, learning hunting skills, discovering the wonders of the earth, listening to the creative spirit that runs through all

life, that my world felt alive with potential, like anything was possible. Imagining a jackrabbit coming
into my path and a half hour later seeing it running
in the distance. Things like that. Life seemed magical."

Mairie smiled. "Like Fenton. That's why I adored
him. He still knows that."

Jack nodded. "The magic is closest to children.
They're still innocent. I remember being like that,
balanced for four years while I lived with my brothers. Then the Mormons found out about me and took
me away. They sent me to school in Utah. I stayed
there for less than a year and ran away. Back to the
Paiutes . . . only I didn't make it. I ran away from the
Mormons only to be caught up in the Christian zeal
of their missionaries."

His smile was sad as a memory filtered through
his mind. "After I tried running away from them
and was caught, I confided in a padre who I thought
wanted to befriend me. I told him about my brothers. About my home. How I felt so out of place con-
fined in a school room, learning about life, instead
of living it. That's when I was sent East, to Washington, to attend a missionary school for indigent
children . . . for my own good."

Mairie's heart went out to the young boy in him.
She could imagine him feeling imprisoned and
yearning for freedom, his choices taken away.

"I'm sure they thought it was all for my own
good," he said, as if reading her mind, before he
resumed eating.

Mairie had finished her food and took another
drink from the canteen to wash it down. "Is that
where you were taught how to act like a gentleman?"

He grinned at her. "Act? You think I am acting?"

Blushing, she replied, "No, not at all. I'm still
wondering how you went from a school for poor

children to being able to conduct yourself in a ... a ballroom. At least, that's how Virginia portrayed you."

"I was the *project* of a wealthy family that wanted to prove anyone could learn proper behavior. It was their version of charity, I suppose. I was tutored for two years with their children. Ate at their table on Sundays. What torture that was ... every single movement, every sigh, every swallow of food, monitored. Any infraction was met with a severe penalty. I guess they thought that was the only way someone raised with Indians could learn."

He reached for the canteen. "I ran away from it all when I was sixteen, but something was born inside me ... a thirst for knowledge. To read. I was in Washington and the public library became my home for two more years. I worked at night on the docks and spent the day in the stacks. That's when I first read Socrates ... *There is only one good, knowledge, and one evil, ignorance.* What brilliance. Didn't take me long to realize that wealthy family was more ignorant than my Paiute brothers. I learned not to judge a book by its cover. Be it literature or the cover a person wears to hide behind."

She sat back and stretched her legs out before her. "Wow ... now it's my turn. You are one amazing man, Jack Delaney." How could she have ever thought he was feral and deranged? What a comedy of errors they had played out between them. "You remained in Washington, then?"

He seemed uncomfortable with her compliment and focused on answering her last question. "It wasn't surprising that when the war started, I would be one of the first to enlist. What foolishness, to think there was bravado in death. Anyone's death. There is nothing brave in dying. I think during battle, it's living that takes all your courage."

He was seated next to her and stretched his legs

alongside hers. She noticed how much longer they were, how his cowboy boots looked like they should be replaced. What an extraordinary man. To quote Balzac and Socrates, here in the middle of the desert. Perhaps because of his sad childhood, he had spent more time in introspection than most others . . . yet it had served him. She felt the love she had vowed never again to feel expand within her heart. She wanted to take him in her arms, to hug him as he should have been hugged since he was born. To applaud him his accomplishments and to be his cheerleader wherever he went.

A sharp ache reminded her she was leaving him within hours. Best not to think of a future when a hundred and twenty-two years separated them. Trying not to allow the sadness to overwhelm her, she asked, "So then you were wounded in the war? At Gettysburg, right?" Better to change the course of her mental wanderings.

He sighed and ran his fingers through his long dark hair. She turned her head and looked at his profile. That same anguished expression, as when she first met him and vehemently denied she was his gift, came over his face.

"I took a saber thrust at Gettysburg. It was . . . the whole two days were insanity. Carnage. I lost all my illusions on that so-called field of honor . . . all my beliefs. I walked away from an infantry hospital, away from the war and the society that created it, to find my soul again."

He gazed at her and smiled slowly. "I know how it is to feel out of place, Mairie. I never felt so alone as during that time. I was surrounded by people who seemed crazed by a blood thirst I never felt. Took me almost five years to make it back here." He looked out to the desert and set his jaw. "This is my home now. I shall remain here."

There it was . . . Jack Delaney lived and breathed

this desert of 1877, and she had to return to her brother and her life. This was his home. Hers awaited at one o'clock this afternoon. She again wanted to take him to her breasts and feel his body next to hers, to actually tell him that she was falling in love with him and didn't know how to leave him.

Hell. She was no longer *falling*. She *loved* him. What was most remarkable to her was that this incredible man thought she might be his gift. His answer. The more she knew of the man, the more her heart opened. And now she was in love ... with a man who could never return it, who she would never again see in her lifetime.

She felt so drawn to him that she was actually now fighting the irresistible urge to run her fingers over his lips, to taste them again, to memorize every detail of his face, to give in finally to what had been torturing her for days. Complete mutual surrender.

He must have sensed her need, for he turned his head and stared at her mouth, her eyes. Slowly, Mairie leaned forward and reached out her hand. Her fingers lightly traced his bottom lip ever so gently. She didn't care any longer. If they could unite right here, right now, under the fading stars and moon ... if they could physically become one, for just this night ...

She began to offer herself to him, when her attention was distracted by a tiny, wavering red light on Jack's chest. Puzzled, she stared at it for an instant before something, some shock of memory, screamed at her to remember and she instinctively shoved Jack on his back.

"*Get down!*" she yelled, just as she heard the bullet ricochet on the boulder, right where Jack had been leaning only a second before.

"Mairie! What the hell was that? It sounded like a bullet hitting the rock." He scrambled to his feet, pulling her with him, and crouched down behind the large boulder.

"It's Harmon," she whispered, fighting the most fear she had ever experienced. "Dear God, he may have traveled into the past to get me, but he came with twenty-first-century weapons. It's a laser rifle with night vision, or something equally powerful. I've seen this stuff in the movies. We can't escape this, Jack . . . not here."

"A gun? Why didn't we hear the sound of powder when it fired?" He was confused, but even more, he was angry. "Damn it. I can't get to my rifle. The horses are too far. We need to get within the cover of the mountain. Sun's coming up . . . we stayed too long."

"Oh, Jack . . ." Sorrow crept into her throat. "It is getting lighter. He'll see us no matter where we move." It couldn't end like this. It simply couldn't. Not here and not now. She prayed for some help, from somewhere.

It seemed futile.

"He can't shoot and chase us at the same time, Mar, he must stop to aim . . . we need a diversion . . . hand me that stick from over there." She whipped around, instantly doing what he directed. She must now place her life in his hands. He had the expertise of war and survival methods she didn't. She handed him the stick as he placed his hat on one end.

This is the survival of war technique he had in mind? What was he thinking? There was no time to explain, nor would Jack understand that Harmon had advanced weaponry to see in the dark and at close range. A scope on his rifle. Night vision binoculars. Who knows what else? Harmon had the advantage. He had the future on his side.

They had the hat-on-a-stick trick.

Talk about trust. She had no other alternative but to listen to his plan.

He continued, "Mairie, I must ask you to stay here, at best out of harm's way, behind this boulder and hold my hat above it with the stick. I'll break for our horses and head for that ravine. If he fires at my hat, then sees me with the horses, you'll have only a few seconds to get to the ravine while he aims again at me. Understand?"

"Got it . . . I think." *This shit only happens in the movies*, she cursed under her breath.

"Oh, and try not to forget my hat . . . ready? *Now!*" He darted around the boulder as she raised his hat into view, waving it like a flag. His hat spun around and off the stick a few feet away from her. Harmon had fired again. Scrambling for his hat, she grabbed it and ran toward Jack with the horses in the ravine.

It worked. Not even a second shot fired. She couldn't believe it as she mounted her horse. There was a great deal to be said about simplicity, she marveled, as they began their ascent in the shadow and protection of the ravine.

"We've only got a little lead now, Mairie. This path is hard and steep. Lean forward often and your horse will instinctively follow mine. We should be at the cave in less than two hours."

The horses gingerly stepped over crevices, rocks, and brush, zigzagging their way up the narrow trail. Breaking the lull of their slow climb, she added, "We may have more of a lead than you think, Jack. He could be miles away . . . which still isn't to our advantage with his weapons, but he's got to come up this mountain the same way and—"

"That's impossible." He interrupted. "No gun could shoot from that far away . . . but you're right, unless he's got an *air-plane* as you have suggested, there's no other way up this mountain."

"I can't explain now. Just trust me. I understand Harmon and now you're dealing with *my* century . . ." Her voice fell off as the horses lumbered on. Explaining anything right now would be useless. Her life was at stake. Maybe Jack's. Harmon was, obviously, insane in his mission and wanted her, perhaps both of them, eliminated now.

At least an hour had passed without further incident from Harmon. Where could that madman be? she wondered anxiously. Jack must have been thinking the same thing.

"Do you suppose Harmon is still a few miles behind us?"

"I can't tell. I've been looking back as often as I can, but there are too many shadows on the mountain to distinguish anything." She twisted back around. "Hopefully he's having the same problem."

Suddenly, a whirling sound preceded the huge fire ball explosion that hit the trail just yards above them. Rock, sand, and debris flew everywhere, embedding in their flesh. The horses, which immediately panicked and reared, were hit with shrapnel, too. Stunned, Mairie watched Jack restraining his steed with all his strength. Her horse turned sharply and began galloping off around the side of the mountain as she struggled to stay balanced.

Holding the mane as tightly as she could, she pulled back on the animal, while they rose up one side of a ravine, and down another and another. "Whoa!" She pleaded. "Stop! Stop! Stop!" She couldn't turn to look for Jack or to see if Harmon was behind her. She was hanging on for dear life as the poor terrorized animal instinctively ran for survival.

A sharp whistle broke Mairie's horse from its run. It began to slow to a canter, then walk, snorting rapidly through its nostrils. Mairie remembered the last time she experienced this exact situation and was relieved to find *this* horse had the good sense to slow down rather than stop dead.

"Mairie, pull back on the reins now!" Jack shouted from a short distance behind her.

He came alongside her and grabbed the bridle. "Whoa . . ." He said deeply. The horses and riders came to a halt, all heaving.

"Are you all right, Mar?" He swallowed.

"I don't know yet. I think so. Except for a few cuts and bruises, I'll live." She exhaled with a forced smile. "And thanks."

"The horses have been injured. Yours has a deep cut in its right haunch. I'll need to treat it, and us, too, as soon as possible." He scanned the horizon to assure their safety. "Fortunately, your horse darted off in a good direction to reach the cave where we spent your first night here."

He couldn't help himself now. He was caught up in the drama, the moment, and this woman, Mairie Callahan. Her life, her love, her gift to him. His mind went back to their first night together. Had he known then all he knew now . . . how differently everything would have played out.

He shook the thoughts from his head and turned back to Mairie. "What in the hell was that blast back there, anyway? Is he so close he could throw a stick of dynamite, or has he got a cannon? How would he get a cannon all the way out here?" He stared at her in disbelief waiting for some explanation if she could offer it.

"Well, I don't know, maybe a rocket or a grenade . . . a cannon, of sorts . . . Jack, it's just one more thing I can't explain in a lot of detail. But it *was* intended to kill us. *Both* of us. This man will stop at nothing now. I know it. He sees me as a threat to the history of the future and you're my accomplice. We'll never get off this mountain alive." Her voice sounded defeated.

"Listen, Mar. I know this terrain better than any white man . . . in *my time.* I'll get us off this mountain

safely and back where you need to be." Looking at
the blood trickling from Mairie's horse, he muttered.
"Damn, more time we don't have ... we've got to
hurry if we're going to be able to hide the jar and
get off this mountain ... past Harmon. Let's get to
the cave and figure our damages."

He picked up the reins and slowly began to lead
her horse closely behind his as she had never released her clutch of the mane.

After what seemed like hours, for the trauma
they'd endured, they reached the cliff and cave.
Mairie held the bridle of her horse, steadying its
head, as Jack used his knife to dig the shrapnel from
its leg. "You have to listen to me, Jack," she said,
struggling to keep the horse from pulling away. "Oh
... I am so sorry," she whispered to the animal, not
wanting to look into its eyes to see the pain and
fright. "Jack, Harmon could be a mile or more away
and still know where we are and how to stop us.
You have been ... terrific ... in this time. The hat on
a stick worked, and your timing has been perfect,
but you can't compete against twenty-first-century
weapons. For over a century, billions of dollars have
gone into the art of killing people, and Harmon is
carrying the results. He's got the advantage and he's
not going to let either one of us live now."

"Have faith, Mairie ... balance," he whispered,
concentrating, as he gently removed the piece of
metal from the horse's leg and held it in his bloodied
fingers. Flicking it behind him, he inhaled and sighed.
"I didn't come all this way to admit defeat now." He
poked his knife around in the small fire he had lit earlier and withdrew it when the tip glowed.

Mairie winced and looked away as he cauterized
the wound. She held tighter as the horse threw its
head and jolted back in pain.

"Whoa, big fellow," he said lowly, and wiped the

knife on the side of his pants. He stroked the animal to calm it and looked to the sun. "Nearly midday. I'll bury the herb inside the cave and then we must descend. We're going to be cutting it close as it is."

She knew time was of the essence now; tending the wounds had been an unexpected delay. "Do you think we can make it . . . really? It isn't just getting off the mountain now to the desert floor. It's getting off without being killed by Harmon."

He looked down the path they had traveled earlier. She watched him studying the terrain and then he wiped his forehead with his shirt sleeve and muttered, "If we have to get to that exact spot, then so does he. He should be heading there, instead of hurling explosives at us. He's not going to make it on time either if he doesn't abandon this mission of his." Shaking his head, he muttered, *"Who the hell is this guy?"*

In that moment, Mairie had a flash of insight that was so great, it was almost comical.

"Jack! I think I've got it!"

When she'd heard Jack's last question, two scenes from *Butch Cassidy and the Sundance Kid* went through her mind. She had always loved that movie, and could actually remember Paul Newman's character muttering the same question during a chase. The other great scene was Butch and Sundance jumping off the cliff together.

Dropping the reins, she said excitedly, "I know how we can get off this mountain and beat Harmon to the landing spot."

He looked over at her. "How?"

"We can jump."

There was a prolonged pause before he repeated, "Jump? Jump off this mountain?"

It was comical. Mairie saw he had that expression of disbelief back on his face. She would have laughed, had she the time to indulge in that release.

"Listen," she began in earnest. "We can use the parachute. All we need is 5,000 feet to jump and we're almost twice that altitude now. If I pull the chord immediately, we can do it, Jack."

"*We* can do it?" He began shaking his head and walked over to his horse. Unbuckling his saddlebag, he removed the earthen jar and started heading toward the cave. "I am not about to jump off this mountain. If I'm going to die, I'll die here, fighting for our lives, not throwing them away by jumping off a damn cliff."

She hurried around to face him and grabbed his arms. "Wait . . . listen. We won't die. You saw me do it. You saw I landed safely—well, except for my ankle, and that was because I landed so hard. But listen to me, Jack . . . this can be done. *You* can jump with me."

Pulling away from her he turned to look for a sharp flat stone to dig. "Mairie, you can jump, if you feel that is the only way you can return, but—"

"Jack, look at me!"

It was the first time she had used that tone of voice with him. Even in the beginning she was trying to pacify him, but now she didn't have the time. Now she needed him to really hear her.

Clutching the jar in his hand, he crossed his arms over his chest. "What?"

"The parachute can hold us both. I'll pull the chord immediately to open the chute. We'll come down faster because of our combined weight, but it will hold us. I promise."

She ran back to her horse and grabbed the satchel holding the parachute. Frantically, she pulled it out, cursing herself for just stuffing it inside instead of folding it, as she had been instructed. "Here," she said, holding up one of the handles attached. "See this? There's two of them and they control everything. What direction, slowing down . . . everything.

That's all I have to do. Pull on the left to go left, the right to go right . . . like the reins of a horse. And when I want to slow down to land, I'll pull them both really, really hard, down between my legs. That will narrow the chute, like slowly closing an umbrella and trapping the wind inside. It's simple, and it's our only way off this mountain now."

"Simple?" He said shaking his head again as if he were crazy for even listening to her explanation. "Throwing myself off this cliff is simple? I'm burying the herb. You can make up your mind how you want to get down."

He turned and left her staring after him.

Mairie sighed with defeat. How could she make him understand jumping was safer than dealing with Harmon? She had been so obsessed with saving her brother that she put both their lives in such jeopardy. So . . . it was now up to her to correct it. Determined, Mairie looked at the rumpled silky material she was clenching and figured it was time to take charge. This partnership must go both ways. Jack had used his intelligence and skill to get them to the cave and successfully hide the jar. Now she must use hers to get them out of this. Somehow, someway, she would make him see it was their only alternative.

Looking at the short distance to the rocks with etchings of the ancient ones, Mairie knew there was no place to go beyond it. This was it. The top floor. They couldn't climb or hide anymore. Harmon was waiting below them. There was no other choice.

They had to jump.

Gathering up the parachute in her arms, she walked into the shade of huge red rocks and began laying it out on the ground. She had to remember everything she had been taught about packing the chute. There couldn't be one misfold, one mistake.

Both their lives depended on it.

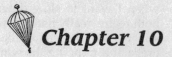 **Chapter 10**

Beads of sweat dripped from Jack's brow and onto the flat rock he'd laid over the spot where the earthen jar was buried. He couldn't believe Mairie actually thought he might jump off a mountain and trust it wasn't absolute insanity. Even though he had seen her do it, he remembered she'd been in this . . . *air-plane*, whatever that was. What she was describing was too uncertain. And yet a part of him wondered if there was enough time to get Mairie to the place she needed to be by one o'clock, and still avoid the ever-present Harmon.

Picking up his rifle, he walked out of the cave and saw her carefully folding that . . . that chute back into the satchel. "So, you've made your decision, Mairie?"

She looked up, and he swore there were tears in her eyes.

Nodding, she said, "There's no other way, Jack. Even you have to admit now there's no hope we can be back on the desert floor by one. Neither of us counted on Harmon relentlessly chasing us *and* having the power to stop us from such a distance. We've lost too much time. I'll completely miss my chance to get back if we try to ride down this mountain, but this way . . . this way, at least there's a possibility."

"A good possibility of being killed." He ran both hands through his hair with frustration. "This . . . this is crazy!"

She stopped packing the satchel and stared at him. "Wait a minute . . . staying here, trying to reason with Harmon isn't crazy? Jack, you're not even going to see him. You won't be able to get a shot off before he kills you."

She slipped her arms into the straps and brought the ones dangling at her sides in between her legs. Buckling them tight, she walked over to her horse to untie that strange hat she had been wearing when he'd found her.

"What if Harmon has already turned back? What if he's there to meet you when you land? You may be killed anyway."

"I'll have to take that chance, and besides . . . only a man like Harmon would sacrifice his own life to stop me from hiding a plant. He can't think beyond what he's been told to do. You must have seen men like him in the war. Men who blindly follow orders without question." She shook her head. "I don't think he's turned back. He's so automated now, he'll miss returning to his own time just to stop us."

He had to admit he'd known men as she described. That kind of thinking had made him turn his back and walk away years ago. But still . . . there had to be another way, just not jumping off a damn mountain into oblivion!

"Jack, I am so sorry for all the trouble I've caused . . . even these horses have suffered." Stroking her mount, she turned her head and looked back at him. Her eyes were wide and he could see tears welling in them. "Please forgive me, Jack. You are the best man I have ever known. My brother Bryan is brave because he is facing his death with courage and trying to live whatever time is left with honor. I see

that in you, too. I just wish that my being here
hadn't endangered you."

"There is nothing to forgive, Mairie," he said in a
somber tone. He wanted to take her into his arms,
to hold her to his chest and taste her lips once more.
One last time . . .

Suddenly, envisioning a life without Mairie Callahan in it seemed empty again.

"You're one amazing man, Jack Fitzhugh Delaney.
And it's been an honor to have . . ." her voice faltered, ". . . to have spent this time with you. Thank
you. Thank you for—"

Everything happened so fast, yet to Jack it appeared to be taking place very slowly, as if it were
a dream. It felt like an eternity, watching the events
unfold before him. He heard the impact of the bullet
hit the side of Mairie's horse. She must have heard
it also, for her eyes became wide with fear as she
held Jack's gaze. The horse dropped to its knees behind her and Mairie went tumbling back over it.

"Mairie!" he yelled out to her, terrified that she
too had been shot.

He reached her only seconds after her head hit the
ground with a dull thud.

"Mar!"

Rolling her over, he saw blood on the rock where
her head had been. He gritted his teeth and tensed
every muscle in his face. Squinting in the sun toward
the valley, he screamed in anguish. *"Harmon, you
bastard!"*

His cry echoed against the mountain and across
the valley, but for the rush of the desert breeze
against the sand, a silence followed. His mind raced.
He had to get them inside the cave to safety. Now
they were trapped on this mountain. Grabbing her
with one arm, he dragged her to the opening of the
cave, his other arm aiming his rifle out at the vast
space before them, prepared to shoot anything that

moved. They had to find cover while he examined her to make sure she didn't have any other wounds.

"Mar . . . can you hear me?" he pleaded, pulling her into the shadows. Resting her against the back wall in the cave, he placed his rifle at his side and began to search for further injuries. Running his hands over her, he tried to probe her body but was hampered by the pack she was wearing. Cursing under his breath, he struggled with the metal and fabric belts until he figured out how the bindings worked. Freeing the straps, he threw the sack to the side and rolled her over to explore her back, shoulders, and sides, anywhere a bullet might have entered.

Satisfied the reason she had lost consciousness was due to hitting her head on the rock when she went down, Jack rolled her back over to face him.

No other signs of blood. She was breathing. A surge of relief went through his body. Unconscious. But alive. He exhaled. He removed the bandana from his neck and with it applied pressure to the small cut on the back of Mairie's head. The bleeding was slowing. It wasn't as bad as he had first thought. "Mairie . . . are you all right?" His voice cracked as he cradled her head in his hands. She didn't answer.

Looking out into the daylight he shook with anger. That son-of-a-bitch shot the horse. But that didn't make sense. Harmon wouldn't have missed. If he wanted Mairie dead, she would be. He was playing with them now . . . taking away, little by little, every hope they had of getting away.

Harmon *was* insane!

All their supplies were tied to the horses. Even the water. He had only his rifle.

His fingers reached out and tenderly stroked her hair away from her closed eyes. Dirt was smudged on her face and he brushed it off gently. He inhaled deeply, exhaling very slowly.

His heart constricted when he thought of losing her, yet it quickly expanded when he thought of how courageous she was ... ready to sacrifice herself for the love of her brother. Maybe that was what struck him the most. He had seen men in battle, heroes who had sacrificed themselves to save another soldier. Those men did it for each other, not for the cause they were fighting. Bravery had nothing to do with politics, he realized. It was human beings coming to the assistance of other human beings. That was nobility. Fighting somebody's cause was the insanity. What a noble warrior princess Mairie Callahan was.

He brought her to his side and sat staring out of the cave, his rifle cocked and aimed for when Harmon made his next move. That madman would have to come around the bend even to get off another shot. Regrets began to flow through Jack's mind. There were so many things in his life he should have done, and still wanted to ... especially experience love. How he wished there was more time, time to really live again. How ironic it was that his life would end less than twenty feet from the spot where he'd sat when he first saw Mairie falling from the sky. He'd been asking the Great Spirit for his hope to be returned. He'd wanted a gift.

He got this incredible woman.

He wasn't cursed. Even though it looked like this day might be his last, Jack glanced down to Mairie and knew he had been blessed. She had come into his life and he had felt alive for the first time in years. She challenged him. Made him laugh. Made him crazy. And so made him want her more than he had ever wanted another woman, more than he had thought possible to want another.

She was ... she was like an angel. An angel of mercy. What an incredible gift.

His chest began to fill with an intensity of purpose he hadn't experienced in ages.

"Damn Harmon to hell," he cursed, refusing to sit back and wait while this woman, this angel from the future, missed her chance of going home. This wasn't a cause. This was justice. Mairie Callahan deserved the chance . . . and Jack Delaney was going to see that she got it.

An idea ran through his head so quickly he thought lunacy must have finally taken him for even conceiving of it. He had no idea if it could even work. She had said it would, it might . . .

"Shit," he muttered, resigned and crawling the few feet to the mouth of the cave. His decision was made. Mairie's horse lay close enough to provide him some cover, if Harmon hadn't gotten any closer.

Steadying himself with a deep breath, he scrambled to the dead horse, untied the canteen, and loosened the rope from the saddle horn. Darting back, he slid into the cave and rolled up next to Mairie.

Harmon must still be climbing to this level. They had time—not much, but enough to pull it off if he hurried. He almost laughed at his own thoughts. Pull off a crazy escapade to outwit an insane man. Sounded about right, considering he was slipping his arms through the bindings of the damn satchel. Tightening them, Jack then crouched in the small space and brought the straps around his thighs, checking them twice to make sure they were fastened the same as the arms.

Once he had the pack secured, he looked down to the unconscious woman. The only way he knew to get Mairie onto the desert floor was to tie her to him. He struggled with her for a few minutes as her unconscious state made her small frame heavier. Sitting on the cave floor, he pulled her onto his lap, her torso against his. He lifted her arms to his sides and positioned her legs over his, along his sides and behind him. Leaning to weigh her against his chest, he slipped the middle of the rope under her thighs and bottom to the front of her. He then crossed it between her breasts, took it up around her shoulder blades, under her arms, then over his shoulders then under his arms. He knotted the thick rope between them against his chest. Resting against the wall of the cave, he breathed heavily.

It was what he'd wanted right before he had first seen Mairie.

Hope . . .

This was it?

If it wasn't so desperate, he would laugh.

He told himself it was now or never. He had to get to the edge of the cliff while Harmon was still climbing. Going over in his mind everything Mairie had said earlier about operating the parachute, Jack touched the exposed metal handle between him and Mairie.

He felt the steady beating of her heart and his own was softened. She deserved this chance. No matter what happened, she had earned the right to go home.

She was an angel.

He just hoped when they jumped, there were other angels to catch them and safely bring them back to earth. At this point he might as well believe that as think some parasol was going to do it.

Grunting, Jack rose to a stooped position and grabbed Mairie's calves to keep her feet from dragging. He hated that when they were exposed, Mairie would be an open target, but he couldn't think of any other way to pull off this trick. He also knew she wanted to jump from the sacred rock, but he couldn't make it that far with her tied to him. He would simply have to walk to the edge of this cliff and jump.

Don't even think about it, his mind commanded. Just do it.

A low rumble began in his throat as he gathered every ounce of daring he'd ever possessed. This was no time to be modest. This was a moment to recall a lifetime of bold adventures. He had run into the unknown during the war. He had trusted the Great Spirit with his life. Now he knew again, when he stepped into the sunlight, all fears had to be left behind. This was about absolute hope.

It's about time you had faith in something again, Jack Delaney, he thought. He looked down to the woman attached to him and grinned. He released her legs. Her neck dropped back and her arms hung lifelessly at her sides. He cupped the back of her head and leaned forward, kissing her gently on the corner of her eye.

"You're going home, my angel," he whispered against her cheek.

They would make it. They had to. He couldn't even allow another possibility to register. He had asked for hope from the Great Spirit, as if it were something that had to be presented to him.

It was now, as he held her to him, that he knew it was always within him. It wasn't dead or gone. It wasn't a gift to receive from somewhere. Hope had just been sleeping inside him.

She was his gift. And for the first time in a long time, he was awake. He was alive with hope. He fortified himself with the thought and gazed lovingly at her sleeping face.

He had no idea it would be so awkward, as he cautiously struggled to the edge of the mountain. *Pull the handle as soon as you jump. Somehow other handles will appear and use them like reins. Pull them hard between your legs to slow down and land.*

Those were the only instructions he could remember. He looked to the shadows on the valley. They could be early or they might be late, regardless, he had to get her back to the desert floor alive.

He stood for just a second or two, knowing he was about to throw himself and this magnificent woman into the unknown. Looking down, his nerve faltered. Hope, Jack Delaney . . . that's all you need, the voice inside him resonated.

From behind a noise made him react instantly.

He made his leap of faith.

Harmon watched as the green-and-white billow unfolded in the sky; a brilliant contrast against the brown desert floor. He dropped to one knee and took careful aim with his high-powered rifle. One shot. That's all it would take to kill them both and stop the alteration of the future. He squeezed his left eye shut and viewed history through his scope.

Searing pain shot through his side as he fell in agony to the ground. A Paiute Indian with bow in hand stepped closer to the dying man and kicked the rifle over the cliff's edge. He watched his brother soar off into Father Sky and began a song for the dead as his heart filled with honor to have played a role in the balance of life.

A part of the prophecy of the ancient ones etched in the sacred rock above had been fulfilled.

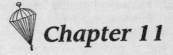

Chapter 11

Gravity worked. Newton's law was right.

They were plummeting toward the earth.

In the instant it took, he held his breath, closed his eyes and pulled the cord. He expected to fall hard and fast. When the chute deployed, the jolting up-lifts shot them like a cannonball higher into the sky. It terrorized him, especially to be dropped moments later with such force he thought the bindings would surely break. Tranquility immediately followed. Nothing but the sound of air rushing over his ears. Finally exhaling, he looked up to the green-and-white material puffed out above them. Damnedest thing. It worked.

Jack held Mairie so tightly to his chest, his natural fear of the unknown and desire to protect her almost made him forget the 'reins' he needed to guide the chute. They dangled out in front of them. *Pull the left to go left, the right to go to the right.*

In spite of it all, he remembered.

Except for riding a horse or traveling in a wagon, his feet had been on the ground his entire life. He slowly eased his hands away. For just that second, letting go of Mairie scared him more than anything else. Hands trembling, he reached out and grasped the handles. Looking down to the earth made him dizzy, so he attempted to focus on the task before him.

He pulled on the left handle.

His vision altered as they turned slightly toward a different view of sky. The clouds he had been using to provide cover now danced so closely. Close enough he thought to reach out and touch them. He didn't even notice when it began . . . the easing of gripping fear. Perhaps that's why his gaze lowered to the mountains. His dizziness was gone, replaced by awe.

This was living a vision quest.

From somewhere in his mind, he saw himself days ago. Sitting quietly on the tallest mountain in his world, looking out over this valley, feeling at one with Mother Earth. But now . . . this was like *being* nature. This must be what the eagle and the hawk felt. Maps couldn't do this justice. How could a drawing ever define what he was seeing?

This was being alive.

He pulled the right handle and felt an almost childish delight in the graceful drift in the other direction. He forgot they were falling at a speed he had never thought a human could experience. All he could think, in that glorious timeless instant, was he was part of something so much larger than he ever imagined. Something exciting and creative . . . his mind was expanding beyond anything he could have ever conceived.

Suddenly the vision quest turned into a nightmare.

White light flashed around them, blinding him at once. In terror, he seized Mairie to his chest as something, some heat, entered his body, racing along his spine and sending an unfamiliar tingling sensation everywhere. He immediately thought he had died, and a part of him wondered how he could think at all if he were dead. His heart slammed against the wall of his chest, as though it might explode through, and his dizziness returned with a vengeance. Clutching Mairie in desperation, he fleetingly thought that death awaited them both, and wasn't all that surprised to see his vision narrow in darkness as he allowed the dizziness to take over and cover in him in soft, welcoming shadows.

It was the perfect silence and the warmer wind that brought him out of it. Jack jerked his head upright and he felt the life force surge through his body. Mairie was still unconscious and he immediately grabbed the handles. He looked down to the ground and saw the earth was much closer. Turning to the mountains, Jack pulled harder on the handle and caught his breath at the back of his throat.

What he saw defied explanation.

Strange lights glittered through the hazy sunlight, and they were coming from . . . from a city of some sort. He had never seen such a large settlement. Pulling the handle harder, they turned sharply and he came fully around. The mountains were still in the same place, but this . . . this city . . . where was this? It seemed from another world.

He had no more time to worry about strange lights and buildings as the ground appeared to be racing toward them.

Pull both handles down hard between the legs.

The command repeated in his head. Those were the last of the instructions. Taking a deep breath, he mustered all his strength and pulled down hard. It seemed to be slowing the descent and he held the downward force as long as he could. When he let up, he felt their bodies falling through the air with more speed and again pulled down. How could he pull all the way between their legs? He couldn't. Not with Mairie attached in front of him. What was he going to do now?

There was no time to ponder the question.

To hell with pulling between the legs. He'd do it at his sides.

He pushed down and held it for so long that the muscles in his arms started trembling, yet he kept up the pressure. Closer and closer the earth came, and Jack thought for certain they would be crushed. He looked up to the green-and-white material and saw that it was narrowing as Mairie had said and knew he had to apply more pressure. From somewhere within him he had to find the strength to pull the lines harder.

Instinctively he raised his legs and brought both arms down straight below his sides narrowing the chute as much as possible. He growled in a primal voice of desperation as his arms shook with the strain. It was working . . . the descent was more graceful, yet he felt unsure he could keep it up until they were on the ground.

The brown desert floor, dotted with sagebrush, flew past his vision and he again felt the incredible, fleeting sensation of being a bird . . . on its awkward first flight. As landing became imminent, he growled again, knowing he had to pull out any last reserves of strength if they hoped to make it alive. Everything, every single thought and sinew of his body, was focused on landing this contraption.

He knew it was possible, Mairie had done it.

The last thing he recalled were his boots slamming into the ground, and he was sure his ankles broke with the impact as pain shot up his body and rammed into the top of his skull. Suddenly he was jerked backward and his legs crumpled under them. His back and head hit the sand as Mairie flopped like a rag doll against his chest. For the second time on this flight, darkness overtook him.

He passed out.

*   *   *

Mairie felt bruised and battered. Her head hurt like hell and she couldn't breathe. She lifted her chin up and gasped for air. She opened her eyes just the slightest bit. The pain increased and she immediately shut them in defense. Her chest ached and she forced her arms to move. Slowly placing her hands in the hot sand, she attempted to raise herself. Everything hurt, and something was restricting her from getting up. She squeezed her eyelids tightly, then opened them to find herself face to face with a lifeless Jack. Her hand felt a rope at her breasts and around her back. Why was she tied up . . . and to him? Fear slammed into her.

"Jack . . ." She breathed his name and touched his jaw. "Wake up. Did Harmon get us?" Fear and confusion overrode the pain and she commanded her brain to think clearly. Why were they like this? She looked down to his chest and saw the thick knot of rope and immediately began to free herself. She had to get Jack away from Harmon. Even as she was struggling with the intricate knot, a part of her wondered why Harmon would leave her arms free to untie herself and Jack. Maybe he thought they were dead.

It never occurred to her.

Terror raced through her system. He couldn't . . . Jack couldn't be dead.

"Jack!" Desperate, she again called out his name as she scrambled to untangle the last few slips of the knot. Finally free, she pulled the rope from her shoulders and back and with a quick look around her, Mairie started slapping Jack's cheeks.

"Wake up. You can't be dead." She threw her head against his chest and had to hold her breath in order to hear his heart.

It was pumping, and she felt his chest expand with his shallow breathing.

"Okay, then wake up," she cried, and shook his

shoulders. "C'mon, Jack. Get up ... get up, get up ..."

He moaned lightly and Mairie froze in mid shake, her eyes clouded by a film of tears. "Please, Jack ... please wake up. That's right, you can do it. I'm here, right here and I need you. We have to get up. Now, Jack ... right now. Come on ..."

His eyelids fluttered once and he moaned louder. "Yes, that's it. Come on. Wake up." She tapped his cheek lighter this time. "Jack ... it's Mairie. *Wake up!*"

"All right," he mumbled. "Stop ... yelling."

Stunned for a moment, Mairie stared at him and then broke into a soft smile. "You're okay ... Thank God, you're okay ... I thought you might be—" She stopped herself short with the thought and continued in a whisper, "Jack, what happened? All I remember ... we were talking in front of the cave ... and ... and I was about to jump ... then I saw this really strange look on your face, Jack ... and I don't remember anything else. What happened? Did Harmon get us?" She began frantically to look around them. "Damn. We've got to get up and get away from here. Open your eyes, Jack. We've gotta move now."

He opened his eyelids and blinked a few times as another painful moan escaped his lips. Mairie winced, sure he was injured somehow, but time was of the essence here. "What happened? Tell me, Jack. What the hell happened? Where's Harmon?"

"Harmon ... he's not here anymore ... at least, I'm pretty sure he's not with us. He was on the mountain just behind us when—ahh ..." Pain wracked his body as he attempted to sit up. "I think I'm going to have to rest here a few minutes more." He fell back down with a groan.

"Jack, I need to know what happened. *Please tell me.*" Her voice was frustrated.

She could only stare and force her mind to function as she listened to his two words.

"I jumped."

It took time to assimilate his muttering. "You did what? You . . . jumped?"

He nodded and sucked his breath in sharply between his teeth. "Yes, I jumped," he repeated, with emphasis on the last word.

"Jumped?" Her brain couldn't get past it, until something new started to register.

A distant noise grew in rapid intensity and Mairie clutched Jack to her as the ground started to vibrate with the thunderous roar. This was no freight train. An earthquake?

"Wha . . . ? What . . . ?" Jack brought his hand up and grabbed her sleeve.

Mairie didn't know who was holding whom for protection. They anchored themselves together to face whatever force was about to descend on them.

"Oooohhh, *shit!*"

She didn't hear Jack's loud objection. They instinctively released each other to cover their ears in protest of the engine's shattering squeal. The air felt still as they gaped up to see the huge white belly of a jetliner flying toward the earth.

An airplane.

She tried to make her brain function, but she was frozen in shock.

"*What the hell was that?*" Jack demanded. He sounded wide awake now.

"An airplane," she managed to whisper, since it was the only cognitive thought she could muster.

She turned her head and stared after the plane heading for a landing at McCarren airport.

It's . . . an . . . airplane, she repeated slowly in her mind. *An airplane!*

She was back.

Joy surged through her body, replacing shock.

She was back!

She forgot about the pain as she scrambled out of the rope and sat up. Looking around her for the first time, she saw that the desert extended further to the mountains. They didn't land in the same spot, but they *had landed.*

She looked down to the man before her who was still staring into the sky, as though he'd lost all ability to speak.

"Jack . . . I'm home," she whispered.

He didn't say anything and continued to stay frozen in shock. She waved her hand in front of his eyes to remind him he was conscious.

"Jack, didn't you hear me? *I'm home!*"

He blinked and barely turned his head to stare into her eyes.

"What . . . the . . . hell . . . was . . . that?"

She giggled and had to stop herself. "I told you. An airplane."

"You . . . you threw yourself out one of those?"

Why did he look and sound like he was about to throw up? Mairie wondered. She dropped beside him. "Not like that, exactly," she said and again put her hands on his shoulders.

"Who cares?" she exclaimed and giggled again. "Don't you get it? I'm back! We did it. We did it. We—" She stopped short and stared at him for a few prolonged seconds. "Ahh, how *did* we do it? We got to my original landing sight?"

What had happened up there by that cave? All she recalled was talking to Jack and then . . . it was all a blank from there.

"I jumped," he repeated while looking back to the sky, as if not believing it himself.

"Did I faint?" She remembered the feeling when the sunstroke hit her, but she didn't remember anything about this.

"Harmon shot your horse and you fell and hit your head. You were out."

She took in the information and started putting it together. "And . . . and you tied me to you and . . . and . . . you jumped? *You* jumped?"

He simply nodded, as though even that was taking more effort than he wanted to expend.

"You saved my life."

He closed his eyes and she fell forward to hug him. Hearing his rush of breath leave his chest, Mairie quickly sat upright. "My God, I can never repay you. You brought me back to my own time, to my brother. We can do this now. We can help him. How can I ever thank you?" Even the word thank seemed inadequate. There should be something, some expression, to describe the magnitude of her gratitude.

"You can hold your hands over my ears," he muttered, then groaned. "Here comes another of your air-planes."

It took them some time to get Jack upright, and Mairie knew they had to move out of the runway flight path as there would be another plane in a few minutes. Jack was bruised and rattled, as she led him north away from the mountains. She had already gathered the parachute and had hidden it behind some brush, since neither had the strength to carry it. For Mairie to support Jack, who had thrown his arm around her shoulders and leaned on her in order to walk, it was enough. She would do anything, whatever it took to help him. He had saved her life . . . and sacrificed his own.

That thought slammed into her when they had begun to walk. Jack had left behind his life. She couldn't get him back to his own time. He had left his Paiute brothers and the peace he was desperately hoping to find with them. Her love for the man increased a thousandfold. How courageous to leap off that mountain . . . just on her word that it would work. And he did it for her. She knew that without even asking. Jack Delaney would have stayed and fought it out with Harmon to the death.

"I saw . . . something," he said through strained breaths, as they slowly walked under the intense sun. "A city . . . something, when I was landing. It had . . . lights . . . strange lights."

"Las Vegas," she automatically answered. "That's what I had hoped to see, instead of O.D.'s place when I fainted. I know the feeling, only in reverse, Jack."

"Wait . . . you are telling me that in one hundred and twenty-two years, O.D.'s small ranch has turned into *that*?"

She nodded, shifting her shoulder to accept more of his weight. "I know it's hard to imagine, but it's true."

"This is . . . is . . . it's unbelievable, Mairie."

"This is the present, Jack. My present and your future." She wanted to hug him in sympathy, but knew she couldn't. "Now you're the time traveler."

In silence they walked further through the desert. They stopped several times to catch their breath and finally Mairie spied a cottonwood tree that could provide some shade. They needed to get out of the merciless desert sun. Although he was acclimated to the desert, the time travel had taken more out of him, and Jack was fading fast.

She helped him sit down, with his back leaning against the trunk, and sat cross-legged in front of him. "I wish I had some water to give you." How her heart ached, to see him in such pain. She knew they couldn't walk any longer in the sun. Especially Jack, since he had taken the brunt of the fall.

"I should have tied the canteen to myself when I jumped, but I wasn't thinking of anything except getting to the floor of the desert."

She smiled tenderly. "Oh, Jack, you did an incredible thing, something I can never repay. You left your time to bring me to mine."

Leaning his head back against the tree, he sighed before closing his eyes. "I didn't know what time it was, or that this would happen, Mairie. I only wanted you to get to the spot where you had landed. Where you said you could get back to the future. This . . . this was not a noble gesture."

She sighed and wiped the sweat from her forehead. "Still . . . what courage it took, Jack. I'm in awe. I know what it took for me to jump out of that plane and I had training."

He laughed. In spite of his bruised body, his shock, his fatigue . . . he laughed. "I had training. Your frantic instructions before Harmon shot the horse. Thanks to you, we're here."

"That bastard," she muttered. "He shot my horse." Shaking her head, her heart filled with remorse for the animal.

"You fell and were knocked out. I dragged you into the cave and that's when I came up with this brilliant plan. Seems the Coyote had a hand in this, too. The future . . ."

She was glad to see a smile still on his face, for she knew he was exhausted. His eyes were closed and his breathing became steady. Within moments he fell asleep, and Mairie sat before him, studying his face. They might as well just stay in the shade until the sun started to set. Without water, neither of them had the strength to make much progress. It would be better to travel at night, she thought. Besides, she couldn't be sure if Harmon made it back or not, and he might be out there looking for them. Or maybe someone from the government would be watching for them. She had waited this long to contact Bryan. She could wait until tonight when she would find a way into the city and locate him.

She studied Jack's jaw and saw the shadow of his beard in contrast to his pale cheeks. He needed this rest. What was he going to think of the world a hundred years into his future? She knew how she had felt in his time, but at least she had some reference by reading books. There was nothing to prepare him for the shock he would endure. All she could do was hold his hand and walk him through it.

She was back.

The thought raced through her mind and she wanted to shout out with happiness. How could she sleep when every nerve in her body was active and alive with gratitude? She couldn't. She simply sat and looked at the man who had altered her life . . . her past, her present, and now her future.

She loved him.

And she couldn't let him know it . . . at least, not yet. She knew from personal experience that Jack would need time to adapt to her present and now, his future. He deserved that time, she thought, imagining his reaction to modern Las Vegas. To blurt out her love for him and overload his emotions would be unfair. Smiling with tenderness, she vowed to be patient.

The huge orange ball of the setting sun appeared to be resting on the crests of Spring Mountain, and the air became cooler as the shadows grew longer. Mairie and Jack continued their trek through the desert, arm in arm, leaving the mountains behind. Neither spoke much, conserving energy, and Mairie wondered how long it would take before they reached some sign of civilization.

It seemed hours had passed. Her mouth was so dry. Every muscle in her body rebelled at movement, yet she continued without protest. She felt she had to support Jack any way she could. If he, injured as he was, could endure this in silence . . . so could she.

But a part of her was wondering how he was doing it . . . from where did this man draw his incredible strength? She remembered his Indian brothers and his inner knowledge of Mother Earth. She knew Jack Delaney was a rare man.

She looked up to the sky and saw stars beginning to appear.

Immediately she remembered sweet Fenton. What had he said to her? Follow the North Star. It would lead her home. Spying it, she smiled while thinking of the boy. How precious those memories . . . she would keep them all, priceless jewels to treasure for a lifetime.

The sound of something registered in her brain and her mental rambling ceased as she concentrated. It was distant and then came closer, a whooshing sound . . .

Cars.

Energy surged through her body. "Jack!" Her voice was hoarse, a mere whisper. "We're gonna make it. There's a road up ahead."

He simply nodded. So great was her need to cross the last rise in front of them to verify the road, Mairie wanted to run, yet she continued to step slowly in unison with him. Patience, her mind commanded. It's there . . . it has to be there.

With great effort, they cleared the incline and together held their breath at the top. One of them, in relief; the other, in disbelief.

A steady stream of traffic raced on Interstate 15 and Mairie almost sobbed with appreciation. She had never been so grateful to see cars and trucks. She wanted to hug each driver, to shout out her joy.

"What are *those*?" Jack demanded in a raspy voice.

Turning to look at his shocked expression, Mairie

grinned. "Cars. Trucks. Ahh . . . vehicles of transportation. Instead of horses and wagons."

"What powers such . . . such things?" His expression remained incredulous.

She wanted to laugh. "Gasoline. Oil, from under the earth. I can't explain it, Jack. Let's just get down there so I can flag one of them down."

"Look at how fast they are going! I . . . I'm going to get in one of them?"

She laughed. She couldn't help it. He sounded like a little kid about to ride a roller coaster for the first time. "Yes, Jack. With any luck we'll both hitch a ride into Las Vegas. Come on . . ." she urged. "This is my world. Trust me."

"Your world is foreign, Mairie."

She turned her head and saw fear in his expression. She knew how he felt. "Listen, Jack," she whispered, "once I realized I was back in time, in your time, I recognized that you were the expert, and I should follow you. When we left the ranch, you were in charge. I thought of myself as your co-pilot . . ." Realizing he couldn't relate to the term, she added, ". . . your relief wagon driver; I had to follow your lead. You're going to have to make that same adjustment now. This is my time, Jack, and I know what I'm doing. You're going to have to trust me. I would never put you in danger."

Taking a deep breath, he nodded. "Just explain everything as we go, and . . ." He paused, putting his arm around her shoulder. "I do trust you, Mar."

She slipped her arm around his waist and hugged him lightly. "Thank you, Jack," she replied, and they began their descent into modern civilization.

She could feel the tension in Jack's body increase as they neared the road. The noise from the traffic became louder, and several times he stopped and took a deep breath. She knew even if he were not injured he still would be shocked to see what the future held. The horse had been the main form of transportation for hundreds and hundreds of years, and trains were a recent invention. To see this had to be a major cultural shock.

"Here," she said, just below a billboard advertising a casino. "Sit here. I'm going to get us a ride."

"How will you do this?" he asked, easing himself to the sandy earth. No sooner had he sat when a loud tractor trailer passed, causing the wind to blow around them. "Not in that," he added in a shaky voice.

Mairie smiled. "I don't get to pick, Jack. Whatever stops for us, we'll use. Don't worry. You'll be safe."

She walked to the edge of the road and waited a couple of minutes until she saw the headlights of a car approaching. Then she flipped back her hair, plastered a smile on her face, and stuck out her thumb.

There was a first time for everything. And hitch-hiking was a first.

Two cars passed, not even slowing down, and Mairie felt disappointment. She was reminded of how many times she had passed by those seeking a ride. Fear. That's what had made her not stop to help another. Seeing no other cars heading north, she took a deep breath and walked back to where Jack was sitting.

Unzipping her jump suit, she said, "Drastic times warrant drastic measures."

"What are you doing?"

She didn't even glance in his direction, as she pulled the heavy dark suit away from her. Cool air immediately made goosebumps rise all over her exposed skin. "I'm doing whatever it takes to get us a ride," she explained.

"Mairie Callahan . . . you cannot stand on a road in your underwear!"

She could only stare at him for a couple of seconds

before bursting out laughing. "This isn't my underwear. Is that what you thought all this time? That I was prancing about in 1877 in my underwear?"

He didn't answer, just continued to look affronted by her behavior.

She shook her head. "Jack, that's another thing you'll have to get used to in this time. There isn't . . . well, your sense of propriety is going to need adjustment. This," and she looked down to her black leggings and white cropped top, ". . . this is considered normal attire at times, even for going out in public. And I was skydiving, so I was dressed appropriately. No one is going to be shocked to see me in this."

"I'm shocked," he muttered. "It's . . . it could be inviting the wrong type of person to assist you."

Her amusement lessened. "That's what is considered a judgment in this time, Jack. To believe that, to say that a woman can't be dressed any way she chooses and still be safe, is unfair and opinionated. Can't you see how thinking like that—" She left off the impending speech when she glimpsed another set of headlights in the distance. Besides, who was she to lecture this man? He'd just pushed a sensitive button within her.

"Okay, keep your fingers crossed for luck," she said, heading back to the road.

"Be careful," he called out to her.

Nodding, Mairie took a deep breath and held out her arm, her thumb pointing north.

It took five more cars to pass before a van slowed. She followed the speed of the headlights until they passed her and the van stopped about twenty-five feet up the road.

"Okay," she yelled to Jack, and raced back to get him.

They limped toward the van and the side door slid open. Music blared from speakers, music so loud that even Mairie's ears were assaulted with the barrage of sound.

Jerry Garcia's stunning guitar solo from "Touch of Gray" seemed to leave the van and envelop them. Jack stood frozen in shock and even to Mairie the amount of sound after so much silence was disorienting.

"Hey, there's two of ya. Didn't see the big guy."

The words were barely audible over the music.

Mairie tried to respond, yet her senses were on overload. Suddenly, the music lowered, and her blood pressure along with it. "Ah . . . thanks for stopping," she muttered. "We're going into Vegas. Can you give us a lift? We've been out here a long time."

There was a pause, and then the voice said, "Okay, but we got to make a stop first. We can take you about fifteen miles and then you can hop another ride or wait until we drop off our equipment."

Fifteen miles closer to her brother, Mairie thought.

"Great," she managed to say, while pulling Jack forward. His body was moving as though she were leading him to his slaughter.

Stepping up into the van, she pushed some wrappers off the back seat and reached out to help Jack. "Come on," she urged. "Get in and sit next to me."

She was glad that the overhead light didn't seem to work. Fortunately, it hid the sheer terror on Jack's face as he followed her instructions. Once seated next to her, the van door slid closed and Jack jumped at the sound. "Relax," she whispered in his ear, pulling him back against the seat.

The van took off and Jack immediately held his body rigid against the motion.

"How long you two been out here?" the driver asked.

"Since one in the afternoon," Mairie answered,

still trying to reassure Jack by squeezing his hand and stroking his arm.

"No shit! Wow!" another young male voice blurted.

"Give 'em some water," the driver instructed.

The passenger opened the glove compartment and a tiny light illuminated the front of the van. Two young men, dressed in jeans, tie-dyed and printed T-shirts, and bandanas around their long hair looked around the floor of the front seat. The younger one, the passenger, pushed his hair behind his ear, grabbed something, and handed it back to her with a smile. His ear was pierced.

"Here," he said, offering her a plastic bottle of water. "You two look wiped."

"Thank you," Mairie said, as the light was turned off. She unscrewed the cap and handed it to Jack.

"Drink," she ordered, trying to bring him out of his frozen posture.

"Who . . . what are they?" he mumbled, just as the music resumed its pulsating volume.

Leaning sideways, she stretched her neck toward his ear and said, "Deadheads."

"What?"

"Deadheads!" her voice shouted over the music, only to have the song end so abruptly that her word rang out in the moment of silence.

The passenger turned around and stared at her. The driver looked at her from the rearview mirror. Both suddenly smiled.

"Us, too . . ." the driver said.

The passenger brought up his two fingers and grinned. "Peace."

Mairie smiled back and raised her own hand. "Peace," she repeated, and almost fell on the floor in laughter when she saw Jack raise his hand.

He held the bottle of water in his left hand and made the symbol of peace with his right. He looked at her, as if trying to judge her reaction. "This is what you did when I first met you," he said in his defense. "I thought it was a greeting."

"It is," she said, and allowed the laughter.

"Is it about cattle? Why are they referring to themselves as dead cattle? You too are a *dead-head*, Mairie?"

"It's not about cows!" Laughing even more, she realized this was going to be more difficult than she had originally expected. The thought became sobering as Jack looked to the driver and his friend.

"What do they mean then? Their heads look quite alive."

She bit her bottom lip to distract her from the waves of laughter that demanded release. "It's just a name, a term, used to label people who follow around this group that's playing."

Hearing the opening bars of "Truckin'," an old favorite song, Mairie managed to say, "I guess I am a deadhead, Jack. Never knew it until now. If the Grateful Dead can get me to Las Vegas, if they can pull off this one . . . then I'll be a dedicated deadhead from here on."

"Where is this deadhead sound coming from?"

"The radio. I think it's a tape."

"What is a radio? That machine with lights on it?"

"Yes. Well, it's . . . like a telegraph. It picks up signals and sends them back. But this is a tape. A . . . a recording, like a phonograph record. Do you know what I mean?"

He didn't answer. He brought the bottle finally to his lips, as if he were attempting to assimilate her words.

She watched him drink and then hand her the bottle. Taking a few mouthfuls, she swirled the refreshing liquid over her tongue and moaned with pleasure. She couldn't wait to get to her room at the Luxor. As soon as she saw Bryan and explained everything, she was going to pamper herself royally. And Jack, too . . . she thought, seeing him steel himself against the assault of sound. He deserved to see that the future could also be quite nice.

Starting to hum along with the music, Mairie looked out the window to the night. At least if she gave herself over to the music she wouldn't keep picturing Jack Delaney soaking in a Jacuzzi. That long wet hair over his shoulders. His eyes shining with pleasure. Sheesh . . .

"Truckin' . . ." she began singing along with the kids in the front seat. Anything to direct her brain away from *that* mental path. He was like an innocent now. Like a child. She had to remember that. Plus, just because she loved him didn't mean it was returned. His actions indicated a little more than like, but far away from love yet.

He did jump, though, and she knew it had been for her. That had to have taken love. Some kind of love.

She couldn't think of it now. Now she had to focus on getting to Las Vegas and finding her brother. Patience. She had to have patience with Jack now.

He was the time-traveler.

Still, the driving beat was stirring up some hormonal reaction that she couldn't deny. She'd just have to remember that she couldn't take advantage of someone with a child's view of his new world. Until he was comfortable in this time, she owed him that respect.

What if he never got comfortable? Suddenly, she was submerged in dejection.

The world, his world, was going to expand with every new experience. It might take him years, maybe even his whole life. How long could she pretend to be just good friends, partners, copilots of this adventure, when every nerve in her body came alive with yearning whenever she looked into his eyes?

It didn't help that he grabbed her arm in that moment, as a cyclist on a Harley passed them.

"A motorcycle," she informed him, patting his forearm like a reassuring teacher.

She had to remember that. She was his teacher now.

His teacher.

Yeah, right . . .

Hard to believe, after everything she had gone through, mentally, emotionally, and physically, that she was capable of being aroused. But she was . . . she wanted to hold him, reassure him, stroke him, calm him, love him . . .

Love.

It was one powerful force.

They stopped about twenty minutes later at a roadside bar and restaurant. Her stomach growled as she and Jack got out of the van. Their peaceful benefactors wished them well and left them on the side of the road as they pulled around the back of the building.

Now what, Mairie thought, as she looked at the few trucks parked on the side of the road. How would they find another ride?

"What is this, Mairie?" Jack asked, standing straighter and wincing. "An outpost?"

She chuckled. "I guess you would see it that way. We've just traveled about fifteen miles in the van, and it's around five more miles to the city. Yeah, this is an outpost. Let's see if we can clean up and get something to drink. I don't suppose you have any money on you?"

"Money . . . ?" He started to reach into his pockets and Mairie grabbed his arm.

"Come on," she said, pulling this wide-eyed man with her to the entrance. "We can at least use the bathrooms. There's running water in them."

She led him through the large glass door into the lobby and Jack stopped short.

"What?" She turned to see his face.

He was staring at a slot machine, the video screen inviting anyone with promises of Lady Luck . . . "Jackpot worth $8000."

Tugging his arm, she said, "It's a game, Jack. Gambling. That's what Las Vegas is known for in this time. Come on."

He didn't budge. "You said you would explain, if I asked. You said that while we were waiting for the dead-heads. I know what gambling is, but I've never seen anything like this."

She exhaled and shook her head. "Okay. People put money into it, pull the arm or push the buttons and the machine eats your dollar. It's a shot in the dark at winning money, Jack. They don't pay out. Come on, let's get cleaned up."

Leading him by the hand through the small casino, with great relief, she spied the sign, "Restrooms." The pleasant thought of using a modern bathroom raced through her mind. How she had taken for granted simple conveniences. They were luxuries. "Here they are, Jack. You go in here, the ladies room is down the hall. I'll be right back."

Jack stood, hesitantly, before the wide door. Suddenly, it drew open from the inside. A burly man with suspenders and a strange, brightly colored hat stopped short and looked at Jack blocking the way.

"You gonna come in or just stand there, buddy?"

"Ahh, excuse me . . . yes. Yes, sir. I'll think I'll come in."

"Another wacko. World's full of them," the man mumbled, as he slightly pushed Jack aside.

The room was bright and cool. There was no foul odor. There was the sound of water rushing. Another man walked in and around Jack to several large white bowls hung on the wall. Jack nonchalantly attempted to watch as the man unzipped his pants and began to relieve himself.

"What are you starin' at, ya pervert?" The man blurted out.

Jack quickly turned away to find himself facing a huge mirror on the wall. For the first time in a long while he viewed himself as large as life. He was accustomed to shaving in a small, cracked and discolored pocket mirror he kept in his saddlebag. He'd seen himself in picture windows on city streets in Washington, but never with this clarity.

His mind went briefly to his life in the desert. Bathing in a waterfall. Drinking from a clear stream. Everything he needed in life was provided by Mother Earth. Now he felt entombed in a cold and clinical prison. In fact, it did remind him of the hospital in Washington where he was taken when he had influenza as a boy.

The dirt on his face and hands brought him out of his memory. He looked like he'd been through the war again, he thought, as he continued staring at his image. Jack Delaney, you are not in a dream, he reminded himself. This is real. Unfortunately, very real.

Beneath the mirror were the washbasins. The man who had grunted at Jack while using the white bowl on the wall now stood beside him at another basin. Jack watched from the corner of his eye. The man pulled a handle under a small box on the wall and a pink liquid fell into his hand. He then pushed a button above what appeared to be a spigot and water began flowing from it. He washed his hands until the water automatically stopped, then turned to dry them with paper he pulled out of a metal cabinet in the wall. The man crumpled and threw the paper into a metal barrel, then turned toward Jack.

"You gotta real problem, fella. Better watch yourself before somebody breaks your face." Leaving Jack with the warning, he pulled the door open, banging it hard against the wall, and stormed out.

"I've got a problem, all right," Jack mumbled to himself. "I'm lost."

Looking down at the basin, Jack figured he'd better get accustomed to it. He went to the wall with the bowls on it and relieved himself. He returned to the basin and washed his hands just as the other fellow had. He splashed his face until the flow of water stopped. The coolness felt soothing as he closed his eyes. Opening them to his own reflection, he saw a worried image of himself.

But for their attire, people in the future didn't look much different, he thought. They were men the same as he was. He just might make it through this, however long it lasted, he reassured himself. A grimace of pain came over his face as he slowly stood upright. He was reminded of the landing he made with Mairie on the ground, and he took a deep breath while drying his face on a rough paper towel. He could really use a bath, he thought, taking one final look at himself in the mirror.

The truth, the reality, of his situation finally hit him.

What if it was for the rest of his life? What if there was no way to get him back?

It was a possibility. A strong possibility.

Turning to the door, he pulled it open.

He was inundated in a sea of people talking, laughing, smoking, drinking, and eating. The aroma of cooking food wafted by. He was starving. Mairie must also be hungry, he thought. There was only one way, one chance. Something within him alerted his instincts and he maneuvered through the casino and back toward the entrance.

Standing in front of the slot machine, he pulled the silver dollar from his dirty pants pocket.

"Jack! What took you so long back there?" Mairie grabbed his arm. "I thought I'd lost you."

"It took me a while to experience all the outhouse improvements, that's all." He raised the coin to the slot.

"What are you doing?"

Grabbing him again, she almost spun him around. "Where did you get that?"

He looked at the coin in his hand. "You asked me to buy them from Virginia. Don't you remember?"

"I wanted one, for Fenton. You bought them both?"

"I thought you wanted them both. Virginia gave me a hard time of it, too."

"That's our only cash right now until I get back to the hotel, Jack. You can't throw it away in a slot machine." She closed his hand tightly around the coin.

He looked deeply into her eyes. "Mairie, this entire adventure has been a gamble. My jumping with you from the mountain was a chance I took and it brought me here, into the future with you. We need to eat. Maybe this silver dollar is supposed to be another chance for us. So much has happened. I swear, something is going to break if I bend anymore."

He watched the light fade in her eyes. "Do what you need to do, it's your dollar," she said, turning away. "I'm going to find us another ride into town."

He watched her walk stiffly toward the bar. Hope. He must draw upon it again because he believed she was his gift. At this moment, his angry and hungry gift.

The coin left his fingers slowly and slid down into the machine. He grasped the handle with his right hand. Pulling down deliberately, his eyes were mesmerized by the flashing colors and sounds emanating from the metal and glass box. Almost in

embarrassment he stepped back from the ostenta-
tious contraption. Pictures spun around, then began
to flip and bounce into place.

"*Bar—bar—bar—bar.*"

What sounded like a firehouse bell started ringing
as a brilliant light flashed around and around on top
of the box. Jack panicked and stood still.

"Winner, winner, winner," the display repeated.
A small crowd of people gathered around him.

"Don't just stand there, take it! Take it, ya fool!"
An old woman yelled at Jack. "Get your ticket!
You're a winner! You hit the jackpot!"

Jack looked at the small white paper the machine
spit out. He ripped it off and turned, looking puzzled at the woman.

"Don't you know anything, darlin'? Take the
ticket to the cashier's box over there and they'll give
you your money! You're the grand prize winner . . .
eight thousand dollars!"

A smile began to overtake his face. He turned to
look for Mairie, who was pushing her way through
the crowd of people toward him.

Strangers slapped him on the back with congratulations. The old woman coyly smiled at him and
remarked, "If I was twenty years younger, son, I'd
ask you to marry me! You an actor or something?"

"Jack! What's happened? You won?"

"This lady says I hit the jackpot, but all I got was
this paper."

"Oh my gawd!" Mairie screamed, as she jumped
up and wrapped her arms around his neck, hugging
him. "I can't believe you, Jack Delaney. You are absolutely amazing!"

He almost fell over with her enthusiasm.

"Oh, oh . . . I'm sorry," she giggled, pulling back
and straightening his shirt. "I was so excited I forgot
all about your back. Geez, and I almost took that
money away from you!"

He pulled her close to him again and laughed, as the truth hit him. He had just won eight thousand dollars! A fortune! The future suddenly wasn't as threatening. "Things are definitely looking better."

Her giggle increased and he saw in her eyes the light return with such intensity that he felt stunned, as though in the middle of a group of yelling and happy people, he and Mairie were standing alone. For just a brief moment the sound around him lessened. The clarity of the crowd dimmed. Nothing seemed as real as the space around him and the woman he was holding. His chest welled with emotion and he pulled her tighter.

"You're a winner, Jack," Mairie said, looking directly into his eyes with her smile.

In that moment, he sure felt like life in the future had something to offer.

They paid the old woman five hundred dollars to claim the jackpot, since identification was required at the cashier's window. With seventy-five hundred dollars all in one hundred dollar bills stuffed into the handbag Mairie had bought in the gift shop, they hired a car to take them the rest of the way into Las Vegas.

Jack, feeling sated by a steak dinner and the money in his pocket, sat back in the conveyance as it carried them north. As the vehicle rode over a hill, Jack was presented with the most amazing sight he had ever seen in his entire life. A city . . . a city of lights, brightly colored and shooting into the sky, this amazing city stood in the middle of the desert. An oasis beyond imagination.

"Oh . . . my . . . God . . ."

Mairie took a deep breath and whispered, "Welcome to my world, Jack."

Why didn't her voice sound excited?

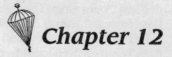 *Chapter 12*

Mairie sat forward in the cab as it pulled into the valet area under the huge Sphinx of the Luxor Hotel.

"Yes, Jack . . ." she answered his excited question. "*That* is the pyramid I was telling you about when you found me."

"It exists!" His voice was awe filled. "And the lights! Look at the lights!"

She was taking out money for the driver and muttered, "I told you." Tension filled her body, and she wished she could share in his childlike wonder, but something that had happened in the gift shop was bothering her. When she'd paid for the purse and the clerk had handed her the receipt, Mairie suddenly wanted to know the date of this remarkable day.

It said seven months later than when she had jumped.

She'd started making a joke out of the mistake, but the clerk assured her there was no mistake. Mairie had wanted to argue, but something held her back. The young woman was looking at her as if she were nuts. She asked a middle-aged woman she met before joining Jack in the restaurant about the date, and the woman had answered the same as the clerk. She asked an old man waiting to be seated for dinner, a young man with a guitar slung over his back. Everyone had said the same thing.

It was supposed to be March. She had been gone four days. That would make it March nineteenth.

Not September . . .

She held his wrist, pulling him away from the base of the Sphinx, and led him through the main doors. Left was hotel check in. Jack started to head for the vast atrium of the pyramid and the escalator.

"What is this place?" he asked in a hushed tone.

She smiled. "I know it's extravagant, but it's a hotel. Come on, I'll take you up to the second floor before we find Bryan. You'll get the best view from there."

She forgot her own worries when she encouraged him onto the escalator and held his hand as they rose to the second floor. There they found themselves at the tall models of skyscrapers, towering ten to fifteen stories high. They were bathed in colored floodlighting, adding to the surreal ambiance, and Jack was nearly overwhelmed.

"Let's go find Bryan," Mairie said. "You can come back later and look at it for as long as you want." It was like an adult Disney World exhibit, and she more than understood his awe, yet she had to connect with her brother and solve this mystery.

"Mairie . . ." Jack's voice was a mere whisper as he viewed the interior of the hotel. "I have never seen anything like this. It . . . it's unbelievable."

She managed to smile. "Yes," she said, looking around at the overstated splendor as they rode the escalator down to the lobby. Walking to the registration desk, she added as they stood in line, "It is spectacular. Even for someone from this time, this is something to behold. Come now," she added, tapping his arm. "It's our turn."

They walked up to the front desk and Mairie said,

"I'd like to speak with Bryan Malloy. He's my brother."

"Certainly, one moment, I'll be happy to check for you," the pleasant-faced clerk answered, and immediately began searching his computer. "You said Malloy . . . Bryan Malloy. Not Mallory?"

"Malloy," Mairie repeated, and spelled it.

After a minute the man looked up at her and said, "I'm terribly sorry. We don't have anyone registered by that name."

"You must," she answered, leaning onto the counter as if she could look into the computer. "Check again. Please . . ."

The clerk began pushing buttons on the keyboard, checking again. "No, I'm sorry. We have no one here under the name of Malloy."

"Check Mairie Callahan, please," she asked in a low voice. She spelled her first name and waited as the clerk ran through the records.

"Again, I'm sorry. I find no Mairie Callahan registered, either."

"Can you look up when they were here? Do you have that information?"

The clerk gave her a suspicious look and asked, "Would you care to speak with our office manager? I'm not privileged to give out that information, but you can put in a request." Picking up a phone the clerk continued, "Let me get the manager for you."

Mairie stepped away from the counter. "No, that's all right. Thank you anyway. Come on, Jack."

"Where are we going, Mairie? Why isn't your brother here?" he asked, as she led him back into the lobby.

"I'm not sure," she answered, looking around the area. Spying what she needed, she murmured, "Come on. I need to make a call."

He followed her while asking, "A call. You need to stop at . . . a rest facility again?"

She was so worried she couldn't even smile at his innocence. "No. I need to make a telephone call. Remember? I told you about them."

"You'll call your brother through the sky and he's going to hear you?"

She could tell he was frustrated by his lack of knowledge and realized that for a man like Jack Delaney, feeling insecure was not a familiar experience.

"Here, sit next to me and watch. I can't explain everything right now, but something's happened to the date. It's not the same as when I left four days ago. Seven months appear to have passed, and Bryan is no longer here in Las Vegas. My things are gone with him. I have nothing—"

"Mairie, we have money. A fortune."

She managed to smile as he sat down next to her at the telephone booth. "Jack, in this time seventy-five hundred dollars is not a fortune. A gallon of milk costs over two dollars. Everything is very expensive."

"It does not!" His shocked expression was comical. "Why don't people just buy cows? You could get a decent milking cow for—"

"Jack," Mairie interrupted. "We aren't in your time. Seventy-five hundred dollars won't last long, especially in this town. Besides, I *have* to find my brother. I'm going to call his friend back in Philadelphia. If anyone knows where Bryan is, Marc will."

She picked up the phone and began dialing. "You see, Bryan and Marc were partners for six years, until Bryan got cancer. Then he took off and Marc was brokenhearted." She turned toward the wall. "Yes, operator, I'd like to place this collect from Mairie." Turning back to Jack she continued, "I know Bryan would have been devastated when I disappeared and would have called Marc for solace—"

"Go ahead," the operator broke in.

"Hello? Marc . . . ?"

"Mairie? Is that really you?" Marc sounded disbelieving.

"Yes, it's me. Where's Bryan? I'm in—"

"I don't want to know where you are," Marc interrupted. "Listen to me, Mairie . . ."

She was stunned by his words and stared at the wall in front of her as she tried to make sense out of what he was saying.

"Don't ask questions. Hang up quickly and call the place where we used to spend Friday nights. Give me fifteen minutes and then call. Do you understand?"

"Is Bryan all right?" She had to ask that.

"Yes. Now, give me fifteen minutes and then call. You understand where I'm asking you to call?"

"Yes," she whispered. "I understand, but—"

She heard a click and then a dial tone.

"Now, what's this about?" she mumbled, hanging up the receiver.

"What happened, Mairie? Did you locate your brother?" Jack leaned toward her with a concerned expression.

She shrugged. "I don't know what happened," she said, and looked back at the phone. "He was acting strange . . . very strange."

"Your brother?"

"Marc. His friend. He just told me to call an old bar we used to hang out at when we were all in college. It's the last place all three of us went to before Bryan and I took off. I'm supposed to call him back in fifteen minutes." She looked at Jack and added in a worried voice, "Something's happened, and I don't think it's good. I mean, how could seven months have gone by in four days? Something's weird . . ."

Her words trailed off as another conversation played out in her head.

"What, Mairie?" Jack asked. "What are you thinking?"

"Right before I left the East Coast, I was at a department store buying makeup and the saleswoman was talking to another worker and laughing. She was saying something about a television show she'd been watching, something about how if we traveled at the speed of light, we wouldn't age, at least we'd age so slowly that Lancome would be out of business. That the people on earth age, but those traveling wouldn't."

She looked at Jack and exhaled. "At the time I thought how odd for a makeup clerk in the mall to be discussing Einstein's Theory of Relativity, but what if that happened to me, to us? Only in reverse, into the past? Suppose whatever that government test was about had to do with the speed of light, with traveling through time at the speed of light? I felt something when I jumped, some unexplainable energy, almost like a shock—"

"There was a light after I jumped, and that's when I lost consciousness." Jack was reaching out for her hand.

Mairie was on brain overload. "Listen, Jack . . . we have to leave here. I don't know exactly what's happening, but Marc sounded worried. *More* than worried. I think we should walk out of here right now and find someplace else to spend the night. Marc wanted me off the phone quickly, as if he thought the call might be traced."

"Mairie, what are you saying? I'm trying to follow you . . . *tele-vision*, tracing calls in the sky . . . I just don't understand."

She stood up. "I know you don't. Let's get out of here," she said, looking around. Every person who passed her now seemed suspicious. "I promise to explain later."

They walked out of the Luxor Hotel and down the

street to another hotel casino. She checked in and paid cash, saying she didn't have a credit card for a house charge. Holding Jack's hand as they rode the elevator to the fourteenth floor, Mairie smiled at him reassuringly.

"It's okay, Jack. Elevators travel at this speed all the time. Nothing to be concerned about. As soon as I get into the room, I have to call information and get the number of Fat Tuesdays, the bar in Philly. You can rest while I speak with Marc."

He looked sideways at her. "And then you'll explain everything?"

She sighed as the doors opened and once more frightened Jack. He would have to get used to automatic doors, she thought. He had so much to integrate, and she was one confused teacher right now. "Yes, I'll explain everything, at least as much as I understand."

He walked next to her down the long hallway in silence. Mairie stopped before a room and inserted the keycard.

"That opens the door?" Jack asked. "You don't use keys?"

"We still use keys," she said, waiting for the tiny green light to appear. "Only certain doors take these. It goes through a computer." The door lock clicked and she opened it. Turning back to him with an affectionate look, she added, "And don't ask me to explain computers. I only sell them. Marc is the computer genius. He can explain them to you."

"I won't ask, Mairie," he said, following her into the room. "I know you're worried right now about your brother. Contact his friend."

She smiled and turned on the light. A bedroom with two queen-sized beds was illuminated. It was an above standard room, with a huge bathroom, Jacuzzi tub included. She was satisfied and threw her purse onto one bed. Sitting on the edge of the bed by the nightstand, she picked up the phone and dialed long distance assistance. She wrote down the number and called out to Jack, "Hey, where are you?"

Jack walked around the wall and watched her finish writing. "I have never seen a convenience of such magnificence. Marble and brass and a huge tub. The future is incredible, Mairie."

She smiled and silently wondered what future she had returned to.

"Are you sure these accommodations are suitable?" he asked with a concerned expression as he looked at the two beds. "Perhaps I should get a room of my own and not jeopardize your reputation?"

Mairie wanted to hug him. "Jack, it's fine. Really. My reputation won't suffer. Besides, I don't want to worry about you. Just let me call Marc and then I'll try and explain everything to you."

Picking up the receiver again, Mairie dialed the number of the bar and waited.

When she finally heard Marc's voice, she felt some of the tension ease from her body. "Now . . . tell me how Bryan is and what the hell this mystery is about."

"Oh, Mairie . . . thank God you are all right. You *are* all right, aren't you?"

"Yes, I'm all right. At least I think I am, but what's happened, Marc? Why isn't Bryan here in Vegas? Tell me how he's doing and tell me the date, because I think I just lost seven months."

She exhaled a long sigh and her chest tightened with apprehension as she waited.

"Bryan is out of remission, Mairie. Started four months ago. He had another bone-marrow transplant, but only time will tell."

"Oh, no . . ." Mairie felt the weight of sorrow descend upon her body. "Where is he? With you?"

"Yes. The fool thought just because he walked out on me to become Indiana Jones that I wouldn't speak to him. Of course he's with me. It's not that bad yet, Mairie. I know the news of you will be exactly what he needs."

"Oh Marc, tell him gently. I will be there as soon as I can. I just have—"

"You can't come, Mairie," he interrupted with that same guarded voice. "At least, I don't think you should until we talk about it. Some . . . some strange things have happened since your disappearance. Too long to go into here, but I think the government is looking for you. You weren't involved in some drug deal, were you?"

"Of course not," she said in her defense. "I know what happened. It was all a mistake, and—"

"I told Bryan that," Marc quickly interjected. "I said our Mairie is far too intelligent to get messed up with that crap, unless there was a dark, mysterious Italian who promised to ravish every inch of her body and—"

"He's not Italian," Mairie interrupted him, shaking her head at Marc's motherly personality and looking at Jack who was staring out the window.

"I *knew* there was a man involved."

"Let's get back to why I can't come see my brother."

"There have been some very . . . suspicious types asking questions. I'm talking Tommy Lee Jones in *The Fugitive* kind of suspicious. Very butch. The kind that seem so driven only the government would want them. Bryan said it was the same in Vegas before he returned. He stayed there as long as he could, Mairie. He hasn't given up hope."

"I knew he wouldn't," she whispered with a sad smile. "Marc, what am I going to do? I have to get my life back. I need to get to Philadelphia as soon as possible. Maybe I should go to the authorities and just clear this whole—"

"I don't think you should announce to anyone you're here. Especially in Vegas. I think you should dye your hair, cut it, and get a whole new identity. They're watching our apartment. Our phones have been tapped. The investigation of your disappearance is extensive, Mairie. The brutes even audited my bank account. Then had the audacity to call my employers insinuating I was in trouble with the government. I still haven't lived that down."

"Oh, Marc, I'm sorry. I . . . I don't know why any of this has happened. It makes me so angry. I was caught up in a military test when I skydived. I think, no I know, it has something to do with time."

"Time? Like on a Rolex? That kind of time?"

Mairie grinned. "Well, I imagine for what the government is spending on this project, every second would have to be Rolex expensive." Her eyes widened. "And it's secret, Marc, top secret. None of us are supposed to know about this testing. Go figure. We're paying billions for this kind of stuff, and it's just another thing they don't want us to know about!"

There was a pause after she finished speaking.

"Ahh, Mairie . . . how would you know any of this? Secret government projects? This is too James Bond. Completely out of vogue, since the Iron Curtain came down. Nobody's doing Bond anymore, dear."

"Oh, Marc," she said, trying to keep the irritation out of her voice. "Will you please forget movies for a minute and listen to me? I know what I'm talking about. Remember me saying I lost seven months? What's that? *Time.* Something is happening."

She waited for Marc to contemplate her thoughts.

"Well, Mairie, I have to admit, my time clock is speeding away. This ol' bod ain't what it used to be, that's for sure. But even the college interns at the company have mentioned time seems to be speeding up. It's not just the old folks anymore. Anyway, let the government keep it a secret. I really don't think I want to understand—"

"Me, either," Mairie said, though something was beginning to stir in the recesses of her brain. It was too bizarre to think about now. Later, when she had time, she'd think about it. She almost laughed out loud at her last thought.

"Marc, did Bryan bring back my things, my purse?"

"Yes. He had a bitch of a time gathering it all back from the authorities. They had confiscated it." He paused. "Do you think it's wise to use your identification now?"

"Talk about James Bond. This is crazy. Are we being paranoid, or what? I can't use my own license and credit cards because the government will hunt me down? What the hell am I supposed to do?"

Silence.

"Marc . . . ? Are you still there?"

"I know how sensitive you are, so you better be sitting down, child."

She sighed with relief. Paranoia. Calm yourself, she thought. "I am sitting."

"You know how Bryan's insurance company is fighting him on his medical bills and cutting back payment on his prescription drugs?"

"Yes, but Marc, speak up, I can barely hear you."

"Speak up? Woman, I am in the middle of a crowded bar. Put a finger in your ear and one over your mouth," he advised in a mock serious voice. "Not the same hand of course, unless you're double-jointed, in which case the man who isn't Italian must be drooling. But darling, you can tell me all about him later. Just *listen*, and if you ever repeat this, I will never french-braid your hair again. Plus I will tell everyone, including your mystery man, you had a crush on John Belushi."

In spite of everything, Mairie giggled. "He made me laugh," she protested.

"Aha . . . had nothing to do with that incredible physique or—"

"Stop," Mairie interrupted, before he could go on with his droll sarcasm and divert her attention again. "Tell me what you don't want me to know."

"Well, I needed to get some fast cash for Bryan's medicine. So I helped out some immigrants for this friend of mine and I got them fake birth certificates, social security numbers. I hacked my way into the mainframe at Harrisburg and another *friend* in the Capitol took care of the rest. I could get you a birth certificate and license in three days and FedEx them out to you." He took a deep breath. "And Mairie, if you tell anyone this, I'll take out a full-page photo ad in the *Times* of you at Cape May in that hideous lime green bikini."

"You can do this, Marc . . . ?"

"The ad?"

She laughed. "No. The fake IDs."

"They are not fake. At least, they are on *record* as being real. The social security card will take at least a week. And yes, I can get you them. I only did it the one time, but I know the right people now. I never thought I'd do it again. Look, Mairie, this was for the parents of children. They came to this country for freedom, got jobs, paid taxes, and they were going to be deported. Kids, and all. It wasn't fair, and they had no idea about the legal system here. By the time my friend contacted me, they had to hide until they could leave and start over in another city. I'm not proud of what I did, but—"

"Marc, say no more. You're a good person, and I love you. So, yes . . . what could it hurt? Get me another ID until I figure out what's happening. I need to get to Bryan as soon as possible. Can you FedEx it overnight to this address?"

"I'll have to contact my friend at the Capitol. Also, you'll have to give up Callahan. Do you mind?"

"It wasn't the name I was born with. I should have had my name switched back to my maiden name anyway."

"You can't use your maiden name."

"I know . . . use . . . use . . ." She looked to the window. "Use Delaney. Mary Delaney. Spell Mary with a 'y.' "

"Don't tell me . . . the one who isn't Italian is a leprechaun?"

She laughed as Jack turned away from the window and looked at her. Cupping her hand over the receiver, she whispered, "Do you mind? It seems I need a new last name."

His smile of sympathy touched her heart.

"I do love you, Marc. Even more now that I know your many talents. Who would have thought, huh? Talk about still waters running deep."

"I have never been still, my love. You have. You're just catching up."

"Well, if you want to hear something really deep, listen to this. I need two IDs. One for me, and . . ." She looked at Jack and tried not to laugh. "And one for the leprechaun. He's coming with me."

"Hmm . . . I wouldn't miss this for the world. Mairie, Mairie . . . quite contrary, how *does* your garden grow? You *do* have a lot to tell me . . . I want to know every detail of your new fellow . . . one of the wee folk. Heavens, I hope *that's* not true."

Mairie laughed and asked Jack his birthday. They might be lost in time again, but at least in this time there was Marc. Comic relief.

She could certainly use it.

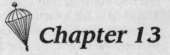

Chapter 13

"Oh, Mairie . . . I must insist!"

He stood at the side of the magnificent tub and pointed to it. "First, you bathe, and then I will. I wouldn't think of asking you to bathe after me!"

She stood with her sunburned hands clutching her hips. Her chin tilted up in defense, and her eyes flashed with intelligence. Jack knew she wasn't about to surrender easily, and he prepared himself for the interaction.

He'd done this before, he thought, while gathering whatever shred of strength remained.

"You won't bathe and leave your water, Jack. There's a drain. I'll have fresh water. Just do it, all right? This perfect gentleman attitude is admirable, and I appreciate it, but let's be real here, okay? You were injured in saving my life. I can never repay the saving part, but I can assist in the healing. The Jacuzzi will ease your muscles, your pain, and you'll recover faster. We both need to regain our strength for whatever follows now. And I haven't got a clue what that might be. I'm just playing this moment by moment . . . and the reality of this moment is shouting at me that you get in this tub and hurry up and heal. There's a time for courtly gestures and there's a time for practicality. Got it?"

She really was spectacular when she became pas-

227

sionate about something. His mind couldn't help but picture her the last time they had kissed . . . the way she had come to him and took as much as she gave. Maybe it wasn't such a good thing after all to argue with her. Feeling his body respond so easily, he thought he might concede the practicality of the situation after all.

This could get embarrassing.

"Fine. I shall bathe before you, but I want you to know that under any other condition I would—"

"Oh, get real, Jack," she said, slapping his arm as she walked from the room. "I'll get you a robe. Good thing this hotel provides them."

He was stopped short as he stared after her. It was the oddest thing. When she'd cut off his little speech, he had the ridiculous sensation of great friendship. It was an intense feeling, almost like brotherhood. But she was a woman . . . this partnership, as she called it, was causing some very unusual thinking. As he waited for her to bring the robe, he realized he had never before felt that height of friendship with a woman. He had felt it as a young boy with his Paiute brother, Hidden Feather, as they grew up and shared adventures, hopes, and dreams. During the war he had experienced that degree of closeness with three remarkable men, all dead now. Four males that he had trusted with everything, even his life. And now to feel that with a woman, along with everything else she brought into his life, Jack almost felt dizzy with the realization.

"Here," Mairie said, startling him.

He reached for the thick white robe. "Thank you." He was almost afraid to look her in the eye, afraid of what she might see.

"We're going to need to buy clothes tomorrow. We can't keep wearing these."

He looked down to his trousers and raised his gaze to her.

Their vision met and locked for a few seconds. It was as if she were touching him. He *felt* her, like an exciting wave of sensuous intensity washing over him. It was mesmerizing and Jack forced himself to blink, to end it. His hand clutched the robe in his fist.

"I trust you . . . to know best. Shopping in the morning it is."

He heard her inhale, sucking in breath between her teeth.

"Do you know what size you are?" she asked, coming closer and running her hand over his shoulder. "Forty-four long, maybe?"

"Forty-four?" he replied, though how he could even think with her hands on him was a minor miracle. Lord, what this woman did to his senses. "I . . . I'm not sure."

"You look like a forty-four," she said, sizing him up, and Jack found himself standing straighter.

"Waist . . . ? Hmm . . . I'd say a thirty-four."

He couldn't think, not with her close proximity. That had to be the reason he took her hands and placed them at his waist. Smiling down at her, he said, "Well, do you think you're right?"

She didn't answer.

They stared at each other for what seemed like minutes. Her hands stayed at his waist while he gently pushed her hair behind her shoulders. It was almost tangible, the current that was heating up the space between them, and Jack sighed with regret. Now was not the time. They were both exhausted. If and when he made Mairie Callahan his, he wanted it to be perfect. She deserved better than this.

"Right . . . well, you remember how to operate the tub?" she asked, recovering quickly as she dropped her hands, though he sensed she was embarrassed.

"Yes, I remember." He smiled at her.

She ignored him. "Okay. Push that button to start it. It's timed for fifteen minutes. If you want more, push it again. Then push the button marked stop to end it. Got that?"

Jack continued to smile. "I remember," he repeated.

"Good. Okay, then. Enjoy yourself." She closed the door.

He laid the robe on the seat of the indoor pot with the remarkable handle. To bring water up fourteen stories with such speed still amazed him. So many new discoveries, he thought as he undressed. Like Mairie . . .

He put off thinking about her until he was inclining in the huge tub. Sighing as the hot water entered his pores, Jack felt his muscles ease slightly. He concentrated on the sensation for a few minutes, not thinking at all, just focusing on the pleasure and pain within him. Finally, he reached out and pressed the button Mairie had shown him earlier.

Holding his breath in anticipation, not knowing what it would feel like, he prepared himself for another taste of the future. The water immediately came alive, bubbling around him like an overactive artesian pool. It was immensely enjoyable.

Resting his head against the back of the tub, Jack exhaled with pleasure.

Now . . . now he could think.

He had read about it from the great poets. He'd heard songs praising it, but he'd never felt it before. How could he understand something he had never experienced? This was new territory for him. All he could do was listen to the words of those who had gone before him. And trust himself. And Mairie. Under the most challenging circumstances, she had conducted herself as well as any man. Better than most.

Jack grinned when he thought she might take that compliment as an insult. Still, he trusted her with his life, felt a deep affection and intimacy whenever he was near her. Plus, he wanted her. Damn, he

wanted her so much right now that he was shocked
his abused body could respond to the admission.

"Damn . . ." he muttered and pushed his hair back
off his forehead. Sweat ran off him, as though taking
his desire and his pain along with it. What was this?
What was happening? Was this it, what he had only
thought of as a gift for a special few?

Was this love?

Was he falling in love with Mairie . . . his gift?

He would have to be careful. Not scare her away.
Patience, he told himself. It would be unfair to push
his cause when her world had just turned threatening. She had to reach her brother and he was committed to helping her achieve that.

And what could he offer her anyway? He was
a . . .

He remembered Mairie's words when she was
desolate in the Indian camp. How they fit him now.

He was a stranger in a strange land.

Mairie stood in front of the window and looked
out to the brilliant lights. It was quite a view and
she imagined Jack standing here while she was
speaking with Marc on the phone. What had he
thought? Was it like she felt when she'd first seen
Star Wars? This had to be like science fiction to Jack.
She pictured him, standing by the tub, staring into
her eyes. What the hell was that about? Remembering how she fought so hard within herself not to
move toward him, to feel his body against hers,
Mairie sighed.

She'd have to be more careful.

Maybe she was in love with the man, but she
couldn't afford to indulge in it or let it show. Now
she had to concentrate on whatever was happening
around her. Had she put everyone in jeopardy? Now
it wasn't just Jack. It was Bryan and Marc.

She wondered again if Harmon had also made it

back, but how could he have? Jack had said her horse was shot about twenty minutes before he jumped. Harmon couldn't have made it back to the desert floor that quickly. He had to be stuck in the past. He had said that was it, the only shot at returning to 1999. He couldn't be back here.

She wondered why the government was still tapping Marc's phone. Did they expect her? Did they know that two people made it? A part of her marveled that her mind was thinking such thoughts at all. She never even gave much thought to government. It was like an absentee parent, only there in an emergency. She realized she was part of the Silent Majority that didn't really question, and now her mind was full of questions.

Like what did they want with her? She decided that she wouldn't dye and cut her hair; she'd buy a wig. She wasn't about to do anything so drastic until she was sure Marc knew what he was talking about. Since she didn't really know if Harmon had made it back, she figured she'd leave it up to Jack if he wanted to alter his appearance.

She would hate to see him cut that hair, she thought, and grimaced as those betraying thoughts of him in the Jacuzzi flashed through her mind. Long, dark, wet hair, sweat dripping from his muscles . . .

She actually shook herself and turned away from the window.

Stop it, she told herself, and walked over to the tall armoire. Opening it, she saw it contained exactly what she wanted and picked up the remote control. She jammed her thumb on the power button and sat on the edge of the bed while watching *Third Rock from the Sun*.

How appropriate, this mindless diversion.

Still, she could hear the sound of the Jacuzzi and the mental picture of Jack Delaney fought for her attention.

She had to let the TV aliens win this one.

As he stepped out of the bathroom, Mairie muted the volume and stood up. "How do you feel?"

"Much better. It really does help, thank you."

She refrained from saying I told you so again. Better to let that one go, she figured, and just take her bath. Picking up her robe from the other bed, she said, "Well, my turn."

He stood, hair slicked back behind his ears and shoulders, clad only in that white robe. Mairie suppressed a groan as he said, "Please, before you leave . . . would you explain what you are watching?" He walked closer to the TV and stared. "What is it?"

"Television," she said in a dull voice. "Like a bunch of still pictures put together and captured by a camera that inverts them, sends them one frame by one frame out to the air, and a signal in this box picks them up and shows it to us as completed picture. There. That's the best I can explain." She walked passed him and grabbed the remote laying on the bedspread.

"Here," she said, slapping it onto his hand. "Use this. Read the words. Channel means finding another picture, another story. Go have fun, I'm going to take my bath."

She didn't mean to be rude or impatient.

She just needed a bath. A *cool* bath.

Her body was inflamed, and she couldn't blame it entirely on her sunburn.

Thirty minutes later, Mairie emerged from the bathroom prepared for another round of twenty questions concerning technology. Instead, she found Jack asleep on the bed, with two pillows propped behind his head. She slowly walked over to him and slipped the remote from his fingers. Holding it over her shoulder, she pointed it at the television and silenced a commercial about an automobile dealership.

Smiling, she placed the remote on the night table

and turned off the light above him. She had left the drapes open so the lights from the casinos dimly filled the room. Jack looked so peaceful sleeping. What a first day he'd had in the future, and he hadn't freaked out once. He was quite a man, she thought. Couldn't have picked a better partner for this bizarre adventure. Even Bryan, she admitted, wouldn't have handled it better.

She admired Jack's strength, his courage.

Reaching out, she lifted a strand of hair off his forehead.

He stirred in his sleep at her touch, emitting a tiny moan, and Mairie withdrew her fingers. She didn't want to wake him. Let him rest, she thought. Tomorrow he'll need it.

Grinning, she turned to her bed and sat down. She towel-dried her hair and threw the damp towel to the rug before pulling down the bedspread. Wearing only the robe, she placed a clean towel on the pillow and finally slipped in between the sheets.

A moan of pleasure escaped her lips as she glanced at Jack to see if he had heard. His breathing remained steady. Letting out her own breath, Mairie looked around the modern room and once more smiled. How heavenly this felt . . .

She was home.

Almost.

He awakened with the sun and stared around him for a few seconds before coming to full alertness. It wasn't a fantastic dream. He really *did* travel to the future. His body was still sore, yet much better, he thought as he stretched. His attention was captured by the woman asleep in the next bed, and he turned his head. Her hair was spread out on the pillow like a dark silky fan. Her face was peaceful, her mouth slightly open as even her jaw relaxed.

He smiled. She certainly was a woman who liked

to voice her mind. He propped himself on his elbow to see her better. Jack's own mouth dropped open as he saw that the top of her robe was gaping, almost exposing her breasts.

He knew he should turn away. A friend, a partner, would allow privacy.

A potential lover would feel the yearning in every fiber of his being.

There could be no doubt that he wanted to consider himself a potential lover as his body instinctively reacted to the tantalizing picture she presented. What would she do, he wondered, if he stroked her hair to awaken her? Would she jump in fright at the intrusion? Or would she melt against him, as she had done at the stream? He had no more time to wonder, as she sighed deeply and turned on her side away from him.

Grateful that she had made the decision easy, Jack looked around the room and again saw the magic box in the dresser. What a fascinating invention. He must remember to ask Mairie about the scantily clad women he had seen displayed on the story about this hotel. The box spoke to him and had invited him to come to the show. Did one refuse such an invitation? He certainly didn't want to, yet he couldn't imagine asking Mairie to attend such an entertainment.

Glancing once more at her sleeping back, Jack reached for the thin black control device and pressed the red power button. Instantly the box became alive with color and movement. He couldn't hear anything this time and thought it was a good thing, since Mairie was sleeping. He didn't want to wake her up just yet. She needed her rest, and besides, he wanted to see if he could find the hotel story again.

Of course, only to be sure his facts were correct before he asked Mairie to explain . . . even he knew that was merely an excuse. He had never seen women of such height and splendor as the ones with the extraordinary costumes.

He sat for over two hours, watching in silence. He found it very frustrating without sound to try and figure out what the people were saying. As if that wasn't difficult enough, when he changed stories he came to one that appeared to be a fast drawing come to life. He knew from focusing that the black duck was speaking to the rabbit. Strange. Very strange . . . stories of animals who spoke to each other and seemed to be in some sort of competition. Then there was the odd-looking bird racing away from a sad-looking coyote. He decided he liked the coyote better than the bird that never flew, and secretly wished the coyote would finally catch it. Instead, he fell over a cliff with a look of desperation and crashed to the ground.

Very sad indeed. He couldn't help but consider that could have been the ending to his own story, had he not trusted in something, anything, beyond himself. He had to have had *hope*.

"What are you watching?"

Startled, Jack shrugged. "I don't know. It's all very strange."

"Cartoons," Mairie whispered, and stretched as she turned to him.

She was smiling so sweetly that Jack's heart melted once again, watching her adjust her robe and sit up. She had the look of a woman well rested, with her hair covering her shoulders like a dark cape. She looked . . . content.

"Will you explain why the coyote never captures the strange bird?"

She giggled and shoved another pillow behind her head. "Because if the coyote captured the road runner, the story would be over."

"Why does he always have to get hurt? He gets hurt a hell of a lot, but he always comes back."

Laughing, she ran her fingers through her hair. "It's supposed to be funny, provide humor."

"I see." Though he didn't. "I noticed there are many shorter stories, about all sorts of things . . . especially food. I couldn't hear them, but the food looked most delicious, almost as though I could reach out and take it."

She picked up the telephone device she had used last night.

"Hungry? Let's order room service. What would you like? Eggs? Bacon? Ham?"

He looked around the room. "Here? They will bring it here? Up fourteen floors? Oh yes . . . the elevator." The pride he felt in remembering was quickly replaced by the gnawing in his belly.

"Yes. I just have to tell them what we want. Would you like to read a menu?"

Shaking his head, he said, "I have no need. Eggs and ham would be wonderful. And coffee . . . if possible."

"It's possible," she said, and touched several buttons before speaking into the phone.

He heard her order breakfast for two and then she replaced the handle and sat back. "Well, our first full day. What shall we do while we wait for Marc to send us our new identities? Shopping for clothes is a must. Would you like to see the city?"

"Yes. And I received an invitation last night I would like to discuss with you."

She narrowed her expression. "An invitation? From whom?"

He pointed to the television. "From there. They spoke to me and asked me to join them at a cabaret show. I don't know that you would enjoy it, Mairie."

She seemed to stare at him for a few seconds and then she laughed. "Oh, Jack . . . that was a commercial. They weren't talking to *you*, well they were, but they were talking to whomever was watching. It was like a group invitation. You can't take anything seriously that comes out of that box. It's for entertainment."

She threw the cover to the foot of the bed and

swung her legs over the side of it. "We can go, if you want. Maybe tonight."

It was the first time he had seen her bare legs, and he had to force himself to answer. "I didn't think you would be comfortable going into . . . into a saloon."

She giggled and rose from the bed. "And what do you think we were in last night when you won the money? It was a saloon, a bar. This is just bigger and has a show to entertain. This whole town, Jack, is about entertaining . . . while you gamble away your money."

"I'm not going to gamble anymore. We won because it was Virginia's silver dollar."

"It was Harmon's before she got it," Mairie said, walking toward the convenience. "Turns out the man was useful after all, huh? But I'm glad to hear you aren't a gambler."

She closed the door and Jack was left staring at the television. He must remember that the voices were not really speaking to him alone. He felt naive, and wasn't pleased. He would study everything, until he could be of more help to Mairie. And then he would find out if he could go back. He wasn't sure any longer where he belonged. The past, or the future. Maybe Mairie was right . . . don't try and figure it all out, just live in the moment and deal with whatever happens.

Some minutes later, a knock at the door interrupted his thoughts and he rose from the bed to answer it. Tightening his belt around his waist, he stood and asked, "Who is it?"

"Room service."

There was a tiny hole in the door he hadn't noticed last night, and he peeked through it. Startled by the young man's face so close, Jack almost jumped back in shock. Taking a deep breath, he squared his shoulders and opened the door.

"Morning, sir," the uniformed waiter said, as he pushed a cart draped with a tablecloth, and holding covered dishes, coffee cups, a pitcher of juice, and a vase with a single flower.

"Ahh . . . morning," Jack mumbled, speaking in his first *normal* encounter with a man from the future. The aroma of coffee filled his senses and his stomach growled as the waiter arranged the table and uncovered the dishes.

"That will be twenty-four seventy-five, sir. You've declined a room charge, so everything will be on a cash basis." He stood, waiting for his money.

"Twenty-four dollars? For breakfast?" Mairie had said everything was expensive, but this . . . this was robbery!

She came out of the convenience just as he was about to argue the outrageous price.

"I'll get it," she said with a smile to the waiter, and walked past them to her purse.

She took out thirty dollars and handed it over. "Thank you," she murmured, looking at the table. "Everything seems fine."

"Thank you, madam," the waiter said, and headed for the door.

"Is he coming back with your change?" Jack asked, as the door closed behind the man. He was glad to see the back of that . . . that robber, who had happened to take a peek at Mairie's derriere when she'd bent over to pick up her purse. "He had better return with your money, Mairie, or I'll—"

"Calm down," she interrupted. Mairie pulled a chair from a nearby table and patted it. "Here. Sit down and have your breakfast." Sitting on the edge of the bed, she inhaled the aroma coming from her plate. "The change was his tip."

"You gave that man a tip, after he's getting twenty-four dollars for a meal that should cost fifty cents?"

Looking up at him, she grinned. "Jack, this isn't your time. Everything is more expensive, and in a hotel it's twice as expensive. He's not getting the money. The hotel is. He's paid a very small amount and his real wages are from the tips the guests give him. I know it seems like a lot of money, but it isn't, for this situation. Wait till you see how expensive clothes are." She waved her hand at him. "Come on, let's not talk about money right now. Let's eat and get ready to go out. We should be able to find more reasonable stores than the ones in the hotel. Want to go to a mall?"

Still trying to mentally answer her string of statements, he figured he'd reply when he was seated. He picked up the cloth napkin. Placing it on his knee, as he had been taught all those many years ago, he stared at his food, the fluffy yellow eggs, the glazed slices of ham, the browned potatoes, and he thought twenty-four dollars might be extravagant, but he was going to enjoy every morsel.

"What's a mall?" he asked, right before he tasted the eggs.

She was pouring them both coffee, and Jack had to admit he liked the domesticity.

"Shops. Probably more than you've ever seen in one place. Just wait . . ."

Three hours later, Mairie dragged him away from a window showing a display of leather pants and platform shoes. "Come along, Jack. You don't want that."

"I don't want it. I'm wondering how anyone could walk in those shoes."

She giggled. "I had them about twenty years ago. Men and women wore them, and now they're back in style." She knew they made a sight, walking through the mall. A handsome cowboy in filthy clothes, and her in leggings and a cropped top. Still, she wasn't above noticing that even in filthy clothes, Jack Delaney attracted attention. Mainly from females.

"Here," she said, spying the store she wanted. "We'll find something in this place."

They walked into the Gap.

An hour later they walked out, dressed in brand new jeans and light cotton sweaters over colored T-shirts. They carried packages of shirts and cotton slacks for them both. They even purchased light-weight jackets. Mairie had a wonderful time suggesting clothes for Jack, though she'd had to steer him away from the more western shirts. She reminded him they were going east and wanted to blend in there. Plus, to be honest, she was dying to see him in something modern. When he'd come out of the dressing room in jeans, his cowboy boots and a natural cream colored sweater, she'd felt that attraction heighten.

Teacher, she reminded herself.

Teacher.

Who wanted to be a teacher? They never seemed to have fun.

Shaking her head to dislodge the silly thoughts, Mairie said, "Okay, now we need to take care of something *really* important."

"Undergarments?"

She laughed. "Yeah, that too. But first . . ." She grabbed his hand with great affection and led him forward.

Already her tastebuds were activating as she walked up to the counter and breathed, "Haagen-Dazs, Jack. When's the last time you had ice cream?"

"Not since I was on the East Coast. It was a rare luxury."

"Well, here you have a decision to make. You want an ice cream cone? Mmm . . . sugar cones! Or, would you like a sundae? Normally I wouldn't try to influence a person's choice of ice cream, but I can say that if you haven't had ice cream very often, forget the cone. You've already had that experience.

Try the sundae. You won't forget your first sundae."

She looked to the vats of ice cream through the glass case and grinned in remembrance. "It's kinda glorious, and ... and ... well, I don't want to give you any more suggestions."

He smiled down to her. "Then I shall have a sundae."

She watched him begin to salivate as his eyes widened at the exotic abundance of ice cream. "I know I said I didn't want to give you any more suggestions, but I have to offer this one. Don't let your eyes be bigger than your stomach."

He turned and looked at her, as if shocked. "My parents used to say that to me all the time."

"Mine too," Mairie said, feeling that pulling sensation again.

"How strange to hear it from you."

"Some things have survived, Jack. Not everything will be different."

He temporarily lost his interest in ice cream as others came up to the counter and ordered their preferences. "Tell me what has survived. Beyond buildings ... what has survived?"

It was a deep question to be asked in the middle of a mall, especially in front of Haagen-Dazs, and she shut off all thoughts except what to tell him. "I wish I could say that only the good survived, but that wouldn't be true. Generations have brought with them some of those same things you were dealing with in your time. Greed. Arrogance. That stuff we all wish would just go away, so everybody could be happy for a change. But there's a lot of good, too, Jack. Maybe you just have to look a little harder in this time, but you'll see it. You'll recognize it. I don't know that it could change."

He turned away from the counter and crossed his arms thoughtfully over his chest. "That's comforting to know. Yet I suppose it has been all around me.

See that mother and child? See the attention being given? That's the same as in my time, maybe through all time. And that man shaking his friend's hand. That appears the same. Look at the flowers in that cart. They haven't changed at all. Still beautiful." Smiling at her, he added, "I hope you are right, Mairie Callahan. I wish that basically, despite all our differences, people are the same. Don't you think they want the same things? Happiness. Peace. The right to live a life with both."

"I think all people have always wanted that." She wondered where he was going with this conversation.

"As someone who saw a different side of humanity in the war, I will take some time to think about your statements. You see, Mairie, that is one of the reasons I am exploring your time, this future, with you. When I thought about all I had left behind, I could only mourn the absence of my brothers. I had given up hope for civilization, for myself, and now to have you tell me that—"

His words were cut off as shots rang out across the mall. Mairie was so stunned she could only stare at Jack in amazement as he moved into action so quickly it seemed like one movement. Mairie felt him grab her and take her to the hard marble. One moment she was standing upright, listening to him, and in the next she was lying on the floor with Jack Delaney over her.

"What . . . what's going on?"

In a low serious voice, Jack said, "Turn over and move on your belly to that table behind you. Do it now. *Now!*"

Was Harmon back? Was he after them again?

She did as she was told. The shift in authority was swift and natural. Whatever was happening, Jack had more expertise, was better able to handle it successfully. He crawled on his stomach to her and they huddled under a dining table.

"Get down," he shouted at the young Hispanic girl who was peeking over the ice cream counter. Her head disappeared from view.

"What's going on, Jack? Can you see anything? Those were shots, weren't they?"

"Yes," he muttered. "They sounded different, more muffled, but they were definitely gun shots. Wait . . . don't move a muscle. He's running right at us."

Mairie's heart was slamming against her rib cage and she had to turn her head slightly to see a young boy zigzagging his way through the food court as security guards chased him. The boy was holding something in his left hand and a gun in his right as he leaped over chairs or pushed them out of his way. He was about twenty feet from them when Mairie saw Jack move. He placed his hand on the leg of the chair in front of him and she could see the veins in his hand stand out with the pressure of his grasp.

"Jack . . ."

Before she could say more, Jack slid the chair into the path of the kid and he went down like a bowling pin. Before he could scramble to his feet and run, a security guard tackled him and was soon joined by another. Mairie saw the gun being kicked away and Jack stand. He reached out his hand and helped her. Upright, she pulled down her sweater and stared at the scene before her. A crowd was gathering and she pulled on Jack's sleeve.

"I can't believe this. How could this happen now? Come on. We have to get away from here. We can't be witnesses."

He picked up the packages and joined her as they began to walk away. Both were breathing hard from the experience and they each jumped when they heard the voice.

"Hey, mister. Thanks. I'll give you free ice cream. Whatever you want."

Grinning at the young girl behind the counter,

Jack shook his head and muttered to Mairie, "Find me a sundae, Mairie Callahan. I'm about ready for a glorious experience."

"You got it," she answered, shaking her head as they mall-walked faster than the senior citizens. "Ahh, that was some of the not-so-good stuff we've still got around. Perfect time for an example, huh? Sheesh!"

"My glorious experience was postponed," he retorted, as he kept up her pace. "Not a perfect time. Maybe there isn't such a thing?"

She couldn't think of an answer, so she kept on walking while wondering if there was a Baskin-Robbins in the mall. She didn't care if they had to hire a cab. This man was going to have his sundae. He deserved it.

They sat at a table in a Baskin Robbins three miles away from the shooting. Jack was eyeing the sundae before him and Mairie was licking her rum raisin cone.

"This . . . you are right, Mairie. This is glorious!"

"Wait till you taste it," she said, licking the side of her cone to stop a drip. "Though I personally think you overdid it with everything on it . . . but that's just my opinion. I mean, four different flavors over a brownie over a banana, with carmel and hot fudge and pineapple syrups and nuts and cherries and whipped cream and—" She gulped. "I don't know how you can eat it."

"Oh, I can eat it," he said, sticking his spoon into the confection and taking a huge bite.

Mairie stopped licking, waiting for him to swallow.

"Well? How is it? Glorious . . . ?" There was an expression of bliss passing over his face.

He licked his lips in deep appreciation. "Divine is the closest I can come to it."

She grinned, glad that he was enjoying it so much.

"Yeah . . . a peak experience. Just remember the eye-mouth-belly wisdom."

"I will," he said, digging into it with relish.

Right, Mairie thought, as she sat down opposite him. It would be interesting to see how far he gets or if he finishes the entire thing. She looked around the clean ice cream shop and shuddered. She always shook after the fact. Or maybe it was the ice cream. Nope, she'd been scared. "How old do you think he was? Twelve?"

"I would say so. So young. He shouldn't carry a gun without having the responsibility." Jack licked the corner of his lip. "His father ought never to have let him have it."

"He shouldn't have had a gun. Period. His father probably doesn't even know." She didn't know how to explain this one to him. He thought 1877 was violent. How did one explain a society where children carry guns and kill? It was beyond her.

"You were very brave back there," she said, licking the creamy overflow around her cone. "Quick thinking, too." She wanted to change the subject and said the first thing that came to her. It was true, too. Jack Delaney was quite a man.

He was staring at her mouth and Mairie licked the corners of her lips, sure that she must have missed something.

Jack seemed to recover and said, "More like being in the right place at the right time with a chair leg in my hand. You know, this might be the best thing I have ever tasted, Mairie."

Since she had just done it, she recognized when the subject was changed again.

Yes . . . Jack Delaney was quite a man.

Visions of a prim and proper teacher were nowhere within her mind.

She buried her lips into the ice cream and tasted it deeply. So what if it was oral gratification? She needed something.

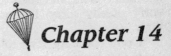 *Chapter 14*

"Here," she said, holding out her hand. "Take it."

She watched him react like a twelve-year-old boy and withdraw. Mairie stuck out her hand further.

"What is it?"

She couldn't help it any longer. She started laughing. It was a terrible habit she had when confronted with a semi-serious situation. She had the irresistible urge to giggle. "Oh, come on," she managed to say, trying so hard to be serious. "It's only Alka Seltzer . . . a bromide thing."

"Thing?" He held his stomach and took a step back. "Until you have a better explanation, I'm not putting them down my throat!"

Geez, he looked so cute in those jeans and white T-shirt, she thought, while biting the inside of her cheek to distract her. She must remember he had eaten the entire sundae in one sitting and was in some discomfort. It was funny, because he'd refused to listen to her advice and she had warned him five times this might happen. She bit down harder, as she needed her wits now to explain this.

"It's like . . . like a bromide. Seltzer. Didn't you ever take anything for an upset stomach?"

"Yeah . . . I threw up."

That did it. She couldn't hold it any longer. Bursting out laughing again, she covered her mouth and shook her head, trying to stop it. "Okay, okay . . ." she finally said and then took a deep breath. "I'm sorry. Really sorry. I'm not laughing at you. Exactly."

"Don't you dare say I told you so again."

He was looking less and less like a funny kid and more like himself. She saw his mouth twitch, just a tiny bit. Even he seemed to be amused.

"All right," she said, with as much compassion as she could gather. "Well, you may very well have that . . . that previous option if you don't take this. It will help. It's like medicine."

"It's *like* medicine?" His words held more of a hint of laughter. "Either it is, or it isn't."

She closed her eyes and tried not to giggle. "It *is* medicine." Opening her lids, she captured his vision with her own. Her voice became more thoughtful. "Why don't you trust me?"

He immediately stopped rubbing his stomach and stared back at her. "I do trust you," he said in a serious voice.

"Then take the pills," she answered with a smile of affection. "Drop them in water and drink it down."

He held out his hand to her.

In that moment, Mairie felt her fondness for him, not the intense yearning for his touch or his attention, but the genuine affection she held for Jack Delaney. He was real . . . he was faithful to his own set of beliefs. He had honor. He could be trusted. Plus he was funny, compassionate, *and* handsome. She liked him, and that shocked her because she liked him as well as she had liked her best female friends.

Maybe a little more.

Where had all her bitterness against males gone?

She picked up the glass of water and said, "Okay, partner. Drop 'em in and watch 'em fizz."

He dropped the big white tablets into the water and watched.

She chuckled as she saw his expression change. "You have to wait till it stops before you drink it."

Relief spread over his face. "Oh, it stops? I thought the damn thing was alive! It's busier than that Jacuzzi thing in the convenience . . . just look at it!"

"I am. I know what it is." Nodding to the glass, she added, "See, it's slowing down now."

He looked skeptically at the glass. "This is some future kind of aid for a queasy stomach?"

"Yes, that's it exactly," she reassured him. "Now drink it."

He brought the glass to his lips and hesitated a few seconds before taking a deep breath. "I trust you," he repeated, not precisely with the same confidence of earlier.

She watched him gulp the liquid and whispered, "All of it."

He was gasping when he finished.

"There you go. Soon you'll feel much better." She took the glass and placed it back on the night table between the beds. Pulling the bedspread down enough to expose the pillows, she fluffed and placed two of them against the headboard. "Now, lie down. Or sit up a little, if it's more comfortable."

"Why do I have to get off my feet? What is this going to do to me?" He was looking worried and Mairie held his shoulders and gently pressed him down on the edge of the mattress.

"It's not going to do anything, except make you burp."

"Oh, wonderful. I'm stuck in a room with a beautiful woman and I'm going to be belching all night?" He started laughing. "How I wish the Cornells could witness this night. After all that tutoring to be such a gentleman." He rubbed his stomach and grinned.

"I am sure continual belching would be frowned upon."

Mairie chuckled. "Yeah, well under ordinary circumstances I'd agree with the Cornells. Witnessing a belching marathon is not my idea of a swell evening, but this isn't an ordinary circumstance, sir. This is your first ice cream sundae."

"And what memories," Jack muttered, trying not to laugh.

"Ahh, you loved it, Jack. Admit it. This is only because you ate the entire thing. I told you—"

"Don't! Do not remind me again." He held his stomach and curled onto the bed away from her.

She heard a long burp and laughed. "See?"

He groaned. "I see that I'm making a pathetic impression."

She stopped laughing and smiled. "Hey, Delaney? You made your impression a long time ago. In 1877. Don't worry about it, okay? Let's watch some TV. Maybe it'll get your mind off it. By the way, thank you for saying I'm beautiful."

"You are. Surely you know that."

"It's been awhile, but I appreciate the compliment. Now, for the TV . . ." She felt ridiculously pleased that Jack thought she was beautiful, and stifled a wide grin.

"No food stories, okay?"

Picking up the remote, Mairie nodded. "Okay, but they aren't really food stories. They're commercials for food, or cooking shows. I guess technically a cooking show could be a food story, but I told you, it's all to get you to buy something. You don't even have to look. You can change the channel any time."

"Do you have one of these devices in your home?" He was sitting up against the pillows as if he felt a little better.

"I have one, though it's in storage right now. I left everything when my brother got sick." Scanning through the channels, she selected a nature show for the middle of the afternoon. Seemed safe. He certainly wasn't ready for a soap opera or Jerry Springer yet.

"Now I am impressed. Imagine to own one of these. One would never be lonely or bored."

"Don't be impressed," she answered, and fell onto her bed. She propped her pillows behind her and sat Indian style. "Almost everyone has one, in every country. It's kind of like that telephone, a communication device. You can see and hear what's happening in say England right now . . . almost anywhere, by the news. I'll show you later. Hey, look . . ."

Except for Jack's occasional burps, they sat in silence for the next twenty minutes, watching the life cycle of the salmon. Finally Jack said, "Will you tell me about your brother, Mairie? Will I meet him?"

She turned her head and saw that he wasn't interested in the program either. "I can see if there's anything else on that you might like."

Shaking his head, he smiled. "I'd really rather talk, if you don't mind. I would like to hear about this person you risked everything to help. He must be quite a man."

"He is," she answered, and smiled as a mental picture of Bryan filled her mind. "He's one of the best people I've ever known, the kind you want to be your friend. He's honorable. Loving. Strong. Humorous. Adventurous." Embarrassed, she added, "I guess you can tell I love him."

"I can." He burped and excused himself.

Mairie grinned. "And he's another man who can burp in front of me and I don't seem to mind. I think you might like him."

"Then I will get to meet him?"

"Yes. We're flying back to Philly as soon as Marc sends us new identification so we can travel."

"But we're traveling within the United States.

Why would we need identification papers? If we're stopped?"

She sighed, not knowing if she could make him understand what had taken place in the last hundred years. "You can't travel on an airplane without proper identification because of . . . it's for our safety, Jack."

He sat up straighter. "Wait. We're traveling on one of those air-planes?"

"Ahh, yeah. Did I forget to mention that?" It was like telling a child that he had to get a tooth pulled.

He shook his head and waved his hand in dismissal. "I don't think so, Mairie. I got in those vehicles to get us here and to the arcade of shops, but this is out of the question. Surely, there are trains, horses even."

She tried not to lose patience. "Jack, we can leave Las Vegas and be in Philadelphia in less than five hours. How long would a horse take?"

Looking shocked, he said, "You must not be serious. You can't get to Philadelphia from here in five hours. Try five months. Hell, it took me years to get back here to the desert."

"I would imagine you stopped along the way." Okay, so some sarcasm was creeping into the conversation. Being the teacher wasn't easy. How was she supposed to explain everything he found curious or different? She couldn't. Soon, he would need a more advanced teacher, someone who could answer his technical questions. Someone who understood the logical, mechanical, left brain. Like Marc.

Sure. How was she supposed to explain *Marc* to him?

"Yes, I stopped. I stopped and worked. I didn't have any plan, except to find my brothers, but still . . . Mairie, to travel across this country in five hours is . . . is unbelievable."

"Well, believe it, Jack. In a couple of days you're

getting on a plane with me and you'll see for yourself."

"We need to discuss this. Explain how these airplanes stay in the sky."

"I can't!" she said with frustration. "Look, even though I sold computers, I never went on a sales call without a tech . . . a technical representative, with me. He did the intricate, scientific presentation. The mechanical stuff that explains how it all works. Not me. I don't know how a plane stays in the air, Jack. I've told you all I know. It's about thrust and how the wind hits the wings. There are engines, like in a train, only really powerful."

Jack could see that she was getting upset. Wanting to end the subject, he said, "So again, I'll have to trust you."

He was pleased to see her smile.

"Are the pills working?"

He sat for a moment and realized he did feel better. "I think they are."

"Oh, goody," she said, and ran her hands down her thighs. "So tonight we can go to the cabaret show? I know how much you want to see it."

He didn't miss the teasing note to her words. "I don't feel that good. We can see it tomorrow."

"Whatever you want. So what would you like to know now?" She grinned. "Sorry if I got a little carried away there with the plane thing. I know all this is frustrating and scary. I just wish I could explain everything better."

Jack smiled. "You're a good teacher, Mairie. I can't imagine how I would explain the train engine to my Paiute brothers. Now you never finished telling me about Bryan. You said yesterday that Marc is your brother's partner. What business are they in together?"

She just stared at him for a prolonged moment,

and then burst into laughter. "Oh, Jack. Love. Their business together is based in love."

Now he stared at her. "Marc is a male, correct?"

"Correct." She sighed. "Look, I know this may seem odd to you, maybe even shocking, considering the time you just left . . . but my brother and Marc are life partners. They live together."

"I'm not sure I understand this," he said, certain he didn't want to head into this discussion with a lady. "I suppose I'll understand better when I meet them. Now, tell me of your family. Are they there in Philadelphia?"

"Everyone's gone now. It's just me and Bryan."

"No wonder you are so close to him. And what about your divorced husband? Does he live there also?"

"I don't know and don't really care. The last I heard he was in Philadelphia and was planning to remarry."

He watched as her expression became pensive. She pulled her knees up to her chin and turned her face to the wall. He paused, allowing her a moment of reflection. She suddenly inhaled deeply and turned back to him with a smile.

"That was a long, long time ago, Jack. I don't think about him anymore. He came into my life for a period of time, and it . . . it just wasn't meant to be forever. We drifted apart. He was engrossed with work and I was busy with mine. We didn't spend enough time together . . . I guess our interests grew in other directions. I believe everything happens for a reason, even if you can't see it at the time. Alan and I served each other for a time, but it just wasn't forever—"

"You don't have to say any more, Mairie. I'm sorry if I pried."

"Actually, Jack, I don't mind at all. The truth is, one day my ex-husband admitted to me he was having an affair and he asked me for a divorce."

"Oh Mairie, it must have hurt you deeply to hear that." He wanted to take her in his arms and tell her the man had been a fool.

"Well, at first, it hit me from out of left field. I mean, I had no idea. Things weren't perfect, I knew that. We were so busy with trying to make ends meet, but I thought we were working on a life together. I guess we were working on a life apart. At least that's how it went."

Her pause gave him a thoughtful moment. He looked down to the floor, avoiding her stare, and rubbed his hands together. "It's a shame to see the future has produced men who no longer believe that a man's word is his honor."

She inhaled and looked to the ceiling. "Come on, Jack. Men have been unfaithful since . . . Adam. It wasn't the fact my husband cheated on me that hurt so much. It was the betrayal of my best friend, or who I believed was my best friend. I once thought all men were like that, without honor in their words. But I don't think that anymore. Surprisingly, I find myself not bitter toward Alan. He served a purpose for me. He was part of a lesson in life I had to learn. There is still decency in this world, Jack. It may be harder to find, but it exists." She added with another smile, "At least, I hope it does."

In the silence after her words he thought of how similar they were. Mairie had been through her war, and he his. Both had emerged scarred but intact. She had walked away from her battle and didn't appear to harbor bitterness. She still believed. She still had hope. He looked up at her with a great tenderness in his eyes.

"*By virtue of her emotions.* Balzac was certainly correct. Mairie Callahan, once again I am drawn to say, you are an incredible woman and are deserving of admiration."

"Well, this is a recent revelation to me, this . . . this

healing." She was looking at him with such warmth. "But I do thank you, kind sir."

Their gazes locked. He felt a pull in his chest so deeply he was sure his body rocked toward her with the ache. She remained still, her arms wrapped around her legs, her head resting on her knees. He couldn't be sure if her eyes said more.

"Did the Alka Seltzer work?"

"Quite well. I'm actually feeling much better."

"Good." She sat up quickly, slapping her knees with both hands. "We need to get busy and do something. This is Las Vegas! We should be out on the town. Here—" She tossed his sweater to him.

He jerked with the interruption and tore his eyes away.

"Perhaps you're right. It might be best to get out of this hotel room and get some air . . . and a drink." He was most relieved she had ended the intensity of that moment. He slapped his legs in agreement and rose from his bed.

"I've got an invitation to a burleyque, madam. I would be honored if you would accompany me." In a theatrical gesture, he put his arm out for her.

"I would be delighted to attend with you, Jack Delaney." She looked up at him, smiled grandly, and touched his arm. "But first, I must don my disguise. Let me get my wig. We're traveling incognito."

It was so strange to see her with blond hair. It was a complete transformation. He preferred her long, straight black hair falling over her shoulders.

"Mairie, your appearance has altered so much with that light hair. If it were not for your dazzling blue eyes, I might not recognize you tonight." With a grin he added, "Your carriage awaits, dear lady." He again offered his arm and she took it.

Quietly he shut the door behind them.

*   *   *

Mairie loved walking next to him, her hand resting on his strong arm. She felt happy, secure, and protected, and thought about what she'd said to him minutes ago in the room. The bitterness really was gone. Six years she had carried it like a stone around her heart. She actually felt . . . lighter, she thought as the elevator doors opened.

"Jack, wait a second. Let me help you." In the elevator Mairie stood before him and raised her arms to the back of his head. "Your hair. It's got static from pulling on your sweater."

"Oh, what's that?"

He leaned slightly toward her with an ease which surprised her. It was as though they had been married for years. Yet she knew she went flush when she saw him caressing every detail of her face with his eyes. That same flush was creeping down her body, inflaming her senses. She wondered if he was searching for the familiarity under the blond wig and if he could pick up on her desire.

"There. That's better." She slid her fingers down the length of his hair and patted his chest to confirm he was now presentable. Her hands lingered briefly and she had to use every ounce of willpower not to caress him.

She watched him stand erect, never taking his eyes from hers and she was sure he trembled. An ache grew so intense within her when the beating of his heart pounded against her palms that Mairie almost moaned.

A synthesized tone announced their stop.

Saved by the bell, she thought. With a deep breath she declared, "I could really use that drink now." Mairie turned out into the lobby. She felt his hand reach out and stroke the length of her arm as she stepped forward. She sensed for an instant his hesitation in holding her hand, then he followed behind her.

This is definitely going to be some evening, Mairie Callahan, she thought to herself.

They wound up at the cabaret show in the hotel. She thought of Bryan, in Philadelphia, out of remission, and felt a pang of guilt. After speaking with Marc, she decided not to chance going back to the cave. If the Feds were looking for her, they would be watching that area. And nothing, absolutely nothing, was going to prevent her reunion with Bryan. She knew there was nothing she could do until Marc sent the new IDs, yet a sadness took hold of her. How she missed her brother. Soon . . . soon she would hold him in her arms and explain everything.

Mairie immediately ordered a Long Island iced tea and told the scantily clad waitress to keep them coming. She couldn't help but sense the young woman's flirtation toward Jack as he asked for a beer and a shot of whiskey. Mairie didn't blame her, for Jack Delaney was an attention grabber. He'd had hers ever since she'd laid eyes on him. Suddenly, instead of feeling insecure, Mairie felt a rush of pleasure that Jack Delaney was her date. She could say that. It was an almost-kind-of-a-date . . . she was with him, a man from a hundred years ago, a remarkable man, a charming gentleman. She actually loved his old-world gestures. They were genuine.

This night might be torture, to be this close to him, to feel everything that was coursing through her mind and her body, and to hold back.

Her seven months of celibacy suddenly felt like seven years.

After her second drink, she actually relaxed and grinned at Jack's stunned expression when the floor show started. The women were all tall and beautiful and wore stunning bejeweled costumes of elaborate feather designs. She sat and wondered how they managed to walk in the heavy contraptions. But she had to admit they were lovely and she hoped they got paid a lot of money to prance around in those high heels. Their feet must kill them. Then the magician came out and did a decent imitation of Siegfried and Roy's tiger act. Jack was amazed and Mairie giggled. Okay, she was on her second drink, but his astonishment was so precious, and she was . . . damn, was she getting drunk?

Trying not to laugh, she straightened her wig and took a deep breath. She had to keep up with Jack and not make a fool of herself, but the wig did make her scalp itch and she wanted to tear it off her head. She must look like some retro Farrah Fawcett wannabe, but it wasn't all that expensive and she couldn't see spending hundreds of dollars on a better one. Still, it seemed a shame that she had nice clothes somewhere, clothes like the other women in the audience were wearing, and her hair when styled was decent, and makeup . . . when the hell was the last time she'd worn makeup?

"Mairie?"

Stunned out of her pity party, Mairie jumped and looked at Jack. He was smiling at her.

"Don't you think we should eat something?"

She stuck her index finger under the flap of wig by her ear and scratched. "You think you can eat now?" she asked over the applause, as the crowd showed their appreciation for the magicians.

"I think *you* should. I'm not very hungry, but you haven't had anything today since your ice cream cone." He reached over and tenderly tugged the corner of her wig back into place around her face. "Something light?"

She nodded, wishing he would touch her again. His fingers had brushed her cheek with such thoughtful familiarity that she almost moaned. "Right, I'll get us a menu."

"I was looking at this." Jack stated, pulling a small plastic card from behind the centerpiece.

"Okay, lemme see," she said, to hide the fact that she was distracted by matters that seemed much more important than food. She forced her eyes to focus on the printed words and blinked a few times when she looked up at him. "They only serve appetizers during the show. No dinners. Shall I order for us?"

"Please," he answered with a lazy smile. He really seemed to be enjoying himself.

She stared at his mouth for the longest time. In fact, she probably would have continued if Jack didn't suddenly raise his hand slightly to flag the waitress. Naturally, the woman came immediately and couldn't have been more helpful in suggesting which appetizers were the house specialty.

Mairie sat glumly while watching the interaction. Maybe Jack was right, maybe she needed food. Two drinks on an empty stomach must be the reason she was feeling this defensiveness, as if Jack Delaney belonged to her. How immature. She wasn't a young girl. She was a woman.

Right . . . a woman with two Long Island iced teas in her, forced to sit next to a gorgeous man whom she was in love with and must not show how she felt. She wanted another drink, as more beautiful women in costumes followed the magical act to do another number.

Jack was mesmerized. Hey, she couldn't blame him.

Their food came quickly and Mairie studied the array of appetizers. Fried mozzarella sticks. Buffalo wings. Fried shrimp. Cris-cut fries. Fried zucchini and onion rings. Ranch sauce, marinara sauce, cocktail sauce. The jalapeño sauce was for the buffalo wings.

"It smells wonderful." Jack inhaled the aroma of the food.

"Everything is fried," she said, and wondered if her voice sounded like a whine.

"Is something wrong?" His expression showed concern.

She wanted to say that yes . . . something *was* wrong. She was getting tipsy. She was miserable in her wig. She couldn't possibly compete with the showgirls or even the waitress for his attention and wanted to take him back to the room, where he was all hers.

Talk about childish.

Concentrate on the food, she told herself, and picked up a mozzarella stick. She pointed to each food with her other hand, identifying them with the corresponding sauce. Dipping the cheese stick and swirling, she raised it to her lips. "They're best with the ranch sauce, Jack. Try it. It's . . . finger food."

She closed her eyes as she bit down and savored the taste. Melted cheese dangled between her lips.

"Interesting," he said, squinting at her.

Now I've got his attention, she thought triumphantly. That, or I'm really making a fool out of myself. At that moment the oh-so-cute waitress brought them each another round of drinks.

Perfect, she thought, and picked up her glass.

"And these, Mairie?" he asked, holding up a buffalo wing. "This is a bird of some sort. I've had buffalo, and this isn't it."

She laughed and took another sip of her drink. "One of the many paradoxes in life, Jack. Buffalos don't have wings, yet you're holding one. Actually, it happens to be named after the city of Buffalo in New York."

"Why Buffalo?"

"I don't know," she answered truthfully.

"Ahh . . ." he said, and dipped it into the jalapeño sauce.

Before she could warn him, he bit into it.

"Wait, that's hot," she said, and marveled as he calmly chewed. "You don't think that's hot, spicy?"

He grinned and swallowed. "Mairie, I like hot. Remember, Mexico isn't far from here. I'm used to hot foods. And it's a hell of a lot better than prairie dog."

She picked up her glass. "I'll drink to that."

Holding him by the arm, she rested her head against his shoulder and squeezed. "This has sefintely been dome evening, Dack Jelaney. I mean, Jack Delaney." She corrected herself and then giggled at her own spoonerism as she fumbled with the electronic lock.

Smirking at her inebriated state, Jack carefully took the key from her and successfully opened the door. "You're as giddy as a schoolgirl, Mairie Callahan."

"Thank you, my good man." She threw the purse into a chair and flopped down on her bed. She sat for a moment and evaluated her condition. "I think I'm going to be sick," she stated matter-of-factly. Falling back onto the bed, her arms flung above her head she continued, "I never should have eaten that fried food on top of the alcohol."

"Would you like one of your Alka Seltzer? I can speak from experience, it tastes like hell, but works wonders." He grinned foolishly.

She burst out laughing. "Best commercial I ever heard."

"Then I shall prepare some for you, madam, and return henceforth."

This is absolute insanity, she thought, as she pulled the wig from her head and tossed it across the room. *I can't believe I'm living this. This man is incredible. Back in time, forward in time, and having the time of my life.* The room started to spin and Mairie struggled to keep herself coherent.

"Mairie, are you awake?"

She slowly opened her eyes to see Jack with a fizzing glass in his hand.

"God, you are beautiful," she mumbled inaudibly.

"I'm sorry, Mairie, I didn't hear you."

"Nothing." She struggled to sit up.

"Let me help you, Mar."

She felt the care in his embrace as he put his arm around her shoulders and placed the glass to her lips. She swallowed a gulp.

"Egads. You're right. It does taste like hell." She crinkled her nose. "And the bubbles tickle."

"Just finish it. If I did, you can. It's a miracle medicine. You'll feel better in a little while."

She closed her eyes as he tipped the glass for her to finish the last swallow. She felt so cared for in his strong arm. She was entirely safe. There was no assuming here. She knew Jack Delaney's intentions were honorable. He was a rare man, indeed.

Hearing him place the glass onto the night table she felt him turn back. What a state of bliss . . . presently, chemically induced . . . nevertheless, bliss, she thought. She couldn't force her eyes to open. How she wanted this moment to last. But what a sight you must be, Mairie Callahan, she chided herself.

She felt his finger touch her bottom lip when he brushed away a drop.

"I'm glad to see you haven't lost the rest of your head." He said, noticing her wig on the floor.

She lazily opened her reddened eyes and looked across the carpet. They both burst out laughing and a huge belch left Mairie's mouth.

"Ooops!" she said coyly, covering her lips. "Did that come out of me?"

"Indeed it did, madam. Now, don't you feel better?" He smiled at her reassuringly.

"Excuse me, Jack. I'm sorry . . . really, really sorry. My behavior tonight has been appalling. Now I think I *will* be sick." She pushed back on his arm to lie down on the bed in embarrassment. She knew she would hate herself even more when the hangover woke her in the morning. But that was timetraveling. Stay in the moment, she reminded herself.

Heck, it had worked before.

"Jack, will you do me one more favor?" She stretched herself up to the pillows and turned to see him standing beside her bed.

"Anything, Mairie. What do you need?"

He stood, looming above her, having already removed his sweater, and was now unbuttoning his shirt. Oh, not *that*, she fought her own thoughts, and quickly rolled over.

She paused and spoke softly. "Jack, would you just . . . just hold me tonight?" It sounded so female, but it was what she wanted in this moment, to be held.

He froze in mid-button and looked down at her. She truly was a temptation. He wouldn't be a man if he didn't notice her long black hair fanned against the pillow; the expression on her face, her smooth skin that was turning tan. She had the look of absolute serenity about her. She *is* a goddess, he thought, then reminded himself he respected her completely.

Jack lay on the edge of the bed next to her. Mairie didn't move. He slowly eased onto his side and fit his body against her. He felt how well his framed hers. Gently, he placed his arm across the pillow above her head. Mairie lifted her head and softly rested against his arm. The perfume in her hair filled his senses. Gritting his teeth, he drew a deep breath and slowly exhaled. A quiet moan escaped. As though it were the most natural thing in the world, Mairie reached behind her hip, took his hand in hers, and pressed his arm around her waist.

"Thank you, Jack Delaney," she sighed sleepily. "Good night."

"Good night, Mairie Callahan, and thank you." He closed his eyes.

He waited a few seconds and then whispered, "You are an incredible gift."

His last words went unheard through her slumber.

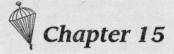

Chapter 15

"Let me entertain you . . ."

She awoke to a deep baritone voice singing in the shower. It was Jack, she realized, and snuggled deeper into the pillow. He was singing the opening song from the show they'd seen the night before. Groaning, Mairie opened her lids and slammed them shut immediately as light pierced through to her aching brain. Her hangover alarm echoed relentlessly through her body. Suddenly, from behind the pain, an image came to her consciousness. Something she had seen in the second her eyes opened. She had to make sure. She shielded her eyes with her hand and squinted into the sunlit room.

Jack's bed hadn't been slept in.

She remembered, sort of remembered, asking him to sleep with her last night.

Another deep groan escaped her lips as thinking made her head pound harder. She sensed her blood pumping through her veins and every nerve ending in her body told her reality was here and she wished she wasn't.

She didn't! She couldn't have! *She did!* The proof was right there, and he was singing in the shower! Hearing the faucet squeaking off, Mairie lay in bed completely still, attempting to ease the torture and figure out what the heck had happened. Obviously, she'd had too much to drink. She wasn't going to punish herself for that, since she'd had one hell of a week so far, but this . . . what had she done?

She'd made a complete fool of herself.

"Good morning, Mairie. You're awake. It's a beautiful day, and I feel great!"

His greeting had the opposite effect on her. More evidence that *something* had happened last night, but what? Part of her was pissed that she couldn't recall much more than falling into bed. It had to have been an incredible experience. What a shame she couldn't remember any of it. Just her luck, to suffer this embarrassment and be left with a blank memory.

"Good morning," she murmured, as nonchalantly as she could manage. "Are you finished in the bathroom?" She needed to make an escape.

"Yes. The convenience is all yours."

Okay, she thought, all she had to do was somehow get up and walk past him. The getting up part seemed monumental. Forcing her body to move, she barely opened her eyes as she sat up. She was in her jeans.

Her jeans!

Blinking at her legs, she thought, there's no way he could have gotten her jeans off and back on again . . . she would have remembered something about *that!* Relief swept through her body. Nothing had happened. At least, nothing serious. Now her embarrassment was merely from getting soused. But she could deal with that. She couldn't deal with the other. Not that, and not drunk. If it ever happened, she would make sure she was stone cold sober. She didn't want to miss a second.

"Morning," she whispered again with a weak smile, and walked past him to the bathroom.

"How are you feeling, Mairie?" he said in a cheerful tone. Way too cheerful for her sensitive ears.

"Fine, I guess. I'll know better once I wash this

hangover out of my head." She shut the door behind her. She didn't mean to be rude, but she needed privacy and a shower before she would feel human again. That, and an industrial-strength painkiller.

Using the bathroom phone, she ordered breakfast for him, a pot of coffee for her. She turned on the shower water and steam immediately began filling the air. Her clothes almost peeled off her body. Spending over twenty hours in jeans didn't exactly enhance her sleeping experience. Yet she remembered a flash of something. A security. The feeling of being so protected, almost cherished, when she fell asleep.

She hoped that wasn't her imagination.

When she emerged from the bathroom in her robe, she saw that Jack was clad in jeans and a pale yellow T-shirt. He was sitting at the table, drinking his coffee and reading the complimentary newspaper. He looked up as she entered the bedroom and smiled.

"Shall I pour you some coffee, Mairie?"

"Thanks." Her head still throbbed and she knew she'd have to get down to the hotel gift shop to purchase something for the pain. She just couldn't drink that Alka Seltzer again.

"Did you pay for this?" she asked, seeing his breakfast was half eaten.

Again he smiled as he placed her filled cup in front of the seat opposite him. "I even tipped the waiter. Just as you did yesterday."

She sat down and tightened her robe around her. "Good. I'm glad you're learning the customs here."

He set the folded paper down beside his place setting then leaned back. "You're a good teacher." He seemed to look even deeper into her eyes as he raised his coffee cup to his lips.

Yeah, that's a good one, she thought. Some education. *Hard Liquor 101.*

She tried to smile, but even that hurt. "Jack, I'm sorry if I did anything . . . well, anything silly last night. It's been some time since I've been drinking."

"Stop apologizing. You were . . . delightful."

Somehow, the way he said "delightful" made her wonder again if it were possible to perform the jeans trick without her knowing. No, Jack wouldn't take advantage of her. She knew that.

"Mairie, when you feel better, I would like you to explain this war I've been reading about." Offering his plate, he changed the subject and asked, "You don't want anything to eat?"

In her best etiquette she attempted not to recoil. "Oh, please—no, thank you, but you go right ahead." She didn't want to see or think of anything fried for a very long time. "What war?" she asked, as she sipped the restorative black liquid.

"All this reporting of murders across the country. I am reading stories and statistics. I was wondering if that's why you're getting us identification papers. Is the country at war again? Is that why the young boy had a gun yesterday?"

She could only stare at him. It would seem that way to someone from his time. "It's an undeclared war, Jack," she murmured, holding the cup with both hands.

"That must be why I haven't seen anyone in uniform," he stated, while absentmindedly rolling the newspaper into a tube.

She shook her head. "I don't know how to explain this, but you experienced a bit of it yesterday in the mall. Guns are everywhere. It's like . . . like Tombstone all over the country, and no one knows what to do about it."

"I don't wish to get involved in another war. I have no fondness for guns myself, I use one only for hunting, but we may need to protect ourselves as well. I left my rifle back in the cave. Perhaps I should purchase a weapon?"

"No." The word rang out in the room and Mairie was shocked at her tone of voice. She didn't have the right to tell him what to do.

"I'm sorry," she again apologized. "That's really your decision, but they won't allow you on the airplane with a gun."

"Now I'm sorry. I've upset you." He tossed the paper to the floor and added, "We won't discuss it any further." He paused. "But there is something else I wanted to speak to you about, if you don't mind."

She smiled, thankful for his perception. She really didn't have the mental strength right now to explain modern day gun ownership. "Of course, I don't mind. Just nothing too heavy. I have a . . . a headache this morning."

"Ahh . . . to be expected, my dear," he smiled slyly, "one of the evils of drink." He winked at her. "However, I shall endeavor to pamper you all day until you've recovered, madam."

"You seem so chipper." She appreciated his thoughts and hoped her voice didn't slightly tinge with jealousy.

"I feel very well, though I could do with a good shave." He rubbed the stubble on his chin. "I'll need to find a barber or get myself a razor today."

She thought he looked quite dashing with the couple days' growth. How ironic, it was a fashion statement these days.

"And also, please do not take offense, but last night I noticed all the ladies dressed more formally than in these jeans, as you call them." He paused, taking a sip of his coffee, as though doing a temperature check on how she was handling the delicate insinuation.

"And . . . ?" She wasn't about to help him, since

she had no idea where this one was leading.

"And I thought perhaps we should purchase a dress for you. I know you are trying to be frugal with the money, but you do wear dresses, don't you?"

"Quite often, in fact." She couldn't help sounding a bit offended. When she looked up from her coffee, she saw his intention was sincere and was touched by his sweet offer. "Jack, that is your money. You don't need to spend it on—"

"Mairie," he interrupted, putting his cup back onto the saucer. "I wouldn't even have it, if you didn't ask me to purchase those silver dollars from Virginia. It would be an honor. And you could assist me in finding a tailor. I need a suit. Haven't worn one in years, yet I see in all the advertisements men do wear them. The styles for men haven't changed much in all these years. Women, on the other hand . . ."

He let his words trail off and Mairie said, "I would imagine many of the current fashions are shocking to you. Like me wearing pants. You know, I wish I could have this discussion with you, but I have to get dressed and go down to the gift shop for some Advil, a . . . a pain medicine. I must admit to nursing a hangover." She smiled sheepishly.

"I'll go," he said, already pushing back his chair.

"No, I'll go," she said, taking her coffee with her as she got up and moved around the room. "I'll just throw on my jeans and shirt. I'll be right back."

"You never answered me."

She turned around at the dresser. "About what?"

"Allowing me to purchase a dress for you. If you feel better tonight, we can have a nice dinner at one of the restaurants here. I have read that there are six different ones in this hotel. One appears to be quite nice."

Smiling, she said, "That's very kind of you. I

would be delighted to wear a dress and have dinner with you tonight. Thank you, Jack. But first let me get something for my head.''

She took her clothes into the bathroom to change and, seeing herself in the mirror, she groaned. How in the world was she ever going to pull her act together enough to go shopping and look dazzling by tonight.

Miracles.

She needed one.

In the gift shop, she bought a razor, Advil, and some Lifesavers for her dry mouth. As she was standing at the counter to pay, she noticed a stack of postcards. Most were of the city at night, with the glitter of Las Vegas at different locations. She idly looked them over as she waited for the person in front of her to pay. Her attention was drawn to a shiny white postcard with red lettering.

> Go Beyond Reason to Love.
> It is safe. It is the only safety.
> T. Golas

How odd to find that in a rack of tourist post-cards, she thought. She had it in her hand when the cashier called out to her.

"Are you ready?"

She placed her few items on the counter and nodded, yet her thoughts were on that postcard. What an extraordinary thing to read, on this morning too. For some weird reason, she felt like it was a message for her. Probably everyone who read it felt the same way. She was just being foolish.

As she walked out of the shop, Mairie spied a water fountain and took out the Advil. Popping three into her mouth, she gulped water and swallowed. The lobby and casino were already busy and she headed for the elevator. Riding up to the room, she couldn't get it out of her head.

Love was the only safety?

The thought stayed with her for the remainder of the morning and into the afternoon.

Jack was so attentive to her every need that Mairie felt almost guilty for only suffering from a hangover. He patiently waited as she tried on several dresses, not wanting to see what she had purchased. He said he preferred to be surprised later in the evening. She'd found something terrific, a clingy black dress with long tapering sleeves that wrapped tightly around her wrists. It had tiny covered buttons that started at the deep V neck and ran down the front of the flared skirt to her ankles. It was simple, yet elegant. She even bought an inexpensive pair of black high heels. When Jack saw her stop at a makeup counter, he insisted she buy a few items and she so wanted them that she told him the money he spent would only be a loan. She intended to repay him when she got to Philadelphia, no matter how much he protested.

Mairie didn't know if she felt better because the Advil had kicked in, or because she was going to dress up and have another date with Jack. For if last night was an almost date, tonight was the real thing.

They came back to the room around three o'clock. Mairie was initially surprised that Jack assimilated everything so well, without overloading his brain. He certainly was a remarkable man, but even he was glad to return to the room and sit down. Shopping had drained them both.

Looking at the garment bags on the bed, surrounded by packages, he grinned. "I suppose it's about time I had a suit. It may feel strange to wear one again. Been almost ten years."

"Really?" Then she remembered he had said yesterday it took him years to make his way back to

Nevada and the Paiutes. "Well, you'll look smashing tonight. The salesman in the department store assured me of that." Since he had wanted to be surprised, she'd thought she might as well be the same. She had placed Jack in the hands of a well-dressed clerk and had left them for an hour as she went dress hunting.

"Let me hang them up," she said, and reached down to grab the hangers.

Jack immediately stood. "Here, I'll do that. Rest, Mairie."

She looked at him and smiled. "I can do it. I'm not sick. In fact, I feel much better."

He took the hangers and walked to the closet. "Good. I'm glad you can enjoy the evening."

"We'd better call for reservations," she said and picked up the phone. "What time shall we have dinner?"

He closed the closet door and walked back to the bedroom area. "Is six too early?"

"Not at all." She began dialing the gourmet restaurant. After a few minutes she had their reservation secured and she leaned back against her bed pillows and sighed.

She reached for one of the packages and began rooting. "Here's your razor. You use it just like the old-fashioned ones, except it's safer. I'll show you if you want."

He chuckled. "I would imagine I can figure it out. If I have a problem I'll call you. Though I still find it strange that you plaster something under your arms as part of a daily routine. And tooth powders have been replaced by paste." He sat on his bed and ran his fingers through his hair. "You're sure I shouldn't cut my hair, Mairie? I haven't seen many males with longer hair. Do I look like those deadheads? I think I should cut it."

Her heart constricted at the thought. "Do whatever you wish," she said as casually as possible. "I like your hair. It's . . . you."

He seemed to be thinking about it and she mentally crossed her fingers that a haircut was not forthcoming.

"I'll think about it," he finally said. "I do want to blend in."

She laughed. "Oh, Jack. Someone like you will never blend in. You're far too unique to blend in anywhere."

"I thank you for your compliment, Madam, but that sort of defeats our purpose in Philadelphia. We're supposed to blend in, are we not?"

Was he teasing her? She couldn't tell much from that mysterious smile.

"Once you thought of me as a wild man, though I now understand your confusion. I am sorry for the way I treated you when we first met, but you did drive me almost beyond my limit of patience."

She joined his laughter and thought back to their first meeting. The desert, the climb, the waterfall. *Don't think about the waterfall*, she told herself . . . though the picture of the back of Jack Delaney, nude, washing the paint from his body, would never leave her mind.

"I'm going to soak in the tub," she announced, and quickly stood up. She took the bags to the low dresser and separated his items from hers. He was so silent that she thought he might have fallen asleep and she was surprised to turn back to the room and find him staring at her.

"Enjoy your bath, Mairie."

Was she still hung over, or did his eyes hold a look of deep desire? Don't think about it, she told herself, as she smiled and walked into the bathroom with her things. She would shave her legs, wash her hair, and still have time for a nap. Some inner guidance told her to be well rested for whatever followed.

She hoped she could leave her teacher role behind for the night and just enjoy being in the company of the man she loved. Loved . . . even thinking about it stunned her. What a blessing Jack Delaney was, to have come into her life from a hundred years ago and show her that an equal partnership with a male was not only possible. It was natural.

He was *her* gift.

Maybe Jack was right, maybe the Indian's Coyote god was a trickster, after all.

Coming out of the bathroom, she heard his rhythmic breathing before she saw him. Jack was asleep on top of the bedspread. His legs and arms were crossed, and his chin fell forward to his chest. Smiling, Mairie grabbed one of his T-shirts from the dresser drawer and hurried back into the bathroom. She slipped into it and was pleased that it came to the middle of her thighs. Putting the robe back on, she walked into the room and headed for her bed. How perfect. If she set the alarm for five o'clock, they could both be well rested for this *date*. That's what she was calling it. This was an official date.

Now all she had to do was fall asleep and not imagine Jack Delaney spooning her as he had done last night. She remembered that. It was a memory and a feeling she would never forget. She slid between the cool, clean sheets and sighed with contentment as her head hit the pillow. In spite of everything, the government, Bryan's illness, everything . . . she felt blessed. Her life had been altered with that first jump. And what about Jack? What courage it had taken for him to jump. He had done it for her, and that fact still stunned her.

Strange, how one's life could change in an instant of trust.

*   *   *

The annoying noise roused him from a very enjoyable dream and Jack leaned up on his elbow to silence the thing. "I can't stop this time piece from chirping," he muttered.

Mairie groaned and reached out her arm to smack it. Blessed peace followed and Jack dropped his head to the pillow. "Do you need to use the convenience, Mairie?"

She moaned sleepily. "I already took my bath. You use it. You need to shave and take a shower." Waving her hand at him, she added, "Gimme five more minutes."

"Don't fall back asleep. Jack Delaney is not known for being late to his engagements, Miss Callahan." He grinned as he got up and saw that she had snuggled once more against her pillow.

"Five minutes," she whined like a little girl. "Just five minutes."

He was still grinning as he walked into the convenience and closed the door behind him. He bet she fell back asleep. He turned the water on and began his preparations for the evening. Strange . . . he hadn't felt this excited about anything in a long, long time. Something told him that tonight was going to be special, and he was going to make sure it was. After everything she had been through, Mairie Callahan deserved to be treated like the fine lady she was. It had been a long time since he'd courted a woman, but he remembered.

Somehow he knew all his gentlemanly expertise would be put to a test, for courting Mairie would be a unique experience. An experience he was more than ready to explore.

No more than fifteen minutes could have passed when Jack stepped into the bedroom from the bath, wearing the hotel robe and towel-drying his hair. From beneath the thick cloth he saw his way to the end of her bed. "Madam . . . your toilette awaits."

Not hearing her reply, he slung the towel around his neck, still holding it with both hands. His eyes cast upon her sleeping. Not much was left to his imagination as she lay on her side atop the comforter, embracing a pillow. He could not withhold his glance from tracing the slope of her hip and thigh. She was in nothing but his T-shirt and her undergarment. She fills my clothing better than I ever will, he thought to himself. He quickly turned and sat on the end of his bed when she inhaled and began to stretch.

"Hmmm . . . did you say something, Jack?"

"Yes, Mairie . . . I did. I said I'm finished with the convenience. It's all yours now." He hoped she didn't detect an inflection of guilt in his words.

"Mmmm, okay. I'm up. I'm moving. Really—" She mumbled off in half slumber.

"Mairie Callahan, I threw you over my shoulder once, to get you where we needed to go, and I can do it again." He figured an authoritative tone would more likely wake her and at the same time take his mind off her revealing position. "If that is what I must do, Mairie, I'm prepared to do it."

"And perhaps I'll enjoy it this time." She murmured into the pillow.

"Mairie, you're still sleeping. I can't make out what you're saying. I thought you were looking forward to our engagement this evening." He fought the urge to turn and look at her again. Would she call his bluff? He was cleanly shaven, bathed, and well rested. His instinctual desires were now wide awake and it was becoming more difficult to ignore her beauty and form. "Mairie, please—"

"All right, all right. I'm awake." She sat upright and ran her fingers through her hair.

"Would you like to call for more coffee?" Why didn't he think of ordering coffee before? It would have been better than starting with the caveman approach.

"No, thank you, Jack. I'm sorry I snapped at you," she said with a yawn. She stood and walked to the dresser across the room. His T-shirt fell to her mid-thighs, and he couldn't resist gazing upon her.

"Mairie, don't you think you should put your robe on?" he asked.

She stared at him from the reflection in the mirror. "Oh Jack, please, don't be such a puritan. The way I'm dressed, by today's standards, is entirely acceptable. Don't tell me you've never seen a woman in her night clothes. You have, haven't you?"

Jack directed his eyes to her face. "Of course . . ." He paused, "Of course I have. I mean, yes. Well, it's just a matter of . . . it's just the way I was brought up. A lady—"

"Oh, Jack, chill out. A modern lady's sensibilities are not that fragile. If I were embarrassed in front of you, I'd have slept in the robe. But I'm not embarrassed. You're sitting on the end of the bed and I can see your legs. Why are you upset that you can see mine?"

"Because, Mairie, where I come from, women aren't accustomed to showing their legs to their husbands, much less men they've known only a few days." He responded seriously.

Mairie gathered her makeup and walked to stand between his legs. She smiled tenderly down at him. "You've been handling this future shock so well. I keep forgetting the life you left behind had such a radically different view of cultural propriety." She tousled his hair. "I'm so proud of you. You're doin' great." She sighed deeply. "And I can't think of anyone else I would want to escort me to dinner tonight. You are a gentleman in the true sense of the word, Jack Delaney, and I appreciate that."

He watched her completely as she turned away.

"By the way, Jack. It's kind of cute the way you keep calling this the *convenience*, but these days, we refer to it as the bathroom." She smiled at him again and closed the door.

"Whew." He'd made it. He'd wrestled with Indians, crossed hot deserts in sand storms, climbed mountains, and fought in hand-to-hand combat, and he had never felt so close to being conquered in his entire life. It was difficult enough to watch her walk across the room, in his shirt, but when she stood between his legs, he was almost certain she could sense every nerve in his body paralyzed with desire.

Mairie Callahan not only inflamed his body, she'd ignited his soul. Chill out, she said. Perhaps a dip in an ice-cold river would do him well right now.

He abruptly stood and went to the closet. Removing his suit, he laid it carefully on the bed. Better to busy himself by dressing than to envision the distraction of Mairie's scantily clad form and coquettish manner. Holding his newly tailored trousers in his hand, he stopped walking and stared at the closed *bathroom* door.

He couldn't recall a time he had hungered for a woman this much. Just thinking about the closeness of her body, knowing she wore nothing underneath that thin shirt, remembering the shapely slant of her waist, hips, and the descent to her thigh made every muscle in his body ache for her. He thought back to the night of the Paiute celebration, how she had looked at him, flirted with him, bewitched him. He had wanted her then, in his time, but he wanted her more in this one. It went beyond wanting. It was a passion. A timeless passion.

As the thought raced through his brain, Jack felt a rush of emotion come alive that he had believed dormant within him. He realized he wanted this night to be special for more than Mairie. He also wanted it for himself. He had spent so much time alone in the last ten years, needing to separate from society and its demands, satisfying himself only with women who understood he was moving on. Now he wanted something more . . . he wanted to feel vital again, to know intimacy with this remarkable woman who had fallen into his life.

He dressed deliberately, ensuring every seam and crease was exact.

Now for the tie.

He'd always had a problem with these and felt they were too similar to a noose. Nor could he understand why something so confining was still in fashion. However, the white shirt collar folding down was much more comfortable than the raised stiff collars he was accustomed to wearing. He placed the narrow silk tie around his neck and began the procedure of folding and knotting. It took three attempts before he was successful.

Looking into the mirror, he wondered why the clerk had assured him this outrageous colorful design would impress his lady. *My lady*. Those words resounded in his head.

Yes, he thought, looking into the mirror, he believed he would like Mairie Callahan to be his lady. He reached behind him for his suit coat and slipped it on. Buttoning the double-breasted jacket, as the clerk had called it, he stood back and surveyed his reflection.

He wanted everything to be just right.

The dark blue suit fit as if it had been tailored for him. The shoulders tapered to his waist and the material hung perfectly to his upper thighs. He saw how the contrast against his white shirt set off the swirling colors in the tie. The clerk had been right, and Jack thought he did resemble the pictures he had seen in the store of a properly dressed gentleman of 1999. He fit right in; no one would know he was a recent arrival to this century.

Except for his hair.

He pulled it back and saw he looked much better, more in keeping with others he had seen. He went to the closet and picked up his worn old boots. Untying the short black leather lace above the heel, he brought it with him to the mirror. He gathered his hair at the nape of his neck and looped the lace once around before pulling it taut.

A satisfied grin reflected back at him.

Yes. All he needed now was that fancy toilet water he'd been talked into purchasing by the clerk. *Bvlgari.* He couldn't even pronounce it. Made by someone called Chanel. Well, Chanel must be a wealthy person, for this small bottle had cost him over seventy dollars.

Splashing a little on his hands, he patted his face and neck and thought he was finally finished. Until he looked down to his feet. Those shoes . . . Mairie had insisted he needed a new pair and when he asked her which ones she liked, she picked out the soft shiny leather moccasins with tassels. He bought them.

Slipping his feet into them, he had to admit they were comfortable, almost like wearing slippers . . . and they did look smart with his attire.

All right. Back to the mirror.

Again checking his reflection, Jack was finally satisfied. More than satisfied. Even though he'd almost choked when he had to pay over six hundred dollars for this ensemble, right now it was worth every nickel. He looked . . . modern. And he eased his conscience by telling himself he not only needed a proper suit, but he would have it for the next twenty years. Mairie was right. Everything cost a fortune here.

Tonight was not the time to be miserly. Tonight he was courting his lady.

Listening to Mairie in the bathroom, and the

sound of the device that blew out hot air to dry one's hair, he knew he had some time yet before she made her appearance. He stood in front of the mirror and practiced how he would greet her.

"Good evening, Miss Callahan," he whispered with a smile. "Your radiance all but dims the stars in the velvet desert sky."

He scowled and shook his head. "Good evening, Miss Callahan," he began again. "I am honored to accompany such a vision of loveliness." That's better, he thought. Now he was ready to court her. Still he didn't want his greeting to come out sounding like a bunch of posies.

"Flowers!" How could he court his lady without them?

His mind went blank until he suddenly remembered the flower shop in the hotel lobby. Glancing back to the bathroom door, he could still hear the contraption whirring and knew if he rushed he could make it back before she was finished.

Grabbing a fistful of money, he jammed it into his pocket and hurried to the door.

When Jack Delaney courted a woman, he *courted* her.

Mairie patted her hair in place and assessed the style in the mirror. Since her black hair was straight, she didn't try and fight it by attempting something curly. Better to stay with smooth, shiny and elegant . . . but she did pull one side behind her ear to expose one of the tiny pearl studs she'd purchased. It was a good imitation. Now for her makeup.

Applying a razor-thin stroke of eyeliner to her upper lid, she realized she hadn't felt this kind of excitement in a very long time. Probably not since before her marriage. She remembered the desire to look beautiful, to impress, to seduce. Strange, how what she was feeling now was different, even heightened.

"Maybe because you love the man," she muttered to herself.

Jack had already seen her at her worst. He was her friend, her partner. They had made an intimate connection that usually took months to achieve. They had shared so much, as if they'd been an established couple, and *now* was their first date? Everything was in reverse.

Why didn't that surprise her? Was there anything about her relationship with Jack Delaney that was normal?

She picked up the slate eyeshadow and lightly defined the crease at the top of her eyelid, then brushed a soft cream color onto her lids and under her brow. The effect was exactly what she wanted, she thought as she stroked the mascara onto her lashes. Softly dramatic. She wondered if Jack would think so, since she figured only flamboyant women in his time painted their faces. Well he would just have to get used to it, she decided and then remembered how he seemed to appreciate her without makeup.

Again she recalled standing between his legs and touching his hair. It hadn't been planned, yet he'd looked so flustered by her appearance in his T-shirt, that she wanted to reassure him with a gesture of compassion.

Compassion was becoming a desire for intimacy. She had felt it in her body as it responded to the electricity coming from his. The nearness of him had been almost overwhelming and she had to fight the urge to bend down and place a kiss on the top of his head. Dear God, how she wanted to feel his arms around her again.

Sighing, Mairie decided she was becoming a wanton where Jack Delaney was concerned. She applied blush, a faint lip liner, and a mocha-colored lipstick. Standing back, she looked at her reflection and smiled. Clad in her new black demi-bra and slip, she adjusted the underwires and thought how uncomfortable wearing a bra was since she'd spent so much time without one. She looked to her dress hanging on the back of the door and decided to forgo the sheer black pantyhose she'd bought. Way too hot in the desert, and she didn't want to sweat tonight. Spraying herself lightly in strategic spots with the small bottle of perfume, she whispered, "Tonight must be perfect."

Tonight was her first date with the man she loved.

She unzipped the garment bag and pulled out her dress. It was so beautiful. The perfect black dress, bias cut georgette with fifteen tiny covered buttons down the front. Slipping her arms into it, she started buttoning when she heard someone knocking on the door.

"Jack," she yelled out. "Would you see who that is?" She fastened another button and added, "Be careful."

The knocking continued. "Jack?"

He didn't answer her. Alarmed, she opened the door and stuck her head out. "Where are you?" she asked the empty room.

She heard a mumble from the other side of the door. Stepping over to it, she looked through the peephole and saw him standing there. "What happened?" she asked through the door.

"I forgot the key."

"Okay," she answered in a loud voice. "Hold on." Mairie scrambled back into the bathroom and sat on the toilet seat while quickly slipping her feet into the slinky T-strap high-heeled sandals. They added three inches to her height and she stood up while fumbling with the last few buttons.

"Mairie?"

She heard his muffled voice call out her name and answered, "Yes . . . I'll be right there." What was he doing in the hallway? This was not the way she wanted to make an impression. Rushed and flustered.

Taking a deep breath, she patted her hair one final time and opened the door.

Ready, or not, it was time to begin . . .

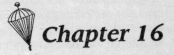 *Chapter 16*

He took her breath away, and her ability to speak. Standing there, looking so handsome and classically dressed that he could have graced the cover of *GQ*, he held a gardenia in his hand and smiled.

"How lovely you are," he paused for a moment of appreciation. "Simply exquisite."

"Jack," she quickly recovered. "You look so... handsome." She stepped back from the door and smiled. "Come in."

"Mairie, you are more lovely than this blossom. Truly." He returned her smile. "Even it fades before your beauty," he added, handing her the corsage and closing the door behind him.

"Thank you, Jack." Feeling a blush of pleasure rise to her cheeks, she looked down to the fragile blossom and whispered, "How did you know this is one of my favorite flowers?" She grazed the soft petals across her lips and took in the scent.

Mairie stepped back into the room and he followed her. She sensed his presence like an irresistible attraction she was helpless to fight any longer. Standing before the window, she turned to him.

"Would you help me put it on?"

"Certainly, Mairie, I would be honored."

He didn't take his eyes off her as he joined her.

Mairie found herself following the way his body moved, the elegant way he carried off the sophisticated suit, how his hair was pulled back, making him appear contemporary. He looked so . . . so different, almost altered, yet preciously familiar. It was as though she had always known him, yet was now recognizing him for the first time.

As she extended the flower, his hand gently wrapped around her fingers and lingered for an instant. He drew the stem from her hand and removed the stick pin. She felt him tremble slightly when he placed his fingers beneath the thin material at her neckline, and she shivered deep inside with the intimate contact of skin to skin.

"Ouch!" Feeling the stick of the pin, she flinched and then laughed.

"Oh, Mar. I do apologize . . . it's been quite some time since I—"

"It's all right, Jack." She looked back up into his eyes. "You didn't hurt me."

"I would never hurt you, Mairie." As soon as he returned her gaze the intensity came back with a powerful merging. "You're my partner. I . . . respect you."

It was as if nothing else in the room existed at that moment, except his vision penetrating every barrier of doubt or resistance she ever had in her life. It was as though he could see beyond all of it, into her mind, her heart, her very soul. She felt a tug from the center of her breasts as she fell into his soul-filled eyes.

"I trust you, Jack."

His smile was tender. His expression held a hint of something she was almost afraid to identify, in case she only imagined it.

"You are safe, Mairie," he said in a low, rough whisper.

It was a moment frozen in time as the words from

the postcard seemed to whisper through her mind.

Go beyond reason to love. It is safe. The only safety.

Could this be happening? Could the messages she was receiving be true? She only knew for certain that she had never wanted another as she wanted this incredible man who stood before her.

He reached up and his fingers gently, ever so gently, caressed her face in a silent, urgent plea. "Say something . . . please."

It was so clear for her now, and her answer was so simple.

"Yes."

His eyes searched hers, as though wanting to make sure, and Mairie did something that could only have been intuition. Slowly, with purpose, she reached up and glided her hands around the base of his head. Her fingers entered his hair and she heard his quick intake of breath. Gently, imploring consent with each fraction of motion she applied, she brought his face closer to hers. The magnetism between them grew stronger as they neared, like two powerful forces on a course that must be traveled, no matter the outcome. She felt something so intense, so compelling rushing through her body that she knew this moment was privileged, that nothing in her life had ever come close to comparing.

His eyes never broke contact as his face barely touched hers. She could feel his breath upon her skin while they stared into the depths of each other's souls.

Oh, what she saw nearly stopped the beating of her heart!

It was as though she had waited her entire life for this moment, this recognition.

"I want you, Mairie Callahan." He whispered the words into her mouth. "I want you so much I've got to tell you even though it may scare you and end this. I have never desired another woman as I thirst for you." His eyes held a look of wonder.

Her breath left her body in a rush that was almost surrender. She knew deep within her that if she proceeded, her life was again going to alter. A part of her held back, a tiny wave of uncertainty. Where she was about to travel was the unknown, for this was beyond anything she had ever known existed. This was undefinable. It could only be experienced. The uncertainty increased along with the intensity as he continued to hold her gaze, and she wondered how to trust the unknown.

Suddenly she remembered she had jumped from a plane, been thrown back in time, survived, and made it back somehow to her own time. It went beyond comprehension. She couldn't understand it or explain it to anyone else. She had done it.

Inhaling him, she closed her eyes and barely grazed the corner of his lips with her own. "Go beyond reason to love," she softly breathed against his skin, as she moved her lips over his mouth, along his nose, under his cheekbone, feeling the electricity between them build even more. "It is safe. The only safety."

He moaned in response. "Oh, precious lady . . . you *are* safe."

It started out as a gentle greeting of lips, a hesitant tasting, but soon it became a mutual supplication, a surrender, a homecoming. Jack quickly demanded a response and she gladly gave it—clinging to him, her heart singing with joy. She bonded to him, relishing the feel of his chest against her breasts, his hard thighs pressing hers, as his arms encircled her with a restrained strength.

Mairie was astonished by the ripples of pleasure that seemed to pulse from deep within her and race along her skin. Jack moaned again, as if he also felt this stunning sensation. The kiss became fast and hard, as if each couldn't get enough of the other, and when they broke away and again stared into each other's eyes, they were gasping for breath.

Without words they again came together, this time demanding more. His hands traveled over her back and into her hair, pressing her closer. Her body melted into his as her fingers clutched the fabric at his chest. They were hungry, starved for each other, and whatever barriers remained were dissolving.

It was frantic, and clothes became impediments that must be removed. She unbuttoned his jacket and pulled it over his shoulders and down his arms. Trapped for a moment, she lured him to her and kissed him again with a ravenous passion she never knew existed within her.

She stripped the jacket from his arms and threw it to the chair. He immediately reached for the buttons on her dress. "Help me, love, for I want you so desperately right now I might tear this from your body."

Her fingers fumbled along with his and the only sound in the room was their heavy breathing. When enough were unbuttoned, he slid his hands under the edges of the material and eased it off her shoulders. She brought her fingers to the middle of her chest, unhooked her bra, and allowed him to remove it. Mairie closed her eyes, threw her head back, and inhaled through her teeth as his hands produced currents of pleasure along every nerve ending he touched. It was a slice of heaven . . . the feel of his touch . . . slowly, torturously slow, grazing only the tiny hairs of her skin with his warm hands along her sides and exploring the small of her back and hips. She shivered but gave no resistance and withdrew her limbs. The dress fell to the floor and Jack exhaled with a deep moan as he gazed at her body.

"Come with me, Mairie," he said in a low voice. "Come let me love you."

She only had to smile her consent. He picked her

up, stepped over her dress and laid her gently on her bed. "What about dinner?" she whispered with a giggle.

"Do you care?" he answered with a sexy grin, as he stripped off his beautiful new clothes, threw them to the chair, and untied his hair.

Dear God, he was magnificent, she thought, shaking her head as his mouth captured hers once again and demanded her surrender.

This time she gladly gave it.

The setting sun cast fiery reflections across the room, as their lovemaking became feverish and hands became instruments of discovery and pleasure.

She felt the heat of his breath as he grazed down her torso with his lips. Like a cat he brushed his head and face back and forth across her. Her body became an altar, as his long hair caressed her skin and she arched her back in pleasure, offering herself to him. There wasn't a centimeter of her he did not worship and tears ran down her cheeks as she experienced an orgasmic flight beyond the limits of her body.

"You are exquisite," he whispered, gliding up the length of her body. The wonder on his face was now replaced with awe.

He slid his fingers firmly between hers and pressed her hands to the sheets, while gently covering her body with his. His lips found hers once more and Mairie thought surely this was heaven on earth, to be loved, joined, with another so gracefully. When he entered her body, her back again arched to receive him and the ancient, sacred ritual began, slow and deliberate, as Jack held her hands and captured her gaze.

"Beautiful, so beautiful," he whispered, his expression of wonder still bathing her with passion. "Thank you . . . thank you . . . thank you."

Tears filled her eyes, tears of gratitude to experience this divine union. *"This* is so beautiful, Jack."

Her body moved in rhythmic answer to his inviting thrusts. It was a primal dance, earthy and sacred, and they were willing participants, yielding to each other's movements.

The moon rose, basking the entwined lovers in iridescent white shadows. Time faded with the moment of merging, receding like the desert sun as Mairie and Jack released a passion kept too long under control. It was timeless and Mairie reveled as Jack threw back his head, filling the room with a primitive cry.

"Mairie . . . !"

Power filled her, a feminine power of mutual giving and receiving, and her mind, body, and soul took flight along with him . . . anywhere he was, she would follow.

And he took her to a height she had never known. *Paradise . . .*

She felt Jack's entire body relax against hers as he rested his head on her shoulder. Their bodies rhythmically twingeing from climactic pleasure as they descended from their admission.

Mairie lovingly stroked Jack's hair as he caressed her sides and slid his hands behind her shoulders and held her closer. His body slowly and naturally withdrew from hers and they lay in silence, the beating of their hearts in unison the only sound filling their senses.

Mairie stroked his back with the lightest touch and softly whispered, "I love you, Jack."

He lifted his head and gazed at her. She sensed absolute adoration in his eyes as he slowly, tenderly kissed her lips. A kiss that defined she was cherished. She knew she had never been so loved before. It was as if he were the one she had been talking to all those years in the secret recesses of her heart. The *one.* The one she believed existed, but resigned herself to thinking was a myth, never to be found in this lifetime. But here he was, with her . . . now.

This was the confirmation for why she had traveled back in time. She went beyond reason to find love. And it was safe. Safe.

Love was safe!

He rose slowly from the bed. "Come with me, Mairie . . . I want to adore you completely." He took her by the hands. She stood before him on shaky legs and he embraced her once again. Laying her head against his chest, she felt the vibrations of his deep voice. "Come bathe with me. I shall anoint you with oils and perfumes."

He led her gracefully by hand to the bathroom. She followed willingly.

He filled the tub and she stood behind him, encircling his body with her arms, as they waited. Words were unnecessary. They were communicating now on another level that needed nothing beyond touch.

Steam filled the air as she lay with her back against his chest and hot water covered their bodies like a blanket. He was massaging her shoulders with the sponge and scented gel she had purchased for bathing. Their bodies slid together and she ran her hands down his legs, memorizing each muscle, each endearing mole or scar that made him unique.

Peace descended upon them, so tenderly sensuous, until they both could feel the exquisite tension building again, coming over them in a wave that couldn't be held back. Turning to him in the water, Mairie slid over his body and captured his mouth.

"I'm hungry," she whispered, stroking his damp hair off his forehead. She reached for the phone and ordered room service. "Wait till you taste a pizza," she said, after hanging up and slipping back into his embrace with a giggle.

"I'm hungry only for you."

Their mouths met in an intimate mating. The hunger in their bodies was forgotten as the hunger in their minds and senses demanded attention. The scent of the soap, the heat of the water, the slippery texture of skin were enhancements that banished all thoughts of food.

She smiled down to him before kissing him again. "I want you," she murmured into his mouth, as his hand slid over her back in a wet caress.

His lips touched hers and lifted into a smile. "You have me," he answered. "I think, dear lady, you always have ..."

It was an insatiable passion.

"All these people! So many in one place!" He stood in the middle of McCarran airport and seemed frozen in awe. "Why, it's like a city itself."

Mairie giggled as she pulled on the sleeve of his sweater and pushed her sunglasses up the bridge of her nose. "Come on, Jack. We've got to find our gate." She led him through the throng of traveling passengers to the departing flight monitors. Her eyes scanned down the list. "Okay, there we are. Gate fourteen. Follow me, we have to pass through security now."

They stood in line and Mairie could sense Jack's tension as their turn arrived. "Just place the bag on the belt and then walk through the metal detector. It's okay, Jack, if you have any change in your pockets, put it in the dish they offer."

"Why? Do I have to pay them to go through?"

She smiled. "No, you'll get it back."

"Sir?" They both turned to the security agent.

She watched as Jack placed the new canvas bag they had purchased onto the belt. He took out his change and placed it into the dish and then took a deep breath before walking through the detector. Thank God they didn't have anything to declare, for

Jack looked so unwary and suspicious that she saw they spent time examining the contents of their bag.

The security agent handed him back his change and Mairie walked through. Picking up the bag, she handed it to Jack and said, "Well done. Now all we have to do is check in at the gate and get our seat assignments. Then we're on our way."

Even wearing sunglasses, he looked pale and nauseated, she thought. And he hadn't yet gotten on the plane. She reassuringly threaded her arm through his as they walked past gates announcing departures and lines of arriving passengers who impatiently wove their way to baggage claim.

"You'll be fine, Jack. I promise. Look at all these people. They've just done it and they look fine."

"They don't look fine, Mairie. They look grim."

She giggled as she adjusted her ponytail out the back of the baseball cap she wore as part of her disguise. "That's only because some have to make connecting flights, and others just want to get home."

A short loud beep startled them, and Jack jumped to the side as a courtesy electric cart carried an elderly couple along the terminal. Mairie bit the inside of her cheek not to laugh. She figured if the situation were reversed, she wouldn't want some future being to think she was so amusing in her naïveté. But it wasn't easy.

"Come on, it's okay, Jack," she quietly said, once more taking his arm and leading him down the terminal. "Once you get on the plane you'll be fine. This . . . this is just the frantic processing of passengers. Look, we're almost there. Gate twelve. Two more."

She could feel his muscles under her fingers tense even more.

"I'm fine," he muttered. He didn't look it.

They walked in silence the rest of the way. When they arrived at their gate, there were passengers in line and they got in the short queue. Mairie opened her purse and took out the tickets.

Jack stood at her side as she handed the tickets across the counter and said, "We need our seat assignments, please."

The airline employee smiled back at her and glanced shyly at Jack. The woman studied their tickets and started typing on the computer. She looked up at them and asked, "May I see some identification, Mr. and Mrs. Delaney?"

It was the first time someone addressed her by her fake name, and she experienced a moment of surprise before she slid a plastic card across the formica counter top, along with a piece of paper, and held her breath. The young woman looked at Mairie's new Pennsylvania license and Jack's new birth certificate, then glanced up at Jack. "Do you have any photo identification, Mr. Delaney?"

Blinking at the airline attendant, Jack began to stutter. "Ahh—"

"His wallet was stolen while we were vacationing here in Las Vegas." Mairie broke in. "We're pretty upset. We could only get this copy of his birth certificate and had to have it FedExed to our hotel just so we could get back home. The authorities assured us this would be acceptable. Is there a problem?"

"Well, no, it's just that we're supposed to get a photo ID. But the birth certificate will be fine. I'm sorry you had such a bad experience here in Las Vegas." The attendant slid the paper back to Jack. "Have you any bags to check?"

"No, we only have the carry-on." Mairie breathed a silent sigh of relief and looked at Jack. She was glad she'd learned to think quickly on her feet. It was a sales thing.

"Very good. Would you like a window or aisle seat?"

Exhaling, Mairie smiled. "Window would be

great. Do you have the emergency exit row available? My . . . my husband would love the added leg room.''

The clerk smiled prettily at Jack and then glanced at her computer screen. "Let me see what I can do."

Within two minutes they were thanking the woman and walking away. They had done it! It was clear sailing now, Mairie thought as she followed Jack to the large window.

Looking out as the plane was prepared, Jack touched his fingers to the glass and whispered, "Tell me again that something this big will stay up in the air."

She slid her arm around his waist and leaned her head against his shoulder. "Oh, Jack . . . do you think I would ever let anything happen to you now? I'm your partner, remember? I've got your back . . . and you're safe."

He leaned down and kissed the top of her head. "I couldn't ask for a better partner, *Mrs. Delaney.*"

She smiled and looked up at him. His eyes held an expression of love. Even though he hadn't said the words, Mairie knew he loved her. Nothing had ever felt this real, this true, in her life. She didn't care any longer about being his teacher. He would have lots of teachers now. She wanted to share his life, wherever they wound up.

"Hey, it worked, didn't it? No one questioned that we're married. Especially here, where there are wedding chapels on every corner. It could have happened."

"Yes," he whispered, looking back to the plane. "It could have."

Mairie was shocked to realize that she wished it were true. She was glad when they called out the boarding, though Jack once more became nervous. "All you have to do is follow me," she said, as they got in line and handed over their boarding passes.

In the jetway, Jack kept breathing heavily, as if preparing himself for battle, and Mairie wanted to hug him. Instead, she entwined her fingers through his and said, "This is like a portable bridge from the terminal to the plane. See? You can make out the side of the airplane now. We just step into it and find our seats. That's all there is to it, Jack."

"Right," he mumbled, as he cautiously ducked through the door hatch. "I'm going to fly."

She laughed. "No love, the plane's going to fly. You're going to sit back and enjoy it."

Jack rolled his eyes.

"Welcome," the lovely attendant said, with a bright smile for Jack.

"Thank you," he said, and bowed his head slightly.

Mairie tugged on his hand. Really . . . the way every female reacted to him was ridiculous, yet she wouldn't change a hair on his head. Especially his hair, she thought with a grin, as they walked through first class and entered the coach section.

Jack moved stiffly, following Mairie down the narrow aisle. He could feel his heart slamming into his ribs and his stomach muscles clenched in fear. His brain was telling him that it must be safe for all these many people to do it daily, yet his belly was shouting at him that people were meant to stay on the ground. He didn't care how Mairie described it. It didn't matter if the plane flew or he did . . . how could something this big stay in the air?

"Here we are," Mairie announced in her continually cheerful voice. She took the cloth satchel from his hand and deposited it in a small compartment over the seats. He knew she was trying to ease his fears, yet her blithe manner was beginning to grate on his already raw nerves. Of course he wouldn't tell her for fear of hurting her, and he'd vowed never to do that to this amazing woman. She was his gift.

After a life without, he knew how to treasure such a rare gift. Even if it meant following her onto this bizarre machine and entrusting his life to it. Mairie had assured him the parachute would work. It did. So, in a sense, he'd already flown. Okay, he was seating himself in a metal contraption and *flying* across the country.

"Now, these are the seat belts, Jack. We need to buckle up."

He held the gadget in his hands and placed them together as he had seen her do. Nothing happened, and the straps fell to his lap.

"No, here," she said, and reached over to slide the flat piece into the larger one.

He felt like a child. "Thank you," he answered, and looked out the small window. He could see the long expanse of white metal wing along with men who were working somewhere under the belly of the plane. Hearing thumps, he turned to Mairie and said, "What is that? What is happening?"

She shook her head and grinned. "They're just loading the luggage and cargo into the bottom of the plane. It's nothing, Jack. Relax."

"Hmm." He watched the other passengers take their seats. No one else seemed frightened, not even the children, who, he noticed, buckled their seat belts quite easily. Perhaps his nervousness was not necessary, he thought, and leaned his back against the cushion behind him. After all, if children could travel through the air without fear, he surely could.

He watched everything . . . the pretty women in uniform who walked up and down the aisle like train conductors, closing the compartments by the ceiling, talking to passengers, checking those seat belts. He showed his when the woman looked at him. Why did Mairie roll her gaze upward? Wasn't he supposed to show it?

He heard a male voice suddenly start speaking and looked around him in fright.

"It's the pilot," Mairie whispered and patted his arm. "Just listen."

He did. The man said they would be departing shortly, that they would be traveling at an altitude of thirty-one thousand feet and their traveling time would be five hours and forty-three minutes. The weather in Philadelphia was cool and clear and sixty-two degrees.

He leaned over and whispered to Mairie. "Surely, I didn't hear correctly. He said thirty-one thousand feet. *In the air?*"

She nodded. "That's right, Jack. We'll be above the clouds."

"But the planes we saw in the desert were not that high!" Nothing could fly above the clouds.

"Those were coming in for a landing. We're taking off . . ." She pointed her finger up and grinned. "Just relax. Everybody knows what they're doing."

"Everybody but me," he muttered and looked out the window as the plane started backing away from the gate. His stomach again began twisting.

The pretty woman in uniform stood in the aisle and demonstrated how to fasten the seat belts, adjust masks, and identify exits. He immediately picked up from the seat pocket in front of him a copy of the safety features she mentioned and started reading.

He wasn't pleased by what he read.

"All right, what is this about a water landing? Why would they say this unless a crash were possible? This seat is a flo-ta-tion device. Explain this, Mairie. And please be honest."

He could see she was struggling to answer him.

"Just tell me. Are these instructions in case we crash?"

"Oh, Jack. You above all should know there are no guarantees in life. The chance of that happening are so slim you shouldn't even worry about it. They just have to provide those cards in the event—''

"So it is *not* safe?"

The pilot's voice came back into the cabin. "We're next for takeoff, ladies and gentleman. Enjoy your flight and thank you for flying with us."

"Jack, please. You must try and relax. Everything is going to be fine." Mairie took the card from his hands and slid it back into the pocket and looked at him carefully. "Please, love. *Relax.*"

Jack stared at her wide eyed, still pondering his instructions. "The lady says I may have to operate this door. Mairie, I don't know if—"

"Don't worry about the door, Jack. If it's necessary, I'll open it. But it won't be necessary." Mairie's words faded as the engine's roar overwhelmed his hearing.

"Dear God," he moaned, as he braced himself against the reverberations.

"Those are the engines I was telling—" Mairie stopped herself short as she watched the look of absolute panic on Jack's face.

He stared straight ahead and gnashed his teeth as the engines' thrust propelled them forward. He was moving at a speed he had never encountered in his life. How does a human being travel like this and survive? His knuckles were turning white, gripping the chair arms as he felt the lift of the airplane's nose.

"Oh . . . shit," he groaned, when the sensation of gravity pushed him even deeper into his seat.

Although she had a concerned look on her face, Mairie seemed calm. "Jack? Honey, are you going to be all right? You look as though you're going to—"

"Fine . . . Mairie. I'm . . . fine." He forced the words beyond his clenched jaw.

She reached over to his rigid hand and began to massage it. With her arm atop his, she began to hum a song. Her voice was barely audible over the engine's blast. He didn't want to look out the window. It would be better to concentrate on Mairie's pretty voice, he thought. Music does soothe the savage breast. She must know that also.

"Thank you, Mairie," he said, still staring ahead.

"Jack, it will be fine. I promise. You jumped off a mountain using a parachute. Believe me, this is not so bad." Her smile was supposed to be reassuring.

"I've already thought that. It doesn't help."

Suddenly he heard a grinding noise from under the floor of the cabin and jolted in his seat. "What's *that?*"

She laughed. "It's the landing gear. The wheels are going up, that's all."

"That's all," he repeated, and glanced out the window. Everything seemed so far away, even the mountains. He was mesmerized, staring out to the desert. He could even see small towns scattered and those vehicles traveling on the roads. So tiny.

The plane banked and Jack gripped the arm of the chair again. It felt like the thing was falling. "Mairie . . . we're going to crash."

"We're turning, Jack. It's okay."

He let out his breath and felt a sweat break out over his body.

Nothing would be okay until his feet were on the ground again.

Five hours later he stared at the skyline of Philadelphia in awe. As they had neared the city, he kept seeing all the towns so close to one another they appeared attached. Was there no open land any longer on the eastern coast of the country, just small patches of green? How could so many people live so close, in such congestion? No wonder the newspaper stories told of violence. His body felt as though something heavy were settling upon it. Mairie told him it was the pressure in the plane as it descended, yet

Jack knew it was something more. The last time he had been in Pennsylvania, he had been at war. Mostly with himself. An uneasiness haunted him, and he glanced at the woman at his side.

Mairie was excited to be heading back to Pennsylvania, to meet with her brother, and he didn't need to burden her with the ghosts that were starting to creep back into his soul as he neared the place where he'd thought he had slain them. It didn't matter that it was over a hundred years ago. They were ghosts that knew nothing of time.

He heard the grinding beneath him and merely nodded as Mairie informed him it was the wheels being lowered for landing.

"Don't be afraid, Jack. Sometimes it can be a bumpy landing, but it's clear and sunny today, so it should be smooth."

Her smile was endearing. How she had catered to him on this fantastic ride, even when it became quite boring to be looking out the window at the clouds so far below. Then she had told him stories of her childhood, of Bryan, and then of Marc. He still didn't understand completely the bond between her brother and his friend, but he was coming to the conclusion that although it was unusual, he had known of others. Then he had been highly suspicious, but Mairie informed him that such associations were quite common and becoming more accepted. He didn't know that he could accept it himself, but for Mairie's sake he would try. So much had changed in the last century. This was just one more thing he must attempt to understand.

He didn't look out the window after seeing they were over the Delaware River as the plane approached the runway, as Mairie called it. *Runway*. He didn't care for the sound of that, nor the fact that the plane was so low the water rippled with the close proximity. He looked at the large card in the pocket of the seat before him and tried to remember everything about the flo-ta-tion cushion.

Mairie held his arm, leaned her head on his shoulder, and again began humming softly to ease his fears. What a treasure she was, he thought, and couldn't help himself from glancing from the corner of his eye to the window. They were speeding past buildings where other planes were docked. How would they ever stop at this speed that was pushing him back against the seat? Impossible!

"Umph." He couldn't control a grunt as he heard and felt a bump, then another and the plane leveled out, but it was still moving at a tremendous speed.

Then it happened.

A screeching noise assaulted his ears and he was thrust forward. Glad to be wearing the seatbelt, Jack held his breath in moments of fear until he felt the plane begin to slow down.

"You did it!" Mairie announced with a giggle and a kiss to his cheek. "You just experienced your first plane flight. Congratulations!"

He let out his breath and allowed himself a smile of accomplishment.

"There. It wasn't so bad, was it, Jack?"

"I'll let you know after we've gotten out of this flying contraption." He began trying to undo his belt when Mairie stopped him.

"You have to wait until we get to the terminal and the plane stops. I know you must be terribly sore and need to stretch." Her voice sounded sympathetic. "You didn't move the entire flight."

He rested his head on the cushion behind him, closed his eyes and sighed deeply.

"I need a convenience. Quickly."

"I told you there were small ones on the plane. If you had just listened to me and—"

"*Mrs. Delaney . . .*" he interrupted, before she

could finish her I told you so speech, "to use a current expression I heard recently . . . shut up and kiss me."

He loved to make her laugh, to see that sparkle in her eyes, as much as he loved the taste of her lips against his own.

"Gladly," she whispered, staring into his eyes, her mouth inches from his. "The kiss you shall receive. But that won't ever shut me up, buster. You'd miss the fun of me being right."

It was his turn to laugh and he could, now that they were on the ground and pulling into the terminal. "You enjoy tormenting me, don't you?"

"Because I haven't kissed you yet, or that you have to use the bathroom and I'm making you laugh?"

"Both."

Her grin widened, until she looked like a young girl. "Yeah," she whispered, and kissed him soundly.

How he adored this woman.

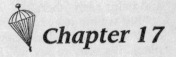

Chapter 17

Mairie held Jack's hand in the cab as they left the airport and picked up the interstate that would take them into the city. They passed the Naval Yard and Jack merely shook his head at the huge gray battle-ships in for repair. She sensed it was just another thing he would have to process later ... the *size* of everything.

"It's different here, Mairie," he said, as if picking up on her thoughts.

"It would be, love," she murmured. "It's called progress." Though as she looked out to the neigh-borhoods they passed, she saw them through Jack's eyes and was suddenly depressed. Graffiti and aban-doned houses. Garbage strewn along the streets. Run-down buildings with billboards attached to them advertising the smooth quality of a certain vodka. It all became sad. "It's not like this where we're staying. Marc has a friend who's in Europe and he's apartment-watching, so he sent the keys along with the tickets. He thinks it will be more safe if we stay there. He and Bryan will meet us. From the address, I can tell it's a nice neighborhood."

Jack smiled. "Marc appears to have many helpful friends. I am grateful for his assistance."

Glad she could distract him from the passing scen-ery, Mairie smiled back. "They call it *the community*.

I guess any group of people that is outside the so-called normal sanctions of society bands together and helps each other."

"But we are not . . ."

"You can say it, Jack. Gay. We discussed it on the plane. It's okay to say it." They would have to talk about this before Marc and Bryan arrived. "Even though you and I are heterosexual, they appreciate our nonjudgment. It makes them want to help us any way they can."

"I'm not judging, Mairie. It's just—"

"I know you're not," she quickly interjected. "I know that these things were handled differently in . . . in the past."

"It's just that . . . this is a highly unusual situation. Such an arrangement as your brother and his friend have is something that would have been kept secret in my time. Discretion would have been used."

"I understand, Jack, but would you want to live your life in secret?" Mairie asked, adjusting the blond wig she had donned in the ladies' room of the airport. It dawned on her that her own life might have to be led in secret now, and it really frightened her. What if she could never *be* herself again? She understood her brother and Marc a little better now.

"Let's not speak of this right now. Perhaps the best thing would be for you to meet Bryan and Marc and decide for yourself. There's no pressure for you to accept it, Jack. Really. I merely ask for you to extend to them the same courtesy you would show anyone else. Besides, I think you'll like them."

He squeezed her fingers. "I'm sure I will. After all, if it were not for your brother, you and I would never have met. I am grateful to him."

"Aw . . ." Mairie snuggled closer to him and hugged his arm, "how sweet. You have such a way with words, Mr. Delaney. It's kind of a lost art in this time."

Jack smiled down at her. "Are you saying, madam, that *shut up and kiss me* doesn't exactly melt a woman's heart?"

She laughed. "Let's just say a woman would have to be in the right frame of mind to hear it."

He leaned down, kissed the top of her head, and whispered, "Even though I am backward in current customs and not educated in the proper etiquette of this particular situation, I will endeavor not to embarrass you in front of your brother, Mairie. I will be a perfect gentleman."

She immediately lifted her head. "Oh, Jack. I wasn't thinking that. I was—"

"Shut up and kiss me." And he stopped any further words she could have said.

Mairie turned from the kitchen counter. "Hey, Jack, check the cabinets and see if you can find the coffee. It might be in the refrigerator, or even the freezer." When she saw the look of bewilderment on his face, she burst out laughing. "Now what?"

He shook his head, as though to bring himself into the present, and stared down at the glass of water in his hand. "All these . . . machines. I know you explained about the current of power that makes everything operate, but to see ice coming out of a door! Fire turned on with a switch at the stove!"

"Ahh, you ain't seen nothing yet. Wait till I cook dinner tonight. I can't wait to show you my culinary skills. Which reminds me, we have to get to a grocery store. Marc didn't have time to stock up for the few days we'll be here." She brushed his cheek with a kiss and opened the cabinet beside him. "Hmm, just instant coffee?"

Taking out the jar, she said, "Okay, we have an hour and a half before Bryan and Marc arrive. Let's do the shopping and add real coffee to the list." Grabbing her wig off the top of her purse, she grimaced. "I can't believe I have to wear this thing."

"It's for your protection," he said, placing his glass on the counter. "Are you sure you want to go outside to shop with your brother coming so soon? Can't we call the room service?"

Smiling, Mairie walked to the hall mirror and adjusted the wig into place. "Jack, this is an apartment. I know it looks like a hotel. I think it even was one years ago, but there is no room service. Besides, I'm so excited I need to keep busy until Bryan arrives. Come on. This will be another experience in modern living."

He rolled his gaze to the high ceiling and sighed. "How exciting. *Another* experience. I don't know that I've recovered from the last."

"This won't be as exciting as the plane trip, but I think you will be surprised."

They found a grocery store two blocks away and Jack was astounded at the amount of food displayed. He refused to accept that this was considered a small store, compared to a major chain outlet. They filled their cart and Mairie found herself enjoying the experience of shopping with a man again. She didn't know Jack had such a sweet tooth. Cookies and a large chocolate cake were added to their purchases. She had also forgotten how much fun a grocery store could provide, or how erotic certain foods could be when lovers explored the produce aisle together.

Lovers. She repeated the word in her mind, as they stood in line at the cashier. That's what they are. She couldn't let her mind wander to the future. For right now Jack was in her life, and she was going to be grateful for every moment. Leaning back against him, she smiled with appreciation as he stroked her shoulder. Yes, she was a blessed woman . . . however long it lasted.

When they left, carrying their bags with them, Jack seemed upset by the amount of noise and confusion on the street. Horns honking. The reverberating bass of blaring radios. People yelling obscenities. Roller-bladers weaving. Police whistles bleating. Ambulance sirens howling. Jackhammers blasting. Mairie was glad they only had to travel two blocks.

Back at the Rittenhouse Square apartment, Mairie and Jack put away the groceries and then she began dinner preparations. She had decided on one of Bryan's favorites, and it was also a dinner that she hoped would impress Jack. Salmon stuffed with crabmeat. She could prepare it in a casserole dish with baby carrots, mushrooms, and shallots and let the honey soy sauce marinate it until later in the evening. That way she could pop it in the oven whenever everyone got hungry.

Wiping her hands on a dishtowel, she looked at Jack. He was sitting at the kitchen table, watching her cook, a huge smile plastered on his face. "What?" she demanded with a grin. "Do you want more coffee?"

He shook his head. "I've had enough."

"Why are you staring at me like that?" She put the dish into the refrigerator.

He continued to smile. "Can't I look at you and appreciate your domesticity?"

"Domesticity?" Funny how not so long ago that remark would have made her defensive. Now she actually liked cooking for a man again. Was she getting soft?

"Yes, seeing you do feminine things makes me smile. I have seen you scale a mountain, fall to the earth not once, but twice, and challenge any male in endurance. You are an amazing woman, Mairie Callahan, and could be intimidating to some men."

She laughed and closed the fridge door. "You saved yourself with that last remark, Delaney, or we could be having one hell of a debate right now."

Jack laughed and walked up behind her at the

sink. He pulled her against him and her back arched in response. "Back to calling me Delaney again, huh? I don't know that I would interpret that as a save." His hands slowly stroked her stomach before cupping her breasts.

Moaning, she turned around and stood before him. Pulling him to her waist, she gently brushed his hair away from his face. "I take it I don't intimidate you?"

His arms slid around her waist and he hugged her, fitting her body tightly with his. "Oh no, my dear. This time may intimidate me until I learn everything I need to, but you . . . you've met your equal, madam."

Mairie smiled and rested her cheek against his chest. "I know," she whispered, right before the doorbell rang.

Startled, she jumped and announced. "It's Bryan!" She moved away a few feet and stared at Jack. "It's Bryan," she repeated, and Jack nodded.

He touched her face and smiled tenderly. "I know you're frightened, Mairie. It's all right. Your brother needs you now, and you'll be strong for him. Answer the door, sweet one. You can do it."

It was as though he knew she was keeping herself busy, not speaking about it, avoiding it. He must have known her heart was breaking, and was trying to divert her attention from what she must now face. Bryan, out of remission.

Mairie smiled and nodded as the doorbell rang again. "Thank you, Jack."

She ran to the front of the apartment.

"Hey, kiddo."

She steeled herself and was surprised to see that Bryan didn't look as bad as she had feared. He'd lost weight, around twenty pounds, was pale, but he wasn't as sick as she'd imagined. "Oh, Bryan," she called out, and threw herself into his arms.

She couldn't stop the tears as she clutched him to her and muttered, "How I've missed you. Bryan . . . Bryan . . ." She couldn't stop saying his name. "I thought . . . I thought I'd never see you again."

Stroking her back, he whispered into her hair, "Did you really?"

She shook her head and sniffled. Pulling away, she looked into his beautiful eyes and said, "No. I was just scared. Somehow I always knew I'd see you again. Oh, you look wonderful!"

"It's seeing you that's wonderful. You look great!" Bryan brought her close and again hugged her in a surprisingly strong embrace.

"And so there isn't even a how-do-you-do for someone who lit novena candles for nine days straight and isn't even Catholic?" A deep mock-serious voice behind them demanded a response.

"Marc!" Mairie held out an arm and she was enveloped between them. "Bless your heart for everything you've done. I can never repay you."

"Inviting us in would be a start, child. Besides, I'm dying to meet this mystery man. He is with you, isn't he?"

She giggled and wiped at the corner of her eyes. "Yes, he's with me. Come on in."

Mairie held Bryan's hand tightly, as if she were afraid to let it go, and led them through the apartment to the living room. Jack stood waiting for them by the sofa and Mairie's heart expanded with even more love.

"Bryan, may I present Jack Fitzhugh Delaney. He saved my life."

Bryan and Jack each walked the few feet separating them and extended their right hands.

"How do you do?" Jack asked with impeccable manners. "It is a distinct pleasure to meet you."

Bryan pumped Jack's hand and answered, "The pleasure is mine, along with a debt of gratitude I can never reciprocate for bringing my sister back to me." Bryan looked at Mairie and shook his head, as if still not believing she had been lost to him.

"Your sister exaggerates greatly, sir," Jack said with a friendly grin.

Laughing, Bryan answered, "I could really tell you some stories from her childhood. But never mind that, and please . . . no need for 'sir.' Call me Bryan."

"Such nice manners," Marc whispered to Mairie. "And gorgeous. Look at that hair."

Chuckling, Mairie hugged Marc and whispered back, "Be gentle with him, you old lecher. *Everything* is new to him, especially you."

Nodding, Marc moved forward and extended his hand. "I'm Marc Hayward. Thanks for bringing our Mairie back to us."

She watched Jack exchange pleasantries with the men and could see that he was surprised. Bryan was handsomely masculine and Marc was stylishly arty, yet also masculine. The couple complemented each other well, both tall, one with dark hair so like her own and the other blond and fair. Neither was overt in any way. Mairie's heart swelled with love. Three of her favorite people. Together. Her eyes filled with tears she couldn't hold back.

"Mairie, Mairie, quite contrary," Marc called out in his favorite expression for her. "What brings these tears to your lovely eyes? Certainly not the sight of three good-looking men who are singing your praises? You should be rejoicing."

"I am," she whispered. "I'm just so grateful . . . for all of you."

Marc came back to her and hugged her again. "And we're grateful for you, child. So dry those tears and let's have a reunion." In almost an inaudible whisper, he added, "Wherever *did* you find him?"

Taking a deep breath, she smiled and walked back

to her brother. "Let's all sit down and talk. We have quite a story to tell you."

She watched as Marc came up to Bryan and took his jacket. He helped Bryan lower himself to the sofa and then threw his own jacket with Bryan's onto a side chair. "What can I get everyone to drink?" she asked, smiling at Jack as he sat in the matching chair. "We have coffee and soda and juice. I even found some tea."

"Oh, Mairie, I'll get it," Marc announced coming up to her and pushing her lightly toward the sofa. "Go sit with Bryan. But don't you dare start the story until I return," he added as he walked in the direction of the kitchen. "We've been anticipating this for days and I do not intend to be left out, just because I've volunteered to play Hilda the maid ... though you must admit my Aryan features do fit the bill." His words trailed off as he rounded the corner.

Mairie and Jack both grinned and Bryan shook his head. "You'll have to forgive Marc, Jack. He takes some getting used to, I'm afraid."

"I heard that!" Marc yelled from the kitchen.

"You were supposed to," Mairie yelled back and sat on the rug between Bryan on the sofa and Jack in the chair. She patted her brother's foot. "Thank God, I found you."

Bryan's hand rested on the top of her head for a moment. "I know, Mar. Seeing your face a few minutes ago wiped out the hell of the last seven months. I don't understand what happened to you yet, but I knew you'd come back. I never gave up hope."

Sniffling the tears that threatened again, Mairie turned her face and smiled into her brother's eyes.

"She never did either, Bryan," Jack said in a low, respectful voice. "There is a great bond between you."

Mairie turned to look at him and swore she saw

a twinge of sadness in his eyes. Suddenly she realized that he had lost not only his birth family but also his adopted family as well. He was all alone now. She reached out her hand for his and gently kissed his knuckles. "You're family now, Jack. As long as you want, we're here for you. All of us."

"Absolutely," Bryan joined. "Though you may want to reconsider Marc. He can be bossy and—"

"Bite your tongue, big brother," Mairie interrupted with a grin. "Here he comes."

"Talking about me, are you?" Marc asked, as though not really interested. From a tray, he served the drinks and set a plate of chocolate chip cookies onto the coffee table. "The Malloys are up to their old tricks again. See if I care."

"Oh, you know we love you," Mairie chided, and winked at Jack. "We waited for you. Didn't even mention that I traveled back in time."

Marc, about to sit down next to Bryan, froze in mid-act. "I beg your pardon?"

Mairie laughed at her brother's and especially Marc's expression of disbelief as he continued to sit, very slowly. "You heard correctly. I traveled back in time." She leaned forward and took Jack's hand again. "And this incredible man risked his life and left the year 1877 to bring me home. We're . . . we're time-travelers."

Marc looked at Bryan. Bryan looked at Jack and then at her and then at Marc. "You heard that, didn't you? It wasn't the pain pills working overtime? I'm not hallucinating? She said, *time-travelers?*"

Marc held Bryan's hand tightly and answered, "Screw the pain pills, if I heard correctly, we're *all* hallucinating!" He turned to her. "Mairie, you can't be serious!"

She and Jack laughed.

"He *is* quite humorous. You were right, Mairie."

"I told you, but then you know how I love to be right."

Leaning over, Jack kissed her forehead. "And I secretly love you being right. You take such pleasure in it."

"*Excuse me . . . ?*" Marc raised his voice over their conversation. "I hate to interrupt this oh-so-precious Kodak moment, but what the hell are you saying here? You can't travel through time!"

Mairie became serious. "Tell that to the government. I jumped after you, Bryan, and before I pulled the chute, I experienced this blinding white light. I thought I was dying, or had died, when I felt this . . . I don't know how to describe it, this weird sensation in every nerve of my body. I was so scared because I was tumbling, 'cause I forgot to arch my back. Remember how we were supposed to arch our backs right away, Bryan?"

"Oh, who cares about your back, Mairie?" Marc interrupted, as Bryan nodded with his jaw dropped in disbelief. "Get on with it before I call for strait jackets." He grabbed a Coke and muttered, "I wonder where Sydney hides the liquor in this place. I could use a bottle."

Mairie shook her head and giggled. "I found it when we arrived this afternoon. It's in the kitchen. Top cabinet over the refrigerator."

Marc waved his hand. "To hell with it. I don't want to miss a syllable of this. You were tumbling and forgot to arch your back; now, get on with it, woman, while I'm still conscious. I swear I'm close to . . . to the vapors, or something." Waving his hand in a fanning motion under his chin, he looked at Jack and muttered, "How's that for time-traveling?"

Jack threw back his head and laughed, causing Mairie and even Bryan to join in. "Very good," Jack said in between lingering chuckles. He rose to his feet and said, "I'll get the liquor, Marc. You sit and collect yourself. How does a bit of wine sound?"

"Not strong enough," Marc answered, sitting back and holding his forehead. "See if Sydney has a bottle of rum, or something equally potent. It's the least I deserve for watering his plants for the last three months and now listening to . . . to *this!*"

"Mairie . . . what you're saying is too incredible," Bryan said, ignoring Marc who was now shaking his head. "I never even saw you jump. I thought the skydiving school was lying and trying to cover up some foul play. I even thought you might have suffered a mental breakdown and they landed with you and you wandered away. But this . . . this is—"

Bryan struggled for the right word and before he could find it, Jack returned to the room and said in a serious voice, "I will tell you what it is. This is the truth."

He placed the bottle of rum in front of Marc and took his seat. Looking directly into Bryan's eyes, he continued, "I saw your sister fall from the sky. I was on a vision quest and sitting on top of the tallest mountain I had ever seen. I asked the Great Spirit of the Paiute to send me a sign of hope and Mairie came, floating, it appeared, from heaven. My angel—"

"This is too bizarre," Marc muttered, pouring a shot of rum into his cola.

Jack continued. "She is telling the truth, Bryan. Please listen to your sister. She risked her life over and over just to be sitting here right now. I have never seen anyone with more determination, more love, than this woman. And she did it all to get back here to tell you this very story. Trust her."

He smiled down at her and Mairie had to swallow the thick lump in her throat.

Jack looked back to her brother. "I did. With my life. And that trust wasn't misplaced."

Mairie took a deep steadying breath and turned

back to Bryan and Marc. "It happened," she said simply. "I met this man in 1877."

Marc picked up the bottle and poured still more rum into his glass. "This is like living an episode of *The Twilight Zone.* Any moment I expect to hear Rod Serling's voice telling me not to adjust the channels." He gulped the drink. "Except he wouldn't be telling me if I'm not watching it, if I'm bloody well in the damn episode, would he?"

Mairie was half laughing, half crying, and she wanted to reach out and hug her brother and sweet, funny Marc. "I know how this sounds. I fought it myself for days, but it's true. I swear. Everything I'm about to tell you happened."

"I feel like I am in an alternate reality," Marc muttered to himself.

Patting Marc's leg, Bryan said, "Calm down. This is Mairie. She wouldn't put either of us through this unless it was true." Addressing Mairie, he smiled shakily and said, "Go on. You forgot to arch your back . . ."

Mairie smiled her thanks to Bryan and felt Jack's hand on her shoulder in a display of strength and support. As she observed her brother and Marc, she realized they were all connected to one another and smiled through her tears. "I am a fortunate woman to be surrounded by such wonderful people. Anyway, Jack is right. I had to get back here to you, Bryan. I would have done anything to tell you what I learned."

Marc sipped his drink and muttered into it. "Well, it's obvious you learned to arch your back."

Everyone laughed, even Marc, and his words broke the serious mood.

"Yes, I arched my back after I felt that white light enter my body, and I straightened out immediately, and after I pulled the chord I looked for you, Bryan. But you were gone. Everything familiar was gone.

You. Las Vegas. There was nothing but desert.
Everything I knew as my reality had disappeared . . ."

There were no more interruptions, and Mairie and
Jack told their incredible story.

The recounting took hours and they stopped while
Mairie prepared dinner. Marc called it a very long
commercial, and couldn't wait to get back to what
he called the twilight zone. During that time, she
heard Jack and Bryan and Marc talking. Her brother
and his companion were asking questions about
what life was like in the last century. Mairie felt like
the night was almost magical when they all sat
down to dinner and, after praising her for the stuffed
salmon, Bryan and Marc begged them to continue.
Jack became the perfect dinner host intuitively assisting, serving, and entertaining their guests, and
Mairie felt their partnership grow to an even more
expansive level. They worked so well together, their
movements gracefully paired with unspoken syn-
chronicity.

Dinner was cleared and the conversation continued over two pots of coffee, three-quarters of a chocolate cake, and brandy before she and Jack ended
the story with Mairie calling Marc from the hotel
lobby of the Luxor.

Marc looked exhausted. His usually impeccable
hair was disheveled. His sleeves were rolled up and
his shirt unbuttoned. Bryan, surprisingly, looked
better than when he had walked in the door. He
seemed energized.

"You are saying, Mairie, that you hid a jar in a
cave over a hundred and twenty years ago and you
expect to find it now?"

She was tired and her jaw hurt from speaking so
long, but she nodded and said, "It has to be there,
Bryan. You heard Jack. He buried it. We would have
rented a car and driven there before we left Vegas,

but Marc scared me when he told me about the government looking for me. I could only think of getting back here to you and didn't want to take the chance that anything, or anyone, might stop me."

"So what do we do?" Marc asked, wiping his forehead with his dinner napkin. "Send you back there? I told you they're tapping our phone. I know this because I have a friend who gave me this detection device and it registers. Bryan and I decided to leave it on, rather than alert them that we know about it. I wouldn't trust my cell phone, either."

"Area 51," Jack said, looking at Mairie. "You didn't mention that when you told me about Harmon. I didn't want to interrupt while you were telling Bryan and Marc, but what does it mean?"

Marc shook his head and almost whined the *Twilight Zone* theme song. "Do-do-do-do . . ."

"Gimme a break, Marc," Mairie said with a tired chuckle. She looked at Jack and sighed.

"I don't think that anyone knows how to explain it. Only those who have been stationed there or work there could answer that truthfully. It's a highly secret government installation. Something is going on there that they don't want the average citizen to know about—"

"I saw a documentary where this reporter sneaked onto the property and was immediately met by armed guards. They were really threatening and—"

"And aliens are supposed to be there," Marc interrupted.

"You've had too much to drink," Bryan said with a grin.

Mairie leaned closer to them. "What if they're doing secret testing there? On time? Look, I lost seven months. Seven months! I was only back there four days."

No one said anything for a prolonged moment.

"Sydney has a computer," Marc said. "I'm going

on the Net to see what I can find." He pushed his chair away from the table and walked toward the back of the apartment.

"What's the net?" Jack asked.

"Computers," Mairie answered, as Marc stopped and walked back to the dining room table.

"Care to come with me, Sundance? If you can jump off a mountain, you can surf the Net. It ain't that scary."

"Certainly," Jack said, and stood up. Stretching, he looked to Mairie. "Would you excuse me?"

She smiled. "Don't be too overwhelmed by what you'll see. It's only a machine."

"A machine that's changed the world," Marc retorted, defending his passion.

"Granted," Mairie conceded. "Just go easy, Marc. Jack's already been hit with a lot of changes."

She watched Jack and Marc walk away and turned to her brother. "Isn't he wonderful?"

Bryan smiled tenderly. "He's wonderful, and you deserve him. He's your reward, Mairie. Happiness. What a novel idea, huh?"

She grinned. "Right. All those years, Bryan . . . I was so angry. And I feel now as if a boulder has been lifted off my heart."

"So you had to go back a hundred years to heal?" Laughing, he added, "You are one stubborn woman sometimes."

"*Moi?*" Her eyes were wide with innocence.

Bryan became serious in their moment of privacy. "Thank you, Mairie. I don't know if this herb, this plant, will help, but I'm willing to give it a try if it's still there. What you did for me . . ." He shook his head in disbelief.

"I love you," she whispered through her tears. "You're my big brother."

"I am sorry to interrupt," Jack announced as he walked into the dining room. "But Marc said you both should come and see this." He looked shaken.

Mairie helped Bryan rise and whispered, "Sweetie, do you want to lie down now? It's been a long night."

"I'm fine. Haven't had this much excitement since . . . since I jumped out of that plane."

"Jack, would you bring one of the armchairs into the back office for Bryan?"

Bryan protested, but Mairie insisted.

When they entered the small office, Marc turned from the computer. "Wait till you guys read this. I'm going to print it out. You know how much stuff there is on this subject? I mean some of it is wacko, but some of it is real science. Like this one site . . . any of you ever hear of the Montauk Project, or the Philadelphia Experiment?"

They all shook their heads. Bryan sat in the overstuffed chair and thanked Jack, while Mairie took a seat on the rug. Jack joined her and smiled as he stroked her hair. Mairie had to admit she was tired. It had been a full day, and she appreciated his gentle attention. They all listened as Marc continued to read off the computer screen.

"Well, this is long but I'll try to shorten it. Listen to this . . . the origin of the Montauk Project dates back to 1943, when radar invisibility was being researched aboard the USS *Eldridge*. When the *Eldridge* was stationed in the Philadelphia Naval Yard, it was involved in this test called the Philadelphia Experiment. The object was to make the ship undetectable to radar, and while that was achieved, it had some pretty nasty results for the crew members. It was a catastrophe, as far as people were concerned. Death. Burning. Mental disorientation. Those who survived were discharged as mentally unfit or otherwise discredited and the whole affair was covered up."

Bryan was skeptical. "Oh, Marc. Not another conspiracy theory."

"No, listen . . . now they talk about someone I know of, John Von Neumann, he was the inventor of the modern computer and a mathematical genius. It says after World War II he was able to draw on the enormous resources of the military industrial complex."

"This sounds weird, Marc," Mairie conceded.

"Wait a minute. The Germans had this incredible technical knowledge, and after the war some of the scientists came to the States and some went to Russia, and even more defected when east Berlin came under Russian control. That was the beginning of the cold war, and the arms race. This claims the scientists here in the States started a project in Long Island that dealt with time travel. We're talking back in the forties and the fifties and continuing up till today. All this is now under something called the Black Card clearance level, and—"

"Harmon mentioned that," Mairie interrupted in an excited voice. "I didn't know what he meant, and I was too scared at the time to question him about it."

"Well, this explains it," Marc said. "It's just about the highest level of clearance there is, and most people don't even know it exists. And this means, in essence, that it is such a deep black hole project that all the records, everything connected to it, is buried in a black vault and nobody has access to it, not even members of government, without a need-to-know clearance. Listen to this. Here's an account from one of the crew of a battleship the Navy reportedly made disappear in Philly and reappear minutes later in Norfolk. This guy survived and told his story when he was an old man. Name's Carlos Allende . . ." and he read right from the screen for the next ten minutes.

Mairie was horrified to hear about secret government projects and installations on the East Coast, the

West Coast, and in between. How much of it was truth, she would never know, but she did know about Harmon and how determined he was to stop her and Jack. The fact that she was an innocent caught up in a military test meant nothing to him.

Marc took a deep breath and said, "Okay, here's the end. 'The Philadelphia Experiment and the Montauk Project were key parts of American history because they demonstrate what a government is willing to do to have an advantage in war. Whatever the truth really is about these experiments into time travel, Carlos Allende says it perfectly. *'The ultimate truth will be a truth too huge, too fantastic, not to be told. Perhaps one day we the people will be told the truth.'* "

"Sounds pretty far-fetched," Bryan said.

"Yeah? Well so does Mairie and Jack's story. Oh, this is cool," Marc added, as he clicked on another site. "This one goes from time travel and the Pythagorean theorem into Einstein. They jump straight to Einstein's Theory of Relativity, which states that neither time, nor length, nor even mass remain constant additive quantities when approaching the speed of light—"

Mairie sat listening and all she could think of was that Marc's rambling of physics was sounding like the Peanuts cartoons when the adults were talking to the children: *wha, wha, wha, wha, wha, wha.* None of it made sense. It was like he was speaking a different language.

Science.

"Look," she interrupted. "I don't have to understand *how* it happened. I know it happened. I want to know *why* it happened."

"Well, I think it's interesting. Who would have thought that so many people were involved or even interested in time-travel experiments. It ain't science fiction anymore," Marc stated, typing in something else in his search. "Okay, let's look up Area 51."

She touched Jack's hand and smiled. "I know none of this makes sense to you, but don't feel intimidated. If it makes you feel any better, I don't understand it either."

"I'm a simple man, Mairie. I don't have to understand. I'm living proof of this time travel."

"Hey, listen to this one." Marc sounded excited again. "Okay, I've skipped all the alien stuff about Roswell, though that would explain how we got advanced technology for this. All right, here's something definitive. Well, kinda . . . 'According to the U.S. government, Area 51 doesn't exist. It's an Air Force base in southern Nevada. It's also known as Dreamland and is surrounded by the Nevada Test Site and Air Force base. Area 51 has nine large hangars, and this is probably where the Black Book Projects are located.' There's that term again," Marc muttered. "Wow, you ought to hear about the security."

"What I want to know is why the government has granted the security guards authorized deadly force to keep the public out." Bryan sounded serious. "And why my phone is tapped. And why the harassment? What the hell is the reason? Because some technology not yet known to the public is being tested there?"

"Maybe they don't think the public can handle it, that we aren't ready to accept a new or different reality," Mairie said, thinking aloud. "Remember the notions that the earth wasn't flat, or wasn't the center of the universe. Both were met with great opposition. New thinking, thoughts that shake up the old opinions, are always suspect and challenged by the establishment. We want to think we're safe, that we're right. If the public knew that time travel was possible and being used by our government, what else is being done that we have no knowledge about? This is opening a can of worms. If this is released it could threaten the stability of . . . of the economy, religions, government—all our personal belief systems. No wonder all this is Black Carded or Black Booked.''

She looked at the men. ''They aren't going to just question me, are they? They're going to try and shut me up.''

''What do you want, Mairie? You want to blow the whistle on this thing? It probably isn't even known in the top levels of the government. This could be a radical branch of the military, or something,'' Bryan said. ''You want to talk to a reporter, or something?''

She shook her head. ''I want to slip quietly back into my life.'' She looked at Jack. ''They can't find out about him.''

Everyone agreed it was the best plan.

Jack stretched his legs out in front of him and cleared his throat. ''Excuse me, but I think we're getting away from the real issue here. How can we get back to that cave and look for the jar? Then we can all disappear.''

''Jack's right,'' Mairie stated. ''Somehow, we need to get back.''

''How?'' Marc asked. ''After reading this stuff, I'm even more convinced you shouldn't get involved in any way. Don't let them know you're here in the present. How would they, anyway? Harmon didn't make it back, or you would have been picked up immediately.''

''Maybe they have some kind of technology that indicates two people returned,'' Bryan suggested. ''They would think it's Mairie and Harmon, but when Harmon doesn't show up, maybe they think they both died, or something. Like in that Philadelphia Experiment. It was a test, and they screwed up the first time when Mairie was thrown back in time. Maybe Mairie's safe to go back to Nevada. They don't know anything about Jack at all."

"We have to go back," Mairie stated. "Jack and I didn't go through all that for nothing. We have to at least try to find that jar."

"So when do we leave?" Bryan asked.

Marc turned away from the computer with his mouth opened. Nothing came out for a few moments and when he finally spoke his voice was almost a shocked whisper. "You think you're going with them? You didn't get enough of your grand adventures? You're going again?"

"I have to, Marc," Bryan said with a regretful tone.

"Then I'm going, too."

Everyone looked at Marc. His expression was determined. "You took off once, Bryan Malloy, and I'm not about to sit here and wait again. So I suppose we're all going off on this scavenger hunt through time together. Besides . . . this time you need me."

Bryan smiled. "You're right. I do."

"Then it's settled," Mairie declared and rose to her feet. "We're all going. When do we leave?"

"The sooner the better," Bryan said, and Jack helped him stand as Marc shut down the computer. "I'll be glad to get off the East Coast for a while. I've been thinking Tucson might be a good place to relocate. We can check that out after Vegas."

"Tucson? *Arizona?*" Marc stared at Bryan as though he were joking.

"Yes, some place warm for a change."

"Doesn't Arizona have snakes, scorpions and tarantulas, and . . . and desert?" Marc looked horrified.

"It's just an *idea*, Marc," Bryan said with a laugh. "Come on, we've kept these two up long enough. Time for all of us to get some sleep. We have a trip to plan tomorrow," he added, while walking out of the office.

"Why don't you and Marc spend the night here,

Bryan?" Mairie asked, as she followed her brother from the room.

"Yes. It's late," Jack agreed. "Stay the night and we can make our travel arrangements in the morning."

"There is a second bedroom," Marc said. "It might be a good idea, Bryan. You do look tired now."

"Fine, how can I stand up against the three of you?" Bryan smiled. "We'll plan our trip in the morning."

Mairie and Jack almost fell into bed, exhausted from the full day. When she was snuggled against his body with his arm around her, Mairie sighed with contentment and whispered, "I'm glad you like Bryan and Marc. They are both so dear to me."

He kissed the top of her head. "Yes," he whispered back. "They are fine people." He sighed deeply and added, "I still can't believe this morning I was in Nevada and tonight I am sleeping in Pennsylvania. I feel like I've time-traveled again."

She giggled. "Just space-traveled, Jack. Jet lag. Though there is a three-hour time difference."

He chuckled. "Don't even try to explain, Mairie. My brain actually hurt attempting to understand Marc's computer information."

Mairie suddenly became serious. "It doesn't sound good, though. I wonder if I'll ever be able to be myself again, to use my own name. I can't believe I have to go into hiding from my own government. Talk about being in the wrong place at the wrong time. Thank God my money is in mutual funds and Bryan has access to it. Wherever I wind up until this blows over, he can send me money and the government can't touch it."

He hugged her gently. "I'm so sorry you've lost your identity, your life here."

She shrugged. "We're a pair, huh? Now both of us are strangers in a strange land."

They lay in silence for a few minutes and then Jack whispered, "Mairie . . . ?"

"Yes?"

"Do you think you could hire one of those cars for us while we're here?"

"I don't know that I can, unless I use Marc's credit card. But maybe. Why? Where do you want to go?"

"Gettysburg."

She raised her head and stared at him in the darkness. "Really?"

He nodded. "Yes. I've been thinking about it, and when Marc was reading from the computer about the government, I was remembering everything I thought I was fighting for, what we all thought we were fighting for . . . this country, and wondering again about power and its misuse, and the lives that are affected when that happens."

She didn't say anything, just held him close and listened.

"I never believed I would revisit the East Coast. I kept thinking this might be the only chance I have to return to where I lost my soul. Maybe it's time to bury all the old ghosts once and for all. If I can . . ."

How she loved this man. What courage he possessed. He had said she'd met her equal and she wondered if she could match his strength of character.

"We'll go tomorrow," she said and kissed his cheek. She looked at the clock on the night table, saw it was after three A.M. and sighed. Settling back into the crook of his arm, she whispered sleepily, "Anywhere you are . . . I've got your back."

They held each other and drifted off, entwined in more than body.

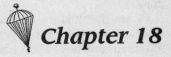 *Chapter 18*

"Stop the car."

Jack stared out the passenger window. "Please Mairie, stop."

Mairie slowed the car to the side of the road and placed it in park. With the engine idling, she looked at Jack and traced his vision beyond the open field to a lengthy ridge. "What is it?"

There was a prolonged silence as she continued to watch him staring out the window.

"I'll never forget his name," Jack finally whispered as he sat, almost mesmerized.

"Tell them I died honorably," he murmured.

Fumbling for the handle, Jack opened the car door and stepped out onto the grassy roadside.

"Who, Jack? Who died?" Mairie implored, reaching too late for Jack's hand.

She stopped the engine and slid across the seat and out the passenger side. "Jack, you're talking in riddles. I don't understand." She slowly walked down the gully and approached him from behind as his gaze remained transfixed upon the hills.

Mairie tenderly placed her arms around his sides and looked over his shoulder to the sunlit knolls.

"That's when I knew that I was dead." Jack inhaled deeply and closed his eyes.

Mairie held tighter and paused as she knew he

was working something out in his head and heart. "But you're here, now, Jack. It's over. It's just history."

"I am that history, Mairie. Living history. I have not had over a hundred years to bury the ghosts of the men and boys slain here. It's been only a little more than a decade since I walked away from this field." A shudder passed over his body. "I can still hear their cries."

Mairie, resting her head against his back, looked around to the peaceful countryside of Gettysburg. "Oh, Jack," she breathed softly.

"Can't you hear them? *Shh...*" He looked around the open field. "Can't you feel them all around you?" A tortured look came over his face. "Listen, Mairie ... for they are here, and my spirit died with them that day."

Jack suddenly took her hand and walked further toward the field. Worried, she followed beside him as he helped her over a weathered post-and-rail fence.

"There's a greater story than the museum and plaques tell, Mairie. So much more. I don't think there's anything heroic about the carnage that took place here. It was madness. *Madness...*"

"Then tell it, Jack." Mairie sat on a rail of the fence and listened intently, knowing somehow this man needed to release it.

Taking a deep breath, Jack squinted toward the ridge and continued. "It was a suicide charge, plain and simple," he began in a low agonized voice, and Mairie knew he was seeing it again, as it had happened.

"I was commissioned a lieutenant in the Union Army. Everyone with an education was, and I commanded a regiment that stood upon that very ridge, not so long ago." He pointed. "We had a wall of cannons over a mile long up there, and we assaulted the Confederate Army camps with artillery for nearly two hours on the morning of July third, 1863. Our guns stopped only by our astonishment. There . . ." and he waved his hand across the field, ". . . in the early morning light, amidst smoke and screams from the depths of hell marched flag bearers and drummer boys. Children. Lee had Pickett send children into battle along with the men, those thousands of men marched in perfect parade formation across this field then up that ridge. There was an eerie silence for just an instant as we gaped. You would have had to have seen it, Mairie . . . we were stunned. Absolutely stunned."

She didn't say anything, entranced by his words. It seemed so real, and she could sense his torment.

"Then someone yelled, *'Come on, Johnny Reb! We got your Seccesh here!'* And the firing commenced." His face became rigid with the recollection and he drew a deep breath.

"God help us, we fired upon them all; men who should have been at home with their wives and children, working their farms, boys who should have been in school learning about anything besides man's inhumanity to man." He paused and looked back at Mairie.

"Madness," he repeated.

His expression was pained and she could see the tension around his eyes, the way the muscles in his cheeks worked as he ground his back teeth to stop the emotion. "It was a fierce artillery barrage. Brother against brother. Yells and screams. Men calling for their wives, sons for their mothers, and begging, pleading, for water, to be put out of their misery. I don't know how they did it, but some actually broke through our line. It must have been a half hour of hand-to-hand combat. Seemed like hours passed. My men were exhausted, most hadn't been home in two years, and I did everything I could to rally and support them."

She wanted to touch him, to wrap him in her arms and take away the horror that was playing inside his head. She thought of the millions who'd carried similar atrocities in their minds throughout history and tears ran down her cheeks. All she could do now was support him, listen, assist him in healing those deep scars.

"I'd just pulled a Reb off Randy Sullivan and turned around directly into the point of a bayonet. This . . . he couldn't have been more than nineteen, this boy thrust his bayonet into my chest. I didn't feel it, Mairie. Not at first. There was mostly surprise and . . . and I grabbed the stock of his rifle."

Jack closed his eyes and swallowed deeply. "We . . . we stared at each other for . . . I don't know, seemed like forever, but it was probably only a second or two. We looked each other right in the eye, past the uniforms, the issues, the commands from our superiors. None of that existed in that moment. It was just him and me. Life and death. And his bayonet was in my chest. I never felt anything like that in my life, that kind of separation from everything but that kid in front of me. It was as if he was stealing my soul. I . . . brought up my pistol and shot him . . . in the chest. Point blank. Just shot him . . ."

His words trailed off and Jack's mouth trembled with the recollection.

"He dropped to his knees, still staring into my eyes. And then . . . then he reached into his jacket . . . it was so bloody, and he pulls out this picture. *A picture!* I could see in his face he accepted his fate, as though he'd known it when Pickett had ordered him on the damn charge. His hand was shaking as he handed it to me. *'Tell them I died honorably,'* he pleaded."

"Oh, God . . ." Mairie's hand covered her mouth

to stop the sobs. She must remain strong for him now, somehow.

"I took it," he continued in a shaky voice, biting the corner of his mouth to control his own tears. "It was a picture of his family. His mother and father and two brothers. And the city and state of his home were written on the bottom."

"Jack . . ."

He didn't hear her, for now that he told the worst of it, it was as though he had to continue, to rip it out of his mind.

"I pulled the bayonet out of my chest and sank to the ground, just holding that picture as that kid died in front of me. All around me was insanity. Men falling. Screams of agony. And I looked at the picture again and knew, I mean I *knew*, that I had nothing against that young man, that under any other circumstances we might have laughed together. He was fighting for another man's dreams . . . and so was I. We were pawns in something so big that neither of us realized it until that very moment."

He ran his hand over his eyes, as if weary. "I knew I was fighting someone else's war. It wasn't mine. Insanity was taking place all around me and I remembered my Paiute brothers. I remembered that once I knew of balance, of peace with the earth, and I threw back my head and starting singing the Paiute Song of Death. Right there in the middle of the battlefield as the Confederates retreated. I stayed there until the ambulance team came and found me. They put me in a cart and took me to the hospital, an old barn with a corn crib filled with amputated limbs. When they had a two-horse load, they carted it away. I sat there for hours and counted how many times they emptied it. Eventually, a surgeon came out and stitched me up, but I knew I was already dead. That's when I got up from that hospital and took to walking . . . and I never looked back until today. I had fevers, hallucinations, but I kept walking. Somehow I had to get back to my brothers. I didn't have a blood thirst, not for campaigns, battles, issues, politics . . . none of it. I had to get home to sanity."

He wiped at the corner of his eye and pinched the bridge of his nose. "It took me awhile, but I realized I deserted. All I wanted after that was to live my life quietly, to work my way back to Nevada."

Mairie jumped off the fence and closed the distance between them. She wrapped her arms around his chest and clung to him. "Oh, Jack . . . You didn't desert. You woke up, that's all. You remembered who you were. Your mind and heart were always Paiute. They took you away to . . . to their missionary schools and tried to make you one of them, but you never truly bought into it, you aren't an aggressor, your people believe in peace. You couldn't be the institutions, the establishment, or what they demanded, you had to be *you*. All you did was wake up, my love, and begin your journey back home."

He held her tightly, so tightly that Mairie couldn't breathe. She pushed back gently on his shoulders and whispered, "It's okay, Jack. It's okay . . ."

Pulling back her hair he clutched it in his hand and looked into her eyes. "Mairie, all of this . . . all of it . . . it seems beyond reason."

Looking up to the trees, she continued to hug him and tenderly whispered, "Oh, Jack, go beyond reason . . . reason can't help now. I saw it on a postcard. *Go beyond reason to love. It is safe. It is the only safety.* Say good-bye to the ghosts. Do it with love . . . Love, Jack, and you will be safe."

Jack pulled back and stared into her eyes. "I love you, Mairie Callahan."

She quickly exhaled into a smile. "I know," she whispered, with as much love as she was feeling.

"I knew when you left that mountain to find me."

Her smiled widened. "Just took *me* four days and seven months in two different ages to remember how completely my heart belongs to you. Thank you, Jack Fitzhugh Delaney, for finding me, for reminding me what love is, what I always wanted and thought wasn't possible. I was so lost. So lost . . ."

"You knew then, huh?" His smile was lovingly provocative. "Ah, how you love being right, my time-traveling *woman*." He chuckled and lightly shook his head. "And heaven help me, but you are an amazing woman!"

"Why, I'm your gift. You said so." She smiled just as provocatively, as she wiped the tears from her eyes. "I love you. And I am your gift. I do believe heaven already helped you. You went beyond reason to love, and found out it's not only safe, it's . . ." She threw her head back and looked up to the sky and then as the word came to her, she quickly stared back into Jack's eyes and smiled, wanting to connect again, wanting him to understand the depth of her.

"It's not only safe, Jack. It's our reward. Our gift." She pulled him closer and kissed him.

Jack moaned and deepened it, challenging her to go with him, to soar to another level. She gladly followed his lead and when they broke apart, Jack muttered roughly, emotionally, "Anywhere, Mairie Callahan, anywhere you are. I would be with you."

She let the tears flow down her cheeks. It didn't matter that her mascara was probably running, that she looked stupid when she cried. Nothing mattered but the truth.

"How about Vegas, and then who knows where? We'll live in the moment and see where it takes us. It worked getting us here, so far. What do you say we go for the adventure of our lives?" She was actually giggling at the thought.

He chuckled, joining in her excitement, and then pulled her closer until his lips were inches from her own. When he looked down into her eyes, that expression of wonder had come over him. She stared at his mouth as he began to whisper.

"Hey, partner . . . I've got your back. You're safe."

She gasped in awe. No matter what the future held, she knew one thing.

She was with her mate.

As they drove away from the field, Jack looked out the window at the passing scenery and said in a quiet voice, "Mathias Boyer."

Mairie took her right hand from the steering wheel and tightly squeezed his left. Now she knew the name of a mother's son, a father's pride, a brother's friend. Mathias was honored and could rest in peace within Jack's mind.

He had walked in his ghost's shoes, seen them as invisible, and had reclaimed his life.

What a gift . . .

He sat in the front seat of the four-by-four and looked out over the desert landscape, some of it so unchanged in the last hundred years, he felt as if he could be home, and some changed so drastically that it ate away a little at his gut. There were so many fantastic discoveries, inventions, conveniences, so many improvements in the lives of those who lived now. Yet something crucial seemed to be missing, and Jack couldn't put his finger on it. Not yet.

He pushed it out of his mind and ran his hand over the leather on the panel in front of him. It wasn't real leather, but that didn't matter. It was still a great machine. He liked it far better than the other vehicles they had used. This one excited him, and this was the first time that he had the opportunity to sit in the front seat while traveling at such speeds. Once he'd gotten used to the motion, he relaxed and started studying the way Marc operated it. He watched how the right foot would push on one pedal to make it go faster and on another pedal to the left to slow it. He couldn't see that Marc did much more than steer it after that, except to operate some lever on the left when he turned.

Jack knew he could do it.

He kept his silence for some minutes, trying to decide how he could ask Marc to hand over the control. Dismissing them all, he decided simply to ask. The worst Marc could say was no. But if he didn't ask, he thought he might never have the chance. He sat up straighter and took a deep steadying breath.

"May I ask a favor, Marc?"

"Certainly."

"Would you allow me to operate this vehicle? Just for a few minutes. I would love to know what it's like."

Wearing a large felt hat, Marc turned to him and pulled his sunglasses down his nose, revealing his eyes. "You want to drive?"

"Drive. Yes. I would like to drive." At least he didn't refuse right away. Perhaps there was hope.

Marc turned back to the road. He then looked behind them in a mirror. "Okay," he said, pulling the vehicle over to the shoulder.

"What's wrong?" Mairie asked from the back.

Jack hoped she wouldn't object, especially now that Marc was stopping the car. In just moments he could be oper . . . *driving.*

"Our cowboy wants to drive," Marc announced to the back seat.

"Oh, Jack, do you think you should?" Mairie looked behind them to see if any others were present to witness.

He nodded firmly. "Yes. It's time I learned."

She shook her head, but Bryan, who sat next to her, piped up, "Oh, Mairie, let him drive. Nobody's on the road right now. Remember when you wanted to learn? Who taught you?"

"You did," she said, elbowing him and grinning. "Okay, Jack. Hope you do better than I did. Poor Bryan almost threw up."

"That was stick shift, kiddo. This is automatic. He'll do fine."

Jack was suddenly filled with a mixture of excitement and fear. He knew he was being trusted with their lives. Now sitting behind the steering wheel, Jack put his hands on it and breathed deeply. What was it Mairie had called him? A copilot? He felt like one in training now. All right, he could do this. He could pilot this marvelous conveyance.

Closing the door, he strapped on the belt and put his foot down lightly on the right pedal.

"You have to shift into drive first," Marc advised through the corner of his mouth. "Between the seats. Press down and shift it into the place marked D."

"Right," Jack said, following the instruction.

He pressed his foot to the pedal. The car moved forward so quickly that he became stiff armed against the wheel to brace himself before he slammed down on the left pedal.

"Take your foot off the brake," Marc said with a laugh, as he braced himself against the leather panel. Everyone was laughing.

"The left is the brake?"

"Oh, geez . . ." Mairie moaned from the back, in between chuckles.

Marc, at least, was willing to be serious, and Jack was grateful.

"Left is the brake. Right is the gas. Don't put both feet on them at the same time. Use your right foot to work both. Take your foot off the brake and *gently* press down on the gas."

Off the brake, off the brake, Jack mentally repeated. He did as Marc had advised and the vehicle moved forward more smoothly.

"There," Marc said with a sigh. "Now, steer! *Stop looking at your feet!*"

Jack looked up and saw they were heading toward the side of the road. He turned the wheel sharply and everyone yelled at once as sand churned up against the metal belly of the car.

"Get back, get back!"

"Go to the right!"

"Stop confusing him!"

Jack struggled for a few seconds and then brought the vehicle back to the center of the lane.

"The white lines are our friends, Jack," Marc said as he collected himself . "Stay in your lane."

Mairie and Bryan were laughing like schoolchildren behind him, and he was glad they thought it was so humorous, but he really wanted to get this right. He'd decided that since he was here in this time, he was going to adjust, and the first thing was to purchase a vehicle. Like this one, if he could afford it. What freedom it would provide. To travel so easily, so comfortably, so quickly . . . anywhere he and Mairie wanted. Yes, he thought, staying within the white lines, they could go anywhere, so long as they were together.

After a few minutes, he saw another car approaching and his stomach muscles tightened with dread. "Someone is coming," he said, tightening his hold on the steering wheel.

"Just stay cool, Jack," Marc advised. "You can do it."

"You're doing great, honey," Mairie said, and stroked the back of his head. "Keep going."

"Go for it, Jack," Bryan cheered.

He held his place in the center of the lane as the smaller car came closer. He could do this, he told himself. He had jumped off a mountain with a parachute. He could pass another vehicle.

And he did.

Everyone cheered and Jack felt very proud of himself.

"I want one of these," he stated, trying to control his grin of accomplishment.

"We'll get a car," Mairie answered.

"Not a car. I want one of these. It is a most . . . excellent machine."

Why was everyone laughing again?

It *was* excellent.

Marc took over driving when the traffic increased. They were traveling west toward the Spring Mountains and Charleston Peak. Jack's exhilaration and excitement at driving lessened as they drove further into Paiute Territory. Only it wasn't Paiute Territory any longer. Yesterday, he and Mairie had visited the tiny reservation in the middle of the city; ten small acres were assigned to the people who had lived on this vast desert for a thousand years. Mairie had been right on the night of the Indian celebration. The Paiute needed to continue to teach their children the balanced way. One day . . . one day, others would listen.

The road was rough on the mountain and they bounced around a lot. Jack thought it was exciting, and so much faster than when he and Mairie had done it on horseback. He saw refuse on the side of the road and it looked so out of place in the pristine desert, as though modern man had left his mark . . . and it was dishonorable to the earth. He became quiet and introspective, wondering if he would not again be, as Mairie put it, *a stranger in a strange land.* He knew he didn't want to stay in Nevada, for it would only be a constant reminder of what had been, and the loss of his Paiute brothers' way of life.

"This is . . . is unbelievable," Marc said, maneuvering the four-by-four over the winding road. "Look at that view. Can't say I could live here, but it sure does take your breath away. You guys did this on horse and on foot?"

"Yes," Mairie whispered, looking out to the valley below them. "It seems so long ago . . ."

"It was a different world," Jack said, and he felt Mairie's hand touch his shoulder in a display of compassion. He knew she understood how he felt. It amazed him that words were not always necessary between them. They were in such perfect attunement, that they often seemed able to pick up each other's thoughts. To have found her was worth it, Jack thought not for the first time. He would have left anywhere, anything, to experience her love.

"Okay, looks like this is it. We can't drive any farther," Marc announced, pulling the vehicle to the side of the road and shutting off the motor. He turned around to the back seat. "Now we walk."

"It's not far," Jack whispered, remembering throwing himself off this cliff into the unknown. "Just around that bend there." And he pointed to the red outcropping of rocks.

"Can you do it, Bryan?" Mairie asked in a gentle voice. "You can wait here with Marc and we'll find the cave."

Bryan opened the back door. "You have got to be kidding," he said with a grin, and slid toward the opening. "You think I came this far to be left in a car?"

Marc shook his head and muttered as he adjusted his hat in the rearview mirror. "We can't just stay in an air-conditioned car, like civilized people. Oh, no . . . it's Indiana Jones again, I see."

"Hey, Marc," Bryan called out, as he stood beside the car. "Notice I'm wearing a baseball cap. You sure *you're* not the one who wants to be Indian Jones? Look at what you're wearing."

Marc got out of the car along with Mairie and Jack. He stood for a moment and looked over the

roof to Bryan. "You know how my skin burns, and
this sun is bloody brutal. I wasn't about to wear a
ten-gallon cowboy hat. Sorry, Sundance." He
glanced at Jack and apologized. "You can carry it
off, while I, on the other hand, happen to look daring and dashing in my felt fedora. If I appear to
remind you, Bryan, of your favorite character, then
perhaps you're seeing the real me. The adventurer."

Everyone stood for a moment of silence and then
burst out laughing.

"What? What?" Marc kept asking, as Bryan came
up to him and slapped him on the back. "You think
leaving Philly and coming out here like this, dodg-
ing government agents and hiking up mountains, is
not an adventure? This ain't a walk in Fairmont
Park."

"Come on, you daredevil, you," Bryan said with
a chuckle. "Let's go find a miracle."

They hiked the remaining distance, everyone conscious of Bryan's shaky condition. No one spoke.
The suspense was undeniable, and Jack realized they
all were acutely aware that everything he and Mairie
had gone through depended on what they found.
Jack wondered if it was a fool's journey, how anything could remain after a hundred and twenty
years, but then he glanced at the woman before him
and felt the strength of her resolve. If it was there,
she would find it.

She was an amazing woman.

They stood before the cave and Jack's heart felt so
heavy he wanted to yell out to relieve the pain.
Above where they were, he could see the ancient
drawings of the ancestors desecrated with bullet
holes. Men had used that sacred place as target prac-
tice and left their cans of beer as further insult. He
knew then what was missing from this time.

Balance.

It was just as Wovoka had predicted. He remembered the words, spoken after the Spirit Dance . . .

I have seen the land of tomorrow and it is troubling. The Indian disappears until only a few are singing the songs of the Father Sun and Sky and dancing the rhythms of Mother Earth.

The white man conquered and forgot how to dance gracefully in balance with the life force. He thought it could be overpowered, instead of honored. Swallowing down the thickness in his throat, Jack turned his attention back to the people around him, knowing he must find his own place of balance now.

"Here it is," Mairie whispered to Bryan, grabbing his hand. "I just know it has to be there. We wouldn't have gotten this far for nothing."

"It's so small," Marc observed in a reverent voice.

Bryan was staring at the opening of the cave. "All this . . . Mairie, it really happened. I mean I believed you, but this makes it so real. No matter what we find, or don't. Bless your heart for all of it."

She squeezed her brother's hand and took a deep breath. "I have been blessed, Bryan. All of it makes sense to me now, even if I had to travel into the past to find my future."

She glanced at Jack and smiled with such love, he couldn't help but reach out and take her hand. "Come . . . let us find your miracle, my lady."

They crawled into the cave as Bryan and Marc squatted at the entrance. It was littered with the debris of both animal and man. Jack went over to the far corner and began digging with the pocket knife he had purchased earlier in the day. How much dirt would accumulate over a hundred and twenty years? Not that much, Jack thought, not in a cave. He continued to dig in the earth until he had gone about six inches.

"Nothing?" Marc called in a dejected voice.

Mairie shook her head. "Not yet. Jack, you'll dig further?"

Nodding, he went back to his task, hoping that the blade would touch something solid, something earthen. Mairie's jar. It didn't.

She sat back on her heels and looked so dejected that Jack said, "I'll keep trying, love. You never know."

"I was so hoping . . ." she whispered, as tears came into her eyes. "Maybe someone found it and threw it away, thinking it was useless."

Hope. There was that word again. Jack renewed his efforts and hit something hard. Mairie sat up with interest.

"What do you think?" she asked in a hushed tone.

He shook his head as he began sifting through the dirt with his fingers. He touched something sturdy and brought up a piece of dirt-encrusted clay. Blowing away the dirt, he handed it over. "What do you think? Could this be it?"

Mairie took the piece and he saw her hands were shaking. "I don't know," she whispered. "Even if it *is*, this means the jar was broken and the plant lost."

"What is it?" Marc asked. "Have you found it?"

Mairie handed over the piece of clay. "It may be part of the pot. I really don't know."

Jack continued to bring up fractured pieces of clay and lay them on the ground next to him.

"It's all right, Mairie," Bryan called out to his sister. "We tried."

"No, it is not all right, Bryan," Mairie answered, sniffling back her tears. "I really thought . . . no, I *knew* it would be here. It was like the driving force in getting back to you, to bring this to you. Wovoka said it would be *part of the answer.* How can an answer just disappear?"

"Come out of there, Mairie," Marc called out. "It's

been over a century. You've done everything you could."

"Here, Mairie, look at this," Jack said, handing her a rounded piece with fragments of wax still attached. "Could this be part of your jar? You did seal it with wax."

She took the piece and, looking at it, sighed deeply. "It could be my jar," she said in a broken voice. "That's it, then. The seal is broken. It's gone."

"My love, I'm sorry." He couldn't find words to comfort her, and he felt helpless.

She shook her head and gathered up the clay pieces. "I . . . I guess it was a long shot for anything to have survived intact all this time."

He could see she was fighting her tears and losing. How he wished with all his heart that her mission of love would have been complete.

Mairie handed the pieces to Marc and Bryan as she left the cave and whispered, "I'm so sorry, Bryan. I'm sorry I led you on this wild-goose chase for nothing."

Bryan took her into his arms and hugged his sister tightly. Jack left the cave and brushed his hands on his thighs while he watched the sad scene of Mairie crying against her brother's chest. He felt helpless, hopeless, as he heard Bryan's whisper.

"Whatever is meant to be, will be, Mar. I'm still going to live every moment I have left."

"*Hey!*"

Everyone turned to see Marc holding something up to the sun.

"C'mere," he said in an excited voice. "You've got to see this!"

They all walked over to him and he held out a piece of clay. "Remember Jurassic Park?"

"Oh, Marc," Bryan scolded, "this is not the time for your movie mania."

"No, look . . ." He placed the fragment of clay in

his hands and held it in the sun. "Look in the wax. What do you see?"

"See?" Bryan leaned closer, along with Mairie and Jack. "I don't see anything, except dirt."

"Not dirt," Marc whispered. "Look closer."

And they did.

"*Seeds*?" Mairie asked in disbelief. "Are they seeds?"

"That's what it looks like to me."

"What does that mean?" Jack asked, not seeing why they were so excited. "They are still useless."

"Not today," Bryan whispered, suddenly grinning like a young boy who had just found his pot of gold at the end of a rainbow. "With the technology today, we can take this to a lab and extract the seeds without damage."

All four looked at each other as the realization set in . . . for in those dark, dry seeds lay the dormant energy of life, of hope.

Mairie looked into Jack's eyes and smiled. Her mission of love was complete. And Jack suddenly realized that hope, like love, really is eternal.

You never give up.

Life, anywhere you find it, is essentially good.

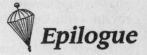 *Epilogue*

Hope.

Sitting on the wrap-around porch of the large ranch house, she deeply inhaled the early summer air and relaxed. Rolling green hills as far as the eyes could see, sparsely dotted with evergreens, painted an awesome picture. In the distance were majestic mountains with lingering caps of snow before an unclouded blue sky for a backdrop. It was pristine splendor and she knew she was blessed to behold it. The purity entered her lungs with a sweetness she appreciated, and she couldn't stop the grin from spreading over her face.

It was such a great story and she couldn't share it, except with the handful of people who had participated ... and they reminisced about the incredible circumstances whenever they were together. Tonight, she was sure that Bryan or Marc would bring up something, some memory, and they would all settle back to time travel. Back to six years ago, when it had all started.

She rocked slowly, enjoying the gentle sway, as she privately time-traveled through the chain of events that had led to all of them being gathered together again tonight. Who would have thought that writing a novel about the Civil War would have been such a blockbuster? That the movie rights would have enabled them to buy this ranch in Wyoming, to develop the seeds into plants and a natural vitamin supplement, to own the patent and split the royalties with the Indian nations? To sit on the board of a foundation?

It never failed to amaze her. Her smile widened as she looked down to the letterhead of the document she was holding.

THE NOW FOUNDATION
PAST AND FUTURE UNITED
AND GIVING BIRTH TO THE PRESENT

The foundation was able to offer the gift of a two-week vacation to terminally ill children and their parents. The kids got an experience of ranch life, of being a cowboy and listening to Indian stories around a campfire. The parents were counseled and given a reprieve from worry and care. And in the fresh juice, served each morning, was BIHA. She had named the supplement they derived from the plant, and she again grinned while thinking of the reactions to her suggestion. They had understood at once.

Believe In Hope Again.

So that's what they did. Believed. More novels followed. More movie options, enabling them to run the ranch and quietly operate a foundation that allowed them to distribute the herb in an altruistic way. There was still a bit of suspense and mystery about it, which Marc enjoyed with great flourish, as evidenced by the resurfacing of his frustrated acting abilities.

"Is that the foundation list for the next group?" Bryan asked, coming to join her in the opposite rocker. He placed a glass of iced tea on the little table between them.

She nodded and handed the paper to him. "Thirteen families. Scheduling with the staff is completed. They'll arrive on Tuesday to set up the cottages. Everything should be fine for the weekend arrival."

Her brother glanced at the paper and then asked, "Are you sure you're up to this right now?"

Mairie smiled, knowing he was concerned. "I'm fine. Besides, I get such pleasure from these two-week gatherings, just visiting with the children and parents."

He grinned at her. "You do look great, better than ever. You don't mind being in the background? You're the brains behind all of this, and to everyone else you're just Mary Delaney, housewife."

She thought of her quiet life and what a perfect cover it was. How peaceful to be an unknown . . . especially unknown to the Feds. "Happy homemaker," she corrected with a laugh. "I love staying at home, tending my plants, living a simple life."

"Yeah, right!" Marc opened the screen door and came onto the porch. "You're simple Mairie, Mairie? I don't think so. And you stay here, thank you, and make the rest of us come to conduct business in *Wyoming*, of all places," Marc added with a western twang, "where the deer and the friggin' antelope play."

Turning her head, Mairie laughed even louder. "Gimme a break, Marc. As if you don't love it. Look at the way you're dressed. That JR Ewing getup may still be in style in Arizona, but it doesn't cut it here. This is real cowboy country."

Marc adjusted his bolo tie and leaned against the railing, very Jimmy Stewart-ish. "Well, *you* decided to make the West our base of operations. I have to fit the part of chairman of the board. By the way, another pharmaceutical company contacted me, making a ridiculously high offer to—"

"We've had this discussion before," Mairie interrupted. "No drug companies are going to get their hands on this and spend years in FDA testing and politics with the AMA, only to charge a fortune when it's distributed."

"But they're already trying to develop their own."

"Those are chemicals," she said, looking out to the rolling hills. "They won't be useful. This has to be natural to be of any benefit. Kinda eliminates any corruption of it, so we'll continue to quietly offer a natural supplement to anyone who might be interested. Besides, it's the kids who really benefit . . . and those who can remember what it was like to be childlike, to believe in magic." She paused and grinned out to the horizon. "Those who still have hope."

All turned in the direction Mairie was looking when the sound of pounding hooves reverberated through the ground.

"Well, well, well . . ." Marc said with an admiring smirk. "If it isn't the Louis L'Amour of the new millennium."

Mairie inhaled deeply with anticipation and attempted to stand up. Both men immediately came forward to assist her.

"Oh, Mairie," Marc clucked, like a mother hen. "Don't you think forty-three is a little old to be—"

"Hush," she murmured, before he could continue. "I'm fine." She walked to the edge of the porch and held a post. "He needed to clear his head," she said, nodding toward the approaching figure."He's about to write the ending scene of his latest book."

Jack raced to the house, over the last hill, up the dirt driveway, and over the rolling green lawn, and pulled the horse to a dramatic halt right in front of the porch.

"Momma, momma! You should see how fast Daddy rides!"

Bringing a hand up to her hip, Mairie grinned. "I've seen it. Don't get any ideas, young man. You only ride fast with your daddy. Promise me."

Marc walked down the steps and caught the five-year-old boy who jumped into his arms. "What are you feeding this child, Mairie? He's as strong as ... as—"

"As his Uncle Bryan." Bryan leaped down the steps to capture his nephew from Marc. Carrying the child, he looked at Mairie and added, "What a joy, to watch him grow."

Mairie's heart expanded. And what joy she received watching her brother experience life, to see him in remission for the last five years. She decided that they could finally drop the remission part. Bryan was a miracle. They were all together again, and for the next few days they would laugh and love and plan.

Her mission of love was a success.

Smiling, she turned her attention to her husband as Jack tied the reins to a post and climbed up to her.

Stopping on the last step, he leaned down and kissed her stomach. "How's my baby?"

She stroked his head with tenderness. What a perfect partner he was. She could hardly believe how happy she was, how much she was loved, and how much she was capable of loving another.

"Your baby is fine. How's our son? He's not going to get sick after all that jostling, is he?"

Jack came up the remaining step and put his arms around Mairie, at least as much as he could. Now seven months pregnant, she found not only her heart had expanded. She didn't care. Carrying this child was another miracle in her life.

"Sick?" Jack asked with a laugh. "The Delaneys don't get sick from a hard ride, madam."

"Oh, I'm not touching that one with a ten-foot pole," Marc said, and sat down in a rocker. "There are children present."

Everyone laughed until they heard a childish whine.

"What does that mean? We don't get sick, Daddy."

Mairie held out her arm to her child.

"C'mere, Fenton."

Her precious son ran toward them and Jack scooped him up in his arms. Holding him, Jack wrapped his other arm around her and looked to his guests.

"Is she an amazing woman, or what?"

Marc called out, "She's amazing, all right. Even if, again, I'm preempted of being her birth coach. All that breathing I learned for Fenton's birth, and at the last minute *you* decide you're strong enough for the delivery."

"You know you would have fainted anyway, Marc," Jack said with a laugh, since Marc never missed an opportunity to tease Jack.

"Probably, right," Marc muttered.

Bryan said, "She's an angel."

Mairie connected her gaze with her brother and smiled her love.

"She's a gift," Jack whispered and kissed the tip of her nose. "Our incredible gift."

Mairie giggled. "She's pregnant and hungry. Who's cooking?"

As everyone walked into the house, Mairie picked up the glass of iced tea and looked out once more to Mother Earth in all her splendor. How spectacular she was. She lived, breathed, exhaled . . . giving life. Filled with emotion, Mairie gave her thanks . . . for being, for another day of love, of joy. What a miracle life is, she thought, as she turned to the door, held open by her remarkable husband.

You can never give up hope.

Anywhere you are . . .

*We are each of us angels
with only one wing.
And we can fly only by
embracing each other.*

Luciana de Crescenzo

Acknowledgments

To Robert Lee Harmon . . . for his friendship and for sharing his views on the Civil War. Even though he is one of the kindest human beings I have met, I kept my promise and used his name for the villain just so he could chuckle.

Phillip Hergett . . . a brilliant writer who broadened my view of the universe and expanded my perception of time. I will always value his friendship.

The Harleys . . . who were stuck with me on a boat for eight rainy days in Belize and showed me true partnership between a man and a woman. It was their example that made me believe such a union was not only possible, but natural.

The Las Vegas tribe of Paiute Indians . . . for the research material they supplied. I ask their indulgence for the way I manipulated time and circumstances. I also acknowledge the beautiful words of Woziwob—a message of hope that withstands time.

The descendants of the Gass Family . . . O.D., Virginia, and especially Fenton made for such wonderful characters.

Kristen Flannery . . . my daughter, my friend.

Thanks for hanging in there through all the years of writing and for always listening to the last chapter and keeping the tradition alive. So glad we "wrote" it this way, this time around.

Lyssa Keusch . . . who believed in this story, and through her editorial skill helped to make it a better book.

Michael Rodriguez . . . for his faith, his friendship, his talents. My buddy, what a blessing Santa Fe was and will be again.

My Cristopher . . . Memory Maker, this book could not have been written without your input and your assistance. Mere words can not express my gratitude, and I look forward to a joyous lifelong "partnership." Thank you, my love.

And, last but certainly never least . . . the Clueless Club, who kept me laughing through all of it.

Calling All Women to the World of
Avon Romance Superleaders!

Would you like to be romanced by a knight in shin-ing armor? Rescued by an English earl with a touch of gypsy blood? Or perhaps you dream of an Indian warrior or a rugged rancher.

Then the heroes of Avon's Romance Superleaders are exactly what you're looking for! And our au-thors know just what kind of women these tough guys need to shake up their lives and fall in love.

So take a deep breath and let the romantic promise of Samantha James, the sexy magic of Christina Skye, the soul-kissed passion of Constance O'Day-Flannery, and the heart-stirring warmth of Cather-ine Anderson plunge you right in the midst of an explosive love story.

OCTOBER

What could be more romantic than an honest-to-goodness Christmas Knight, who lives and breathes to rescue damsels in distress? In her truly magical fashion, Christina Skye makes that fantasy come true for a '90's woman, just in time for the holiday season. See why Virginia Henley said, "Christina Skye is superb!" and why this romance should be on your holiday shopping list!

Hope O'Hara's quaint new Scottish inn is falling down around her ears, but she's determined to get it in tip-top shape for the Christmas crowd. So when she's on the leaky roof one rainy evening, nearly falling off the slippery thatch, her cries for help conjure up a rescuer from across time—knight Ronan MacLeod.

CHRISTMAS KNIGHT
by Christina Skye

Hope screamed. Her fingers burned as she clawed at the roof edge, losing inches with each passing second.

Thank God the rider had come from the cliffs, answering her call.

He rocked forward into the wind while his anxious bay sidestepped nervously along the narrow trail. A branch swept past his head, and he ducked and called out at the same moment he saw Hope.

She did not understand, his words lost against the boom of thunder. Desperately, Hope clawed at the soggy reeds, which shredded at her touch. Her foot sank through a rotting beam and swept her out into cold, empty space.

She pitched down the wet reeds, a captive of the rope lashing down the tarpaulin, her scream drowning out the man's angry shout. As if in a nightmare she plunged toward the ground, spinning blindly.

The great horse neighed shrilly as its rider kneed forward.

Instead of hard earth, Hope felt the impact of warm muscle halting her descent. Her breath shuddered as she toppled forward, clinging to the terrified horse. She was alive.

Breathless, she turned to study the man whom she had to thank for saving her life.

His long, black hair blew about his face, as wet as her own. Darkness veiled his features, permitting only a glimpse of piercing eyes and tense jaw. But the strength of his body was unmistakable. She blushed to feel his thighs strain where she straddled him.

He muttered a low phrase to the horse, the words snatched away by the wind. The sounds seemed to gentle the creature, and Hope, too, felt curiously calmed by the soft rhythm of his speech.

Above their heads the tarpaulin swept free and a four-foot section of packed reeds hurtled toward the ground. The rider cursed and kneed the horse away from the unstable roof, struggling to control the frightened mount.

Hope understood exactly how the horse was feeling. She sat rigid, aware of the stranger's locked thighs and the hard hands clenched around her waist. Dimly she felt the rider's hands circle her shoulders and explore her cheek. Hope swept his hand away, feeling consciousness blur. The cold ate into her, numbing body and mind.

Deeper she slid. Down and down again . . .

Finally, even the rider's callused hands could not hold her back from the darkness.

NOVEMBER

In a rough and tumble world, Catherine Anderson always manages to find a refuge of safety and calm, where love conquers all. Publishers Weekly *praised her as a "major voice in the romance genre." In Catherine's newest historical romance she shows us that even a former gunslinger can learn to love and* Cherish *a woman.*

On the trail from Santa Fe through New Mexico Territory beautiful, sheltered Rebecca Morgan loses everything and everyone she's ever had in the world. She is plucked from danger by rancher Race Spencer, a loner who reminds the young innocent of the wild land. Although she's not ready to trust anyone again, Rebecca is beginning to realize that in this life the love of a good man might be her only salvation.

CHERISH
by Catherine Anderson

"Countin' the stars, darlin'?"

Rebecca jumped so violently at the unexpected sound of his voice that she lost her hold on the quilt. Pressing a hand to her throat, she turned to squint through the wagon spokes at him.

"Mr. Spencer?"

"Who else'd be under your wagon?"

He hooked a big hand over the wheel rim and crawled out. As he settled to sit beside her, he seemed to loom, his breadth of shoulder and length of leg making her feel dwarfed. Drawing up his knee to rest his arm, he turned slightly toward her, his ebony hair glistening in the silvery moonlight, his chiseled features etched with shadows, the collar of his black shirt open to reveal a V of muscular chest. As he studied her his coffee-dark eyes seemed to take on a satisfied gleam, his firm yet mobile mouth tipping up at one corner as if he were secretly amused by something. She had an uncomfortable feeling it had something to do with her.

She expected him to ask what she was doing out there, and she searched her mind for a believable lie. She had just decided to say she had come out for a breath of fresh air, when he said, "You gettin' anxious to go to Denver?"

Her heart caught. Keeping her expression carefully blank, she replied, "I've tried not to count too heavily on it, actually. It could snow, and then I couldn't go until spring."

"Nah." He tipped his head back to study the sky. "Now that we're this close to home, I can take that worry off your mind. We got a good month before the snows'll hit." He settled his gaze back on her face, his eyes still gleaming. "In three days, we'll reach my ranch, and we'll head out straightaway. I'll have you in Denver within five days."

"I'm not in that great a hurry. I'm sure you'll want to get your herd settled in and see to business that's been neglected in your absence. After all you've done for me, being patient is the least I can do."

He shrugged her off. "Pete can handle the herd and anything else that comes up. Gettin' you settled somewhere is my first concern."

Rebecca gulped, struggled to breathe. *Stay calm. Don't panic.* But it was easier said than done. She dug her nails into the quilt, applying so much pressure they felt as if they were pulling from the quick. *Inhale, exhale. Don't think about his leaving you.* But it was there in her head, a vivid tableau: Race riding away from her on his buckskin, his black outline getting smaller and smaller until he disappeared from sight. She started to shake.

In a thin voice, she said, "Mr. Spencer, what if I were to tell you I don't wish to go to Denver?"

He didn't look in the least surprised. "I'd offer you two other choices." He searched her gaze. "One of 'em would be permanent, though." His shifted his bent leg to better support his arm, then began clenching and relaxing his hand as he turned his head to stare into the darkness. "So you probably wouldn't be interested in that one."

DECEMBER

The dark of night is full of romantic promise and during One Moonlit Night *a vicar's daughter has a run-in with a rakish earl. With heart-stopping excitement, Samantha James weaves a beautiful love story that is sure to enchant. As* Romantic Times *said, "Samantha James pulls out all the stops, taking readers on a spectacular roller coaster ride."*

The new Earl of Ravenwood has gypsy blood running through his veins. Half wild, half noble, and completely inscrutable, he is the subject of much speculation. So when the dark lord nearly runs down gently-reared Olivia Sherwood in a carriage accident, she can't help but feel trepidation. Surely there's no other reason for the racing of her heart?

ONE MOONLIT NIGHT
by Samantha James

" 'Tis midnight," he said softly. "You should not be about at this hour."

Olivia bristled. "I'm well aware of the hour, sir, and I assure you, I'm quite safe."

"You were not, else we would not be having this discussion."

Olivia blinked. What arrogance! Why, he was insufferable! Her spine straightened. "I am not a sniveling, helpless female, sir."

His only response was to pull a handkerchief from

deep in his trouser pocket. Olivia stiffened when he pressed it to her right cheekbone.

"You're bleeding," he said.

Her reaction was instinctive. She gasped, and one hand went to her cheek.

"It's only a scratch." Even as he spoke, he let his hand drop. "It will soon stop."

All at once Olivia felt chastened. Lord, but he was tall! Why, she barely reached his chin. She didn't need the light of day to know that beneath his jacket, his shoulders were wide as the seas.

Her pulse was racing, in a way she liked not at all—in a way that was wholly unfamiliar. Quickly she looked away. Most assuredly, she did not wish to be caught staring again.

To her surprise he stripped off one glove and tucked it beneath his arm. He then proceeded to take her hand.

Two things ran through her mind: for some strange reason she thought his skin would be cold as death; instead it seemed hot as fire. The second was that her hand was completely swallowed by his larger one.

"Allow me to take you home, Miss Sherwood."

She tried to remove her hand from within his grasp. His grip tightened ever so slightly.

"Y-you're holding my hand, sir." To her shame her voice came out airy and breathless.

"So I am, Miss Sherwood. So I am." A slight smile curled his lips . . . oh, a devil's smile surely, for she sensed he was making light of her. "And I would ask again . . . may I take you home?"

"Nay, sir!" A shake of her head accompanied her denial. " 'Tis not necessary," she hastened to add. "Truly. I live there, just over the hill."

He persisted. "You may well have injuries of which you are unaware."

"Nay." She was adamant, or at least she prayed

she sounded that way! "I would know it."

He gazed down at her, so long and so intently she could have sworn he knew she'd lied.

He released her hand just when she feared he never would.

"Very well then." He inclined his head, then spoke very quietly. "I'm very glad you came to no harm, Miss Sherwood."

Three steps and he'd disappeared into the shadows.

JANUARY

Constance O'Day-Flannery changed romance forever with the first ever time-travel romance. Full of passion, fantasy, and magic, her novels have delighted millions of readers. Now allow Avon and the Queen of Time-travel to take you back and introduce you to a fantasy lover who will go anyplace and Anywhere You Are.

After the War Between the States, Jack Delaney retreats to the tribal lands of his adopted Indian family to ask the Great Spirit for a vision and peace. What he receives instead is a flesh-and-blood woman seeking adventure who dives from the sky, travels through time, and whose soul is as unfulfilled and restless as his.

ANYWHERE YOU ARE
by Constance O'Day-Flannery

"You came."

Hearing the two words, Mairie stopped breathing and lifted the edge of the canopy away from her head. She imagined that, right? Maybe she was starting to hallucinate from the heat and lack of water. Dehydration could do that . . .

"I knew you would. Thank you."

This was too real. She pulled the canopy completely away and looked behind her, just to make sure she wasn't delusional. What she saw didn't help confirm her state of mind.

A man, some kind of man, was staring at her. All

he was wearing was heavy jeans and boots. Naked from the waist up, his chest and face were painted in some sort of Indian zigzag decoration that was smeared and his hair hung below his shoulders in a matted mess. He looked . . . wild. Crazy. And he was staring at her as if he'd seen a ghost.

Fear entered her system and made the adrenaline start pumping with amazing speed. She had to stay calm. This guy was definitely not from the skydiving school. He didn't look like he had attended any school. Ever. He looked . . . feral.

"Hi." She tried smiling. "Thank God, you found me. I've . . . ah . . . sorta wandered off course, and I need to get back to civilization. Can you tell me where I am?"

"What are you?" The man's voice was low, as though he might be frightened of her, yet he slowly walked around her to stand in front. He squatted down and simply stared, like she was an exhibit in the zoo.

How do you answer that question? she wondered. He must be like a hermit or something. He wasn't an Indian, not with brown hair, streaked by the sun, and blue eyes. Maybe he was crazy. Really crazy. Damn . . . What kind of luck was this?

Stay calm, she told herself. The best way to deal with crazy people is to stay calm. She had no idea where she'd heard that, but it seemed like good advice considering the person before her. "You see, I was skydiving and, like I said, I must have gotten off course so if you could just point me in the right direction I can—"

"You dived from the sky?" His words were filled with disbelief.

"Well, yes. Actually I jumped from a plane and then dived, but that doesn't matter . . . I just need some help here and then I can—"

"What is a plane?" he again interrupted, tilting his

head and staring at her with the intensity of someone examining a bug under a microscope.

She stared back at him, wondering if he was messing with her mind. How could he not know what a plane was? "You know . . . an *air*plane." She pointed to the sky and made hand gestures.

"What *are* you?"

Suddenly, she remembered that she was still wearing the helmet, and pulled it off. Of course, he couldn't see her face. That was it.

"I'm a woman. See . . . ?"

He fell back onto the ground in awe.

She couldn't help it. She laughed. How long *had* this guy been out here, if the sight of a woman had that effect on him?

"Are you God, the Great Spirit?" The words were barely audible.

"I'm not God," she said with a grin. "Though I do like the fact that you would consider God might be female. Pretty enlightened." Compliments wouldn't hurt. "However, I'm just a woman who's lost and looking to get back to civilization. So if you could just point me in the right direction, I'll leave you and—"

"You're my gift. I saw you fall from heaven."

FREE TOTE BAG!

Receive a **free tote bag** with the purchase of four of Avon's romance titles:

CHRISTMAS KNIGHT by Christina Skye (on sale September 9th), **CHERISH** by Catherine Anderson (on sale October 7th), **ONE MOONLIGHT NIGHT** by Samantha James (on sale November 11th) and **ANYWHERE YOU ARE** by Constance O'Day-Flannery (on sale December 9th).

Send in your proof-of-purchase (cash register receipts) for all four books, and the coupon below, completely filled out. Offer expires December 31, 1998.

Void where prohibited by law.

- -

Mail to: Avon Books, Dept. TB, P.O. Box 767, Dresden, TN 38225

Name _____

Address _____

City _____

State/Zip _____

BAG 0698